www.xulonpress.com

Table of Contents

DEDICATION

The author dedicates this book to the three most important people in his life.

First is my wife, Pamela Joyce Shennan. She acted as mid-wife to bring the first book in this series to birth, *SKIP JORDAN and the Veil of Deception*. She did the same for this present volume. Her constant stream of encouragement to persevere even after I sustained serious injuries from a fall on the ice kept me going. Even after several other set-backs, causing me to miss two dead-lines, her prayerful support won the day.

I also dedicate this book to our two children, Shane Christopher, and Joanne Elizabeth. The Psalmist declares: *Behold, children are a heritage from the LORD, The fruit of the womb is a reward. (Psalm 127:3)*

Since I cannot leave them any great wealth or worldly acclaim, I leave them what I have. In the words of the apostle Peter: *"Silver and gold I do not have, but what I do have I give you,"* the fruit of the labour I have poured into this book.

ACKNOWLEDGEMENTS

First of all I give thanks to **Almighty God, Father, Son, and Holy Spirit**, for inspiring me to write this book, and for giving me strength to complete it.

To: **my wife, Pamela Joyce**, for encouraging me during the writing, and putting up with my near obsession till it was finished. She also gave herself to the task of proof-reading with her usual dedication to detail and accuracy.

To: **our son, Shane, and our daughter, Joanne**: Shane for walking me through the technical details in preparing the manuscript, and Joanne for putting up with my frequent references to my writing during our weekly telephone conversations.

To: **Trueman and Gail Browett**, for the initial reading of the manuscript, approving of it, and proof-reading with such dedication.

To: **Robie Atkinson**, my colleague and fellow labourer in the work of the Gospel, who backed me at every turn. His spiritual fellowship and counsel was of more value than he could imagine.

To: **all the friends, family and acquaintances** who in many and various ways gave encouragement and support, I give thanks.

Chapter 1

Near the End

The small lamp Ntambo carried gave more light than anyone could expect. The crystalline content in the stalagmites and stalactites in the great cave took the weak flame and multiplied its light a hundred-fold.

He hurried along toward the narrowing end of the cave and the tunnel leading to what was known as 'The Devil's Chimney.' Practically everything in these hidden chambers had the devil's name on it. This was not surprising, considering that only the devil's work was being done in this habitation of demons. Ntambo's heart was pumping from the exercise and from the urgency of his mission.

Skip Jordan and the others were in mortal danger.

He had to get out of these caverns, the vast majority of which were unexplored and its network of tunnels virtually endless. To the world outside, these caves were non-existent; they were known only to the secret lodges and groups practicing the works of darkness. Branches of the Druid Society, associations of Wicca and a plethora of New Age groups and secret societies *could* know about this place, but only at the higher levels. Others would know if they were chosen to train for the perpetration of some particular deception to be foisted on the church. To any others this habitation of demons and deceivers was totally unknown. Death was the consequence of breaking the code of secrecy.

The path Ntambo was travelling was treacherous; there was dampness in the air and moisture collected on the smooth rocks beneath his feet. As careful as he had to be the urgency of his mission caused him to move more rapidly than was wise. He had slipped and fallen three times, but with only minor inconvenience. His departure from the others had been silent and unobtrusive. Those who watched them could not be aware his intention was to escape, but that would not be the case for long. Once his absence was discovered the number of his pursuers would be such that his fate was sealed. He knew he would not get out of this alive. All he could hope for was to set some markers and warn their friends on the other side of the falls that their party was in mortal danger. Beyond that, he was ready to die.

Ntambo reached the tunnel he believed led to the secret exit. He had not dared to attempt an escape before, not until he had had a vision of what he dubbed, 'the map room.' It was logical there should be such a place, since the almost endless tunnels twisting and turning at random would be confusing even to one who had lived here for years. The walls were covered with intricately painted maps. Seeing them, he realized that the maps themselves were not exhaustive. He imagined they covered only the chambers and tunnels currently in use. The map showed open-ended tunnels, as if there were regions beyond not yet explored.

Referring to a piece of paper he had inscribed with the route he was to follow, Ntambo chose one of several tunnels and moved into it. Immediately, robbed of the reflective quality of the larger cave, he had to make his way with the aid of the dimly flickering light of the oil lamp.

He slowed his pace, for not only was it harder to see the path ahead, but the tunnel began to slope upward. As the way grew steeper his sandaled feet began to slip on the moisture-laden rocks, some breaking loose as he put his weight upon them. At the same time the tunnel narrowed still more, till he began to doubt his ability to proceed. He was a big man, well over six feet tall with broad shoulders and a muscular chest. It would not be difficult for a youth or a smaller man to get through, but for him it became a struggle. Soon he was forced to abandon the lamp and make his way in the dark. If this tunnel did not lead to the surface he was in deep trouble. As yet he could see no glimmer of light to indicate he was near the end of his journey. No longer a tunnel but a vertical shaft, he was grateful for the roughened sides. His hands and feet could at least find purchase, preventing him from sliding to the bottom. He realized he was now in 'The Devil's Chimney.'

It felt like an hour had passed, though it could only have been a few minutes, before faint light from the surface penetrated to where he was. He was sure he must be bleeding from the rough edges of the 'chimney.' His sandals had fallen off and every advance upward caused him pain; his hands, like his feet, felt raw from pushing against the sides to propel his considerable weight upward. He pushed harder than ever, driven by visions of the fate his friends would face if he did not succeed. His lips moved continually as he prayed and rose inch by inch toward the surface. It seemed to him the pain diminished as he progressed. Whether this was due to numbness in his limbs or as a result of his prayers, he could not tell.

At last Ntambo neared the top of the 'chimney.' Sunlight streamed in. A sense of relief washed over him, but the relief was premature. His troubles were not yet over. As he came nearer to the surface he saw there was a sharp protrusion several feet from the exit. A smaller man *may* have been able to squeeze past this obstruction with only minor injuries; a man his size would likely get stuck and die there. If by some miracle he got through he knew he would sustain crippling injuries.

Exerting every ounce of energy he possessed Ntambo reached the point where the razor-sharp rock intruded into the narrow space. Sunlight shone down on it and he was able, at least from his position, to examine it. A faint glimmer of hope rose within him; the protrusion was not part of the geological structure, but a separate piece jammed into a fault. If he could dislodge it he would be able make his way to the surface. The problem was that his strength was waning and his hands and feet were almost numb from the cuts and bruises they had received from the punishing climb. If the hidden portion of the rock was too long, and the fault too tight against it, he would never be able to break it free. He had no choice. He had to try.

While he was making his tortuous way up the 'chimney,' Ntambo had not ceased praying. His lips moved silently, but his heart was pumping out requests to his God with mingled faith and desperation, "Show me what to do?" he prayed.

Almost immediately fragments of scripture came to mind. At the end of his life Samson had prayed for strength to inflict one last blow against the enemies of God. His mind created a vision of that last desperate scene and the words of Scripture provided the description of what had taken place:

Then Samson prayed to the Lord, "Lord God, remember me. God, please give me strength one more time..." Then Samson turned to the two center pillars that supported the whole temple. He braced himself between the two pillars, with his right hand on one and his left hand on the other...Then he pushed as hard as he could, causing the temple to fall... [i]

As the words passed through his mind Ntambo knew God was telling him to pray the same prayer Samson had prayed and to make one last effort to break free from the devilish trap he was in.

Reaching up to take hold of the rock that was blocking his way, Ntambo prayed, "Give me strength just once more to demonstrate your power, and to win one more battle against the forces of darkness."

Never before had Ntambo tested his strength to its limits. Now, cramped as he was in this confined space, he willed every muscle in his body to its fullest potential. Pain coursed through him but he would not desist. With his feet lodged in a crevice and his shoulder pressing against the underside of the rock he pushed with all his might.

It was not enough.

The rock held firm and a sliver of doubt entered his thoughts. Had God indeed told him to pray that prayer; had he just imagined he had heard God tell him to pray the same prayer Samson had prayed? He pushed the doubt aside and pushed even harder against the rock. He was at the end of his strength when a sudden surge of power coursed through him like nothing he had known before. The pain receded and a wave of well-being came over him. He imagined this was what Samson must have felt when the Spirit of the Lord came upon him; when he overcame the Philistine army with the jaw-bone of an ass, and when, at the end of his life, he pulled down the temple of the heathen gods. His muscles were invigorated. Though he felt the strain it was as nothing compared to what he had felt before.

What happened next was as incredible as it was dramatic. A sound like a cannon blast assailed his ears and the great rock blocking his way snapped in two. He heaved the severed piece up through the exit and heard it thud on the ground outside.

Once the obstruction was out of the way the mighty power he had experienced drained from his body. The pain returned; struggling up the remaining distance he at last emerged into the sunlight. He lay gasping for breath on the rough ground scattered with tufts of grass, wild thorn bushes and broken shale. A lizard stared at him from a rock and a rodent scurried away into some low brush. The roar of the waterfall pounded in his ears.

He was indeed bleeding; there were cuts on his hands, feet, and numerous parts of his body. Passing his hands over the cuts, however, he determined they were mostly surface scratches. Once he had caught his breath he would be able to proceed, but losing his sandals in his progress up the 'chimney' was nevertheless going to prove a problem. The rough terrain on this area above the falls would chew up his feet unless he provided some protection for them. Unwinding the cloth he kept wrapped around his waist, Ntambo began to tear it into strips. He wound the strips tightly around his feet and tied them around his ankles. At last he was ready to proceed.

The sun beat down but a light breeze and the spray from the waterfall cooled his wounds. His eyes focussed on a ridge some thirty feet higher than the plateau he was on. The arrangement with Aunt May, Reginald and Angela was that they would frequently keep their binoculars on that ridge. They would look for a distress signal to indicate they were in trouble. All he would have to do would be to create some sort of beacon on that ridge and they would be alerted. Mazimbi had left detailed instructions of how to find the caves. The secret entrance to 'The Lion's Den' would be exposed. They would all be rescued. At least, that was the plan.

However, as he moved forward on his cloth-bound feet, Ntambo became aware he was not alone. A figure appeared some fifty feet to his left; a moment later there were two or three approaching him from the right. Glancing behind him he saw a dozen or more shadowy forms bringing up the rear. The numbers increased to the point where he was being herded, not toward the ridge, but toward the edge of the waterfall. It seemed he was on an island dividing the mighty flow of the Zambezi toward the great gorge. Soon, there would be nowhere to go, except over the edge into the depths below.

Ntambo knew he had failed. There was no way he could warn Skip's aunt and uncle and Angela. Without his warning they would not know they needed to set off the alarm. His pursuers were drawing closer and hemming him in on both sides. There could be only one end to this – his death.

....

Invisible to human eyes, another scene was being played out in the heavenly realms above.

A group of angelic beings were looking down on the scene below. They followed the progress of the large black man as he stumbled forward on wounded feet. On both sides of him, and behind him, his enemies hounded him toward the brink of destruction.

Behind this central group of angels a host of like beings were spread out, it seemed, from one end of the heavens to the other. Opposite these beings of light, fidgety and malevolent, was the opposing force of demons.

One from the central group of angels enquired voicelessly. "Do we have enough prayer support from the children of light?"

"We do," replied the tallest among them. "He-Who-Knows-All has given us leave to act."

"When are we to act?" another asked.

"Soon," the tall one replied.

The situation below was fast approaching critical proportions. The black man's enemies were only feet away from him as they enclosed him on both sides and from behind. Their faces, for the angels could see every detail, were masks of hate. The black man stopped, for he seemed to realize any attempt to escape now was futile. Nevertheless his enemies did not relent. They crowded around him and pushed him forward. At the brink of the gorge they gave him a final push, and the servant of the living God tumbled into the abyss below.

"Now!" said the tallest angel. "The time to act is now!"

What followed was a battle such as human eyes had never seen. Swords made of pure light flashed from one end of the heavens to the other. Two angels of light separated from the rest and sped like lightning toward Ntambo's falling body.

Chapter 2

Dreams

The dreams were coming back and they were worse than ever.

Aunt May and Nancy stood at the open doorway to Skip's room in their nightgowns. They silently debated whether or not to wake him. It was sometimes dangerous to wake someone suddenly when they were in a deep sleep, and Skip seemed more to be in a trance than in normal sleep

Skip rolled over, emitting sounds from his throat that may have been reactions to events taking place in his dream. He groaned often, and once or twice cried out in alarm. Whatever he was dreaming must have been horrific, for there was an unmistakable quality of fear in his cries, appearing so real it was indistinguishable from reality. His voice sounded raw and desperate, as though he were backed into a corner with no way of escape.

Just when Aunt May had decided to make an attempt at waking him he screamed. At the same time he sat bolt upright in bed and seemed to stare through them as if they were not even there.

The time for action had come; Nancy rushed to one side of the bed, Aunt May to the other. Gently they massaged Skip's arms, finding the muscles tense and stiff as a board. They massaged his scalp and cooed comforting sounds into his ear, not sure if anything they did was the right thing. It must have done some good, though, for his muscles relaxed and his eyes began to focus.

"Uh... where am I?"

Nancy said, "You're at home in bed and you just about frightened us to death with your crying and groaning in your sleep."

"They've come back?" Aunt May asked, "the dreams, I mean?"

Skip nodded, unable as yet to give voice to the still vivid images in his mind.

Aunt May sighed, "I think we'd better go downstairs and give you time to recover. I'll make hot chocolate and you can tell us about the dream. Talking about it may settle you."

"Dreams," Skip said.

"What?"

"There were dreams, not *one* dream."

"Well, put on a robe and come down when you're ready. There's nothing like sitting around my kitchen table with mugs of hot chocolate to give one a sense of normality."

Nancy looked distressed, "Are you ...are you...alright Skip?"

Skip nodded, "As Aunt May says, a mug of hot chocolate and sitting around the kitchen table will do wonders."

Somewhat reassured Nancy turned and followed Aunt May down the stairs.

When Skip came down he had obviously spent some time in the bathroom. His wavy red hair was brushed into a semblance of order and he seemed more in possession of himself. He sat down at the table and accepted the mug Aunt May handed to him.

"So," Aunt May said, "It's been almost a year since we got back from Nova Scotia, and you had any dreams. Now they're back. Do you have any idea why?"

"Not really," Skip replied, wrapping his hands around his mug as if it gave him comfort, "but I would guess it is because the victory God gave us over witchcraft is not the end of the fight. There are new dangers facing us."

Nancy shivered, as if memories of the dangers they had faced were still fresh in her mind, "You mean God may me calling us to fight another battle against the enemy?"

"Perhaps, but I wouldn't say 'us.' "There is no need for anyone else to get involved. I am the one having the dreams, so I guess I am the one responsible to see it through."

Nancy gave him a stubborn look, "Now Skip Jordan, you just think very carefully about that. What would you have done if Ashley and I had not been there to support you before?"

Aunt May intruded, "Why don't you just tell us what this last dream, or dreams, are all about. We can discuss who's to be involved later."

"Right," Skip said, "but I warn you, they were not dreams to encourage you."

"I never expected they would be, given the shouting that went on when you were having them. Drink the rest of that chocolate and I'll refill it. We're not likely to get much more sleep tonight, or should I say 'morning.' What were the dreams about?"

Skip drained the rest of his drink and allowed Aunt May to re-fill it. Leaning back in his chair he fixed his eyes on them both, and began:

"The first one was very disturbing. There was this church, filled to capacity. Every seat was taken. Extra chairs filled the aisles and people were standing around the walls and in the foyer."

"A full church was disturbing?" Nancy asked incredulously.

"Wait, just let me finish. The preacher had everyone's attention. He was saying over and over again, his arm stretched out pointing randomly at people in the congregation, 'You have the power! You have the power! Listen everyone, you have the power!' "

"So, what was disturbing?"

"The full church and the preacher was not all I saw. The scene changed, like a camera zooming back to take in the church from above. Swarming over and above the church was a host of demons. The presence of the demons was not as disturbing as what they were doing. They were filled with glee, shooting back and forth excitedly, and rejoicing over what was taking place below. They were laughing, and it wasn't a pretty sound. It sent shivers of apprehension through me."

"What was there to rejoice about?"

"That was the question I asked myself, and I thought it must have been over the message the preacher was delivering. There must have been something wrong with it, though I couldn't tell what. Whatever it was caused the demon host to rejoice."

Aunt May was pensive, "Let me think about it. I agree with you. Such a scene as you observed is more than disturbing – it is frightening. To see demons excited about what a Christian minister is preaching has to be one of the most frightening things I have heard for a long time."

"What else did you dream?" Nancy asked.

"I saw Roger."

"You saw whom?"

"I saw Roger Wilson, our former friend. I don't suppose you have forgotten him, that jolly intelligent guy we all loved? The Roger Wilson that got sucked into witchcraft and has since disappeared."

"What? Where was he when you saw him?"

"He was standing near a great waterfall. I think it must have been Victoria Falls in Africa. I was there when I was very young but the memories are vague. I've seen pictures of it on the internet, though, and in a coffee-table book at Ashley's house. It wasn't that hard to identify."

"What was Roger doing?"

"He was laughing, and it wasn't a pretty sound. It sounded more like the demoniacal laughter I heard in the previous dream. And it seemed like he was looking straight at me. His eyes were filled with mockery – and triumph. His look seemed to be telling me that, even if we won the last battle, we are doomed to failure this time."

"So, Roger Wilson is in Africa."

"It would seem so."

"Do you think we should tell his folks?" Nancy asked.

"I don't think so," Skip replied. "They have been through so much pain in the last year I don't think we should raise their hopes. Besides, what would we tell them? Should I tell them I dreamed Roger is in Africa? What good would that do? I wouldn't expect them to take me seriously."

"I agree" Aunt May said. "We must wait till we have more information, if there is more information to be found, that is. But you've not told us all you have dreamed yet, have you Skip?

"No."

They sat in silence while Skip closed his eyes. They guessed he was trying to decide what, details of the dream to share with them first. He shivered, as if the memory still sent tremors of horror and fear through him. At last he opened his eyes and asked, "Do you remember Ntambo?"

"The African convert who saved your life when you were four years old?"

"Yes. You will also remember the letter he included in the box I keep under my bed; the box containing my mother's journal and other items."

Nancy recalled, "He also wrote you a letter after we returned from Nova Scotia describing how the Lord had called him to support you in prayer."

Skip nodded, "He also gathered some former witchdoctors to support him. They engaged in spiritual warfare to support us in the fight against witchcraft."

"What about him?" Aunt May asked.

Skip shivered, in spite of the hot chocolate warming his insides, "I saw him in my dream." Skip said, and fell silent again.

"Well, what about him?" Nancy asked. There was a touch of impatience in her manner.

Aunt May lay a restraining hand on her arm, "Don't rush him, Nance. Something bad happened in his dream. Just give him time."

Skip sighed and looked both of them in the eye, "I saw Ntambo die," he said.

Chapter 3

Trying to Understand

"So, tell us what happened to Ntambo," James Johnson asked. It was late afternoon of the following day, Saturday, and Aunt May's kitchen was again being used as a gathering place for Skip and Nancy's friends.

Aunt May had dragged a love-seat into the kitchen, and some extra chairs. The living room in this house had not been well planned, getting little light and even less sun. Her kitchen on the other hand got both morning and afternoon sun since it had been built on with windows on three sides. It was the ideal place for the gathering of family and friends.

Aunt May was in the love seat with Reginald Alderman, his arm around her shoulders and her head resting comfortably on his shoulder. With their wedding day only a week away Skip thought they presented a picture of love and devotion good for teenagers to see. It was unusual for a room full of teenagers to be comfortable in the presence of adults, but none of them thought of Aunt May exactly as an adult. Her warm personality and caring demeanour made her seem more like one of them. And since Reggie Alderman was soon going to marry aunt May, he felt part of their group as well. Besides, Reggie had an aura of wisdom about him, and the need for wisdom in the present circumstances was obvious.

Skip let his eye pass affectionately over the others present in the room. Besides James there was Nancy who, as Skip's 'sister,' had taken over the tea and coffee duties of the house, and was proving quite an asset to Aunt May in the kitchen. Ashley Woods, though casually dressed still looked immaculate with every hair in place and a demure expression on her face.

Andrew Wen and Leon Craig had become regular visitors in the past year. Both of their lives had been transformed since their deliverance from witchcraft the previous summer. All in all they were a happy and contented gathering of friends. Were it not for the shadow of gloom that hung over them due to Skip's dream, they might have been care-free and light-hearted.

As it was, all of them had had enough experience of the dark forces of witchcraft not to treat Skip's dreams lightly. His dreams over a year ago had proved accurate and there was no reason to believe these most recent dreams would be any different. To those gathered these dreams were an ominous sign of an evil cloud gathering. Evil had indeed suffered a stunning blow at the Magic Moments Retreat. Christ Himself had appeared as the suffering Saviour and risen Lord when The Veil of Deception had hung over the valley. As a result the forces of darkness had scattered. Yet none of those present in Aunt May's kitchen that afternoon imagined the battle was over. Again, the Deceiver was about to cast a cloak of deception over the world like nothing they had ever seen before. Skip thought the cloak had already been cast and they were only becoming aware of it now.

Nancy poured some lemonade into a glass and set it on the table before him, "I know your brilliant mind is occupied, but we all want to know the details." Her teasing manner was obviously designed to lighten the mood.

Skip smiled at her before turning his attention once more to the whole company, "You all know from the letter I read you earlier what a vital part Ntambo and his former witchdoctor friends played in the deliverance of so many from the deception of witchcraft."

"And mine," said Leon.

"And mine," echoed Andrew.

"Well, in my dream I saw a great crowd of people seething around Ntambo. They were on a high plateau and Ntambo was being pushed ahead of the crowd. It was like they were herding him to a pre-arranged destination."

"What was the destination?"

"They were herding him to a ledge overlooking Victoria Falls in Africa."

"Did they push him over?" Andrew asked.

"From where I was standing I couldn't see everything, but I saw him tip over the edge... and disappear."

"Who were these people?" Ashley enquired.

"I don't know. As far as I could tell they were not from only one nation. I thought I saw Africans, Asians, Europeans, and Orientals. There were some I couldn't exactly identify. It was obvious Ntambo had offended them in some way that had earned their hatred. Their hatred was enough to make them willing to murder him. What such a diverse group were doing all together in the middle of Africa I have no idea."

Reginald removed his arm from around Aunt May and leaned forward, "They were no doubt gathered for some common goal, a conference to discuss shared concerns."

"That may be," Ashley said, "but what kind of conference would be so incensed against one man they were prepared to kill him?"

"Only those united in the service of evil," Skip replied, then asked a question of his own, "But what I want to know is, why me?"

"I'll only be fifteen in a few weeks. Shouldn't these dreams be given to someone older and wiser, like Reggie here?"

Reginald squeezed aunt May's hand as if to confirm something they had discussed privately, before turning his full attention on Skip, "When God chooses someone, Skip, He doesn't do it according to human wisdom, as you well know. When God called you and the girls to rescue those at the Magical Moments Retreat, what was it that encouraged you to continue?"

"Well, it was a lot of things, including the backing you and Aunt May gave us, and the prayers of people I didn't even know were praying for us."

"That is all true, Skip, but I'm thinking of one single thing that made you believe it was even possible."

"If you mean a promise from the Bible," Skip replied, "I'd say it was the one that says, if I can remember it correctly: '*But God chose the foolish things of the world to shame the wise, and he chose the weak things of the world to shame the strong.*' "[ii] "So," Reginald said, "you know God doesn't always use the strong, why would you then have a problem with how old you are?"

"I just thought..."

"You thought there would be a problem because you do not feel any older than a boy."

"I guess so."

"Then listen to what Jeremiah said about his own call into God's service:

'The Lord spoke his word to me, saying:
"Before I made you in your mother's womb, I chose you.
Before you were born, I set you apart for a special work.
I appointed you as a prophet to the nations."

Then I said, "But Lord God, I don't know how to speak. I am only a boy."

But the Lord said to me, "Don't say, 'I am only a boy.' You must go everywhere I send you, and you must say everything I tell you to say.Don't be afraid of anyone, because I am with you to protect you," says the Lord.'[iii]

"Jeremiah also thought being a mere boy would disqualify him from being called of God, but God told him he was mistaken."

Skip sighed, "Thanks, that does make me feel better, but I'll tell you what encourages me most in that passage."

"What is that?"

"The part that encourages me is where God promises to protect him. I don't think the Lord would give me these dreams unless He wanted me to be involved in some conflict, as we all were last summer. If that is true I'm going to need all the protection I can get."

"I also think," Reggie said, "that something else God said to Jeremiah also applies to you."

"You mean..."

"I mean the word God spoke to him at the beginning: *'Before I made you in your mother's womb, I chose you. Before you were born, I set you apart for a special work.'*"[iv]

Skip seemed overwhelmed by the idea, "My mother's journal seems to imply the same thing, but I'll tell you the truth, I've never felt less 'chosen' for anything in my entire life. I feel scared, uncertain. I feel overwhelmed, but certainly not *chosen*."

"That's what you ought to be feeling," Reggie said. "If you were feeling especially chosen you may be tempted to pride, and the Lord could not use you. I do believe, however, He is preparing you for something rather special this time."

Skip glanced at the others in the room. Nancy had an expression on her face that spoke volumes. It seemed to say, "Oh no, not again."

Aunt May just smiled, as though she had some secret knowledge. James' eyes were large, and his lower lip trembled. Leon and Andrew exhibited interest and perhaps a little awe at the turn of events, but no evident alarm. Ashley's expression was sober, as though she was under no delusion as to what all this meant. She had seen what the enemy could do.

Reginald said. "I think some serious conflict is ahead, and we must lean on His promise of protection." He paused then continued, "I just want to correct one idea you have."

"What is that?"

"You have the idea you are having dreams. I don't think that is quite correct."

"What are they then?"

"I think they are visions."

"What's the difference?"

"I'm not sure there *is* much of a difference, except that Scripture makes the distinction. We should always call things what God calls them, even if we don't understand why. I believe what you've been seeing is what the prophet Joel said would happen in the last days before Jesus returns. Let me read it to you." He drew a New Testament from his pocket and read:

But Joel the prophet wrote about what is happening here today:
God says: In the last days
I will pour out my Spirit on all kinds of people.
Your sons and daughters will prophesy.
Your young men will see visions,
and your old men will dream dreams.[v]

"You see, young men will see visions, old men will dream dreams. There is a clear distinction made between the two."

"All of this is very interesting," Nancy said, "and I am sure it is important. But what do Skips dreams, or visions, mean practically? Are we supposed to rush off to Africa, like we rushed off to Nova Scotia last year? Should we try again to rescue Roger from his involvement in witchcraft? Must we try to prevent Ntambo from being murdered, or is that going to happen whatever we do? If we are going to Africa how are we going to *get* there?"

Aunt May smiled at Nancy's monologue, then grinned as she nudged Reginald in the ribs, "Don't you think we ought to tell them now?"

"Tell us what?" The question came as a chorus from all the others in the room.

"Well, Reginald and I are getting married in a week, and we're going on a honeymoon."

"We knew that," said Skip, speaking for the rest.

"What you didn't know, is that we are planning to take you, Skip, Nancy, and Ashley, with us."

Everyone gasped.

"Not exactly *with* us," Reginald corrected.

"No, not *with* us, but they'll fly to the same continent with us, anyway. Why don't you tell them the details? It was your idea to start with."

Reginald put his arm back around Aunt May and drew her close before responding, "May and I are going on an extended tour of Africa, visiting some of the more famous places. We've made arrangements for you to stay with the missionaries that replaced Skip's parents after they were killed."

"But I thought Nancy and I were going to stay at Ashley's house while you are away."

"That was the original plan," Aunt May said, "but Mr. Woods has been called to take extra courses at a summer school. Ashley's mother has decided to go with him."

Ashley's jaw dropped, "I... I was not told about that."

"I think your parents wanted it to be a surprise. They were very grateful when we offered to take you to Africa with us. They think it will be a wonderful experience for you to travel to another continent. I guess you *are* surprised?"

"I don't think that's quite the word to describe it. I'm *more* than surprised. I'm..."

"Amazed, shocked, and you're a little hurt at being left out of things?" Aunt May finished for her.

"I guess that's as good a way of describing my feelings as any other."

"I'll actually see the place where I was born, and see my old friend Ntambo again," Skip interjected.

"I don't think Ntambo lives at the mission anymore, Skip. I believe he got married and moved away, but perhaps he is not very far away and you may still be able to see him."

....

Three months earlier...

Angela Symonds had only been working at the Bartlett Home for three months. During that time her warm personality and bright outlook had marginally changed the atmosphere in the place.

The other workers, most of them having worked here for many years, had become fatalistic in their dealings with the inmates. Angela did not blame them. She understood that working with mentally ill patients for years on end without seeing any improvement in their condition could be discouraging. Worse, it could paralyze a person with a sense of the hopelessness of the work being done here. Any worker exposed to the extreme nature of the inmates' illness would begin to feel a sense of futility. They would conclude that all they were doing was keeping people alive who had no hope of ever living meaningful lives. They were merely extending their existence, but not their lives. As a result most of the workers at the Bartlett Home went about their duties mechanically, treating the inmates as objects rather than people. Angela prayed she would not succumb to the same sense of futility as the rest of the workers had.

The matron on the same shift as Angela, was a good woman in her fifties by the name of Regina Hill. She was efficient, fair in her dealings with the staff, and skilled in handling the often wild behaviour of the inmates. However, she had long ago given up any aspirations of doing any good to those committed into her care. She advised Angela to do the same. "It will save you a great deal of disappointment," she said.

Angela had determined in her heart never to follow such advice, particularly in the case of Raymond Nichol. That gentleman, and Angela insisted on referring to him as such, had suffered some cataclysmic event that had driven him over the edge. His mind had snapped. Now he existed in a semi-catatonic state, with staring eyes and mumbled phrases that meant nothing to anyone but him. They may not have meant anything to *him* either. But this was not always true. Angela had detected lucid moments when Raymond Nichol seemed well aware of his surroundings and even of the events that had brought him here. These occurrences had been brief, but Angela had seized these moments as tendrils of hope to cling to. She took them as an opportunity to pray with him.

The more Angela prayed with Raymond Nichol the more his lucid moments increased. Against protocol she accessed his file and discovered two things about him: he had been a teacher and he had been involved in witchcraft. This information spurred her on to pray with more intensity.

Now Angela Symonds was a very attractive girl; what is more she was young and vibrant with an interest in people that immediately endeared her to those with whom she came in contact. She came into Raymond's room one morning to find him staring at her with both intelligence and interest. For the first time in the year he had been here, he spoke. So his file indicated. His unintelligible mumbling was not considered speech in any meaningful sense.

Mr. Nichol said, "You are a Christian." It was not a question, only the expression of a conclusion he had come to.

Angela's heart beat faster. Was she seeing what her colleagues believed impossible – the miraculous recovery of a chronically ill mental patient? Would he remain lucid long enough for her to help him, or would he slip back into his catatonic state before she could reach him? There was no way of measuring these things.

His next utterance was equally stunning, "Is there hope for me?"

Angela drew closer to him and laid a hand on his arm, "Hope for what, Mr. Nichol?"

"Hope for Heaven; hope for salvation; hope for whatever it is you Christians proclaim."

Joy coursed through Angela and she was about to answer when the glaze of non-comprehension returned to his eyes and he was once more unreachable. However, she was not discouraged. The incident was proof to her that recovery for Raymond Nichol was possible. More than that, his lucidity was focussed on the most vital issue that could occupy the mind of anyone: the issue of his soul's salvation. She determined to spend more time in prayer than ever for this man. Her dealings with him, to date, confirmed her conviction that God had called her to reach out to those whom most people considered unreachable. If she could have seen into the future Angela may have had second thoughts regarding her interest in this man. As it was, she was blissfully unaware of the events that would transpire as a result of her involvement with Raymond Nichol.

Angela Symonds was also unaware, at that moment, of what was going on in the heavenly realms. Far above, but looking down directly at the occupants of room 208 in the Bartlett Home, were two angelic beings. They saw what Angela could not see – two demonic entities holding Raymond Nichol in the grip of madness. For a brief period they had broken the demonic hold on their charge – for he was their charge. That brief period of release had been enough for the girl to perceive the possibility of recovery.

In silent communication the taller of the two angels said, "It won't be long now. He-who-knows-all has plans for this brand plucked from the burning. Though the enemy has used him for evil, his future will be in the service of Truth, though he is to know suffering beyond his comprehension."

"How long before we can act?" asked the other angel.

"Soon," his companion replied. "We'll be able to act very soon."

Chapter 4

The Attack

"You have just *got* to let me come with you," James Johnson said, gripping Skip's shirt sleeve with an intensity that threatened to tear it at the seams, "I couldn't *bear* to be left alone all summer while you go off to Africa."

Nancy grinned at James' antics, "You won't be alone. You'll have Andrew and Leon to keep you company."

"You know what I mean," James responded, impatient of Nancy's lack of comprehension, "I have just got to be involved in trying to get Rodger out of the clutches of the devil. This is a personal thing with me, and you know it."

Skip made eye contact with the girls, "Besides the fact that it is not our decision to make, James, we may never get the chance. We may never get beyond the mission station where we will be staying."

James' eyes expressed exasperation and superior knowledge when he replied, "You know better than that, Skip. I was there when Reggie discussed your visions, and visions they were. God would not have given them to you if he did not intend you to get involved. It is no accident that you and Ashley and Nancy suddenly get the opportunity to go to Africa. It must be the Lord who arranged that."

"Then perhaps you ought to talk to the Lord about letting you come with us, "Ashley said. "If He wants you to come with us, He'll make it happen."

James sighed, "I already have. I'm just not sure it *is* His will for me to go. But I *need* to go."

The four friends were lounging on chairs on the back deck to Aunt May's house. They had not been keeping their voices low, so their voices echoed over the lake and back through the open glass doors into the house. It was not long before Aunt May and Reginald appeared at the open door to see for themselves the small drama taking place amongst the young people.

"You can't force God to agree to what you want to happen," Skip said mildly. "Serving the Lord is not you leading and Him following. It is the other way around."

"I *know*, but I'm having trouble doing that. It just seems right that I should be going. I admit I'm envious of you three going while I have to stay behind.

"What would your parents say about you running off to Africa? Reginald said from behind him, moving forward to stand in front of them. Aunt May remained at the door.

Surprise at the older man's appearance registered on their faces, and James shrugged his shoulders, "I think Mom would be glad to see me go. Since I've lost weight and won't eat all the cake she baked for me, we've sort of grown apart. And she calls me a fanatic for committing my life to Christ. She says I've become a religious nut."

"What about your father? What does he think?"

"Well, Dad wouldn't mind me going. He can afford to send me, but he won't. He agrees with my mother that I've become fanatical about religion. Things haven't exactly been comfortable around home lately."

"So, how exactly do to plan to get the money go to Africa?"

James' shoulders slumped, "I don't know... exactly. I guess I was going to pray Dad would change his mind, or for a miracle, which may be the same thing."

Reginald gave James a kind look and said, "I think praying is an excellent idea, but prayer is not demanding from God what you want. Prayer is a uniting of your will with God's so that anything you *do* want is according to God's will. The apostle John put it this way: *'And this is the boldness we have in God's presence: that if we ask God for anything that agrees with what he wants, he hears us. If we know he hears us every time we ask him, we know we have what we ask from him.'* [vi]

"Do you think you can pray like that, James, if know what you want may be different to what God wants?"

"You mean it is I who has to change what I want to fit in with what God wants?"

"Yes, God's will is always good and right and will work together for our good. God is not going to change what He wants to fit into what you want, but He will change your heart to want what He wants, if you ask Him. "

James turned to his friends, "Will you help me pray?" he asked gently.

"Of course we will!" they all said.

....

"You mean you're going to take us with you to visit your friend Joshua?" Nancy asked. "I thought he only allowed *you* to visit him."

Skip punched Nancy on the arm, playfully, "Joshua told me to bring you and Ashley a long time ago. And seeing James is coming on the trip to Africa with us, I asked permission for him to come along, too."

James gasped, "I'm coming where?"

Skip glanced secretly at the girls, "Oh," he said, pretending forgetfulness, "you didn't know? Oh my, girls! Nobody's told him yet."

"Told me what? Now stop your clowning around Skip. Tell me what's going on."

"Do you think we should tell him now or later, Ash?"

"I think it would be cruel to make him wait *too* long," she teased, "Perhaps tomorrow would be soon enough."

Nancy came to James' defence, "Stop guys! You're tormenting the poor man. Tell him Reginald went to see his Dad, and he has agreed to cover the costs." She turned to James, "You're coming with us, buddy!" Ashley and Nancy squealed with delight and hugged him affectionately. Skip just grinned and patted him on the arm.

When the celebrating had calmed down, Ashley asked, "So, when are we going to see Joshua?"

Skip raised his hands in imitation of a ghoul creeping up on its victims, "When it is dark and there is no moon and the woods are teeming with frightening creatures."

Skip's three friends suddenly descended upon him in playful attack, punching and tickling till he held up his hands in surrender, "OK, OK, I'll tell you."

Laughing, they all settled back in their deck chairs and waited for Skip to speak.

"It will have to be this afternoon after lunch. We're leaving in two days and tomorrow is going to be busy. Put on some walking shoes and take some bottled water." His tone turned more serious, "Get ready for a real treat. Joshua is like no man I've ever known."

The footbridge that had been washed away by the flood had been rebuilt so there was no need to use a boat to get across.

The bridge itself was well constructed, with stone and concrete footings; the foundations would not give way easily even when the river was in flood. The wooden railings and surface of the bridge were likewise made of the strongest and most durable timber available. Walking over it felt safe and the muffled sound of their footsteps somehow comforting.

Ashley lifted her eyes to the blue overhead and commented, "Hardly a cloud in the sky. I just love this time of year."

Not having brought his watch Skip glanced at the sun and judged it was just an hour or so past noon. It was a perfect day for a long hike through the woods. There would be birds and beetles, and the occasional sighting of a deer to delight the girls.

After crossing the bridge and trudging up the slope they reached the edge of the tree-line and Skip went ahead to show the way. Sun filtered through the tops of the trees shedding golden beams of light, while small creatures peered at them from the shadows.

For perhaps half an hour they made their light-hearted way toward their destination; then the atmosphere changed. The sound of the forest dwellers ceased and an eerie silence settled upon them. The beams of sunlight faded and disappeared. Shadows became dark pools that encroached on, and finally swallowed the remaining light. Total darkness settled upon them. Tendrils of fear clutched at their hearts and a sense of doom pervaded the atmosphere. The pungent odour of sulphur assaulted their nostrils, alerting them to the source of their present predicament. They all remembered a previous occasion when fire and brimstone had fallen from a clear sky and the smell of sulphur had pervaded the air. It was the odour and atmosphere of hell itself.

No one needed to be told they were under assault from the forces of darkness. As young as they were they had all faced the onslaught of demons. They had experienced attacks from the Looming Menace, a demonic being intent upon snuffing out their lives. They had faced phantom storms, seen volcanic ash falling from the sky, and seen a Veil of Deception loom over a host of witches and wizards. This, however, was something new and more terrifying; their throats constricted and robbed them of the power of speech.

No one moved, till the silence was broken and the screeching of hellish beings filled the air. The noise they made was not the worst if it; the palpable presence of the beings themselves invaded their space. Though they could not see them, they zoomed past and the wind of their passing brushed the skin of their faces and stirred the edges of their clothing.

Skip at last found his voice, "Hold hands! Stay together!" he shouted above the clamour, but he was too late. Both girls screamed and seemed to have been knocked off their feet. One of them, Skip could not tell which, grabbed at his sleeve and he clutched desperately, managing to get hold of a wrist. James came alongside and got hold of an arm. The other girl's screams faded.

"Pray!" Skip shouted. "With everything that is in you, pray!"

With the exception of that one occasion when the Looming Menace had almost stolen his mind, Skip prayed more desperately than he had ever done in his life. As intense as the battle over the witches retreat had been, he had never imagined spirit beings would have substance. Whatever these demonic entities were they had the power to invade the physical world. He heard Ashley's voice close to his ear crying out and knew it must be Nancy who had been snatched away. If possible, his praying grew more intense, and the blackness turned grey, twilight, and at last the sunlight broke through the tree tops once more. Nancy was nowhere in sight.

They found her five minutes later in a depression near the trunk of a fallen tree. She was unconscious, but her breathing was steady and regular. When her eyes finally opened they all let out their breath in relief, unaware they had even been holding it.

Nancy still looked dazed when she said, "What happened? Where am I?"

Skip was kneeling on the leafy undergrowth close to her head while Ashley and James observed from above.

James knelt and took hold of Nancy's left hand while Skip gripped her right. In this way they helped her to her feet. Only then did it become evident Nancy's ankle was twisted; she could hardly rest any weight on it at all. She cried out in pain when it touched the ground. Ashley knelt down to examine it while Skip and James supported her.

Ashley said, "It is swollen. She's not going to be able to walk on her own. How far is there still to go?"

"Not very far," he replied, turning to James, "If we placed her arms around both of our necks we could get her to Joshua's place without much trouble. What do you say to that, Nance?" Her cheeks turned crimson, something Skip and James hardly noticed but brought a knowing smile to Ashley's lips. Guys were so dumb. They never had a clue.

So, with her arms draped around their necks, each of their hands around her waist, Nancy was half carried to Joshua's lair. Her good leg supported some of her weight as she hopped along while holding her injured ankle above the ground. Only Ashley noticed that the crimson tinge to Nancy's cheeks did not depart until they reached their destination.

When they arrived at the top of the ravine Joshua was already there waiting for them. He seemed to have been aware of their trouble and anticipated the need to carry Nancy down the difficult path to his solitary dwelling. Giant as he was in their eyes, they could not help but notice the gentle way he took Nancy into his arms, or the loving concern that wrinkled his brow.

Joshua never spoke as he placed Nancy on the bunk-like bed and bustled around the tiny dwelling to minister to her needs. He placed an extra pot of water on the stove, retrieved bandages and liniment from a shelf and attended to her injuries silently and efficiently. The kerosene lamp he had set on a stool, shed its yellow light on her finally calm features.

Only when he was done and Nancy's grateful smile assured him she was comfortable, did he turn to the others.

"I only have one chair," he said apologetically, and offered it to Ashley. "The rest of us can use the floor." His six foot six inches of height folded till, resting his back against a wall, he said, "Now tell me what happened."

Skip and James followed his example, lowering their bottoms to the rough boards and wrapping their arms around their knees.

Joshua did not rush them, but waited patiently while Skip gathered his thoughts to reveal the events of the past few days. At last he said, "It was pretty bad, the attack, I mean. I know I was supposed to trust the Lord and not be afraid, but Joshua, I was terrified."

"We all were," Ashley said.

"I was beyond terrified," Nancy said from the bunk, glancing significantly at her bandaged ankle.

"Tell me the details," Joshua insisted.

When Skip and the others described, each from their own perspective what had happened, Joshua said, "They were ghouls, at least a counterfeit manifestation of them"

The young people made eye contact with each other, remembering the almost exact description Skip had given earlier of what had happened to them in the woods.

"I was just joking," Skip said in his defence.

Joshua eyes sparkled with interest, "What were you joking about?"

"We asked Skip when he was bringing us to visit you," James replied, "and he put on a creepy show." If I remember correctly he said something like 'When it is dark and there is no moon and the woods are teeming with frightening creatures.'

"At the same time he raised his hands in imitation of a ghoul creeping up on its victims. It was really quite good, now I think about it, but none of us expected it to actually happen. As Skip says, it was just a joke."

They sat in silence till Nancy asked, "What is a ghoul exactly? I know it is something awful, but I've never actually understood what they are."

"They are mythical creatures, mere superstition," Joshua replied. They don't actually exist, but Satan is capable of producing demonic imitations of them. There must be something mighty important coming up for him to go to such trouble to stop you."

"There is," Skip said. "We're all going to Africa."

"What do you hope to accomplish there?"

"We're not sure, but I've been having dreams, or visions, again, and Africa seems to be where it's at. Aunt May and Reginald are going there on honeymoon, and they're taking us to stay on the mission station where I was born while they're away."

"I want to hear about your visions, Skip, but first let me answer Nancy's question about ghouls."

Ashley went over to help Nancy sit up so she could give better attention to what Joshua was about to tell her. She placed a pillow at her friend's back and went again to sit on the only chair gracing the available space.

Turning to Nancy, Joshua explained, "Ghouls are the hellish invention of human imagination. They first appeared in the original writings of Arabic, Persian, and Indian tales. The Arabic tales of the Thousand and One Nights mentions them. They were creatures conjured up from the dark places of the human mind and believed in by many. They were supposed to lure people into the desert to kill and eat them. They would rob graves and devour young children.

"Now, ghouls do not exist, but demons do. What you experienced out there in the woods was an attempt by the forces of darkness to discourage you from pursuing whatever it is you intend to do in Africa."

"I'm not entirely sure what that is," Skip said.

"Whatever it is God wants you to do in Africa must be very important or the attack would not have been so severe." Joshua glanced at Nancy's injured ankle, "I confess I have never heard of demons actually inflicting physical injuries to humans. A human possessed by demons may be able to do so, but not by direct assault. I must warn you, Skip, the battle you are about to engage in may be several notches more dangerous than what you experienced last year."

Skip's voice was not entirely steady when he said, "We'll just have to trust the promises of God more than we ever have before." All he got for a response was the solemn nods of his companions.

Chapter 5

The Power

"Now you have to tell me about your visions, Skip. I believe they were given to prepare you for what is to come."

For the next half hour Skip related in detail what he had seen in his dreams (he still could not think of them as visions), including the disturbing thoughts he had been having as a result.

"I mean, all three disturbed me for different reasons. I haven't seen Ntambo since I was four years old, and I've only read two letters from him, yet seeing him disappear over the edge of the falls just about tore my heart out. It felt like part of me was going over with him. One thought keeps going around and around in my head."

"What would that be?"

"It is a question. Is God telling us that Ntambo *will* die, no matter what we or anyone else does? Or, it is only what will happen if we don't obey and follow God's leading?"

Joshua closed his eyes and leaned his back against the wall before answering. Birds twittered and complained outside. A squirrel peered at them curiously from the door before scurrying off. Those inside the hut seemed to be holding their breaths in anticipation of Joshua's answer.

At last Joshua shifted his bulk and made eye contact with each of the young people. He sighed, "The Scriptures tell us that God's ways are past finding out, or they are beyond our comprehension. However, God gave us the Bible to guide us in both our thinking and in our actions. There are examples in the Bible of both kinds of visions; those that reveal the unchangeable purpose of God: there are also warnings of what will happen, but where appropriate action can still avert disaster."

"Nancy asked, "You mean it is possible Ntambo may not die in spite of what Skip saw?"

"It is possible, not certain."

"You have something in mind," Ashley said, "some passage in the Bible that may be important?" Ashley had the quieter nature, yet Skip knew, she was observant and could at times discern moods and intentions.

"I do," Joshua answered. "I was thinking of Joseph in the book of Genesis. You will remember God gave him dreams that firmly predicted the honour his father would give him in the future. Nothing could change the fulfilment of those dreams.

Joshua rose from the floor and stood over the Bible lying open on the table. Finding his place, he began to read: *This will happen as I told you. God is showing the king what he is about to do.You will have seven years of good crops and plenty to eat in all the land of Egypt.But after those seven years, there will come seven years of hunger, and all the food that grew in the land of Egypt will be forgotten. The time of hunger will eat up the land.People will forget what it was like to have plenty of food, because the hunger that follows will be so great. You had two dreams which mean the same thing. This shows that God has firmly decided that this will happen, and he will make it happen soon.*[vii] "Nothing could change what God was going to do. He was going to bring seven years of plenty on the land, followed by seven years of famine, but that did not mean the outcome of the famine could not be changed. The natural outcome of a seven year famine would be starvation and death, but what actually happened?"

"Joseph came up with a plan that changed the natural course of events," James said.

"That is right. Guided by God, Joseph came up with a plan that would divert disaster." Joshua went back to reading"

"So let the king choose a man who is very wise and understanding and set him over the land of Egypt.And let the king also appoint officers over the land, who should take one-fifth of all the food that is grown during the seven good years. They should gather all the food that is produced during the good years that are coming, and under the king's authority they should store the grain in the cities and guard it.That food should be saved to use during the seven years of hunger that will come on the land of Egypt. Then the people in Egypt will not die during the seven years of hunger."[viii]

"So," Skip said. A faint tendril of hope was evident in his voice, "My seeing Ntambo going over the edge of the cliff will happen, but I didn't actually *see* him dashed on the rocks and swept away by the waterfall. The outcome *may* be different to what I imagined?"

"Yes, Skip, but you mustn't allow yourself to hope too much. It is a very faint possibility that the outcome will be different to what one would expect after seeing someone going over a cliff. Only a divine act could avert Ntambo's death."

Nancy said excitedly, "I saw a movie once, starring Harrison Ford and Tommy Lee Jones. *The Fugitive*, I think it was called. Harrison Ford was trapped at the edge of a duct overlooking the rushing waters flowing over the wall of a dam. In the movie, Harrison Ford throws himself over the edge in a desperate attempt to escape. He plunges into the raging water and disappears from sight. Everyone assumes the game is over. The fugitive could not possibly survive such a fall. Tommy Lee Jones, however, makes no such assumption. He orders a full scale search. Until he sees the body of the fugitive he will not give up the pursuit – and he was right – the fugitive did survive.

"I know it was just a movie," Nancy concluded weakly, "but it gives me something to think about."

"That's OK, Nancy," Joshua said, returning to his place on the floor, "We are dealing with things beyond human understanding. Only God knows the final outcome, but we can hope, and pray – and believe." Turning to Skip, Joshua enquired, "What else disturbs you about your visions?"

Skip stood up to pace awkwardly in the confined space, "The expression I saw on Roger's face when I saw it against the background of the falls disturbed me. It was so full of mockery and derision. I guess I was hoping there would be some evidence he was having doubts about the course he has chosen. I didn't detect anything of the kind. He looked like he had solidly aligned himself with the forces of darkness."

Joshua said, "You never can tell. The apostle Paul was standing by gloating over the fate of Stephen when he was being stoned. No one would have guessed he was having doubts. In fact he later got letters from the authorities in Jerusalem to those in Damascus.

Those letters would enable him to kill and imprison believers. On the road to his destination, however, everything changed:

So Saul headed toward Damascus. As he came near the city, a bright light from heaven suddenly flashed around him. Saul fell to the ground and heard a voice saying to him, "Saul, Saul! Why are you persecuting me?"

Saul said, "Who are you, Lord?"

The voice answered, "I am Jesus, whom you are persecuting. Get up now and go into the city. Someone there will tell you what you must do."[ix]

"All the while he was raging and intent on his mission to destroy Christians, something was goading him on the inside. He appeared convinced of the rightness of what he was doing but could not rid himself of the nagging doubts. In the end he surrendered to Christ and served him like few have served Him since."

Skip stopped pacing, "So you think Roger may be having doubts in spite of the rage and cruelty I saw in his face."

"It is possible, Skip. Besides, we should never give up on the ones we love. God works in mysterious ways. We are all different, and different means may have to be used to bring each individual to the truth. With some, the truth comes easily; with others God may have to use more extreme measures."

There was silence in the cabin as each of them thought on the lessons Joshua had shared with them. It was almost too much to take in all at once. There was no doubt they were involved in a mighty conflict between light and darkness. If nothing else the demonic attack they had so recently experienced in the woods convinced them of that. And the battles they were still to face were not likely to get easier.

The new perspective Joshua had revealed to them regarding Ntambo's possible deliverance suspended them between hope and despair. It was *possible* he may ultimately survive, but common sense decreed that he would not.

The same kind of suspension between hope and despair applied to their friend Roger as well. They had discussed it among themselves and determined to always refer to him as their friend, despite the antagonism and hatred he displayed toward them. They *had* to believe in his deliverance or any attempt to reach him would be undermined by their unbelief.

The silence was broken by James, "I am still confused about that preacher and the packed church Skip saw. Why would demons be ecstatic over the preacher's message that believers have the power? Isn't that true? When we believe in Jesus we are born again. The Spirit of God enters into us, and we are not living by our own power any more. So, what is wrong with the preacher's message?"

Joshua did not answer immediately. He closed his eyes as if praying for wisdom. When he opened his eyes again he turned his gaze on each of them individually before speaking, "Before I reply I want to ask you all a question." He paused, and they all held their breath in anticipation.

"If you were going to print counterfeit money, how close would you want the counterfeit to look like the real thing?"

"I would say so close it would be almost impossible to tell the difference between the two." A glimmer of understanding was beginning to dawn on Skip.

"Correct. You would want the fake bills to look so much like the originals that anyone but an expert wouldn't be able to tell the difference. When Satan wishes to turn people away from the truth he does the same. He does not always tell obvious lies. His lie would be so close to the truth very few would be able to tell the difference.

"When that preacher declared over and over again, "You have the power!" he was declaring the truth and a lie at the same time. "

"What do you mean?"

"Jesus told the disciples before He ascended into Heaven, *But when the Holy Spirit comes to you, you will receive power. You will be my witnesses—in Jerusalem, in all of Judea, in Samaria, and in every part of the world."*[x]

"The disciples only had power after the Holy Spirit came upon them. It was not *their* power. It was the *Holy Spirit's* power. When the Holy Spirit came upon them they had His power available to them, so long as they walked in the truth and submitted themselves to the will of God.

"If you had the power it would mean you could use that power for anything you want, even if it ran contrary to God's purpose for your life. The devil told Eve in the Garden of Eden that if they ate fruit from the tree God had forbidden them to eat from, they would be like gods. If *you* had the power you could use it any way you liked. You would be like a god. It is the same lie the Serpent told to Eve in the garden."

"So," Ashley said, "the Holy Spirit and His power cannot be separated."

"That is correct. He works His power in and through those who have surrendered to His will and purpose."

"So what the preacher should have been preaching was, 'When you have received the Holy Spirit you will have the power to do anything God wants you to do."

"Yes, it *seems* like the same thing, but there is a world of difference between the two. Telling people *they* have the power is more like sorcery and witchcraft. It is the sorcerer's art, the power of mind and positive thinking that can be exerted by Christians and non-Christians alike. The demonic host you saw, Skip, were rejoicing because they knew the preacher was tapping into the powers of darkness, without knowing it."

No one said anything for several minutes. All of this was almost too much to take in, but if they thought Joshua was finished with them, they were mistaken.

"I have a question for each of you," Joshua declared after a while, "Has the Holy Spirit come upon you yet?"

Nancy adjusted her sprained ankle and said, "We all have the Holy Spirit. If we did not have the Holy Spirit we would not be Christians at all. Christ lives in our hearts by the Holy Spirit or we could not live the Christian life."

"That is not what I asked you," Joshua replied. "You have the Holy Spirit *in* you. You were born again of the Spirit when you put your faith in Christ. What I asked was has the Holy Spirit come *upon* you?"

"We're not sure what you mean," Skip said.

"Alright, let me show you what I mean. Do you remember what happened after Jesus rose from the dead, what He did for them? You will find it in the Gospel of John: *Then Jesus said again, "Peace be with you. As the Father sent me, I now send you." After he said this, he breathed on them and said, "Receive the Holy Spirit.*[xi]

"The disciples received the Holy Spirit when Jesus breathed on them. They *had* the Holy Spirit. He was *in* them. Yet almost two months later He tells them: *"...but you will receive power when the Holy Spirit has come upon you; and you shall be My witnesses both in Jerusalem, and in all Judea and Samaria, and even to the remotest part of the earth.*[xii]

"When Jesus breathed on them the disciples had the *presence* of the Holy Spirit; after the Holy Spirit had come *upon* them they had the *power* of the Holy Spirit to accomplish the work He had called them to."

"What you are saying," Ashley concluded, "is that we lack the Holy Spirit's power to do His work. Then how were Skip, Nancy and I able to rescue James and others from the Magical Moments Retreat if the Holy Spirit was not involved?"

"Oh, the Holy Spirit was *involved*, alright. You will probably never know how much prayer was offered for you, or by how many. Skip told me that not one of you knew exactly what you were doing. You trusted the promises of God and followed Him the best you knew how. God used you in your weakness and brought glory to Himself.

"I think, though, that what you are about to face in Africa will require you to be instructed more fully in the working of the Holy Spirit. You will need to have the *power* of the Holy Spirit as well as His *Presence*."

"I guess you are going to tell us how receive the power of the Holy Spirit?"

"Yes I am. Let us all kneel around Nancy, since she can't come to us. We are going to pray for the Holy Spirit to come upon you in power.

....

Two months earlier...

Angela Symonds had been praying harder than she had ever prayed for anyone ever before.

The brief periods of lucidity Raymond Nichol had displayed to date had not been long enough for her to get through to him. If getting through to him was even possible. Angela, however, had begun to bank on achieving the impossible. At the same time she was aware her interest in Raymond, as she thought of him now, was beginning to take on the nature of an obsession.

She was careful to fulfil all her duties to the other inmates, but again and again her thoughts returned to the former teacher who had lost his mind. He had *almost* lost his mind, she reminded herself. She was convinced his whole mind, and his whole personality, was imprisoned somewhere behind the cloak of madness visible to the outside world. All she needed was to find the key to let him out.

As careful as Angela was to hide her special interest in this one inmate it was beginning to be noticed. Regina Hill, the matron on her shift, remarked to her one day, "You do know, Angela, nothing can be done for these people? Only the extreme cases are sent here. They've slipped beyond the possibility of any human help."

Angela sealed her lips. Any answer she gave would betray her radical approach to the treatment of the insane. At the very least she would be seen as someone who did not 'fit in;' better to let the matron's remark pass as of no consequence. That being so, she did say silently to herself, "Yes, beyond *human* help. With that I can agree. Help from Heaven is another matter altogether."

Angela began to plan for the next episode of lucidity Raymond would have. None of the other care givers had reported anything unusual about his behaviour, apart from the general symptoms of insanity. Either there had been none, or they had not thought it significant.

Angela thought it was. She focussed on that one occasion when he had asked if there was any hope for him. She had written it down in her notebook:

He had asked, "Is there hope for me?"

Angela had responded, "Hope for what, Mr. Nichol?"

His reply had been stunning, "Hope for Heaven; hope for Salvation; hope for whatever it is you Christians proclaim."

So, anything she said when he emerged from his madness had to be in answer to that question. She would have to pray for guidance to say the right thing in the simplest way possible and in the time available. Already some phrases had begun to come to her. I'll tell him, she thought, "Jesus died for you. He shed his blood to save you. The only unforgivable sin is to reject him, and die without changing your mind."

....

The two heavenly beings above room 208 looked down at the scene with anticipation. The time to attack was drawing near.

The former teacher sat, as usual in a chair by the bed. He was staring blankly at the wall when the girl entered.

Above his head and on both sides demons hovered, gleefully laughing at the girl's paltry attempts to reach the man's mind. She had no idea what she was dealing with. They were aware that this servant of darkness, in his few lucid moments had turned his mind in contemplation of the Enemy. He was thinking of changing sides and aligning himself with the forces of Light. That must not happen, for if the Enemy recaptured his devotion he would do great damage to their master's cause. They were ready to prevent any penetration of the cloak of madness they had cast over him. Angels were present, but a host of demons waited to prevent their interference.

Meanwhile the angels watched the girl approaching their charge. In silent communication the taller of the two said, "It will not be long now."

His companion asked, "Is the girl ready?"

"She is almost ready. Her mind has been prepared and she is ready to strike the moment his mind is freed to receive her words. She is new to spiritual warfare but she is a chosen instrument. He-Who-Knows-All has given her understanding."

The other angel swept an arm to one side, indicating the host of demons gathered to prevent any action on their part, "What about them?"

His taller companion made a dismissive gesture, "Reinforcements are on their way."

Chapter 6

The Dark Deceiver

To Skip Jordan Aunt May looked more beautiful than he could have imagined. She was radiant as she said her vows and pledged her love to Reginald Alderman.

The church was only half full but everyone present had a special connection with the bride and groom; their loving support pervaded the atmosphere.

As Reginald lifted the veil to kiss his bride Skip thought of the veil in the carved chest under his bed – his mother's wedding veil. Seeing his mother's twin sister getting married was almost like being present at his own parent's wedding. His heart-beat quickened as the preacher declared Aunt May and Reginald, 'husband and wife.'

When the ceremony was over, Skip and Ashley assisted Nancy down the aisle and through the door to the church hall. Her ankle was bandaged till the sprain healed. Her green eyes flashed as she reluctantly allowed her friends to take hold of her elbows and assist her progress down the steps into the hall, "I should have brought my crutches. I hate to be treated like an invalid."

Skip smiled teasingly, "Just think how undignified that would look, Nance. You would be bouncing along like Hop-along Cassidy? How humiliating would that be?"

Nancy made a deprecating noise in her throat, "I don't know anything more humiliating that being helped along by two self-satisfied friends."

"You're calling us self-satisfied? Why Nancy, whatever do you mean?

Nancy's face broke out into a grin, "Oh, I'm just kidding. I'm really grateful for your help. It's just that I'm wondering what I'm going to do when we get to Africa. I have visions of being left behind when the rest of you go off on some exciting adventure."

Ashley said soberly, "I'm not sure 'exciting' is the word to use. Try using the words, frightening, dangerous, or impossible to describe it, but *exciting* is not a term I would use. What Skip saw in his vision wasn't exactly comforting. I think we're headed for some spiritual conflict that I, for one, do not feel prepared to face."

"I agree, Ash, but we don't have much choice, do we? Not when we have a chance of rescuing Roger, however faint that possibility may seem. The Lord has carried us through before. We'll just have to trust that He'll do so again."

"I know that, Skip. I'm just not going to pretend we're going on some carefree adventure. The enemy is not going to leave us alone if we plan to assault one of his strongholds." She glanced significantly at Nancy's ankle. "As you can see he is capable of causing physical injury."

"You're right, Ash, but we can't focus on Satan's power. We have to remember that Christ in us is greater than those against us."

Their discussion ended when they reached their assigned places in the reception hall and helped Nancy into her seat. The table was loaded with food and they entered into the celebration with the gusto of teens convinced that every meal was their last.

The usual speeches and humorous anecdotes interspersed the eating and merry-making. Even Skip gave a short speech, telling how Aunt May had nurtured him after the death of his parents. He joked about how Reginald had surreptitiously stolen her heart while he, Skip, hadn't been looking. It was a warm and wonderful time when visions and demons and death retreated to the edges of his consciousness. They were all allowed some welcome relief from spiritual conflict and their spirits were refreshed.

Nancy forgot her injury for a time, and how she had got it. James revealed his funny side, enjoying his non-fat image and just had himself a good time. Ashley, though quieter by nature, entered into the fun and the joy of the occasion.

In the midst of all this, Skip found himself experiencing strange and new sensations. He had always been completely at ease in Nancy and Ashley's presence. Sure, they were girls, but he had never treated them differently to the guys he spent time with. They were part of the gang, friends like the others. Now, looking at them in their wedding finery he saw them with new eyes. They were beautiful young women and there were times he felt awkward and confused in their presence. Most of the time he could react normally, as he always had with them before. But now, like the time in the woods when Nancy had been injured, he felt tongue-tied and uncertain of what to say.

The feeling passed, and as the evening wore on, he began to feel normal again. Aunt May and Reginald left to go to a hotel; Ashley's folks would soon be taking them to their place for a sleep-over, and they began to talk about what had happened in Joshua's cabin.

"I've never met anyone like him," Ashley said thoughtfully. "He is a giant physically, but it is not his size that made an impression on me. There was something in his eyes that drew me to him."

"That's exactly what I felt when I stumbled on his place when I was only six," Skip replied.

Nancy said, "I don't know how he lives alone in that tiny cabin of his. I'd go crazy in less than a week, but he seems to thrive on it."

"He's not alone, Nance. Most people wouldn't be able to stand it, but with him it's a calling. I think he touches more people through prayer and communion with God than some do in a lifetime out in the world."

"What got me," James said, "is what happened before we left. It was wonderful when I gave my life to the Lord in the valley, but I've never felt God's power the way I did when we prayed for the Holy Spirit to come upon us."

"I've always known the Holy Spirit was in me since I became a Christian," Ashley said, "but He came to me in that cabin in a way I never thought possible."

"All we had to do was ask, and He came," Nancy said, a sense of wonder in her voice. "I guess we shouldn't have been surprised. Jesus already told us He would."

Skip pulled his New Testament from his pocket, "You mean that passage in the Gospel of Luke? Let me read it to you:

"'*So I tell you, ask, and God will give to you. Search, and you will find. Knock, and the door will open for you. Yes, everyone who asks will receive. The one who searches will find. And everyone who knocks will have the door opened. If your children ask for a fish, which of you would give them a snake instead? Or, if your children ask for an egg, would you give them a scorpion? Even though you are bad, you know how to give good things to your children. How much more your heavenly Father will give the Holy Spirit to those who ask him!*[xiii]

"We asked and received. It was that simple."

"Turn to the passage in the Gospel of John, Skip, the one that says we will be able to do what Jesus did."

Skip turned the pages till he found the place, *I tell you the truth, whoever believes in me will do the same things that I do. Those who believe will do even greater things than these, because I am going to the Father. And if you ask for anything in my name, I will do it for you so that the Father's glory will be shown through the Son. If you ask me for anything in my name, I will do it.*[xiv]

"That's the one," Ashley confirmed. "It's a good thing we went to see Joshua before leaving for Africa. I don't think we would have been prepared for it otherwise."

Skip's manner changed. His voice becoming serious, almost gloomy, "I'm not sure anyone can be ready for what we're likely to face in Africa. We are only human and are open to deception if we do not keep alert and completely dependent on the Holy Spirit to guide us."

James looked intently at his friend, "Something is bothering you, Skip. What is it?"

Skip hesitated, wondering if it was the right time to share his misgivings. Aunt May and Reginald's wedding had been a refreshing interlude; if he shared his depressing thoughts the gloom may spread to them all. Seeing their attention fixed on him, however, he realized it was too late. His gloom had already spread, so he told them what was bothering him, "I was thinking of the *Looming Menace*."

Alarm immediately registered on their faces, particularly on those of Nancy and Ashley. Nancy's grandmother had suffered an attack from that demonic entity and in her view was responsible for her death. Ashley's father, a gifted minister of the Gospel, had been sent into a catatonic state for some time because of that dreadful "messenger of Satan," as Skip thought of it.

"You think he'll come back?" Nancy asked. Her voice sounded raspy, as if her throat had suddenly constricted.

"No, I don't think he, or it, will come back. For some reason I think the *Looming Menace* has been taken out of the picture. No, in spite of the attack we suffered in the woods I think we have come off very lightly so far." Skip sent an apologetic glance toward Nancy and the plaster cast encasing her ankle. "I think that was meant mainly to frighten us."

"In that case," Nancy said, "it succeeded. I've never been more terrified in my life, even considering all we went through to rescue James and the others at the Retreat."

"Something worse is coming," Skip said, aware he had killed any feeling of celebration lingering from the joyous event of aunt May's wedding. He regretted it, for he was certain there would be enough doom and gloom in the future to satisfy the most dedicated of pessimists.

....

Aunt May lay comfortably in Reginald's arms, exulting in the reality that she was now Mrs. Reginald Alderman. They were in the honeymoon suite of the local hotel. Everything about the wedding ceremony and the reception had been perfect, and the furniture and appointments in the room were luxurious. It had been almost eleven years since the death of her husband and baby. She felt in her spirit (she had felt it for some time now) the release to move on. God did not intend tragedy to loom over one's life and steal the capacity for renewed joy. The memory of her dead loved ones was sacred, and would always occupy a special place in her heart, but she had learned to love again.

For the next two months May Alderman would be travelling with her new husband, getting to know and adjust to life with this gentle, godly man. The prospect thrilled her, tempered only by a lingering doubt. She was loath to express it, especially now, on their long anticipated wedding day. Yet she was no longer single, and Reginald deserved to be party to all her concerns, as well as her joys. She suspected, too, that Reginald may already have sensed, may even share, some of the doubts she was having. She squeezed his hand.

"What is it, love?"

"I ... I was thinking..."

"What were you thinking about?"

"I don't want to intrude on the happiness we have found together."

Reginald turned her to face him, fixing her with a look so filled with love her heart seemed to skip a beat, "We are one now, my sweet, and our happiness includes sharing everything, even our doubts and fears."

"I know that. It's just that I'm wondering if we're doing the right thing. I mean, going off on our own and leaving the young ones to fend for themselves."

"A frown creased Reginald's brow, "How long have you been feeling this way?"

"Oh, I don't know. It's just been something nagging at me under the surface. What do you think?"

Reginald grunted as he thought about it, "I think they will not be alone. First, they are going to stay at the mission with Bob and Rhonda Lucas. Also, I have no doubt they'll hook up sometime with Ntambo, and perhaps with some of the former witchdoctors he gathered around him to pray for them before."

"That's not entirely my concern," aunt May responded. "Given the content of Skip's dreams, I expect they'll try to locate Roger. If they do they will be headed into danger. They've already faced a demonic attack. It can only get worse."

Reginald stirred, "Let's go sit on the couch and we'll talk about it."

Aunt May looked contrite, "I'm sorry for bringing this up, especially now."

"I think this is a great time to bring it up. We can start our married life dealing with issues that arise together."

Once settled on the couch, Reginald said, "Tell me what happened when you felt this way before."

"You mean when Skip and the girls disappeared into that valley in Nova Scotia?"

"Yes,"

Aunt May snuggled up closer to him, "Well, I was scared and worried when they didn't get back when they were supposed to. I felt I should have been with them, that I had failed in my responsibility by letting them go off alone."

"What did you do?"

"I prayed and cried to the Lord into the early hours. At last He directed me to a Scripture about Elisha and his servant being surrounded by the Syrian army, but there were more angels protecting them than the soldiers confronting them." She smiled, "OK, I get your point. My being with them would not have protected them any more than they were being protected already."

"That's true, but what else happened?"

"I had a vision of two angels going before and behind. Skip and the others didn't return for another three days, but I had peace till they finally turned up."

"So, what's your problem now?"

"I guess I don't have one anymore."

Reginald smiled, "That's good, but I'll tell you what we'll do. We'll pray for them every morning and evening while we're traveling, and at any other time the Holy Spirit prompts us to pray for them. If He gives us any sense of danger we can always adjust our itinerary and come to their aid."

"You would do that for me?"

"What do you think, my love? Do you think I married you just to do my own thing. We are one, now. Besides, now that we're married Skip and Nancy are as much my children as they are yours."

Aunt May kissed him on the cheek, "You're a very wise man, Reginald Alderman."

"And so are you, Mrs. Alderman, and beautiful besides."

Aunt May laughed, and snuggled up closer, "Now you're just flattering me."

....

The demonic presence, had it been visible to human eyes, would have appeared more as a dark shadow than a being with defined outline and features. It was like a dark blob of evil shifting shape as it moved through the house belonging to Ashley's parents. The four young people it had been assigned to would be sleeping here before flying to Africa in the morning.

The demon moved from room to room, gazing intently at each occupant till at last deciding the dark haired beauty named Nancy was to be the primary target. She was the more emotional and impetuous by nature and so more easily influenced. The greatest threat at this point was a united onslaught of these four youth against the works of the master. The Prince of Darkness had assigned this dark deceiver the task of sowing discord amongst this tightly loyal group of believers. If it was discord the Prince wanted, then discord is what he would get.

The deceiver waited till Nancy had fallen into a deep sleep, before overshadowing her and entering her dreams.

Chapter 7

Miracles and Mayhem

One month earlier...

The Director stared at Angela from across the heavy oak desk with a stare she could only interpret as malevolent.

He was Angus Bartlett, the director and founder of *The Bartlett Home for the Mentally Insane*. At least, that was the name he had originally planned to call it, but the government and other agencies had vetoed that designation. Referring to 'political 'correctness,' they had unmercifully denuded the original name to the unspectacular *The Bartlett Home*. Since all the funding for the project came from the government he had no other alternative but to bow to their wishes. To Angus Bartlett, however, it would always be *The Bartlett Home for the Mentally Insane,* and he encouraged all his staff to refer to it as such.

"I consider," he explained to any who would listen, "all who enter here to be incurable. As a psychiatrist, and the foremost in my field, I state categorically that all who reach this state of mental illness are incurable and irretrievable from their condition of insanity. They will forever be unable to re-enter society without dire consequences to themselves, and to those with whom they come into contact."

Angela Symonds, this stunningly attractive young intern sitting across from him, had committed an unforgivable offense: she had somehow disproved his basic premise. By so doing she threatened his credibility, and so his career. Radical action was called for.

Raymond Nichol had miraculously and inconveniently come back from the deep well of insanity; he had returned to absolute normality. There was only one thing he could do about it, or rather, a series of actions that would save him from public disgrace and professional ignominy.

First, he had written into Raymond Nichol's file that he had been misdiagnosed by the physicians and psychiatrists that had sent him to this facility (completely ignoring the fact that he had been one of those affirming that diagnosis). Second, he had written letters to the government agencies underlining what he had included in the file.

His last action was presently in progress: Angela Symonds had to be discredited and dismissed.

From Angela's point of view the director was a frightened and disillusioned man. Raymond Nichol's recovery was completely beyond his understanding. His atheistic mind-set made him a stranger to God's power; when he was confronted with it he was forced to consider God's existence. The existence of God was the one thing he could not endure. If he once admitted His existence he would have to submit to His moral code. The only code he wished to follow was the code he had formulated for himself. In Angus Bartlett's world, Angus Bartlett was king.

In the waiting room, and as she waited for the director to get down to business, she had allowed her thoughts to drift to the miracle that had taken place in room 208.

She had been waiting for that one lucid moment that would last long enough for her to answer clearly the question Raymond Nichol had asked previously: "Is there hope for me?" She had been praying for it and expecting it. Nevertheless, when it came it was so radical in nature, and so obviously a work of God, she was stunned and speechless. She had intended to waste no time and immediately declare the truth she had rehearsed so diligently. As it was she was unable to say a word for almost a minute.

The first thing that happened was the sudden change in atmosphere. Angela had always sensed oppression in all the rooms occupied by the inmates. Only her constant and dedicated prayer had saved her from its effects; it was like she was moving in a bubble where the oppression could not reach her. On the day of Raymond Nichol's deliverance the bubble had expanded to include the entire room.

Raymond Nichol had been sitting in the stuffed chair, at ease and in his right mind. He had been waiting for her; she found out later that he had been lucid for some time before she had arrived.

"At last," Raymond said, "I was afraid you may have been off duty."

"I...I..."

"I believe you have something to tell me." He leaned forward, his hands resting on his knees, "I have been having dreams about you. In them I was told you had a message to share that would wipe away my sorry past and give me a future and a hope. I have been sitting here trying to control my impatience."

"I...I..." Angela said again.

Raymond frowned, "Ms. Symonds, are you alright?"

"I...I... have been praying for this, Mr. Nichol. You must forgive me. I was expecting a... gradual... recovery."

"And instead, you got this." He spread his hands in a gesture to indicate his fully recovered sanity.

"Did you... were you aware," Angela asked, "what was going on when you were..."

"When I was crazy? You mean when I was insane did I know what was going on around me?"

"Yes."

A shiver went through Raymond's body before he answered, and a tremor of fear passed over his face, "I've got to know you quite well while the madness was on me. It wasn't always, but I had these flashes of awareness of my surroundings. It was usually when you were praying. I would come out of my stupor and find your head bowed and your lips moving."

"Were you... aware of anything else?"

Raymond Nichol shivered again, "I was attended by a host of demons, horrible creatures that cackled in glee at my predicament. I knew their power, since I had dealt with them before. You see, I was involved in witchcraft, and knew some of them intimately. That is why I cried out once when my understanding returned to me briefly."

"When you asked if there was any hope for you?"

"Yes."

"Mr. Nichol..."

"Call me Raymond."

"Uh... Raymond... I'm taking a chance not answering your question right away, except to say yes, there *is* hope for you. Jesus Christ came to save sinners, even the chief of sinners. But I've been praying about what to say to you when you came out of your... stupor."

"It was madness, insanity. You can say it Ms. Symonds"

"You can call me Angela."

She had been standing in the middle of the room, almost frozen to the spot in wonder at the transformation she was seeing in this "incurable" inmate. Now she drew a chair to where she could face him, and sat down. Her astonishment at this man's sudden recovery had settled into a wonderful sense of gratitude. Her passionate nature resurfaced.

"As I said, I have been praying about what God wanted me to tell you when you... came back. And I think you need to understand what has happened to you and why God allowed you to be 'gone' for almost a year."

"You mean God planned this for my good?"

"Yes I do. I believe God has a plan for your life, but you were not in a condition to receive it. I don't know what your history is, but I would guess you were very angry at God."

"Go on Ms... I mean Angela."

"There is an account in the Bible concerning a man, a king, who went mad for seven years." Horror registered on Raymond's face as she said this, and Angela reached into her uniform to retrieve her pocket Bible, "It is found in the book of Daniel, about a king Nebuchadnezzar, who had a vision. It is rather a long passage, but it is very important for you to understand what's going on. Leaning forward she began to read:

These are the visions I saw while I was lying in my bed: I looked, and there in front of me was a tree standing in the middle of the earth. And it was very tall. The tree grew large and strong. The top of the tree touched the sky and could be seen from anywhere on earth. The leaves of the tree were beautiful. It had plenty of good fruit on it, enough food for everyone. The wild animals found shelter under the tree, and the birds lived in its branches. Every animal ate from it.

"As I was looking at those things in the vision while lying on my bed, I saw an observer, a holy angel coming down from heaven, He spoke very loudly and said, 'Cut down the tree and cut off its branches. Strip off its leaves and scatter its fruit. Let the animals

under the tree run away, and let the birds in its branches fly away. But leave the stump and its roots in the ground with a band of iron and bronze around it; let it stay in the field with the grass around it.
" 'Let the man become wet with dew, and let him live among the animals and plants of the earth. Let him not think like a human any longer, but let him have the mind of an animal for seven years.
" 'The observers gave this command; the holy ones declared the sentence. This is so all people may know that the Most High God rules over every kingdom on earth. God gives those kingdoms to anyone he wants, and he chooses people to rule them who are not proud.'
"That is what I, King Nebuchadnezzar, dreamed. Now Belteshazzar, tell me what the dream means. None of the wise men in my kingdom can explain it to me, but you can, because the spirit of the holy gods is in you."[xv]

Angela paused in her reading, "Nebuchadnezzar was a very proud king who served other gods, as I suspect you have. Daniel told the king the tree was all about him and his kingdom. He would lose his kingdom and become like an animal, but after seven years he would be restored to it and rule once again."

"So that's what I've been these past months," Raymond interjected, "an animal?"

Angela gave him a compassionate look, then returned her eyes to the passage before her. Skipping over half a chapter she began to read again:

All these things happened to King Nebuchadnezzar. Twelve months later as he was walking on the roofof his palace in Babylon,he said, "I have built this great Babylon as my royal home. I built it by my power to show my glory and my majesty."

The words were still in his mouth when a voice from heaven said, "King Nebuchadnezzar, these things will happen to you: Your royal power has been taken away from you. You will be forced away from people. You will live with the wild animals and will be fed grass like an ox. Seven years will pass before you learn this lesson: The Most High God rules over every kingdom on earth and gives those kingdoms to anyone he chooses."

Immediately the words came true. Nebuchadnezzar was forced to go away from people, and he began eating grass like an ox. He became wet from dew. His hair grew long like the feathers of an eagle, and his nails grew like the claws of a bird. At the end of that time, I, Nebuchadnezzar, looked up toward heaven, and I could think normally again! Then I gave praise to the Most High God; I gave honor and glory to him who lives forever. God's rule is forever, and his kingdom continues for all time. People on earth are not truly important. God does what he wants with the powers of heaven and the people on earth. No one can stop his powerful hand or question what he does.

At that time I could think normally again, and God gave back my great honor and power and returned the glory to my kingdom. The people who advised me and the royal family came to me for help again. I became king again and was even greater and more powerful than before. Now I, Nebuchadnezzar, give praise and honor and glory to the King of heaven. Everything he does is right and fair, and he is able to make proud people humble.[xvi]

When she had finished reading Raymond Nichol said, "So you think God dealt with me as he did with Nebuchadnezzar. You think He allowed madness to come upon me for seven or eight months instead of seven years till I learned to honor Him?"

"Yes, I do." Angela said.

"I may not have lived among animals," Raymond reflected, "but I lived among much worse. I was in the constant company of demons from hell."

Angela then made sure he understood the Gospel, the Good News of God's salvation. She explained that Jesus had already paid the full price for his sin, and that his rebellion against God had been fully paid for. She turned to some special verses in the Gospel of John and read them slowly and repeatedly : *He came to the world that was his own, but his own people did not accept him.But to all who did accept him and believe in him he gave the right to become children of God.They did not become his children in any human way—by any human parents or human desire. They were born of God.*[xvii]

When Angela was sure Raymond had grasped its full meaning she urged him to call on the name of Jesus, assuring him from another verse in chapter three: *Those who believe in the Son have eternal life, but those who do not obey the Son will never have life. God's anger stays on them."*[xviii]

Just as the joy of salvation registered on Raymond Nichol's features, the door to room 208 slammed open and the director, Angus Bartlett, stormed into the room.

"What in damnation is going on here!" he screamed.

Angela brought her thoughts back to the present. The director was still glaring at her, but now he was almost spitting words at her. She had missed the first few sentences but there was no mistaking the force of his anger, or the intent of his speech:

"Angela Symonds," he said, managing to make her name sound like a curse, "you are a great disappointment to me. I never thought when I took you on you would try to undermine the foundation of the work we do here."

"But..."

Angus Bartlett waved his hand, "There is no need for you to speak, Ms. Symonds. I called you here merely to inform you of the action I have taken."

Angela fumed at the director's summary dismissal of her point of view, but then committed her fate to her Lord. God knew how these events would play out. It was He who had brought Raymond (that was how she thought of him now) out of insanity, and delivered him from demonic oppression. Angela had no doubt the Lord had done this because he had a plan for his life, so whatever happened to her she had to believe He had a plan for hers also. So she kept silent.

"I will tell you," the director continued, "what I have done and what I am going to do about this sorry business.

"I have already written letters to all the relevant government departments, and to the Association of Psychiatrists, declaring Mr. Nichol was mistakenly sent to this facility. As a result, He will not have to go through the lengthy process of being uncommitted. He will be ejected from here without fan-fare."

Angus Bartlett took a deep breath and intensified his already intense glare, "So you can forget about making any wild claims, Ms. Symonds. If you try to say there has been some kind of miraculous recovery from insanity, you will be ridiculed. With my reputation as the foremost psychiatrist in the country you will not be taken seriously." He took another breath.

"And that brings me to what I'm planning to do with you. Of course, your employment is immediately terminated, but that is not going to be the end of it. Details of your reprehensible behaviour will be entered on your file, and letters will be written to every agency in the country declaring you to be unreliable and unprofessional. To sum it all up, Ms. Symonds, your career is at an end. You will never work in your field in this country ever again, and I would venture a guess, in most Western countries as well."

In spite of her faith this last bit of news caused a heavy weight to settle upon her heart. As she made her way to the staff room to empty her locker she could not prevent tears from running down her cheeks.

....

High above the Bartlett home the two angelic beings who had affected Raymond Nichol's deliverance looked down upon the scene.

The battle had been intense and long. Even with the reinforcements arriving to support them the demons holding the former teacher captive were reluctant to leave the field of battle. They had possessed him body and soul before and they did not surrender him up easily.

As they watched Angela's despondent figure heading toward the staff room, they turned to engage another angel hovering near them. In silent communication they accepted their assignment to protect Raymond Nichol, and their new companion's charge to protect Angela Symonds. They would be working in concert, for He-Who-Knows-All intended they never be separated. They would be a team to perform His will and engage the enemy. They would also be available as advisors to the youthful team heading for a stronghold of darkness in the centre of the African continent.

As Angela walked down the sterile corridor of the Bartlett Home, she had no idea of the danger and excitement that lay in her future. Joy and tears were waiting just around the corner.

Chapter 8

The Four Bulls

Nancy awoke in the room she shared with Ashley in a troubled frame of mind. Her dreams had been filled with images and emotions that were disturbing.

There had been no ugliness or terrifying creatures in her dreams, apart from an insubstantial shadow that seemed to hover at the edges. No, to the contrary, her dreams had been filled with memories of happy times, from the time she had seen Skip Jordan when he was barely past four years old, to the present time when she was living in the same house with him as his "sister."

Though she had been the same age as Skip, she remembered gazing through the fence at a sad little boy whose parents had been killed far away in Africa. Her grandmother had informed her of these facts, not expecting her to understand. But she *had* understood, even at that early age. Her own parents had also been killed. Perhaps they had not died at the hands of rebel soldiers, but the auto accident had made her loss just as final. From that time on a bond was formed between them, this dark haired girl with green eyes, and the red-headed boy next door. They had become inseparable, Nancy spending more time with Skip and Aunt May than she did with her grandmother in her own home.

Happy times had followed; there had been games and picnics and summer activities, evenings sitting at Aunt May's kitchen table working together on homework projects. They could not have been closer had they been related by blood. Perhaps they had been even closer than that, for the sibling rivalry that often exists between brother and sister was missing in their case. As they had remarked to each other on more than one occasion, they were "inwardly connected."

When Ashley Woods came into the picture, and later Roger Wilson and James (Chunky) Johnson, that state of affairs did not change. Nancy had been secure in the knowledge that what she and Skip shared was unique and unbreakable. Nothing appeared on the horizon to threaten that security – not until last year when they had been approaching the age of fourteen.

She, Ashley and Skip, had launched out on that dangerous mission to rescue Roger and others from the evil of witchcraft. Nancy had always tried to project a tomboyish image, till the stirrings of approaching womanhood came upon her. It was then, on that mission of mercy, that she began to see Skip as more than a friend, and more than a brother. These feelings had not been clear and defined at the time; just confused and unfamiliar. Her feminine nature, suppressed by her efforts to appear as just 'one of the guys,' surfaced.

At the same time she began to notice how beautiful her friend Ashley was, with a soft and gentle nature that contrasted with Nancy's more flamboyant, outgoing persona. With this awareness came a hitherto unfamiliar emotion – envy.

Now the three of them were approaching the age of fifteen, and she had noticed Skip's perception of his two female companions was changing. There was a blend of wonder and mild confusion when he looked at either one of them – or both of them together. It was as if he were trying to figure out how the ugly ducklings had suddenly turned into swans. He would look at them, then away, embarrassed when either of them noticed his gaze.

Nancy sat on the edge of her bed and looked over at Ashley's still sleeping form. Her friend's soft blonde hair spread out on the pillow to frame her lovely face. With the images in her dream still fresh in her mind Nancy realized her own perceptions of her friend had changed. She had always considered her as the closest and dearest of friends. The bond between them had been almost, but not quite, as strong as that existing between her and Skip. With a twinge of regret Nancy was beginning to see her not so much as a friend, but as a rival.

In her dreams, as vivid as life itself, Nancy had seen frequent images of Skip and Ashley moving off together. She had frantically tried to keep up. No matter how much effort she put into it she could never shorten the distance between them. Always, in the pit of her stomach, was that sinking feeling that Ashley was about to steal from her the greatest earthly treasure she had ever possessed – her love for Skip Jordan.

As Ashley stirred and finally opened her eyes, Nancy tried to restore her former feelings for her friend, but all she could see was a beauty and gentleness that outshone her own. She knew Ashley would always be her loyal and devoted friend, but Ashley's beauty and sweet nature was something else altogether. They had the power to frustrate her dearest wish, and deny the fulfillment of her most fervent longings.

....

Skip Jordan stood on ground he had not trod on for more than ten years. It gave him a bitter-sweet sensation. On the one hand it was thrilling to be where his parents had worked and laboured. On the other hand, this was the place where his parents had been killed.

Aunt May stood beside him, waiting for him to process his emotions as he looked out over the mission compound. She and Reginald were here for only one day. They would be leaving next day to continue their travel itinerary. Skip was grateful for her presence. There were a few things he wanted to discuss with her, as he had discussed all of the life issues he had passed through.

"You have something on your mind, Skip?"

Hesitating a little, he answered, "Yes, aunt May. I do."

Aunt May waited, giving him time to process what he wanted to tell her. It had always been like this, between the aunt and her nephew. They never rushed into conversation, thinking carefully before raising concerns, and Aunt May could tell something was troubling him.

"Aunt May," Skip said at last, "did you notice something odd going on between Nancy and Ashley on the trip over here?"

"What kind of oddness, Skip?"

"Do you remember speaking to me a year ago, after that business in Nova Scotia, when you said to be careful around the two of them because..."

"You mean because they were having more than friendship feelings about you?"

"Yes. At the time I hadn't a clue what you were talking about. Now, I can see things are changing between us. And it is not just on their part. I've been a little confused myself. Things are somehow different. On the way over, and later at the Harare airport, they hardly spoke to one another, and when they did their words were sharp and cutting. Aunt May, we are into some serious business here. We can't afford to be squabbling. And the truth is, I don't know how to deal with it. I was always able to speak to them as equals, like each of them was just one of the guys. That has changed. When I look at them I feel breathless, and I often find myself stammering."

Aunt May sighed, and a curious expression spread over her face, "Skip," she said, "it is called puberty. You know what that is, right?"

"Of course I do. I just didn't relate it to what's being going on, is all. You think that's what happening with Nancy and Ashley, and with me, too?"

"I do, and with James as well."

Skip looked up, startled by this revelation, "What has James got to do with it?"

Aunt May drew Skip over to sit on a bench constructed of a long sheet of shale perched on two rocks, "Haven't you noticed how James has been looking at you lately?" Skip shook his head.

"I would guess he is attracted to one or other of the girls and he sees you as a threat."

Skip's mouth hung opened, "I...I... never imagined..."

Aunt May grew serious, "Skip, this is just the kind of thing Satan is good at. He uses our natural urges against us. God has placed within us the desire to love someone special; He has made us so we will naturally desire to marry and have families. These urges and desires surface around the time of puberty, when a girl becomes a woman, and a boy becomes a man. Girls usually start a little ahead of boys, which is why when I spoke of my concerns regarding the girls last year, you had little idea what I was talking about." She paused.

"Nancy and Ashley started to go through puberty a year ago, about the time we went to Nova Scotia. Now you're experiencing the same thing. Girls were just girls to you before; now you see them as attractive young women. Satan delights to take these natural urges and twist them into something ugly.

"It just happens that these changes are taking place at the same time you are about to begin an onslaught against one of his strongholds. Satan is obviously trying to use these natural changes to sow dissention among you. United you stand, divided you fall."

Skip's shoulders slumped, and he turned an appealing gaze on his aunt, "What am I to do, Aunt May?"

Aunt May considered the question before answering, "Reggie and I are leaving in the morning. Why don't you raise the matter at evening prayers? That way you'll have our support, and the Lucas's can give you the benefit of their experience as well. One thing is certain, to delay dealing with this will lead to disaster.

There was a mild tension in the air when they gathered for prayers in the mission house that evening. Everyone seemed to sense something unusual was about to take place. Besides Skip and Aunt May's conversation earlier nothing had been said to the others. Yet their spirits were sensitive to a subtle change in the atmosphere.

Skip himself was experiencing an odd familiarity with his surroundings. Though he had been very young when he had last lived in this house, each room contained items that evoked memories. He remembered the sideboard with intricately carved designs against one wall. There was also a picture of his parents standing in front of the mission house. The present missionaries, Bob and Rhonda Lucas, had not removed it, in honour of the ground breaking work Skip's parents had done in establishing the mission

The large dining table in the centre of the room was also a relic of his parent's tenure here, and of his father's skill in carpentry.

Bob Lucas was a well-built man of average height with a bald patch on his head, bushy eyebrows, and a gleam of devotion to Christ in his eyes. He laughed easily, worked hard, and shared the Gospel with the natives with a sincerity that was unmistakable. His wife, Rhonda, was a pretty woman of slight build and a warm personality that drew people in. She also had a gift for one-on-one evangelism. She visited in the surrounding villages, and, in her quiet way, had won many of the women to Christ. They had been here more than ten years, arriving soon after the Jordan's had been killed. This was especially remarkable since, at the time the rebel bands had not entirely left the area.

After dinner, when the table had been cleared and everyone was ready for evening prayers, Bob raised his hand, "Before we proceed with the Scripture reading, I believe Skip has something to share with us."

Skip's throat constricted. He had thought he was ready to talk about the tensions he had been sensing amongst the four of them, but now he hardly knew how to proceed. He cleared his throat, "Uh, I... I'm not sure how to begin..."

Aunt May interjected, "Skip has noticed, and so have I, that the four of you are not getting on together as well as you used to." Having brought the matter out into the open, she directed her gaze back to Skip for him to continue.

"Yes. I... I'm sorry to bring this up in front of the adults, but Aunt May and I thought we may need some help from those older and wiser than we are." He appealed to each of his friends with his eyes, and they each dropped their gaze to the floor.

"I... mean, we're hoping to rescue Roger and whoever else we can reach from this witchcraft thing. We can't do it if we're not talking to each other and have hard feelings against each other. We've got to get this settled."

Reginald said, "Skip is right, and the only way you can do that is to be totally honest. No matter how embarrassing it is, you have got to let it out."

Nancy's cheeks flushed. Ashley's cheeks were almost as bright. James just looked uncomfortable.

Rhonda Lucas moved behind the girls and placed an arm around each of them.

Skip said, "Come on guys, what's been going on?"

Nancy slowly raised her eyes to meet those gathered around her, "I... I've been... having dreams." Rhonda squeezed her shoulder, encouraging her to continue."

"They... they're embarrassing."

"It's all right, Nance," Skip said, "We're all friends here."

"It was about Skip and Ashley." So she told her dream in detail, including the dark shadow flitting around the edges of her dream. By the time she was finished there were tears in her eyes and Rhonda Lucas's arms were wrapped around her, "It is all right

Nancy," she said compassionately. "We all have to deal with these things from time to time."

It was then that Ashley's quiet voice was heard, "I... I had... the same dream," she said, "only it was Skip and Nancy who were moving away, and I who could not close the distance."

Reggie removed his arm from around Aunt May and leaned forward, his face alive with interest, "Two girls have the same dream, but with reversed roles? What does that sound like to you, Bob?"

"What interests me," the missionary said, "is the dark shadow Nancy saw at the edge of her dream." He turned to Ashley, "Was it the same with you?"

Ashley nodded, "It was more like a dark blob that shifted shape. I never saw it close, but in my dream I was always aware of its presence."

"Same with me," Nancy agreed.

Quiet reigned in the room while they all thought of the significance of what the girls had told them.

"Could the dark shadow have been a demonic presence?" Aunt May asked.

"I believe it was," Bob Lucas responded.

"The question is," Rhonda Lucas said, "is what can be done about it?

"I think... I have an answer to that," Skip said hesitantly.

All eyes turned to him.

Looking apologetic, Skip continued, "I was at the library paging through a book of fables when I came across one called 'The Four Bulls.' " He glanced at the other three young people significantly.

"You're calling us beasts, are you?" James said in an attempt to lighten the mood.

"The way we've been acting, perhaps we are," Skip replied. "But no, we're not beasts, but being human we're open to certain temptations, and I think this fable may help us to understand what's been going on."

The adults in the company seemed as eager to hear what Skip had to say as the rest of them.

"There were these four bulls," Skip began. "They were always found together for they truly loved each other. When you saw one of them, the other three were always close by.

"Now there was a lion in the area who would dearly have loved to eat the bulls, but he knew he was no match for the sharp horns of four bulls together. They would tear him to pieces in no time. He would have to come up with a plan to separate them."

"I think I know where this is going," James said.

Skip ignored the interruption, "For a long time the lion lurked around in the tall grass, licking his lips and trying to come up with an idea that would finally transform those bulls into a tasty meal. His stomach groaned when he thought of it. At last he decided on a course of action.

"Creeping up as close as he could in the tall grass to one of the bulls grazing slightly apart from the others, he whispered, 'The other bulls don't like you!'

"The lion did this repeatedly with each of the bulls till at last he saw that his strategy was working. The bulls began to look with suspicion at each other, and slowly began to draw further and further apart."

"You don't have to tell us the rest," Ashley interjected.

"I will anyway," Skip said. "When the other bulls were not close enough to pose a threat, the lion was able to eat them one by one."

There were several moments of silence before Skip continued, "There is also a Scripture I believe the Lord gave me from the book of James: *So give yourselves completely to God. Stand against the devil, and the devil will run from you.*[xix]

"I know we think we cannot control what we dream about, but if it is the devil giving you a dream, we can get him to go away. First we have to give ourselves completely to God."

James coughed to get attention, "I have to... make a confession." He glanced shyly at Ashley, and then more directly at Skip, "I have to admit I've been a little jealous of you, Skip, and a little resentful."

"Why on earth would you be jealous of me?"

"Well, I like Ashley really well and both of them... well...they both seem to have all their attention fixed on you."

These were no easy revelations, especially in the presence of adults. They all seemed to understand, however, that absolute honesty was vital if they were to continue as friends. Ashley's astonishment at James's confession was complete. Nancy was more humiliated than embarrassed. Her secret feelings for Skip were now out in the open and Ashley had more or less admitted she felt the same.

It was left up to Aunt May to say the final word, "Now you know what to do, don't you?" She looked them all in the eye. "While it is natural for you to have these feelings at your age, you are too young to take any of them seriously. You have got to do what the verse Skip quoted tells you. You have to give yourselves completely to God, then you will be able to resist the devil and he will flee from you." She turned to the girls, "Do that every night before going to bed and the devil won't be able to invade your dreams. Let us pray now so you can focus on what is really important – doing the will of God."

Chapter 9

Swallowed

The tall black man strode purposefully down the pathway toward the mission. Beside him was his sister's boy, Themba. It was more than ten miles distance from his sister's village to the mission. The two of them had been walking for almost an hour, yet the man's steps had not faltered or his pace slowed. The boy was left to keep up as he was able.

Ntambo felt an urgency he could not shake.

He had awoken early. His wife snored gently beside him; their newborn infant slept quietly in the hand-made crib beside her. No, neither of them had disturbed him. The animal noises had stilled before the dawn; even if there had been any he was so accustomed to them they would not have penetrated his sleep. Something else had brought him suddenly into full consciousness. He rolled gently off the sleeping mat so as not to disturb his wife and went to stand outside the entrance to their hut.

Be still and know that I am God[xx] a word from the book of Psalms settled on his spirit. For years now he had begun his day this way, remaining still so his inner ear could hear His voice. Most times he had to wait some time before he heard it. Not now. Almost immediately the Voice spoke: "*Go and get your sister's boy and go to the mission. You are needed there.*"

"Why must Themba go with me, Lord?" The answer was a simple, "*Go!*"

His sister's village was a mile in the opposite direction to the mission. So he left immediately. On his return, with Themba in tow, he had gently shaken his wife awake and informed her of where he was going.

Now Ntambo allowed his mind to search for the reason he was being sent to the mission. He was in the habit of visiting the mission three or four times a year. On his last visit he had been told of the tentative plans for Skip and the girls to stay at the mission. His aunt and new husband would go on a more extended tour of Africa, leaving the young people in the care of Bob Lucas and his wife. Was the Lord urging him to go the mission for them? And was the command to bring Themba with him because he was of the same age as Skip and his friends? Did that also mean they were being called again to assault one of the enemy's strongholds?

One thing was certain; the compulsion to enter into spiritual warfare was building. If Skip Jordan and his companions had arrived at the Mission, his compulsion and their arrival were almost certainly related. It may mean he, and his nephew Themba, were meant to join forces.

Ntambo felt a combination of urgency and excitement stirring within him. The urgency was caused by the Voice he had heard this morning; the excitement arose from the anticipated meeting with Skip Jordan. Though he had fought battles in the Spirit on the boy's behalf, he had not seen him for over ten years. He remembered him as a four-year-old boy, but he'd had glimpses of him a year ago when he had those visions on the mountain. He was tall for his age with a head of red hair and a firm set to his jaw. As young as he was, Skip Jordan, and his friends by extension, seemed to have a call on his life that was beyond human reason. The only explanation for it was in the Scriptures: *Brothers and sisters, look at what you were when God called you. Not many of you were wise in the way the world judges wisdom. Not many of you had great influence. Not many of you came from important families.But God chose the foolish things of the world to shame the wise, and he chose the weak things of the world to shame the strong.He chose what the world thinks is unimportant and what the world looks down on and thinks is nothing in order to destroy what the world thinks is important.God did this so that no one can brag in his presence.*[xxi]

Themba hurried to catch up with his uncle and drew up alongside him, slightly breathless, "Uncle, why are you bringing me with you to the mission, and why are you in such a hurry?"

Ntambo glanced at the young man before answering. The early onset of manhood was beginning to show on the boy. His shoulders were broader, his limbs muscular, and a sharper intelligence shone from his eyes. Sweat was on him now from the forced march, causing his dark skin to shine.

"I do not know why," he answered at last. "I only know the Voice I hear when I am still before God in the morning, has commanded me to bring you. Perhaps it is because you are the same age as the red-headed boy or perhaps..." He caught his nephew's eye, "Perhaps God is calling you as well?"

"To what is God calling me, uncle?"

"That," Ntambo said, "is for you to find out, and for God to reveal. As for the urgency, the Voice I heard this morning was full of it. When He speaks in that way I know there must be no delay."

They had come now out of the jungle and stood on the rise overlooking the mission station. The morning air was clear and fresh, with no clouds to obscure the direct sunlight. Though the two observers were fifty yards or more away from the group gathered near the gulley it was like seeing them through the lens of a magnifying glass. The sight that met Ntambo's eyes gave instant justification for the urgency he had felt, and he careened down the slope, leaving Themba to follow as best he could.

....

Meanwhile...

Angela Symonds Nichol lay on the bed in the cabin, aware of the roar of Victoria Falls only half a mile from where she lay. Her head was spinning from all that had happened in the past month. She and Raymond had been married for one week, and they had spent their honeymoon in this idyllic spot, taking in the beauty and grandeur of the African landscape.

Raymond had gone for a walk in the park grounds where paths and look-out posts gave tourists a grandstand view of the mighty waters plunging into the depths below. He said he needed to think of what lay ahead, apologising that their wonderful honeymoon was drawing to a close. They would be facing dangers from now on she could hardly imagine.

Thus it was that she had time to reflect on the whirl-wind events that had taken place since Raymond's radical recovery from madness, his conversion to Christ, and their brief romance ending in marriage.

Angela had always expected to have a long engagement and a large wedding when she married the man of her dreams. However, the events of the past months had been anything but normal. She had never expected to be engaged in spiritual battle to free a man from demonic powers. Neither had she expected to have her career end so suddenly and so ignominiously.

Angus Bartlett was esteemed so highly in the public and professional arena that his declaration that Raymond Nichol had been misdiagnosed was accepted unquestioningly. All the usual red tape to affect the release of one committed to a mental facility was dispensed with. Within days he was free to leave the Bartlett Home as easily as if he had only been there for treatment of the common cold. Bartlett's letters to the appropriate official bodies, and to influential leaders in the psychiatric field, had effectively ended all Angela's hopes for employment in her field.

Angela had received this all with surprising equanimity, mainly because of the third thing she had never expected; she had never expected to fall in love with Raymond Nichol. Without a job for any foreseeable future, it was almost with surprise she discovered she had formed an attachment for the man once locked into madness, but now a trophy in God's Hall of Fame.

In the world, those in a Hall of Fame reach that distinction by their own character and their own efforts. In God's Hall of fame, sinners reach that distinction through God's mercy and a demonstration of God's power. Angela's faith and prayer for Raymond's deliverance had been, Angela realized, only a very small part of a greater design. Both she and Raymond were being drawn into something bigger than both of them.

In spite of all this, agreeing to marry Raymond Nichol had not taken place without a great deal of heart searching. She had always been schooled not to act in haste. "Lord," she had prayed, "I don't want to get out of your will. All of this is happening too quickly. I'm suddenly without work; I love a man who has only recently emerged from madness, and I feel like I am standing on the edge of a cliff with nowhere else to go but forward. My career is in ruins behind me and this man has asked me to marry him. I hardly know him and have no idea where binding myself to him may lead. I am afraid it may lead me out of your will and into disaster. Oh Lord, please help me."

The surprise Angela felt was not that she received an answer, or that it came so quickly. What surprised her was the form it took: "*Child,*" the quiet Voice echoed in her mind "*do you know my Voice?*"

She had heard this Voice often before, even as a child. Her mother had instructed her even then as to how to discern between the voice of the enemy, and the Voice of the Spirit, "When God speaks it is always gentle, sometimes insistent, often urgent, but never hurried. The enemy will always try to rush you when your emotions are at a high, and in the middle of a crisis. Whatever is disturbing you, act on what the Scripture tells you: *Be still and know that I am God.*[xxii] When you do that you will be prepared to hear His Voice."

Acting on her mother's advice Angela thought of the Voice again, asking her if she *knew* His Voice. Scripture verses from the Gospel of John came to her: *When he brings all his sheep out, he goes ahead of them, and they follow him because they know his voice. But they will never follow a stranger. They will run away from him because they don't know his voice."*[xxiii]

She was one of the Lord's sheep; she was a child of God and ought to know the Shepherd's Voice: *My sheep listen to my voice; I know them, and they follow me. I give them eternal life, and they will never die, and no one can steal them out of my hand.*[xxiv]

"Yes, Lord. I know Your Voice," she replied.

"*Then obey my Voice and go with this man.*"

So Angela had obeyed and married Raymond Nichol, this unremarkable, ordinary man with an extraordinary history. He had been a man in willing subservience to the Devil; now he had been recaptured to serve the living God. And she, Angela Symonds Nichol, had been chosen to walk by his side. A mixture of excitement and fear passed through her. In spite of her certainty that she had done the right thing in marrying him, she knew the path that lay ahead of them would be fraught with danger, and even death.

A key turned in the cabin door and Angela raised herself up and sat on the edge of the bed as her husband entered. He stood still for several seconds gazing down at her before swiftly coming to her and taking her into his arms, "I can hardly believe I have found you at this stage in my life," he said.

"You didn't find me," Angela said, drawing back so she could look into his eyes, "God brought us together. For what purpose we are still to find out."

"Wouldn't that be so that we could love each other and live happily ever after?" He raised a quizzical brow.

"That, too, though I'm not too sure whether the ever after is going to be in this life, or the one beyond."

Raymond's demeanour changed, "You're not regretting you married me are you?"

"No, I'm sure about that. I do think though, given your past and miraculous deliverance, we're not destined for an easy ride."

He released her and turned to gaze through the window at the mist rising from the falls, "Perhaps I was wrong to draw you into this. You can have little idea of the forces arrayed against us. I haven't had time to tell you all I was involved in – or all I have done."

Angela moved up behind him, placing her arms around his waist and pressing her cheek against his back, "Raymond, I married you because I love you, but also because God told me to. I don't know what lies ahead but I am going to enjoy our life together and leave the rest in His hands. I don't need to know all that has happened in the past. Just love me, and let us follow our Master together." He turned and kissed her and all the longings of his past, present and future was in that kiss.

After a long while Angela asked him, "What do we do now?"

"Wait," her husband said. "We just wait."

....

Aunt May and Reginald had left with Bob Lucas shortly after dawn to catch their flight from Harare Airport. Rhonda Lucas had gone off with a few of her helpers to visit some of the surrounding villages; there were new converts to encourage and Bible classes to conduct.

The young people were left to explore the compound, and beyond, with Skip trying to guide them. Drawing on vague memories from when he was only four years old, he searched for the place he and Ntambo had hidden from the rebels so long ago. This was to satisfy his friends' curiosity, and his own need to reassure himself that the memory was more than a product of his own imagination.

However, his mind was only half on the matter at hand. What happened in the dining room last night, and the girls' confession of their more than sisterly feelings for him, was playing havoc with his emotions. Added to that was James' admission he had special feelings for Ashley that, at the time, raised further confused feelings within him.

Also, there was that vague feeling of guilt Skip had not confessed to. What good would it have done if he had admitted there were not *two* girls growing prominent in his thoughts lately, but *three*? It was crazy, but Julia, the girl who had given her life to save her friends from the mind-altering effects of the *Veil of Deception*, haunted him. The thought of what *might* have been if she had not died, would not leave him. Also, he was not accustomed to thinking about girls as more than good friends and buddies, so he was not prepared to deal with fantasies of three beautiful girls all at once. Now, their beauty, their sweetness, and their effect upon him were befuddling.

What made it worse was that he had not even shared his problem with Aunt May. Growing up, he had always shared his inward conflicts with her, and there had been a few. The manner of his parents' death had left him with significant emotional issues to deal with. He knew Aunt May would have had a common-sense answer to his dilemma. Then, why had he not told her?

"So, where is it, Skip?"

"Oh, ah..." Skip shook himself mentally to bring his thoughts back to the present. He stopped and surveyed the terrain. The mission property became irregular at this point, sloping gradually downward to a raised ridge before plunging into a deep gully below. Ntambo had dug a trench through the ridge to ensure water in the rainy season would not back up into the mission compound, but be channelled into the gulley.

Lifting his arm Skip pointed ahead, "The trench Ntambo dug begins over there and goes right through the break you see in that ridge. The place where Ntambo hid me from the rebels is close to where the ridge begins."

Nancy and Ashley ran excitedly toward the spot Skip's pointing finger indicated. He and James followed at a more leisurely pace.

It was hard to find the actual spot, since grass had grown in some places, and the edges had caved in at others. Ten years of only limited maintenance had obscured any unusual features in the sides of the trench. However, by clearing away some of the debris, Skip and James thought they had found it. It was a hollowing out, large enough to partially hide the body of a big man like Ntambo, and create an earth overhang covered with grass. The overhang would have helped to hide the man and the boy, especially at night amidst frantic rebel activity, and the shadows cast by flaming torches.

To Skip it appeared an ineffective hiding place to have saved his life all those years ago. Ntambo had insisted in one of his letters that the activity of angels had been responsible for their deliverance, and not just the shallow cave he had dug. By the looks of things that was a distinct possibility. Perhaps angels *had* been there to save his life, and that would confirm his mother's conviction that God had a purpose for his life. That being true, Skip thought he had better find a way to put aside all the emotional complications that were part of his life at presence. He was convinced he and the others were headed into a spiritual conflict such as they had never known before. In the light of that they could not afford to bicker amongst themselves.

Skip's thoughts were interrupted by the sudden unsteadiness of his feet.

At first he thought it had something to do with his legs, as if they had suddenly become weak. Seconds later he realized it was not his legs that were unsteady, but that the earth beneath his feet was moving. A glance at the others confirmed this; they were swaying in an attempt to keep their balance. They looked like passengers on the deck of a ship being pounded by giant waves. If this was not bad enough, things rapidly became worse. Cracks began to appear in the ground.

Skip could not judge how far these cracks extended; all he knew was that the distance was too great for them to make it to solid ground. A great rumbling assaulted his ears and he could not suppress a cry of alarm. The earth between the cracks collapsed, and Skip knew that the earth itself was about to swallow them.

Chapter 10

Glimpsing the Way Ahead

Themba could not move for seconds after his uncle's sudden rush down the slope toward the mission. His brain was still trying to provide an explanation for his uncle's behaviour, till he directed his gaze to where his uncle was headed.

The sight that met his eyes acted like a trigger and his legs propelled him like a shot toward the tragedy playing out below. He had no idea what he could do when he got there, but his feet seemed to act independently of his brain. Besides, his uncle was a man of God; whatever was going on down there he would know what to do.

When Themba arrived seconds behind his uncle the situation was more dramatic, and more horrific, than he had thought possible. Four young people approximately Themba's own age were sinking into a deep hole about fifty feet across. He watched as the earth crumbled and sank beneath their feet. Dust rose in a cloud to obscure half their bodies, while the sun caused the hair of one of the boys to appear more like a flame than hair.

The earth continued to sink, not rapidly, but steadily, the fine sand beneath them leaving them no foothold. They could not progress to the edges of the hole. By now the walls of the sink-hole were too high and too steep to climb.

His uncle's booming voice intruded on Themba's thoughts, "Do not fear! You cannot fall far!" The sound of his words rose above the roar of the sinking ground.

The faces of the young people trapped in this terrifying funnel of death turned to Ntambo, their expressions registering non-comprehension. How could they not fall far, unless the sinking sand ceased its downward movement? It was moving faster now, not slower. Indeed, the fine nature of the sand itself was beginning to swallow their feet, their calves, and their knees. Themba saw the red-headed boy pushing against the sand that had risen to his waist.

"You cannot fall far!" Ntambo boomed. "Look up, put your faith in God!"

One by one four desperate faces lifted their heads to gaze heavenward.

It was then Themba saw a wondrous thing: the sand continued to sink, but the four young people remained in the same place. The sand that covered their lower bodies travelled down again, till first their knees, and then their feet were exposed. The sand continued to sink, till they were standing on – nothing.

Themba had seen many things in his short life, but nothing like this: The feet of the white skinned youth seemed as steady as if they were standing on solid ground, while the earth continued to sink beneath them.

"Now walk toward the edge of the hole," Ntambo instructed. The noise of the sinking earth was diminishing as it went deeper, so he did not need to raise his voice as much. As the young people obeyed, it was strange to see their shoes connecting something solid beneath them, while to Themba's eyes there was nothing to connect with. The God his uncle served was indeed the Almighty God. And yet that was not the only wonder. As they progressed to the almost sheer edge of the hole they were lifted up till they were able to step unhindered onto solid ground.

Not a word was said by any of them as they all stood looking down into the sink-hole, till the sand was no longer visible. All they could see after a while was a black void that spoke of a depth beyond their imagination. All they could think of was that it sank down into the very depths of hell itself.

The girls both had tears running down their cheeks; the red-headed boy and the curly-headed one bore stunned expressions on their faces. There were just no words to describe what had just happened to them. They simply turned and followed Ntambo into the mission house and gathered around the long table in the dining room. Even then, no one said anything for a long time. They just sat, staring at the dim reflection of their faces in the polished mahogany surface of the table.

At last Skip raised his head to stare into the eyes of Ntambo, a man he had not seen in more than ten years, "Wh... what just... happened?"

Ntambo drew a ragged copy of the Bible from the pouch strapped to his waist, "What happened," he said in a voice as filled with awe as the others around the table felt, " is just one of the enemy's lying signs, and one of God's amazing miracles."

The blonde girl was trembling. Themba could see her hand shake as she raised it to move a strand of hair that had fallen over one eye, "Please explain," she said.

Ntambo turned the well-worn pages of the volume in his hand and read:

The everlasting God is your place of safety,
and his arms will hold you up forever.[xxv]

"You mean," the brown haired girl asked, "God was holding us up so we could not fall any deeper into the hole?"

Ntambo nodded, "He also raised you up so you could get back on solid ground."

"How did you know that?"

Ntambo raised his Bible, "The same way I know anything about the wonder of how God works. I know from what He has caused to be written in this book."

The curly-headed boy asked, "What about the rest of it. Was that real? If God had not held us up, where would we have gone?"

"That is not so easy to answer," Ntambo replied. "Most, if not all that the devil does is a lie. He counterfeits the miracles God performs, but I also think believing the lies of the devil can bring us into real danger. If you had not raised your eyes to Heaven and trusted in Him, you may have sunk to – I know not where."

Themba felt a question form on his own tongue, "Uncle," he said, "what act of God was Satan trying to copy out there?"

Again the big man paged through the volume in his hands. When he had found the place, he said, "Certain men opposed Moses, who called on God to prove to the people God had sent him. This is what happened:

The Lord said to Moses and Aaron, "Move away from these men so I can destroy them quickly."

But Moses and Aaron bowed facedown and cried out, "God, you are the God over the spirits of all people. Please don't be angry with this whole group. Only one man has really sinned."

Then the Lord said to Moses, "Tell everyone to move away from the tents of Korah, Dathan, and Abiram."

Moses stood and went to Dathan and Abiram; the elders of Israel followed him. Moses warned the people, "Move away from the tents of these evil men! Don't touch anything of theirs, or you will be destroyed because of their sins."So they moved away from the tents of Korah, Dathan, and Abiram. Dathan and Abiram were standing outside their tents with their wives, children, and little babies.

Then Moses said, "Now you will know that the Lord has sent me to do all these things; it was not my idea.If these men die a normal death—the way men usually die—then the Lord did not really send me.But if the Lord does something new, you will know they have insulted the Lord. The ground will open and swallow them. They will be buried alive and will go to the place of the dead, and everything that belongs to them will go with them."

When Moses finished saying these things, the ground under the men split open. The earth opened and swallowed them and all their families. All Korah's men and everything they owned went down.They were buried alive, going to the place of the dead, and everything they owned went with them. Then the earth covered them. They died and were gone from the community.The people of Israel around them heard their screams and ran away, saying, "The earth will swallow us, too!"

Then a fire came down from the Lord and destroyed the two hundred fifty men who had presented the incense.[xxvi]

"Will the hole remain? How are we going to fill it in?"

"I think you will find," Ntambo answered, "the hole will be gone when we go back outside."

"Another 'lying wonder,' " the red-headed boy said. He seemed to be gaining confidence. The set of his jaw spoke of determination; his shoulders drew back and his chest pushed out. Themba recognized the look in his eyes. It was the same look he had often seen in his uncle's eyes when he was facing trouble. It was the bold look of a believing heart.

When they went outside again, as Ntambo had predicted, the hole in the earth that had almost swallowed them up had disappeared. There was nothing to indicate that anything at all had taken place.

....

Ntambo arranged for them to meet with the Lucas's after Bob had returned from the airport.

In the meantime the young people were left to get acquainted. For James and the girls Themba was the first black African boy they had ever seen at close quarters. Even those they had seen at a distance in Canadian streets had been a far cry from this boy from a tribal village. He was dressed only in a loin cloth. Wherever he went Themba carried a small bundle tied to the rope that held his loin cloth in place. It was a thin blanket, the only extra clothing he ever wore. He released this now and threw it over his shoulders in deference to Nancy and Ashley who seemed a little taken aback by his simple manner of dress. His toned body was muscular, and his calloused feet were a wonder to them. Never having worn shoes over rough paths and rocky terrain had made the soles of his feet hard as leather.

"My name is Themba," he announced in his heavily accented English.

They all repeated their own names, and Themba said them over and over till he had approximately mastered the pronunciation of each of them. Skip was "Skeep," James came out as "Jaams." Ashley and Nancy were, "Arshley and Narncy."

The girls giggled and the guys chuckled as he tried to get his tongue to say their names correctly, but it was all in good natured fun. Themba in his own turn grinned as they tried to get the pronunciation of the first letters in his name correct. At the end of it all, any cultural barriers and first-meeting strangeness had disappeared, and the beginning of a lasting friendship had been born.

The rest of the time till Bob Lucas returned was spent in exploration and drawing on Themba's rich understanding of his culture and values. He even took them to the village that had been established as a result of the Rebel raid that had ended in the death of Skip's parents. The Mission leadership had deemed it wise not to have local people too closely associated with the mission. They thought many of the local people would not have been slaughtered had they not been living in the mission compound.

So the young people spent a fascinating and thoroughly enjoyable afternoon together. They were careful, however, to avoid one area of the mission property – the place where the earth had almost swallowed them alive. Though it was unlikely the enemy would employ the same tactics again, they thought it best not to provide him with another opportunity. They couldn't be sure that area was not particularly susceptible to that kind of event.

When Bob Lucas returned and they were once more gathered around the table in the dining room, they shared with the missionary couple all that had happened in their absence.

When all the details of their harrowing experienced had been explained to the missionaries, it dawned on Skip how incredible it all sounded. There was no physical evidence any of it had ever happened. The ground that had sunk beneath their feet was as solid now as it always had been. Had the story been told to anyone other than Bob and Rhonda Lucas, he was sure they would have been accused of hallucinating. As it was, a deep furrow of concern appeared between Bob's eyes. He caught Ntambo's eye, then that of his wife, and grunted.

Ntambo merely stared back.

"Are you sure," Bob said at last," that it is a good idea to go on this journey with five young people with little experience? What do they know of engaging the powers of darkness?"

This was the first time Skip had heard of any such planned trip, though he was certain such a trip would have to be taken at some point. He had discussed it with Aunt May and Reginald. Though they were not entirely comfortable with the venture, they considered it inevitable in the light of Skip's dream. He suspected that a lot of the time on their travels would be spent in prayer for them. He wondered though, how Ntambo had been brought into it. He was sure Aunt May had not written to him, and there had been no talk of it before the arrival of the big African and his nephew. He did not have to wait long for an answer.

"I have heard His Voice once again in the stillness," Ntambo replied. "I am to take Skip Jordan and his friends to The Smoke that Thunders." He paused, "It seems Skip's guardian has not told you all the young people have gone through before. They have engaged the powers of darkness before, and they have prevailed. The ways of our God do not follow the path of human wisdom. Though they are young, they have been chosen of God to engage the enemy."

"What about me, uncle?" Themba asked eagerly. "The reason you brought me with you, was that I could go to the Smoke also?"

Ntambo gave his nephew a penetrating stare, and there was a troubled tone to his voice when he spoke, "I did not know when the Voice spoke why I was to bring you with me. But when the Voice spoke again, I knew. Yes, nephew, you will come with us. The Smoke that Thunders is waiting for us."

Bob Lucas had not lost his troubled expression, "You are taking them to the Victoria Falls? I take it you know of the rumours, and of the legend?"

Ntambo replied simply, "I know."

"You know you will be taking them into extreme danger, and in the light of what happened today, don't you think you are taking too much of a risk?"

"I must obey the Voice," the big man replied.

The missionary's shoulders relaxed. He knew when Ntambo spoke of the Voice no arguments would prevail. He turned to his wife, "Can we get out of our meeting with the Superintendent, love?"

His wife shook her head, "The Superintendent will not be in the country for long, Bob. The other workers are coming from all over, and you know there are some vital concerns that must be settled."

Bob sighed, "Is there no way you can delay your departure for a week? I could drive you then."

Before Ntambo could reply, drums from the nearby village began to sound. They brought with them an atmosphere of urgency, and a pounding that seemed to enter the bones.

"We must leave at first light and we will walk. The drums are announcing our departure. There will be villages to welcome us on the way, and we must meet with the former witch Maleka, and the others. They will have information and words of wisdom."

"You mean the drums are sending a message ahead that we are coming?" Nancy asked.

Themba answered before his uncle could respond, "It is our way of sending news between villages. There are no telephone lines in the jungle, so the drums do it for us."

"And what is this about the Smoke-That-Thunders?" Ashley enquired.

Rhonda Lucas turned to her, "It is the African Name for The Victoria Falls. It was called that long before David Livingston discovered the falls and named it after Queen Victoria. The Smoke-That-Thunders is the translation of the African dialect, 'Mosi-oa-Tunya.' "

Skip had been thinking about the missionary's reaction when he was told they were going to the Victoria Falls, so he asked, "What are the stories and legends you mentioned earlier, Mr. Lucas? You didn't sound too happy about us going there."

Bob Lucas sighed, "I didn't want to tell you, but since you are going there anyway I suppose you need to know. Tribal traditions, rumours, and stories told by some who claim to have been there say there is a secret entrance hidden by the falls. They say it is near a part of the falls called, 'The Devil's Cataract.' They say it got its name because the devil's work is done there. There are rumours of caves and hidden entrances and witchcraft practiced with terrible consequences."

"You say there are rumours and legends and stories," James spoke up. "Is there any truth to it? Why would the authorities allow tourists to visit there if the stories are true?"

"For two reasons," Bob replied. "The first is that most people don't believe the stories, least of all the officials that make decisions like that. Of course, they don't want it to be true; they make a lot of money from the tourists. The second reason is that tourists are apparently not in danger, only those who are searching for the entrance, and meddle in what is being practiced there."

"So that is why you are worried about us going there," Skip said. "We are going there to meddle."

"Exactly," Bob replied.

Ntambo said, "That is why the drums are speaking. They are calling to my friends, those who were witchdoctors before coming to Christ. They will be able to tell us more about what is going on there."

Rhonda Lucas adopted a common-sense voice when she said, "Well, now, if you are leaving at first light, I guess you had all better get to bed."

So they trooped off to bed, their thoughts occupied with the strange and awesome things they had discussed around the dinner table.

Chapter 11

Setting Out

Skip and James looked curiously at the girls in the early morning light as they emerged from the mission house.

The case Nancy and Ashley had shared containing their jeans and other casual wear had somehow been mislaid at the airport. All they had to wear was skirts, dresses, and a few frilly blouses.

The Lucas's two sons were away at boarding school in the States, and were lodging with friends during the summer holidays. Rhonda Lucas had taken one look at the girls and declared, "You can't go on a two hundred kilometre hike in those. You'll have to put up with what's available."

What was available turned out to be Khaki shorts and shirts, with hiking boots and camouflage hats that belonged to her sons. Rhonda said, "Johnny and Jeremy chose not to come home for the holidays, so it's their own fault if these get worn out while they're away."

Nancy and Ashley indeed looked different. Skip felt a sense of relief. The boys' clothing hid most of their feminine curves; the boots looked rugged, and the hats shadowed their pretty faces. He could pretend once again that they were just buddies, as they had been to him before. He could forget they were two beautiful creatures who made his heart skip a beat and his brain to go all fuzzy.

"You look..."

"Weird," Ashley supplied.

"No.... I would say.... comfortable."

Nance gave Ashley a conspiratorial look, "I think he means dowdy... unattractive..."

"No. I didn't mean..."

"Forget it, Skip," James cut in. "They're just having you on. They know they look good. They're just trying to embarrass you."

"I got it," Skip said, and he grinned good-naturedly, "come to think of it you do look somewhat... dowdy, and maybe a little..."

He broke off when both the girls came on either side to punch him, laughing all the while. It was good to see. Their open confessions before Aunt May and the others two days ago seemed to have restored the warm friendship they had enjoyed before. They may not have forgotten their dreams, and the dark shadow lurking in them, but they had come to terms with what was really happening.

Themba regarded his four new friends curiously. The form their teasing took was unfamiliar to him, due to the vast difference in his own village culture and those across the sea. That being true he could still recognize true friendship when he saw it. Glancing down at the walking shoes Skip and James were wearing, he decided they would come apart long before they reached the thundering waters. His people had learned to make much more durable shoes from old car tyres discarded by the city folk. They seldom needed them, for the rough terrain they often walked had toughened their feet. However, they did at times encounter sharp, rocky ground that required a little more protection.

The girls would be fine with their heavy boots, but Skip and James would need something more than the flimsy footwear they were wearing.

Rhonda Lucas came out of the house, followed a few minutes later by her husband. A spectacular red glow was beginning to emerge from behind the low hills, and from the jungle on the eastern perimeter of the mission. The sun would soon bear down on them, its heat causing them to make use of the canvass water bags Themba and his uncle carried. They had thought it more prudent to bear the extra weight to spare those unaccustomed to the rugged demands of terrain and distance.

Ntambo stood apart, ready to leave, but waiting patiently while his charges said their goodbyes. He wanted to reach the first stage of their journey before nightfall.

At last the farewells and prayers for safety and protection were done. Skip and the others trudged behind Ntambo while Themba brought up the rear. A feeling of excitement went with them. In spite of the dangers ahead they could not shake the idea that they were on an adventure quite foreign to the lives they had lived in Canada. It would no doubt wear off in time, but for now it was theirs to enjoy.

....

Joshua the hermit returned to his hut in the hidden ravine conscious of a prodding sensation in his spirit. It was a sensation familiar to him since he had learned to live in the quiet centre of God's Presence. The prodding was a call to prayer, or more correctly, to intercession for those God had given into his care.

Some would question whether he could care for them when he was separated from them by thousands of miles. However, Joshua knew that caring and protection came in many forms, none greater than that provided by earnest intercession.

In Joshua's cloistered life, visions and dreams were rare. They were not generally needed. The calling God had laid upon him was that of direct communion through fellowship with God's Son. The Holy Spirit communicated God's will to him by enlightening the teaching of Scripture, and by the prodding he was presently aware of.

So Joshua did not often see visions or awake having dreamed dreams to communicate Heaven's revelation. Nevertheless, the impressions he was receiving were just as clear. His imagination, aided by the Spirit, supplied a picture to his mind's eye. He could "see" them moving forward to engage the Prince of Darkness in a conflict that would inflict losses on both sides. As his spirit absorbed these things, the prodding turned to a weight that pressed down on him, driving him to his knees. A cry issued involuntarily from his lips. For the next several hours Joshua groaned and wept and cried with inexpressible longings and unimaginable grief.

It was only when no more tears were left, and when they had dried upon his cheeks, that Joshua knew his prayers had been effective. Skip Jordan and his companions had been granted the protection of Heaven.

....

Raymond Nichol and his wife of only ten days occupied their time acting as the tourists they could only partly claim to be.

Yes, they were on their honeymoon. Yes, they were fascinated by the biggest waterfall in the world. Yes, they enjoyed the spectacular scenery and the spray that had prompted the natives to name the waterfall The-Smoke-That-Thunders. Yes, the thundering roar that reached their ears as millions of gallons of water plunged into the gorge below was awe-inspiring.

No, they were not totally taken up with these things. Both Angela and Raymond knew they were here for a more sinister purpose. So lately delivered from the Powers of Darkness, Raymond, and now Angela, were about to confront those forces that had held him captive for so long. Angela could not prevent the thrill of trepidation that passed through her. God's power was indeed greater than all the hosts of hell, as she had witnessed in the miracle of Raymond's transformation. Still, it was unwise to become over confident in dealing with the devil. She remembered a passage in the book of Jude, about those who took the devil's power too lightly. She had memorized it: *Not even the archangelMichael, when he argued with the devil about who would have the body of Moses, dared to judge the devil guilty. Instead, he said, "The Lord punish you."But these people speak against things they do not understand. And what they do know, by feeling, as dumb animals know things, are the very things that destroy them.*[xxvii]

Angela was lying contentedly in Raymond's arms on the lone couch of the cabin in the lounging area. Idly running her fingers over the back of his hand, she asked, "Ray, sweet?"

"Yes, my love?"

How long will we have to wait? I know I should be just enjoying our time together and not thinking about..."

"Not thinking about what is to come?"

"Yes, but I was wondering..."

"What are you wondering about?"

"I was wondering if we really have to fight this battle. What if we left it all and just went back to Canada and lived our lives. I love you and I confess I'm afraid something will happen and I'll lose you."

Raymond squeezed her tightly, "I'm afraid that is not an option, love."

"Why isn't it an option?"

"Angie, just think about it. What would have happened if you had given up and not prayed for my deliverance? You're afraid to lose me, but if you hadn't persevered would you even have me at all?"

"I guess not."

Her husband moved to sit beside her so he could look into her eyes as he explained.

Still holding his hand, Angela could feel the emotion in his body, and see the intensity in his eyes.

"I need to explain something to you, sweet. It would have been far better to never have got mixed up in witchcraft in the first place. I could have lived my life quite contentedly, but blissfully unaware of the spiritual forces arrayed against the human race. I could have been a Christian, serving the Lord in the safe confines of a church community."

Angela experienced a sinking feeling in the pit of her stomach. She knew these things. She knew where he was going with this and could not disagree. She had often told people the same thing. It was just that now she had so much to lose.

Ray continued, "That is impossible now. I have been deeply involved in the works of darkness. I have hurt more people than I will ever know. It is like ripping open a pillow and letting a strong wind scatter the down feathers abroad. One could never gather all the feathers together again. Most would be gone forever. I'll never know how many I have led along the path to destruction."

Tears came to Angela's eyes. How could she love this man so much after such a short acquaintance? How could he have gained so much maturity so soon after being delivered?

"I can't fix that, Angie. I can't bring them all back from the pit, but with God's help, I may be able to prevent others from being drawn into it."

"Of course, you're right, my love. Forgive me for putting my own interest ahead of what's most important."

"I understand. I have struggled with the same thing myself. Having found you at this stage of my life, and under such dramatic circumstances, I wanted to drop everything else. I wanted to take you off somewhere so we could be by ourselves."

Tears were in Angela's eyes when she said, "If you did do that Raymond Nichol, I would still love you to the end of my days, but I love you even more now for choosing to put Christ first."

That ended the conversation for a while. They simply sat side by side, basking in the peace and contentment that had settled upon them like the mists of the great waterfall beyond the window.

Inevitably, though, Angela's thoughts drifted toward the battle ahead, "Tell me something, Ray. This isn't the first time you have been here, is it?"

"You mean, to see the Victoria Falls?"

"No, I mean this is not the first time you have been to the secret place somewhere near here, where the work of the devil is being done."

Raymond Nichol drew a breath before answering, "Actually, Angel, this *is* the first time. I have never actually been inside the tunnels and chambers reported to be somewhere in the region of the Victoria Falls. However, once I had risen to a certain level in the fraternity of witches and wizards, I was made aware of a number of these centres all over Africa, Europe and Asia and all over the world. This one was mentioned as particularly effective in accomplishing its mandate."

"Would you tell me what kind of devilish work is being done here?"

A look of regret passed over Raymond's countenance when he said, "I think it is better I do not tell you now. You will know soon enough before this business is over. I will tell you though, that we are waiting for some young people to arrive whose paths I have crossed before."

"Who are they?" Angela asked.

"Young people I should have listened to long before now."

....

Skip was not suffering from culture shock as much as the others since, as young as he had been, something of Africa had seeped into him. Having been born in Africa he was technically an African, though he had lived most of his life in Canada. And perhaps the love his parents had had for Africa and its peoples had somehow been communicated to him. He was nevertheless suffering some disorientation. Village life in rural Africa contrasted so radically with what he had been accustomed to in Canada he found himself moving in a kind of fog.

They were welcomed in every village they entered, mainly because Ntambo was well-known and well-loved for his faithful ministry toward them over the years. Most of the opposition he had encountered in his early forays into evangelism had dissipated.

The occasional witchdoctor opposed him, but since he had won the hearts of the people there was not much they could do.

They were all lodged in a guest hut and tended to by the village women, with a head-man making sure they were looked after.

For Nancy and Ashley the lack of privacy was a particular trial.

"I can't believe," Nancy said, "that whole families live in the same hut with no place to do personal things away from the eyes of the others."

"I was speaking to Themba about that. He says sometimes more than one family occupies the same hut."

Skip was close enough to hear most of what the girls were saying in softer tones, "Don't you think the women would wait till the men were gone before attending their personal needs. If you want us to leave, just tell us."

"It's not just that," Nancy sighed, "It's the whole idea of not having any personal space."

Skip thought for a bit then said with a conspiratorial wink at James, "I think I may be able to do something about that."

All it took was a word or two with Ntambo, who in turn engaged the head-man in conversation. The result was a partition constructed of bundles of grass tied together and stretched across one end of the hut for the girls' use alone. From then on the same arrangement was made at every village they entered. It seemed to Skip the gratitude Nancy and Ashley displayed toward him for his small contribution to their feminine sensibilities was out of all proportion to its value.

"It was no big deal," He said when they both gave him a warm hug for his efforts.

There were other adjustments they all had to make on their first trek on the African continent. The floors of the huts they stayed in were made of dried cow-dung. They had a polished finish, either by constant use, or by some art known only to the village people themselves. It was surprisingly clean and smooth to the touch, but the ground beneath it was hard and unyielding. All they had to sleep on was a grass mat, and for the first week of their travels they awoke after little sleep with their bodies aching all over. After that it was not so bad.

Besides all this was the heat.

"I thought the summer heat was unbearable in southern Ontario," Ashley opined, "but to actually agree to a three hundred kilometre walk in the middle of an African summer, and so close to the equator, makes me a candidate for the Looney Bin."

It was uncharacteristic for Ashley to complain, but no one could blame her. Their handkerchiefs were soaked from mopping their brows; damp patches under their arms and down their backs gave evidence of how their bodies were reacting to the heat.

In contrast, Ntambo and Themba only bore a fine sheen of sweat on their mostly exposed bodies. They also did not seem to feel the rigor of the journey, whereas the rest of them fell into deep sleep on contact with their sleeping mats, despite the hardness of the ground.

The long daily walks eventually toned their muscles and the unpolluted air they breathed was good for their lungs, and gave them a feeling of well-being.

They also grew closer as they headed north. They talked, laughed, and helped each other over rough terrain. There were streams to cross and rivers to wade through. A holiday mood swept over them, and a sense of adventure.

Skip made it a point to either walk beside or ahead of Ashley and Nancy. That way he did not have to be confronted with their good looks. Their boyish garb failed to completely veil the charm of their femininity. James and Themba brought up the rear; he and Ntambo often walked together. The mood was not always so light hearted, however.

Trudging along behind Ntambo Skip sensed a change in the black man's demeanour. Hurrying to catch up Skip touched Ntambo on his elbow, "Is there anything the matter, my friend?" This was the way the African had always addressed him as a boy, and it was the way Skip had come to address him on this journey.

Ntambo glanced down at him affectionately, but his expression was still stern, "Did you notice the man in the last village who stood apart from the rest when we were entering?"

"You mean the one with the head-dress and the coloured robe?"

"That is the one."

"What about him?"

"I did not see him last night, and he was not in evidence this morning. I asked the head man what had happened to him. He said he had left before sundown on some urgent business in another village."

"And you think his business had something to do with us?"

"I do. He was a powerful man before the Gospel turned the hearts of most of the people to Christ. He certainly is not our friend, and I am afraid that when we arrive at our destination, we will not be unexpected."

"Is that bad?"

"It is very bad."

Chapter 12

The Lion's Den

The humidity increased as they passed from the plains into the jungle area. Up to that point the abundance of game had been breathtaking, and the scenic wonders that met their gaze inspired a sense of wonder.

The Baobab trees were wonders in themselves. Pointing at several in their path Skip commented, "I did an internet search. Their trunks can be as thick as thirty feet in diameter, and some are hollow at the bottom to form a kind of cave."

"They don't look like trees at all," James said, "at least not ordinary trees. They look as if someone took them and planted them upside down. The branches look more like roots."

Skip said, "The seed pods hanging from the branches contain cream-of-tartar; they ferment after the spring rains."

Themba chuckled in his deep-throated manner, "The giraffe and elephants eat them like that. Many times I have watched them eat the seeds and get drunk. It is a strange and funny sight to see. "

Nancy and Ashley both said, "Really?"

Themba nodded, "The rains are past, and you will not see it, but my father took me often to see them. He wanted me to see what happens when someone takes strong drink. He said it steals wisdom from the mind."

There were other wonders, too, among them the great balancing rocks. Nancy stood and gazed on one beside the path they were following, "How on earth did those rocks get on top of each other? It looks as if some giant decided to arrange them like that."

Indeed, it was a sight to see. A rock the size of a large house served as a base for another half its size to rest upon it. It, in turn, had a boulder almost as large resting upon it.

"The rocks speak," Ntambo's deep voice intruded.

"How do they speak?" Ashley asked.

"They speak with the voice of reason. It seems impossible that those rocks just happened to land on top of each other. And they say something to my heart."

Skip cast a respectful glance toward the big black man, "What do the rocks say to your heart, dear friend?"

"They tell me that nothing is impossible with God. The things that are impossible for *us* are possible for our God to perform *for* us. Skip, take God's book in your hand and read where the boy with a demon was cast out."

Skip knew what Ntambo was referring to. He had spoken with Ntambo about the passage only that morning. Removing his Bible from the pouch on his belt, he found the place and read: *When Jesus and his followers came back to the crowd, a man came to Jesus and bowed before him.*

The man said, "Lord, have mercy on my son. He has epilepsyand is suffering very much, because he often falls into the fire or into the water. I brought him to your followers, but they could not cure him."

Jesus answered, "You people have no faith, and your lives are all wrong. How long must I put up with you? How long must I continue to be patient with you? Bring the boy here." Jesus commanded the demon inside the boy. Then the demon came out, and the boy was healed from that time on.

The followers came to Jesus when he was alone and asked, "Why couldn't we force the demon out?"

Jesus answered, "Because your faith is too small. I tell you the truth, if your faith is as big as a mustard seed, you can say to this mountain, 'Move from here to there,' and it will move. All things will be possible for you."[xxviii]

"So, what are you saying? Are you saying we are heading into demon territory and therefore we are facing impossible odds?"

"Then why...?" Nancy began.

"I'm not finished, Nance. I think Ntambo is trying to tell us we cannot face what lies ahead in our own strength. What we are dealing with here is not something difficult that we can somehow get through by cleverness. We are not facing the difficult, but the impossible. We can only win this fight by..."

"By having faith in God," James finished.

"Exactly," Skip acknowledged.

Ntambo smiled in a way that may have indicated pride in students showing some progress, and turned to proceed on their journey.

The others followed silently, sobered by the reminder of what lay ahead.

The plains teamed with wildlife.

Herds of wildebeest, zebra and impala were visible in the distance. Once they saw vultures circling. An hour later they saw them barely fifty yards away fighting over the carcass of an Impala. There were hardly more than bones and horns left by the time they happened upon it.

"Lions made that kill not long ago," Themba said. "They can't be too far away."

"Is that why you and your uncle are carrying spears?" James asked.

They had all noticed when they set out from the last village that, apart from the supplies and water bags, Themba and Ntambo both carrying long spear-like staffs. They had sharpened iron heads about ten inches long.

"Assegais," Ashley said, "they're called assegais. I read about them on Wikipedia. They are used for war, and for hunting."

"And for protection," Themba added. We're in lion country, though I don't think the lions that killed the Impala are much of a danger now. They have eaten and may not be hungry enough to pay us much attention. No matter, it is better to be prepared."

Hyenas were also in evidence. They lurked at a distance from the vultures, waiting to get what was left when they were done.

Nancy shivered, "They give me the creeps. They look so... evil."

Ntambo turned to inform them, "They're not the nicest of God's creatures, but like the vultures they perform a valuable service. They get rid of the rotting flesh that could spread disease."

"I still don't like them," Nancy said. "I've heard they creep into campers' tents and bite people in the face."

"That is true," Ntambo responded, "but in the wild it is for us to take precautions. We know the nature of the animals living here. We must always be watchful so we will not come under their power."

"Oh, oh, I can sense we are about to be taught a lesson," James said with a comical expression on his face. "I think you find lessons in everything you see, Ntambo."

"Lessons are written by God into everything He has made," Ntambo replied. "If we are alert, we can learn much that will help us in our walk with God."

"So what is the lesson we can learn from the lions, the vultures, and the hyenas," Ashley asked.

"Like we know the nature of the animals, so we also know, from Scripture, the nature of Satan and his demons, and we must prepare ourselves and be alert. If we are not we may come under their power. As God's book tells us: *Control yourselves and be careful! The devil, your enemy, goes around like a roaring lion looking for someone to eat.*[xxix]

"Never stop praying as we move toward The Smoke that Thunders. Word will have reached those doing the devil's work that we are approaching. They are not going to let us get far before they try to stop us."

Skip noticed the direction they were taking led directly toward a vast area covered by dense jungle growth. Out here in the plains one could see wild animals approaching. It would be different in the jungle. With dense undergrowth and abundant greenery a predator could get mighty close before one would be even aware of its presence. Perhaps they should have waited for Bob and Rhonda Lucas to return from their conference before setting out. A trip by road in the mission van would have saved them all this danger, and got them to their destination sooner.

They would also have missed all this beauty, and the close fellowship they had enjoyed so far. Besides, Ntambo had been guided by the Voice, and perhaps this was the least dangerous option of the two. It was impossible to know for sure. There were also the drums. Ntambo had used them to arrange a meeting with some of the former witchdoctors in one of the villages in their path.

Before they could get close enough to the jungle to take refuge there, a new terror descended upon them. Perhaps 'descend' was not the proper term. It came in the form of a dark cloud, but it was not like any cloud Skip had ever seen. It came not from the sky, but along the ground. Rising about thirty feet from the earth it crept toward them, an evil smell preceding it. Black as night, a luminescent green mist moved under it.

All except Ntambo stood frozen as the cloud advanced. It developed wings to either side to cut off any possibility of escape. It kept moving, threatening to enclose them in a ring of death. Skip had no doubt the cloud posed, not merely a threat to their well-being, but that it meant to kill them.

Skip's heart beat like a drum in his ears. He was sure the others were feeling the same sense of impending doom as he was.

Ntambo had a completely different reaction. He moved toward the advancing cloud as if he were confronting an army. He stood still and raised his assegai in both hands and uttered a sound that drowned out the noise of thundering hooves. Herds of wildebeest and zebra were fleeing for their lives; ahead of these the impala were disappearing in the distance.

As the last notes of Ntambo's battle-cry faded, Skip saw the cloud cease its advance. It stayed in one spot but was anything but still, like a living thing it seemed vexed that it could not move forward. The green mist at its base rose higher into the cloud and the cloud itself seemed to roll like waves of the sea unable to break upon the shore.

It would be untrue to say Skip and the others were not terrified, but as they watched Ntambo with arms raised, comprehension dawned and the fear dissipated. It became clear that the only thing preventing the malicious cloud from swallowing them was the raised arms of the big black man. Power greater than the cloud emanated from him, holding the cloud at bay; it was unable to advance.

An understanding of what was taking place dawned upon Skip his heart began to beat more normally. A well-memorized Scripture came to him at that moment: *My dear children, you belong to God and have defeated them; because God's Spirit, who is in you, is greater than the devil, who is in the world.* (1 John 4:4 – NCV)

Ntambo believed that promise. He was allowing God's power to work through him.

But as time went on a curious thing took place. As strong as Ntambo was his arms could not maintain their raised position; as he let them fall the cloud advanced again. With an effort he raised them up again and the cloud retreated. Ntambo and the cloud seemed to have reached a stalemate. As long as he could keep his arms raised the cloud went back; when his arms sagged, the cloud advanced.

Suddenly a solution dawned upon Skip. Turning to Themba he gripped his arm and said urgently, "Themba, you are the strongest among us. Kneel down behind your uncle. James and I will stand on either side of him. We need to help keep his arms raised."

Without question Themba did as he was told, falling to his knees and hunching over so his uncle had somewhere to sit. With no rocks or fallen logs available, it was the only option.

"James," Skip shouted. "Get on that side of Ntambo and ease him down onto Themba's back. Nancy, Ashley, get ready to help us when we need you." No one resisted his shouted commands.

When Ntambo was seated on his nephew's back his arms were at a level he and James could reach, "Now James, we are going to keep Ntambo's arms raised for however long it takes. Nancy and Ashley can help in relays when we get tired."

So that is what they did. The only problem was that Themba had no one to relieve him. His uncle was a big man, and the weight he bore must have been crushing, but not a murmur escaped his lips. Bent, with his knees and hands digging into the ground, he held his position while the two white boys gripped his uncle's arms and held them steady. Even they began to flag after a while, but they held on and called to the girls to help them.

The evil cloud kept moving back until, in apparent defeat, it disappeared like a puff of smoke blown by the wind. Only then did Ntambo lower his aching arms, and the others breathed a sigh of relief. He stood at last and Themba staggered to his feet. He rubbed his hands together and brushed the sand and gravel from his knees. He stood and arched his back; it no doubt ached from bearing his uncle's weight. There was, however, a look of triumph in his eyes when he caught the others' gaze. Like a warrior from the past, he had prevailed.

They had all prevailed. Ntambo squeezed the arm of each of them in a silent display of pride and gratitude for their bravery under pressure.

Ashley turned to Skip, "How did you know what to do?"

"I didn't at first, but then I remembered an incident in the Bible. Joshua and the Israelites were fighting the Amalekites down in the valley." He fumbled in his belt pouch for his Bible. "But let me read it for you, if I can remember where to find it." It took a minute or two while the others watched him search, but at last he grunted with satisfaction, "Here it is," Skip said, and began to read:

At Rephidim the Amalekites came and fought the Israelites.So Moses said to Joshua, "Choose some men and go and fight the Amalekites. Tomorrow I will stand on the top of the hill, holding the walking stick of God in my hands."

Joshua obeyed Moses and went to fight the Amalekites, while Moses, Aaron, and Hur went to the top of the hill.As long as Moses held his hands up, the Israelites would win the fight, but when Moses put his hands down, the Amalekites would win.Later, when Moses' arms became tired, the men put a large rock under him, and he sat on it. Then Aaron and Hur held up Moses' hands—Aaron on one side and Hur on the other. They kept his hands steady until the sun went down.So Joshua defeated the Amalekites in this battle.[xxx]

"It was brilliant of you to come up with that at just the right moment," James commented.

"It wasn't brilliant of me at all," Skip replied. "Jesus promised the Holy Spirit would bring things to remembrance when we needed them. Besides, it was Ntambo who knew what to do. If he hadn't raised his assegai and held the cloud back, I may never have remembered what Aaron and Hur did for Moses."

Ntambo turned from their youthful exuberance, saying over his shoulder, "We must reach the jungle village before dark," before striding toward the tree-line ahead of him. They all followed.

No one said much along the way, in spite of the unfamiliarity of the jungle path and the wild-life encountered. They were too occupied with thoughts of how close they had come to being swallowed by the evil cloud.

"That's the second time we've almost been swallowed up," Nancy said once, "first by the earth, and then by the cloud."

"In spite of our deliverance," James said, "we were in real danger. What do you think would have happened to us if the cloud had not been driven back?"

"Something awful," Ashley said, and they all fell silent.

Nevertheless there was plenty of noise even if they themselves kept quiet. Parrots in brilliant plumage squawked, small creatures rustled in the undergrowth, and the drumbeat of hooves sounded in their ears as some larger animal fled in alarm from their approach. Light from the late afternoon sun was visible through the tops of the trees, but for the rest they moved in a twilight world of half-light. It was an exhilarating experience, but they never forgot for a moment they were in mortal danger. They were moving against evil forces far stronger than they; were it not for their confidence in God's guidance and support they would have given up long before this.

The jungle path led to a large clearing and in the clearing was the village where Ntambo intended to meet with his friends, the former witchdoctors.

Children played in the dust in the last light before sundown. Naked babies crawled in the doorways of huts under their mothers' watchful eye.

From a great hut in the centre of the village came the sound of singing. The harmony between women's voices and the baritone, tenor and base of the men was captivating. The young people from across the sea had never heard the like, though Skip had vague memories of the same. No doubt, a church service of some kind was in progress. The melody of *What a Friend we Have in Jesus* and *Jesus is a Rock in a Weary Land* emanated from the great hut while they stood and waited. They could not proceed any further till the headman of the village emerged and welcomed them, so they stood and soaked in the music devoid of instruments. However, the matchless harmony of the singers created the illusion of an orchestra.

Time slipped by, the sun sank beyond the trees, but still the singing continued. The words were in the local dialect, but the hymns were well known to the visitors waiting outside. They listened to *Rock of Ages*, *Wonderful Words of Life*, and, *Tell Me the Story of Jesus* till darkness settled, yet no one was conscious of the passing of time. Their spirits were lifted and their hearts blessed.

The glow of lamps appeared in the huts before the music ceased; the resulting silence felt as if the gates of Heaven had just closed, and each experienced a vague sense of disappointment.

"I could have listened to that forever," Nancy said dramatically. "That was the most beautiful singing I have ever heard."

No one else said anything for the head man emerged from the great hut carrying a Hurricane Lamp, and approached the group. Stopping a few feet from Ntambo he bowed his head briefly before saying, "Welcome to our village. I apologize for the delay in coming to greet you. We were practicing for the annual gathering of the churches in this region."

Ntambo bowed his head in like manner, "The singing was itself a welcome, my friend. You could have offered us no greater welcome than what we heard when we arrived."

Once the appropriate pleasantries had been uttered the visitors were shown to the hut they would occupy for the night. Word of the special needs the girls of the party required must have preceded them. The grass partition affording them privacy was already in place.

"Once you have been settled," the head man said, you must come to the great hut. A feast has been prepared for you. Your friends have already arrived, great one, and are waiting for you."

The respect Ntambo received wherever they went was impressive. Skip knew, however, that it had not always been so. In the early years of his witness for Christ he was pelted with stones, mocked and driven out by the villagers. Now, as the power of the Gospel had transformed lives and peace had settled on those areas where it had prevailed, he was held in peculiar regard.

Before leaving for the great hut Ntambo described the five former witchdoctors he had summoned to meet with them. He went into great detail concerning their characters, and the part they had played in interceding for Skip and the girls in their attempt to rescue their friends.

"I just want you to know," Ntambo said seriously, "the kind of people who will be supporting us as we enter into the enemy's stronghold. They have all suffered greatly for the cause of Christ and know how to intercede with power. Without them we dare not proceed."

When they entered the great hut, the former witch Maleka was the first to speak. "So, Ntambo, the one who speaks for the Great-Great-One, you have brought the chosen ones for us to meet."

"I have brought them," Ntambo acknowledged.

"And it is rumoured," said a short man, later identified as Mohapi "you intend to go into the Lion's Den." It became evident as the night progressed that Mohapi seldom spoke, but when he did it was always with significant insight.

"It is more than a rumour, bold one. We so intend."

No more was said as food was brought and they ate and drank in mute fellowship. Skip, however could not help thinking of the last words Mohapi had spoken. There was such a thing as the *Lion's Den*, and they were all going to go into it.

Chapter 13

Gathering Support

All evidence of the feast they had enjoyed had been removed. They were now all seated, lotus fashion, on mats arranged in a circle. The arrangement gave Skip an opportunity to examine the other members of the party. All of them at some point must have worn the witchdoctor's garb of feathered robes and horned head-dresses. Now they wore common dress with the addition of an embroidered blanket-like cloak. The embroidery somehow identified their tribe of origin.

While the horns and feathers were lacking, this in no way diminished the nobility of their bearing, but rather increased it. No longer did they need the witchdoctor's garb as a badge of honour; the honour was etched on their faces, and their bearing announced it. They were now the ambassadors of Christ.

The former witch Maleka was the most notable of the group; her features bore an almost fierce devotion to the Christ she now served. She had resisted Ntambo's preaching for more than seven years before finally surrendering to the claims of Christ; the others had opposed Him for only two or three. The intensity of her resistance to Christ seemed to be the measure of her intense devotion to Him now.

Mohapi was a slightly overweight man who was shorter than his companions. He had a boldness of expression that seemed to compensate for his lack of height. He leaned forward with rapt attention to everything that was said, drawing back if something impressed or astounded him. No one needed to guess at his reactions; they were plain for everyone to see.

Ntambo had spoken of the tall gangly member of the group, Mazimbi. His skin was as black as night, and his eyes dark pools staring out from a gaunt face. His gaze was nevertheless warm and engaging.

The fourth member of the delegation from afar was Marimba. Marimba was almost as tall as Ntambo, but with chocolate brown skin in contrast to that of Ntambo, whose skin bore a yellowish hue. He had the bearing of a warrior, with broad shoulders and muscular limbs.

Skip finally fixed his gaze on the last member of the group, Ntombeni. Of average height and build there was nothing average about the passion for the Gospel that shone from his eyes. Hidden by an extra garment he always wore, Ntambo had revealed, were innumerable scars he had suffered for the cause of Christ.

It was Ntambo who opened the discussion.

"You have rightly concluded that my nephew and I, together with these from across the sea, are headed in the direction of the fabled, 'Lion's Den.' I, personally, have no knowledge of it. My father was the witchdoctor in our village, and I heard of it from him. I was rescued from that darkness before I could get involved, though I had already decided against it.

"So I do not know how to reach this stronghold of evil. I only know it is located at, or near, the 'Smoke that Thunders.' I will need your counsel and guidance to find the place, and to know how to confront the evil that lurks there."

An intense silence followed Ntambo's speech.

Though there were the normal sounds of village life outside, their minds had filtered them out. Only the issue before them engaged their attention. Knowing the issues at stake, these four men and one woman were not about to enter lightly into a battle such as this.

"You are quite sure this is what He-Who-knows all wishes you to do?" Mazimbi asked, his gaunt features underlining the importance of his question.

"I am sure," Ntambo said simply.

"Then we must prepare ourselves for a battle such as we have never encountered before," the former witch Maleka said. "But what are we to do about the young ones? Have we the right to involve the innocent in this matter" She fixed her gaze on Nancy and Ashley, "Are you aware of what faces you if you continue?"

"Nancy stared back at the older woman, "We have faced this kind of thing before, but no, we are not fully aware. It is just something we cannot avoid."

Ashley added, "We were not prepared before, and we are not prepared now. We have put our faith in God, and that is all we know for sure."

"Wisely answered," Maleka said, "but is that the only reason you are doing this?" Her eyes flickered toward Skip, at the same time noting the flush that tinted their cheeks at her question.

Skip realized this former witch had discerned the emotional dynamics between him and the girls. It was indeed something that could cause problems. He was not even sure of his own motives with regard to Nancy and Ashley. It was further complicated by James' strong attraction to Ashley. Hadn't they settled that when they had confronted it at the mission?

"If you are to prevail in this fight," Maleka continued, "put all of your youthful desires out of your minds. It is the one thing the enemy can use against you."

Ntambo swept that aside, "The young ones are already involved. It cannot be avoided. What I want to know is if you, my fellow soldiers of the Cross, are willing to be involved?"

"That, too," Mohapi replied, "cannot be avoided. Since you cannot do without our support, we cannot withhold it." Nods from the other followed his declaration.

"Then let us proceed."

"The 'Lion's Den,' as it is called," Mazimbi said, "is really a vast network of caves beneath the ground under and beyond the 'Smoke-That-Thunders.' "

"How does one gain access to it?"

"Before we answer that," Mohapi said seriously, "you must tell us all that has taken place since you first felt compelled to begin your mission."

Ntambo paused, "I was not involved from the beginning, but the red-headed one can tell you of one attack from the powers of darkness." He turned to Skip, "We need the support of these friends. You must tell them all. Leave nothing out."

Skip began with his dream, his recognition of the Victoria Falls (known to the others as The Smoke that Thunders), his recognition of Roger Wilson, and Ntambo's apparent fate. His account drew gasps of alarm from those who had not yet heard it, including Ntambo. Skip had not had an opportunity as yet to share it with him.

Indeed, he had been putting it off. But now, in the light of Ntambo's command to tell all, he had no other option. He told it in detail – the crowd hounding Ntambo to the cliff, and how he had seen him disappear over the edge.

They were all visibly upset. It was clear all five of the former witchdoctors were having second thoughts regarding lending their support to the mission Ntambo and his companions were pursuing.

Mohapi leaned forward and spoke directly to Ntambo, "Did you know of this, O man of God? Have you known the end of the path you are following and still determine to go forward?"

Ntambo, while obviously surprised by the revelation of his impending death, did not seem unduly moved by it, "This is the first I have heard of it, you who have been scarred in your service for Christ. Let me ask you if those scars, and the thought that there may be more of them in the future, will prevent you from continuing to do your Master's bidding?"

Mohapi leaned back as the significance of Ntambo's question impacted him, "Nothing has stopped me till now," he said. Throwing off his embroidered blanket he stripped himself of his upper garment, revealing the terrible evidence of the opposition he had received to his bold preaching. The young people gasped. They had never seen anything like it. Skip and James suddenly felt their throats constrict; Nancy and Ashley dropped their gaze to the earthen floor, unable to continue looking at the evidence of so much brutality. Ntambo had told them Mohapi was scarred, but they had never imagined anything like this.

Mohapi replaced his upper garment and threw the embroidered blanket back over his shoulders, "I would rather die than depart from the path my God has called me to walk."

Ntambo had made his point, "Now you know why I must not shrink from continuing on this journey, even if death lies at the end of it." He turned to the girls, "Tell what you told me on the way here. Let these faithful servants of God know of the spirit that entered your dreams."

Nancy spoke first, telling of the dark shadow lurking at the edge of her dream, and of the envy and resentment that had risen in her heart when she awoke the next morning, "I think, for a time, I actually hated Ashley, who is my dearest friend."

Ashley said, "I had the same dream, and the same feelings. I thought Nancy was stealing my friendship with Skip from me. For a time, until we got it out in the open, Nancy became my enemy."

Next, James told of the demonic attack they had experienced in the woods on their way to Joshua's cabin. "I know there are no such things as ghouls, but for some reason these demons were *posing* as ghouls."

At this point Ntambo took up the tale and told of how the sinkhole had almost swallowed Skip, James, and the girls. "Just before we arrived here," he continued, "an evil-smelling cloud tried to cover us. If it had succeeded we would have perished."

The silence following Ntambo's words was broken by Mazimbi. His gaunt features and eyes the colour of night seemed to add to the solemnity of his voice when he said, "You cannot go alone into The Lion's Den. I will go with you."

No one protested. The manner of his telling it made it clear he was responding to some inner compulsion. No arguments would have changed his mind.

"But first," Mazimbi continued, "I will let the drums speak. I have two hundred faithful people who will pray night and day until the battle has been won."

"I have three hundred." Maleka added.

"I have one hundred," said Marimba.

Mohapi had two hundred and Ntombeni had one hundred and fifty.

Skip was impressed. To think that these shepherds in the dark continent of Africa could call upon so many faithful disciples to pray in relays around the clock was astounding – and humbling. At his home church in Canada it was difficult to get even a dozen out of a hundred church members to attend the prayer meeting. Even considering the vast territories these shepherds of God's people commanded, their commitment was astonishing. Five pastors were able to call upon eight hundred and fifty prayer warriors to join the fight against the forces of darkness. He felt both shame at his own commitment to prayer, and a challenge to give himself more to prayer in the future.

Ntambo asked, "So, we have your support?"

"You have it," Maleka said. "The drums will be speaking for a long time."

....

Unknown to those gathered in the great hut there were five angels gazing down at them from the heavenly realms. Two were assigned to Raymond Nichol, one to his wife, Angela, and the other two were responsible for Skip and his friends.

The tallest angel and his companion had been assigned to Skip and the girls on their former venture into the Valley of Deception. Now they had been joined by those assigned to Raymond Nichol and his wife.

Communicating without audible speech, the tallest angel said, "We are soon to be joined by five others of our kind. Three of them are for the protection of the big man, Ntambo; the other two are for the one called Mazimbi."

"So there will be ten of us assigned to this group alone," one of the angels asked. "How much support can we count on?"

With so many praying, we have been assigned three thousand by the Lord of Hosts to support us."

"That many?" said another, "He-Who-Knows-All must expect great resistance."

"The number assigned to us," the tallest angel replied, "depends entirely upon those committed to pray. Without those who pray those we are called to protect will almost certainly suffer defeat."

....

Angela leaned her back against the headboard of the bed and watched Raymond pace up and down in the limited floor space of their cabin.

He had been restless lately, and impatient, though she knew his impatience was not with her. He was expecting something to happen, or for someone to arrive, and the delay was like a weight pressing down on his mind. He was new to his faith in Christ and had not yet learned the secret of casting his burdens on the Lord. She had only partially learned it herself.

Rising from the bed Angela went to him. Stepping in his path she put her arms around him. Bringing her lips close to his ear, she said, "Still, my love. Don't get so worked up. Whatever is going to happen will happen in God's time. We have to learn to trust Him."

Raymond took a deep breath, "I know, sweet. It's just that the longer we delay the more likelihood there is that my presence here will be discovered. They will eventually, but I don't want them to know yet. When they do they will know about you, then who knows what they will do? I can protect you better when the others arrive."

Angela had asked him before who "they" and "others" were, but he had been vague in his answers, saying he would explain later. For now it was better that she knew as little as possible.

"At least tell me who you are expecting to arrive. You said something about young people you should have listened to before. Who are they, and what part did they play in your previous life?"

Raymond sighed, and his shoulders relaxed, "I guess I can tell you that much. Come sit down and I'll tell you what I know."

Clearing away the photographs they had been examining earlier, they sat on the bottom end of the bed. Taking her hand in his he spoke slowly and distinctly. "Those I am expecting to arrive..." He paused. "Don't ask me how I know they are coming, I just do. They are former students of mine. I used my science class to draw most of the students into witchcraft. Only a handful resisted, but none more than Skip Jordan and two friends of his, Nancy and Ashley.

"There was something unusual about the boy, and it was not just that I knew him to be a Christian. There were other Christians in the class and they were not taken in by the spells and enchantments I used. Skip Jordan, on the other hand, seemed to have natural leadership skills, and something else besides.

"Now that I've become a Christian myself and remember what I learned from the Bible before getting into witchcraft, I have a better idea of what made him different. People like Moses, King David, Isaiah and others were specially called by God to do a special work. They were called and equipped to do that work and were given an anointing, if that is the right term."

"The Holy Spirit came upon them," Angela supplied. "Samson killed a lion and defeated the Philistines only when the Holy Spirit came upon him. The prophets only spoke as they were moved by the Holy Spirit. Is that what you think this Skip Jordan had?"

"I think so," Raymond replied. "Whatever it was, the girls, Nancy and Ashley, had some of it, too. I could not penetrate their defences."

"I arranged a magical retreat, protecting the invitations with spells and enchantments, so no one would know its location except those invited. Skip and the girls managed to break the spell. They actually turned up at the retreat and destroyed everything. That's when I went mad, and ended up where you found me."

"Were they working alone?"

"As young as they were, I think they had a network of adults supporting them. Skip's guardian, whom he called Aunt May, was the principal one. I suspect there were others beside her, perhaps more than I thought at the time. He obviously didn't know a lot about witchcraft; he didn't seem to know what he was doing some of the time. He still prevailed against us, so I think he was not alone."

"And you think," Angela said, "Skip and his friends are coming here?"

"I'm sure of it, but I can't think what is delaying them. I know they were at the mission station where his parents were killed ten years ago. I expected the present missionaries would bring them here by Jeep, but perhaps they are coming some other way."

"What do you think they are coming to do here?"

"I expect they are coming to rescue their former friend, Roger Wilson from the clutches of the devil, though I don't think they have much hope of doing so. Roger has plunged far too deep into the black arts to be easily pried away."

"And who is this Roger Wilson, Ray?"

"That, my sweet, will have to wait for another time; I once saw him as my greatest triumph, but now every memory of him fills me with shame. God forgive me for what I did to that boy."

....

The drums sent messages all night long; in time they seemed to be pounding in their heads, and not in the village outside. At first it seemed impossible to sleep, but soon the pounding, blending with their heartbeats, took on the form of a lullaby; they fell into a deep sleep.

At first light the young people were still a little groggy, yawning and sighing as they ate and prepared for the march ahead. Themba, on the other hand, was bright and cheery. To this kind of life he was born. The hard trail never bothered his calloused feet and the early mornings never made him reluctant to face the day. His eyes were bright with anticipation as if he expected the day to be filled with adventure and excitement. He regarded Skip and James' footwear with amusement.

The rough trail and constant walking had rendered their walking shoes useless. With the appearance of a magician pulling a rabbit out of a hat, Themba withdrew two pairs of car-tyre sandals from his carrying sack. Skip and James beamed at him with grateful smiles. They had been wondering what would happen when their tender feet were forced to make contact with the ground beneath them. Ashley regarded the sturdy sandals with longing. The boots they wore were still in good repair, but their feet, ankles and calves would sweat from being confined. The heat and constant walking made them feel they were walking around in a sauna and not in boots at all.

Nancy never said a word; all she did was gaze at Themba with her expressive green eyes, and then glance down at her feet. Themba got the message, went off to confer with the village head man, and returned carrying another two pairs of sandals. With relief, they pulled the boots from their feet and donned the more practical footwear. With sighs, they exulted in the cool air over their feet and lower limbs. Themba just beamed at them, as proud as if he had brought them some of the treasures from King Solomon's Mines.

As they set out Mazimbi took the lead. He had more intimate knowledge of the trail from this point on. He also knew of the entrance to the Lion's Den, and had been in the caves beneath and below the Victoria Falls before. Ntambo walked behind him, his giant hand gripping his assegai more tightly now that they were going through dense jungle.

Skip and James followed close behind Ntambo, the girls sandwiched between them and Themba, who brought up the rear firmly gripping his assegai.

With his mind focussed on what lay ahead, Skip began to feel a little overwhelmed. The enormity of what they were doing, and the consequences they may suffer as a result, made him wonder if he was being courageous, or just foolish. He and the others must be crazy for making an assault on a major stronghold of Satan. In spite of the attacks they had sustained from the enemy already, their journey to Africa and their trek over plain and through jungle, had felt more like adventure. Yes, there may be danger, but that made it kind of exciting. Now remembering his dream and how he had seen Ntambo hounded toward the edge of a cliff and pushed over, he was suddenly filled with trepidation. What kind of a fool was he to even *be* here?

Turning to James, Skip asked, "What did you think of the meeting with the former witchdoctors last night?"

James had been occupied with his own thoughts. It took him a few seconds to refocus on what Skip had said to him, "I think they didn't much like the idea of Ntambo pressing on, even though he knows he will die."

"It is not certain he will die," Skip said.

"But... you saw him in your dream. You saw him go over..."

"I may not have seen everything there was to see," Skip said desperately. He knew he was clutching at straws. Though he had not seen him for ten years, the last week in his company had confirmed a bond that had not diminished with the passing of time. He could not bear it if Ntambo died. *When* he dies, a voice in his head told him. But perhaps... There was no perhaps, and a heavy weight settled on his heart. It was hopeless to imagine that perhaps he would fall on a ledge, or some other impossible event would happen to save Ntambo from death. Now he felt as if he was part of a funeral march. A sense of impending doom settled upon him.

As if sensing the cloud of fear and despair behind him, Ntambo turned to regard Skip while continuing his relentless march toward whatever awaited him, "Do not despair, my young friend," He said. "Our future is all in the hands of the One Who died for us."

Chapter 14

Uncovering the Past

They walked all day, pausing only for brief periods of rest. Mazimbi seemed possessed with a sense of urgency, pushing them to the edge of their physical endurance. It was totally unlike the leisurely pace Ntambo had kept them to till Mazimbi had taken over.

Only when they had emerged from the jungle and the sun was sinking below the horizon, did Mazimbi call a halt. Setting up camp only amounted to collecting wood for a fire, digging into the soft earth for a bed, and retrieving their rations for a simple meal.

The girls were exhausted, flopping down with muttered longings for a hot shower, perfumed soap, and soft clothing more in keeping with their feminine sensibilities. All they got was a cold, meandering stream, and a change into another set of the borrowed masculine clothing they had been washing and wearing all week.

Skip and James did not fare much better. Weary to the bone, their sweaty clothes clinging to their bodies, they fell to their knees and gratefully removed their back-packs. The cold stream refreshed them and a change of clothing revived them, but they knew they would not take long to sleep that night. The unusual sleeping arrangements would not keep them awake

Gathered around the fire Mazimbi began to talk, the flames giving a yellowish tinge to his dark skin. He spoke with earnestness, and with certain knowledge. His former life had been saturated in the demonic and cloaked with deception. He understood the forces at work and the resistance they were certain to encounter. An hour ago the drums had started up again, a distraction from the sounds of animal life around them. It was also a reminder that communication in deep Africa, though ancient, could be as effective as the conveniences of the modern world.

"I must tell you," Mazimbi began, "of the dangers that lie ahead. You have heard of the Smoke-That-Thunders, or what the white man knows as Victoria Falls. It is a place of great mystery, and of great beauty. The beauty of the Smoke, as we often call it, also hides a great evil. Only a few of those who have delved into that evil know of its existence."

Mazimbi took a deep breath, his gangly frame bending so he could engage each of them with his dark eyes, "It is strange that the white man's name for the place that hides the entrance to the Den of the Lion is, 'The Devil's Cataract.' Many people from many lands have been into the evil place hidden by the cataract's raging torrent, and by the odd rock formation beneath it. Yet, it still remains the most secret place of evil in all of Africa. If any were to reveal its location they would be sought and killed.

"It was either by accident or God's Providence that it was called the Devil's Cataract. However it came about it is an apt name, for it hides the entrance to a vast network of hidden caves where the devil's work is done."

Skip made a noise to indicate he had a question.

Mazimbi's eyes swept over him, giving tacit permission.

"You said those who reveal the entrance to the Lion's Den will be sought and killed. Is not that what you are about to do for us? Will you not be sought and killed if you lead us there?"

"What you do not understand," Mazimbi said, fixing Skip with a disconcerting stare, "is that I am *already* dead. They can do nothing to me that has not already taken place."

The rest of them, all except Ntambo and Themba, looked back at him with astonishment.

"What on earth can you mean," Ashley asked her eyes wide with non-comprehension.

"He means," Ntambo supplied, "he has already given his life up to Christ. He may still be living and breathing, but he no longer counts his earthly life as important. His real life is the one he shares with Christ. The earthly life he lives now has already been given up."

"You mean he already thinks of himself as dead, so he is not afraid of what anyone can do to him?"

"Yes, Nancy, that is how Mazimbi thinks. It is as God's book says: '*Think only about the things in heaven, not the things on earth, Your old sinful self has died, and your new life is kept with Christ in God.*' "[xxxi]

While Ntambo was speaking Mazimbi reached into the folds of his embroidered cloak, extracting a crumpled piece of paper. He handed it to Skip, who smoothed it out and examined it in the flickering light of the fire.

"It is a poem," Ntambo said. It was given to me by your father before he died. I gave a copy to Mazimbi when he first turned to Christ. I think you ought to read it, Skip. It was one of the last things your parents gave to the people of Africa."

His hands trembling now, Skip read aloud:

"I am already dead – my life is hid with Christ in God –
So don't think your jibes and criticisms hurt me.
My real life is far from harm – my old life died.
My new life is raised with Christ. Jab a dead body
And see the reaction you get. So prick me with scorn,
Jab me with contempt; kick me in frustration – all
You'll get is silence.

Yet from another realm my true life sends a message,
Bled from the very heart of God – "I love you!"
No matter that your frantic acts of hate have pierced
My hands and feet, and crowned my head with thorns –
I love you! My new eyes see way past your outward acts,
And past the fields of resentment in your divided heart;
I see the soul for whom Christ died.

Your hate is but a symptom of your need, but weaker than
The love the Holy Spirit sheds abroad in this unworthy heart.
My secret weapon – love – will pierce your hating armour
And show your heart its need. No weapon formed
Against me can prevail; you see, I'm dead, and my life
Is hid with Christ in God."

Tears sprang to Skip's eyes, "This was written by one of my parents, and I have never seen it before. Why was I not given a copy?"

"It was in the box with all you mother's belongings."

"I haven't examined everything in that box," Skip said. "I wanted to savour everything in it so I could really take it all in. Now I am sorry I did not read it before."

"Do not grieve needlessly, my friend. It is God's design that you should read it now. He is preparing you for what is to come. It is your father who wrote that poem. Reading it you can see into his heart. No one took your father's life from him, or that of your mother. Your parents willingly gave up their lives long before they were killed."

Skip could not help the sobs that suddenly issued from him. Ntambo's words stirred something in him that had remained hidden for more than ten years. Nothing had penetrated to that depth in his soul before. He realized later there had been a pool of grief over his parents' death that had never been released. The question as to why God had allowed his parents to be so brutally murdered had never been answered. Now it all gushed forth with unrestrained emotion, the tears streaming down his face and dripping on his clean shirt. His body shook with each successive sob.

Skip's black companions looked on impassively, their tribal cultures giving them a deep understanding of what he was passing through. They knew they were seeing a process of cleansing that would set him free from the hurts of the past.

Nancy, Ashley and James, however, bore expressions of bewilderment. They had never seen Skip break down before. At one level they were embarrassed. It was like seeing someone naked for the first time. At another level they felt helpless, knowing there was nothing to do but watch. That was their collective reaction.

On an individual level Nancy later marked this moment when her regard for Skip made the leap from admiration, liking, friendship, companionship, into something deeper. It was the moment when the crush she had had for Skip changed from a girlish fantasy into what only a woman can feel – love.

At the time Nancy could not have described it in that way, only that something had changed in the way she saw her best friend.

Ashley became aware that what she felt for Skip was a crush – nothing more. She honoured him, liked him, respected him, and enjoyed his presence. Her fixation upon him before, she realized, were just the girlish fantasies of a girl in the process of turning into a woman. She glanced across at James, and began to see him in a new light.

James knew the bond between him and Skip had grown stronger. He did not analyse it; he just accepted that he was getting to know his friend on a deeper level.

In time Skip's sobs diminished till they ceased altogether. He drew a handkerchief from his pocket and wiped the evidence of his emotion from his face. He felt as if something heavy had lifted from his heart. His parents had not been cheated of a life of service. They had given up their lives willingly for the One Who loved them. He was not yet fifteen years old, but he felt the stirrings of a devotion to God he had never known before. His father, and his mother, had blazed a trail for him to follow.

Mazimbi spoke, jarring them all back to present realities. "The drums have spoken," he said.

Indeed, the drums had ceased their steady beat, making way for the normal sounds of an African night. Crickets chirped, small creatures scurried in the underbrush, even a lion's roar and the maniacal laugh of a hyena.

"The drums speak of a white man waiting at the Smoke. He has with him a woman of great beauty."

"What of this man?" Ntambo enquired. He could interpret the language of the drums himself. Either he had not been paying attention, or he was setting the stage for Mazimbi to reveal their message.

"The man has been enquiring after a boy, almost a man, with hair the colour of fire. He has been waiting and expecting this one and his companions to arrive for many days now. He is expecting him to arrive with several of his friends."

"Who in the world could that be?" James asked. No doubt you are the one with hair the colour of fire, but how would he know you were coming?"

"And who is the woman of great beauty with him?" Nancy enquired.

Skip did not enter the discussion that followed. Even Themba had his ideas as to the identity of the strangers who had enquired about them. Skip kept silent. For one thing he was having memory flash-backs. His imagination replayed vivid scenes of their last encounter with the forces of darkness. He saw Julia laying down her life to save her friends and others from the mind-altering effect of the veil of deception that had hung over them. The memory caused a pain of regret that he would never see her again, at least in this life.

He saw again the amazing revelation of Jesus Christ that had swept the veil away and displayed first the Lord`s ignominious death, and then His glorious resurrection. His mind-pictures shifted to his former teacher, Mr Nichol, reduced to a pathetic figure in the grip of abject fear. The madness shining from his eyes had been a terrible sight to see, and evoked a deep sense of pity and regret at a wasted life. True, he had led thousands astray, and some would say he deserved what he got. He had drawn young people into the destructive practice of witchcraft. It was nevertheless tragic that any life should come to such a pitiable conclusion.

A thought suddenly intruded into his mind, and he rejected it immediately. It could not be that Mr Nichol was the one waiting for them at their destination. That would mean...

The thought was interrupted by the breaking up of the campfire discussion. It was time to retire to their hollowed-out beds in the sand. They would be up at first light to start on the final leg of their journey. Tomorrow they would arrive at the Smoke-that-Thunders. Soon they would be exploring the entrance to the Lion`s Den, the location of one of Satan`s most secret strongholds. The identity of the mysterious stranger would also be revealed.

In spite of the exhaustion they all felt, sleep did not come immediately. Their minds were too full of what Mazimbi had revealed about what lay ahead of them.

`That poem you father wrote," Ashley whispered in the dark, "made quite an impression on Mazimbi, don't you think?"

"I would say it was more than an impression," James put in. "I would say he is living it. I would guess it was something of a shock to you, Skip?"

"No, I wouldn't say it was a shock. It was more like a window being opened to let in the light. I saw things I had never seen before.

It answered questions I have been struggling with all my life. I never even discussed them with Aunt May."

"What kind of questions?" Nancy asked.

"Skip took a breath before answering, "Questions as to why God allowed my parents to be killed in such a brutal manner, and why they had to die in the first place. They were doing such a great work. Why should their work be cut off so suddenly? They could have done so much more for the people of this land if they had only had time."

Themba had dug out his bed in the soft sand a short distance from them, close to his uncle. So it was a surprise when his shadow, created by the glow of the moon behind him, loomed over them.

"You are mistaken," the tall black youth said.

All eyes turned to him as he squatted so he could be heard without raising his voice, "Your father died, but he still speaks more loudly than if he had remained alive. And your mother's sweet presence is still spoken of by all the women in the tribe."

"How...?" Skip began.

"What Mazimbi and my uncle have not told you is that another box, besides the one your mother left to you was discovered among the ruins of the mission."

"If that is true," Skip said, frowning, "why was it not sent to me?"

"It was filled with books written in the writing of your father. In it was a letter, but it was not addressed to you."

"To whom then was it addressed?"

"It was addressed to the elders of the churches, and to those converted to Christ through the witness your parents had borne to Christ."

"What did the letter say?"

"It said the hand-written books were to help the church in case he and his wife were killed. He said the books contained instruction on how to apply the Word of God to our lives. They contained encouragement, rebuke, comfort and warning. Because of those books, the church in this region, and beyond, are stronger. My uncle, inspired by the words in those books set out with boldness to tell of the Christ Who died that others might live. If your father had lived, his words may not have been taken as seriously as they were after his death. Without those books, Mazimbi, Maleka and the others may never have been converted."

"But surely the churches could have gotten all that from the Word of God itself. Why were my father's words necessary?"

"Do you not know, my friend, what the Word of God says about preaching?" Suddenly, Themba appeared much older than his tender years. He had never said much, except in the general chatter of youth, but now he displayed wisdom those older than he seldom gained. He spoke from certain knowledge. He quoted, in English, from the Bible: *In the wisdom of God the world did not know God through its own wisdom. So God chose to use the message that sounds foolish to save those who believe.*[xxxii]

"In another place it also says: *So faith comes from hearing the Good News, and people hear the Good News when someone tells them about Christ.*[xxxiii]

"And in still another place it says: *And Christ gave gifts to people—he made some to be apostles, some to be prophets, some to go and tell the Good News, and some to have the work of caring for and teaching God's people. Christ gave those gifts to prepare God's holy people for the work of serving, to make the body of Christ stronger. This work must continue until we are all joined together in the same faith and in the same knowledge of the Son of God. We must become like a mature person, growing until we become like Christ and have his perfection.*[xxxiv]

No one said anything for several seconds, till Ashley asked, "So you are saying God gave teachers to explain his words?"

"There are a few who can search out the truth for themselves, but mostly God raises up teachers to make the Word of God plain. Everyone in the church is at a different level of understanding. Your father's books gave instruction long after his death. His words are still doing so."

Themba retrieved a folded sheet of paper from the folds of the blanket draped over his shoulders, "From early childhood I have been taught, not only to memorize God's Word, but also to take your father's instruction in how to apply that Word to my life."

"May I see that?" Skip asked, reaching out his hand.

Themba returned the paper to its place, "You cannot read it in the dark. Besides, it is written in my tribal language. You would not understand the words that are written. Your father's words have been translated into the tribal languages of this region, and beyond."

Skip withdrew his hand, "This is too much for me to take in all at once, but I thank you, Themba, for explaining things to me. I guess my father was a great man, and I never got to know him. I think I just felt cheated I didn't get to know my parents, and that their deaths were so brutal."

"Your father's greatness, Skip Jordan, came from his devotion to Jesus Christ, and from his faithfulness to God's Word. In his writing he always urged us not to consider him as anything more than a servant of his Lord."

Themba had another surprise for them. Reaching into his blanket again he retrieved what appeared in the dim light to be a book, "My uncle asked me to give this to you. It is the book he read when he first opened the box. It is written in English in your fathers own writing. Now we must all sleep. We have a long journey ahead, and Mazimbi wants us to reach The Smoke-That-Thunders before nightfall."

In spite of the many thoughts swirling around in his head, Skip slept, and it was a sleep without dreams.

Chapter 15

The Smoke That Thunders

There was not much conversation on their journey next day. Skip's thoughts were on the revelations he had received the night before and increasingly on the book his father had written. The rigour of travel prevented him from stealing more than a few glances at it, but the few paragraphs he read transported him into another world. His father's insights into the Word of God were amazing. He felt as if he had never understood a verse before, until a phrase from the book shed light on it.

The experience both saddened and gladdened his heart. He was sad that he would never get the chance to sit side by side with his father and get to know him; he was glad because Ntambo had promised he would be given the box with all the original books inside. They had been translated into the tribal languages of the region, and beyond, so now he had a rich inheritance from both his parents.

He determined he would no longer eke out the treasures in the box his mother had left him. By so doing he had missed the poem that could have comforted his heart long before this. From now on he would bury himself in a study of all his parents had left him. A verse from the Psalms came to mind:

The lines have fallen to me in pleasant places;
Indeed, my heritage is beautiful to me.[xxxv]

In spite of the sense of loss he had suffered for all those years, he felt now his parents had made it up to him. They had left him a spiritual treasure that would enrich him for the rest of his life. It was indeed something beautiful he had inherited. He also had the settled conviction that he was going to need everything it had to offer him.

Ntambo, too, was for the most part silent. Skip caught an occasional glimpse of his countenance and it was expressionless, though the set of his jaw showed stolid determination. It reminded Skip of a Scripture verse describing Jesus as setting his face like a flint toward Jerusalem. Jerusalem was where He was to die, but He pressed determinedly toward it.

It occurred to Skip that Ntambo was doing the same thing. Skip's own vision, or dream, appeared to predict Ntambo's death at the falls, yet Ntambo was not trying to avoid it. Like his Lord he was pressing on to embrace his destiny, even if that destiny led to his own death.

Glancing behind him he was surprised to see James and Ashley striding together in animated conversation. Something had changed between them that could not be accounted for. Nancy trudged on alone with Themba bringing up the rear. Skip thought perhaps he should slow his pace to keep her company. Before he could act on his impulse, however, powerful memories of Julia came to mind and he quickened his pace again. It was strange how memories of her kept intruding on his mind. It was not just that she had been incredibly good looking. He kept seeing in his mind's eye her sacrificial attempt to save her friends from the Veil of Deception. When the evil influence of the Veil began to steal their minds, Julia had aggressively tried to knock them down to break its spell. Her attempt had led to her death, but not before she had seen the glory of Christ beaming down on her; and not before she had seen the glory of Christ to the saving of her own soul.

A year ago Aunt May had asked him if he had loved Julia. At the time he could not answer, not really understanding what love was. He had little more understanding of it now. Only one thing was certain: he could not deepen his friendship with Nancy yet. Nancy had always been his closest and dearest friend, and she was fast becoming more than that. It was too early to call it love yet, but she was now constantly in his thoughts – except when thoughts of Julia intruded – like they had a moment ago. First, he had to figure out why thoughts of the dead girl kept blocking any deepening of his relationship with Nancy. He had to keep his distance till he could resolve his conflicting emotions. His actions, however, were causing Nancy some pain. He could see the hurt in her eyes and in her expression when he failed to walk beside her. He had always done so before, and the change in his behaviour was disturbing her.

Skip prayed silently, "Lord, help me to understand what is going on."

He was startled when the answer came in the still, small voice the prophet Elijah had experienced on the mountain. It formed clear words in his mind, though it made no sound, *"Time, Skip. In time you will understand. Until then just believe there is a time for every purpose under heaven."*

Skip recognised the phrase as coming from the book of Ecclesiastes. He dug his Bible from his pack, found the place, and read:

There is a time for everything,
and everything on earth has its special season.
There is a time to be born
and a time to die.
There is a time to plant
and a time to pull up plants.
There is a time to kill
and a time to heal.
There is a time to destroy
and a time to build.
There is a time to cry
and a time to laugh.
There is a time to be sad
and a time to dance.
There is a time to throw away stones
and a time to gather them.
There is a time to hug
and a time not to hug.
There is a time to look for something
and a time to stop looking for it.
There is a time to keep things
and a time to throw things away.
There is a time to tear apart
and a time to sew together.
There is a time to be silent
and a time to speak.
There is a time to love
and a time to hate.
There is a time for war
and a time for peace.[xxxvi]

The thrill of hearing God's voice in his soul brought peace to Skip's soul. He did not need to know all the answers yet. Whatever the reason for his near obsession with Julia, it would all be revealed in God's time. For the present he could at least remove the hurt from Nancy's eyes. Slowing his pace, Skip allowed James and Ashley to pass him till Nancy drew abreast of him. The grateful smile Nancy gave him was confirmation enough that he had acted wisely. Nothing would be gained by causing her grief. They were still young, and in time God's purposes would be revealed. Now it was enough just to enjoy the strong bond between them.

"So, you finally had pity on me, did you?"

"Not pity," Skip returned, "it just didn't make sense to let my best friend struggle on alone." He continued. "Maybe it's time to give it some serious thought. We'll have to put aside every distraction and concentrate fully on what lies ahead."

"I agree," Nancy said, her face regaining that natural glow and excitement that was the hallmark of her persona. Her whole body seemed to have gained new energy; her trudging gait was transformed into an eager stride. She and Skip were back on a firm footing and she looked as if she was ready to face anything, "Whatever we have to face, Skip Jordan, we can do it together. I'm not going to allow the enemy to separate me from my friends ever again."

There was no need for Skip to respond. The comfortable companionship they had always enjoyed was restored. Either in conversation or in silence they felt a connection that can be stated, but never explained.

A minute or two later Nancy nudged Skip with her elbow, "Do you see what I see up ahead?"

Skip looked up," Oh yeah." A few yards ahead of them James and Ashley were walking side by side, their hands clasped together. Skip prayed this was not going to complicate things any more than they were already.

Gradually they became aware of some changes in the terrain and in the sounds around them. The ground began to slope upward, and a gentle roar became audible, increasing in volume as they proceeded.

Anticipating a question, Ntambo turned to inform them, "We are approaching the Smoke-That-Thunders. We have almost arrived at our destination."

Coming to a halt at the top of a ridge, Mazimbi turned to address them all, "There are many who serve the Prince of Darkness in this region. Keep alert and pray. From this point on there will be dangers, seen and unseen."

It was evident Mazimbi's pace was slower once they were on the march again. He stopped frequently and seemed to sniff the air as if he could tell by smell what lay ahead. His actions affected them all, heightening their sense of danger and making them all more alert. Conversation dwindled to nothing and Skip was sure everyone was praying.

Ntambo, too, was exhibiting signs of extreme caution. Glancing behind him, Skip saw Themba casting his eyes all around, his grip on his assegai intense. All the while the roar of the giant waterfall ahead grew louder and it was clear why the natives had identified the sound as thunder.

They passed through a heavily wooded area till they entered a large clearing. The reason for Mazimbi's sniffing of the air immediately became apparent. A pungent odour they could not at first identify assaulted their nostrils. It was strong and unavoidable; it caused them to hold their breath and pinch their noses. At least, that is what the four companions from across the sea did. Mazimbi, Ntambo and Themba registered no reaction at all. The source of this odour became evident when, out of the surrounding trees, emerged hundreds of warriors bearing spears. Each dark body was covered with what appeared to be various shades of mud. They must have got the mud from a swamp, Skip thought, the odour emanating from rotting leaves and the putrefying remains of drowned creatures.

The most frightening aspect of these warriors, however, was not their odour, or even their overwhelming number. What sent a thrill of fear through Skip was the fierce expression on the faces of those warriors close enough for him to see. Their teeth and their lips curled up in a snarl as of a wild beast about to attack its prey. His throat constricted, almost choking him as he realized these were not just curious warriors investigating their presence. They were here to kill them.

Most noticeable among them was a giant of a man wearing the regalia of a chief. He held his spear aloft, as if bringing it down would be the signal to attack. He was not here to talk. He was here with his warriors to wipe them out.

Mazimbi and Ntambo displayed no fear. Even Themba came up from the rear to stand beside the two older men. His expression was wooden, not showing an ounce of emotion. Skip felt Nancy's hand grope for his. It was shaking so hard he could feel the tremor up to his shoulder blades. At this point James and Ashley had moved to the left and he dared not shift his gaze to take in their reaction. He guessed, however, they were just as stunned and frozen to the spot as he and Nancy were. Just because Mazimbi and the others showed no emotion it did not mean they had none. It was the nature of their race not to show emotion in a crisis. They had been taught from infancy not to show any reaction when confronted.

Skip kept his eyes fixed on the giant with his spear held aloft. He could hardly breathe, waiting for the arm to come down as the signal to attack.

What happened next was just as shocking and inexplicable as the sudden appearance of the warriors had been. The first evidence of something unusual taking place was the change of expression on the face of the chief, then on the faces of his men. Their fierce demeanour changed completely. They took several steps back, and Skip could only describe the look on their faces as stark terror. In seconds they turned and fled into the dense growth of trees and undergrowth behind them.

The chief was the last to leave, but even as he turned to run he looked back. In spite of his great size it was clear he shared the confusion and terror that had routed his men. The one thing in his favour was that he had not been the first to run. Only when they had all disappeared into the bush did he follow suit.

No one said a word for a long time after the departure of the warriors. The shock and fear that had coursed through their bodies and numbed their minds took time to dissipate. Nancy seemed to realize she was holding Skip's hand and released it self-consciously. Her nails had dug into the palm of his hand and it ached from the intense pressure she had exerted. It took several minutes for the friends to begin breathing again.

James said in an uncharacteristic, tremulous voice, "What... what... just happened?"

"I have absolutely no idea," Skip said. "I thought we were dead, for sure."

"We have been given help from Heaven," Mazimbi said in his heavily accented English.

"Mazimbi is right," Ntambo agreed. "No warrior of that tribe would have fled for anything less."

"You mean...?" Ashley asked hesitantly, "You mean they saw something we did not see?"

"Yes, I think they saw an army they knew they could not resist."

"That reminds me," Skip said, "of something that happened before." He dug in his pack again for his Bible. It is something that happened to Elisha and his servant." Finding the place he read: *Elisha's servant got up early, and when he went out, he saw an army with horses and chariots all around the city.*

The servant said to Elisha, "Oh, my master, what can we do?" Elisha said, "Don't be afraid. The army that fights for us is larger than the one against us."

Then Elisha prayed, "Lord, open my servant's eyes, and let him see."

The Lord opened the eyes of the young man, and he saw that the mountain was full of horses and chariots of fire all around Elisha.[xxxvii]

"You mean the army with horses and chariots were really angels protecting Elisha and his servant?" Nancy queried. "You think what happened to Elisha has just happened to us?"

"I'm sure of it, Nance, but you must know that. This is not the first time angels have protected us. We could never have rescued James and the others without help from heaven."

Mazimbi interrupted, "We must continue our journey. We are very close to the Thunder now."

Indeed, as they proceeded along the rough trail the noise of the waterfall increased till it seemed to pound in their ears. Conversation became difficult, so for the most part Skip and Nancy kept silent, enjoying companionship without words. Yet Skip could detect a certain embarrassment in Nancy's demeanour. Moving his mouth closer to her ear, he said, "What is the matter, Nance?"

Her cheeks took on a deeper shade of crimson as she replied, "I... I didn't mean to hold your hand... like that."

"You couldn't help it, Nance. You were frightened and I was the closest thing to hold on to."

"It was just... nice, is all."

It dawned on Skip what she meant. In spite of the pain to his palm the touch of her hand had felt, as she had said... "nice." Warning bells sounded in his brain. He would have to be more on guard next time, but was it wrong to feel pleasure in the touch of this girl who had been his close companion for most of his life? Glancing at James and Ashley still holding hands he suddenly wished Aunt May was here. He needed to have a talk with her. He was moving into emotional territory he had no idea how to traverse. He could not afford to make any mistakes now, or for James to make any either, not with what he knew lay ahead of them. He was well aware how Satan could take the most innocent things and turn them to his advantage.

His thoughts were distracted by a shout from up ahead, even louder than the roar of the waterfall. Hurrying forward they were all confronted with a most amazing sight. Kneeling on the ground before Mazimbi and Ntambo in abject fear was a man Skip could not doubt had been one of the warriors surrounding them half an hour earlier. He was babbling something in his mother tongue that was unintelligible to him, but which the two black men seemed to understand perfectly. The stench of the mud on his body rose up to meet Skip as he approached, and a spear lay uselessly on the grass beside the trembling warrior. The whites of the man's eyes showed as they rolled back, the mindless terror he was feeling distorting his face.

Mazimbi leaned forward and shook the man, barking a command at him. It took several minutes to bring him to a somewhat calmer condition, but he refused to stand. He kept bowing in complete submission to the two men, and to the rest of them. At last Ntambo seemed not to be able to endure the man's animal-like fear any longer. Going to him he raised him up bodily, as though he were but a child, and spoke directly to him in a clear, calm voice. At last the man stopped babbling and Ntambo eased him down again. Seeing a fallen tree beside the trail Ntambo and Mazimbi sat the man down on it. Positioning themselves on either side, they started talking to him. Now silent, he nodded his head in agreement with almost every sentence.

"What are they saying to him?" Ashley asked Themba as he stood silently observing the scene.

Themba turned to her, "They are telling him of the Great One Who sent His Son to the earth to pay for all the wicked things this man has done."

"Has he said what frightened Him?" Nancy asked.

"He is talking now and he says they all saw a great army of warriors in shining white robes. They had swords that flashed like lightening and they could be seen as a great cloud surrounding the clearing where we stood. They were not standing on the ground, but came from the sky. They heard a voice warning them not to harm us."

"That is just incredible," Ashley said, "but I shouldn't be surprised. After Skip read that portion from the Bible I felt sure that was what had happened. To have it confirmed by one who actually saw it is what is amazing. As Skip said, we've been protected by angels before."

The discussion was cut short when Ntambo and Mazimbi called them over and introduced them to the now much calmer warrior whose name was Furingi. They confirmed what Themba had translated for them, that an army of heavenly beings had surrounded them, and a Voice had warned them in their own tongue to leave their intended victims alone. He knew some English, but not enough for comfortable conversation, so Themba appointed himself translator for his foreign friends.

It was late afternoon and the light was beginning to fade, so they lit a fire, dug depressions in the sand for sleeping, and prepared to spend the night where they were.

The campfire discussion was mostly Ntambo and Mazimbi giving Furingi further instruction of how Jesus had paid the price for his sin, and to explain the presence of the angels. The excitement of the day, and their dramatic deliverance by angels, had wearied them both physically and emotionally. Ashley was the first to yawn, but it set them all off and it seemed best for them all to retire for the night.

When they arose at first light they had breakfast and started on their way. After passing through several hundred yards of a dense growth of trees they emerged onto a grassy plateau and then walked up a steep rise. Even before they reached the top they could see a great cloud of mist rising up hundreds of feet in the air. And then they were standing on the edge of a great canyon plunging hundreds of feet to the river below, appearing more like a silver ribbon from that distance. Their eyes did not stay long on the scene below, the sheer magnificence of the view ahead drawing their attention. The girls let out a gasp at the sight that met their eyes. Millions of gallons of water plunged over the edge on the other side of the gorge, the roar of its passing vibrating their ear-drums. Spray collected on their skin and drenched their clothing.

Skip knew Nancy wanted to say something like, "I've never seen anything so magnificent in all my life," but speech was impossible this close to what he knew was the largest waterfall in the world. Speech, however, was unnecessary; her expression said it all.

In spite of the magnificence of the view a dark thought passed over Skip's mind. He had seen this place before, not in actuality, or only in pictures. He had seen it in his dream. Superimposed upon the raging torrent of water he had seen the scowling face of his former best friend, Roger Wilson. He remembered, too, images of Ntambo being hounded over the edge of the cliff into what the local people called 'Mosi-oa-Tunya', or 'The Smoke-That-Thunders.' He shivered, and it was not because of the dampness of the mist; it came from the realization that he and the others were about to clash with the forces of darkness as never before.

Chapter 16

Into the Jungle

Angela Nichol was kneeling by their bed in prayer when she heard the key turn in the lock and her husband entered. He was in a state of subdued excitement as he said, "Angela, my sweet, they are here."

"Who are here?" She asked, though she knew who he was referring to. He had told her of his former students and how they had challenged and overcome him in his former involvement with witchcraft. She had just not been able to figure out how he had known they would be here thousands of miles from their Canadian homes. She had asked him about that and he could give her no answer. He had just *known*. And now he was telling her his 'knowing' had been confirmed.

"Why, Angela, I told you about them, Skip Jordan and his friends, though of course they are not alone. They've come with some black men from down south from here. I've been talking to some of the local people. It seems I am not the only one who has been expecting them. They say the drums have been announcing their arrival for some days now."

Angela rose from her knees and turned to hug Raymond, planting a kiss on his cheek, "So what now?"

"Why, we go and meet them..." He paused, no doubt sensing what she was feeling. They were having a wonderful honeymoon, though the shadow of the impending battle with spiritual forces loomed over it. She had been able to keep that thought at a distance till now, refusing to allow it to dilute the pure joy she had in finding a man she truly loved, though she'd need a life-time to get to know him.

Their short acquaintance before the wedding no longer bothered her; she had asked for and received guidance from God on that score, and it was enough. She could trust God for the future. But now the arrival of the young people he had been expecting meant she could no longer evade a new phase in their relationship. They would have to confront, together, whatever lay ahead.

Raymond became suddenly tender, and apologetic. Leading her over to their bed he drew her down beside him with his arm around her shoulders, "I am so sorry, my love. I wanted this honeymoon to be perfect for you, and I've gone and overshadowed it with walks to discover when the young people will arrive. There should have been more romantic walks together."

Angela gave him a tender kiss on the lips, "It has been perfect, Ray. I have been able to push all the other things aside and just enjoy being with you. That time is over now, and I don't want you to be filled with regret. It is a miracle you are not in that awful place I used to work in. You have been rescued by the power of God and He has brought us together for a purpose."

"You're so sweet, my love. I don't deserve you."

Angela looked him in the eye, "Just don't exclude me from those walks you've been taking anymore. I know you've been trying to protect me, but we need to be together as much as possible, particularly in times of danger."

"You are sure of this?"

"I am. I've actually memorized a portion in the Bible to convince you."

"Well then, my love, give it to me straight."

"God preserve me from being a nagging wife, but I think this is something we need to agree on." Taking his hand in hers, Angela quoted:

'Two people are better than one,
  because they get more done by working together.
If one falls down,
  the other can help him up.
But it is bad for the person who is alone and falls,
  because no one is there to help.
If two lie down together, they will be warm,
  but a person alone will not be warm.
An enemy might defeat one person,
  but two people together can defend themselves;
a rope that is woven of three strings
  is hard to break.'"[xxxviii]

Raymond sighed, "There's not much I can say to that. You are much more versed in the Bible than I am. You are free to instruct me whenever you think I need it, and I won't accuse you of nagging."

"Well then," Angela said. She stood and pulled him to his feet, "Let us go on one of those walks together to find this Skip Jordan and his company of friends."

....

Skip and the others stared at the mighty torrents of water plunging into the gorge for some time. The spray drenched their clothing and wet them from head to foot, but still Skip could not pull himself away. He remembered another waterfall where they had been drenched in like manner, just before entering the valley to confront the evil that had trapped their friends a year ago.

By the goodness of God they had prevailed that time; Skip sensed, however, that the battle this time was going to be much more intense. Everything they had experienced so far, at the mission and on their journey to this place, convinced him the forces of darkness were gathering for an assault aimed at their total destruction.

His thoughts were interrupted by Nancy tugging at his sleeve and indicating the others were drawing back into the trees. They walked for ten minutes or so into a clearing where the roar of the waterfall was not quite so intense. They were able to dry off as the morning sun warmed them.

Furingi began to chatter away in his native tongue, engaging Ntambo and Mazimbi in animated conversation. It was somewhat one-sided however, since he appeared to be trying to convince the two men of something.

"What is that all about?" Skip asked Themba, whose attention was fixed on the three men.

Still looking ahead of him, he replied, "He wants us to come to his village. He says he wants us to tell his people what we have told him of Jesus, and of a kingdom not of this world."

"Wouldn't that be dangerous?" Nancy asked.

"It could even be a trap," James said. "They failed to kill us earlier, and this is his way of finishing the job."

"I don't think so." Themba turned his attention to James. "This man was too frightened by what he saw. He knows he is dealing with a power far greater than anything they have known before. He has heard the Gospel message, and I think he wants the people in his village to hear it, too."

"Then why isn't your uncle agreeing right away?" Ashley asked.

"I think my uncle is just taking precautions. He wants to know what accommodation will be provided, and if Furingi thinks his chief will carry out his orders in spite of everything."

"What orders?" There was a note of alarm in Skip's voice.

"It was not the chief's decision to attack us. There is some kind of organization that has control of most of the villagers in the region, so Furingi says."

"Ashley shivered, "We're in the minority here, aren't we?"

"No we're not, Skip reminded her. "I read you that Bible passage about Elisha and his servant. God opened the servant's eyes to see there were more on his side than the army gathered against them. Also, Furingi told us there was an army of heavenly beings around us to protect us."

Ashley looked ashamed, "You're right. I just forgot for a moment, but I can't help feeling a little nervous about what is happening. If we go to this man's village, we'll be surrounded by the people who tried to kill us."

"We must pray that God has changed their minds about that," Themba said. "It seems my uncle has agreed to Furingi's request. We are going to his village."

Ntambo came over and spoke to them. His face for once showed some emotion, "Mazimbi and I now have an opportunity to preach the Gospel in Furingi's village, but you do not need to come. Furingi assures us we will all be safe, but he may not be able to speak for the chief and the head council of the tribe. You could be in danger if you come."

"If we don't come with you what will we do?" Nancy asked.

"Themba will take you to a village near here. Mazimbi has preached there before and they will welcome you. You will be safe with them."

"What you are saying," Ashley said, "is that the people of Furingi's village may kill you and you are going anyway."

Ntambo gave her his most direct gaze, "Yes. We cannot allow fear for our own lives prevent us from declaring the good news of salvation to all who believe."

"Then I, for one," Ashley declared determinedly, "want to come with you."

When the others echoed Ashley's intention, Ntambo said, "That may not be the wisest thing. If you go with Themba and something happens to us, you will be free to proceed with your mission."

Skip said with finality, "*Nothing* is going to happen to you yet, Ntambo."

A stunned silence followed Skip's words as they all realized what he was referring to. In his dream he had seen Ntambo being hounded over the cliff edge above the raging torrents of the Victoria Falls. If Skip's dream had been a real vision of things to come, and they all believed it was, going to Furingi's village would not end his life. That would take place later... if the miracle they were all praying for did not occur.

Ntambo let out his breath, "Then we must leave immediately. Furingi's village is several hours away."

In took, in fact, a little over two hours of trudging through tall grass, thorn-infested brush, and densely-wooded areas to arrive at their destination. Rips in the fabric of their borrowed clothing caused Nancy and Ashley to utter typically feminine cries of alarm at their deteriorating appearance. Nothing could be done about that till they once again returned to civilization.

As they approached the valley where Furingi's village was located, Furingi halted and once again conferred with Ntambo and Mazimbi. It seemed he wanted to go on ahead and return when he had explained to the chief and elders of the village the reason for their coming. It would have been normal for anyone to suspect a trap; Furingi was about to betray them. When he returned they would be surrounded and killed as had been their original intention. Ntambo and Mazimbi had no such reaction. They seemed confident that Furingi was sincere and was following the traditional manner of introducing strangers to the tribe.

"What do you think?" James asked Skip. "Can this man be trusted?"

Before Skip could reply, Themba answered for him, "My uncle can be trusted. He knows these people, and knows how they deal with outsiders. I heard my uncle and Mazimbi talking. They think there is little danger of betrayal. Furingi's description of the heavenly beings was too real. He is too afraid of them coming back to betray us now. It would be the same with the rest of the warriors."

"I hope and pray your uncle is right," Nancy said, clearly nervous about the whole situation.

Ashley struck a confident note, though it was expressed in her usual gentle manner, "We mustn't forget the protection God has given us in the past. He is not about to abandon us now."

It was late afternoon by the time Furingi returned. He had a grin on his face that did a lot to relieve the uncertainty they had been feeling. He was almost bouncing with excitement. He told them the chief was eager to meet them. Preparations were being made to receive them with honour. Accommodations had been arranged, including woven grass divisions to provide privacy for the females of the party. There would be a feast tonight to welcome the visitors."

All of this and more Themba translated for his friends.

In spite of all the details Furingi had communicated, they were not prepared for what they saw upon entering the village. A large central amphitheatre was surrounded by the typical grass huts. The village itself was much larger than any the visitors had encountered to date. Row upon row of huts could be seen far beyond the central ring of dwellings. The late afternoon sun cast a golden glow upon the whole scene, causing the huts, and the people gathered, to appear like a mythical city inhabited by golden inhabitants.

What caused Skip and the others amazement, however, was not the general appearance of the village, but the manner in which the people gathered greeted them. The amphitheatre, created by the ring of huts surrounding it, was jam-packed with people. Skip thought they must have come, not from this village alone, but from smaller villages scattered throughout the entire region. He imagined messengers must have been sent far and wide to summon the people to this place.

Even the gathering of so many people was not as wonderful as their posture. Every individual, including the chief, was kneeling on the ground. They all had their foreheads pressed to the ground in the obvious attitude of submission. A low rumble emitted from their throats, the volume increasing in waves as of a vast congregation participating in worship. Nevertheless there was the unmistakable note of fear mingled in the sound.

Suddenly Ntambo's voice rose above the sound arising from the multitude before them. There was a note of alarm and command in his voice that seemed to crack like a whip. Instantly the voices of those gathered ceased, and Ntambo's voice took on a timbre that carried to the outer edges of the amphitheatre.

Themba drew his friends closer to him and translated, "My uncle is rebuking the people for treating us as if we were gods, not mere human beings. He is telling them we are just people as they are, but that we are messengers of the living God and have Good news to share with them. He is encouraging them to return to their huts for the night, and gather once again in the morning. He will then tell them of the Great-Great-One, Who came down from Heaven to set them free from the powers of darkness and transform them into children of light. He says, for now He will tell them the name of this Great-Great-One Who came to set them free. His name is Jesus."

Not a word was uttered after that; the only sound was the rustling of the minimal coverings they wore, and shuffling as they rose to their feet and began to disperse. It took several minutes till the space before them was almost empty. The chief, still wearing his regalia of chieftainship, and several of his advisors, had not moved, unless their trembling limbs could be interpreted as movement.

Ntambo spoke to them kindly, focussing his attention on the chief.

Themba said, "My uncle is attempting to calm their fears. He says the heavenly beings they saw will not harm them, and will be their protectors also if they receive the message he will deliver in the morning. He is asking for them to provide accommodation and food until then."

As if loosed from bands of iron, the chief came alive. He was a giant of a man but he took on the demeanour of a child, eager to please. He bowed several times to Ntambo and Mazimbi and once to the younger members of the party. After a few minutes he grew calmer and spoke more seriously to Ntambo.

Themba translated, "He says he is honoured to receive messengers so exalted as to be protected by beings as mighty and powerful as those they were confronted with before. He says all his people will be gathered in the morning. In the meantime we are to follow him to the royal hut kept for the visits of chiefs from other villages. He also wants to know the name of that One Who was to set them all free. He heard it the first time, but cannot remember. My uncle is telling him that the name of the deliverer is Jesus."

By the time they reached the hut reserved for them the sun had painted the western sky in spectacular hues of red and orange. The cloud formations on the horizon looked like tinted citadels, with columns rising, it seemed, to heaven. They stood gazing at it for some time before entering the lamp-lit interior of their night accommodation. Two tribesmen soon arrived to erect the grass partition Ntambo had requested to provide the girls with some privacy.

Before long the food began to arrive. Skip thought there was far more of it than their small party could consume in a week. The purpose of such abundance seemed more to be a sign of the honour in which they were held than an accurate assessment of their needs. Only the most exalted of visitors would be treated so royally.

Apart from the sadza, a corn-base meal the friends had learned to endure rather than enjoy, there was a variety of meats and fruit that mingled in an aroma so enticing their mouths began to water.

There was chicken, beef, and what Mazimbi identified as Springbok, a deer greatly prized by the locals. There were various fruits as well, including papaya, known here as Paw-paw. There was chopped avocado settled in tender pumpkin leaves.

Ashley's attention was drawn to some wooden bowls containing spiny looking pieces that were dry and crackly.

"These are Mopani worms," Themba said, taking a few in his fingers and popping them into his mouth.

"Ugh!" Ashley said with disgust, and turned her attention to another bowl with what seemed like wriggling insects.

"Flying ants, with the wings pulled off," Themba said again, popping one into his mouth.

Glancing toward Ntambo and Mazimbi, Skip saw the unmistakable signs of amusement on their faces, and in their eyes. Till now, Ntambo had obviously catered to their Western sensibilities by arranging with the villages they visited to provide food for them more in keeping with what they were accustomed to. Fortunately, there was now so much variety and abundance now that they could pick and choose what they ate.

"Are you sure," Nancy asked of Ntambo once they had begun to consume the sumptuous meal, "we are not just being 'fattened up' to be killed later? I mean, do we really know these people have changed their minds about killing us? It certainly looked like they were ready to do so when they first appeared."

Ntambo's normally expressionless face broke into a smile. He regarded Nancy with some amusement, "Dear Nancy, after seeing all the miracles God has performed for us, you are still doubting? Do you remember in the Bible when God's people were facing a great enemy, Samuel the prophet prayed for them and God delivered the enemy into their hands? After they defeated the enemy, what did Samuel do?"

"I... I'm... not sure."

Ntambo quoted:

After this happened Samuel took a stone and set it up between Mizpah and Shen. He named the stone Ebenezer, saying, "The Lord has helped us to this point."[xxxix]

"I... I wasn't really doubting, Ntambo. I... I've just never been faced with such fierce warriors before. I've never been so scared in my life. Well, maybe I have once before when we were on our way to the Valley-of-Witchcraft in Nova Scotia."

"You mean when we were trapped in the labyrinth and were faced with the roaring lion?" Ashley asked.

Nancy nodded, "And later, when there were so many tunnels to choose from and I thought we'd never find our way out into the sunlight again."

Mazimbi said in his deep voice, "The warriors were much more frightened than you were. There may be a few who will report to those who sent them to attack us, but most of them were too frightened by the appearance of the angels to even think of attacking us now. You saw how they all grovelled on the ground when we arrived."

"So you think," Skip commented, "they will all gather in the morning to hear Ntambo's message."

"I am sure of it. Even those who are still loyal to their masters of the Brotherhood will not dare to disobey the chief's summons to appear."

Once their appetites were satisfied and their thirst quenched a drowsiness came upon them and they settled down for sleep. A fleeting thought passed through Skip's brain that perhaps this was the design of all that abundance of food. Once they were asleep their enemies could pounce and would not encounter much resistance. The thought passed quickly as he slipped into deep slumber.

Skip awoke suddenly with a sense of alarm in the middle of the night. He was sure he had heard a sound, like a scuffing movement at the entrance to their tent. Before he could say anything a lamp was lighted and Ntambo hung it on a wire suspended from the roof. In its light they saw the village chief. He was bowed low on the ground, with an expression of intense longing on his face. As the others roused and turned their attention to his grovelling form, he spoke in his native tongue.

"What is he saying?" Skip asked Themba, who was lying beside him.

"He is asking for something," Themba replied. He is asking for a name."

"What name is he asking for?"

"In your language," Themba said, "he is saying, "Tell me His name again!"

....

Aunt May and Reginald arrived at the Victoria Falls Resort just as the sun was going down.

Once their luggage had been brought into their room and the attendant had gone, Reginald said, "May, are you certain we should have interrupted our travels to come here now?"

Aunt May shrugged, feeling somewhat regretful for disappointing her new husband who had planned to give her a grand tour of Africa. True, they were still in Africa, but it was uncertain how long they would have to be here, and whether or not they would be able to complete the itinerary he had planned.

"Not entirely," she replied, taking his hand and gazing wistfully into his eyes, "I had an unsettled feeling about letting Skip and the others embark on such a dangerous mission. I know they have

Ntambo with them, and as soon as the Lucases are done with their Missions conference, they will be here to support them. But I was having second thoughts. I'm not sure now whether it was God urging me to come here, or if it is just the usual worry parents have for their children. I may just be Skip and Nancy's legal guardian, but they feel just like my own. Even Ashley and James have spent so much time at my house I have come to regard them as more than just visitors.

"So you are not sure, but you wouldn't be able to fully enjoy the trip while you were uncertain about their safety?"

Aunt May nodded, "Can you forgive me? I know the tour was a special gift you wanted to give me. I can't help but feel, though, that we are needed here at this time." She planted a tender kiss on his cheek.

Reginald was about to respond when there was a knock on their door.

"We haven't asked for any room service," aunt May said, "who could that be?"

"Only one way to find out," Reginald responded, moving to the door and opening it wide.

What met their eyes caused Aunt May to gasp. Of all the people in the world the person she least expected to see, with a beautiful woman bringing up the rear, was the one standing now tentatively in the doorway. It was none other than Raymond Nichol, the teacher who had deceived his pupils and drawn them into the depths of witchcraft.

Chapter 17

The Gift of Weakness

What first surprised Aunt May was the former teacher's demeanour.

He seemed apologetic and uncertain of his reception. From Skip and Nancy's accounts of Raymond Nichol's witchcraft practices she assumed he would be bold and confident. She had only ever seen him in a parent-teacher situation before.

She gained a clue to his timidity when he said, "I know you may not have anything to do with me, Mrs. Alderman, considering my previous involvement with your nephew."

The golden haired beauty behind Raymond Nichol stepped forward, "He's a very changed man, Mrs. Alderman. If you knew what God has done for him recently you wouldn't hesitate in welcoming him."

Aunt May liked this young woman immediately. She had a freshness and candour about her that was appealing.

Raymond Nichol said, "May I introduce my new bride to you, Mrs. Alderman. Her name is Angela. I believe we need to offer you congratulations as well. I believe you've also been married recently."

"May," Reginald said, ushering the newcomers in and closing the door behind them, "I believe we can talk better while we're all inside."

"Forgive me," Aunt May said, "I must admit your appearance is somewhat of a shock. May I enquire how you knew my new name?"

"Oh, I recognized you when you arrived and I asked the man at the desk."

"Well, there are only two chairs in the place. Why don't you and Angela sit on them, and Reginald and I will sit on the bed. And I suppose we had all better start using first names. Please call me May, and this is my husband, Reginald, often called, Reggie."

They talked for well over an hour, against the roar of the waterfall and against the glowing reds and oranges of an African sunset.

When darkness had fallen, Reginald suggested they all go to the hotel restaurant and continue their discussion there.

Once they were all seated in the plush surroundings of the hotel dining room, Aunt May asked the question she had been wanting to ask for some time now, "Have you seen any sign yet of Skip and the others?"

Raymond Nichol leaned forward, "We haven't seen them, no, but we've heard tell of them. I've been asking around since we arrived a week ago, and two days ago they were seen no more than a mile or two from here. The word is that they've headed back into the jungle in the company of two black men."

"One of them would be Ntambo," Reginald said. "We know about him."

"That's the name. The other one is a man of some renown by the name of Mazimbi. It appears he was deeply involved in the black arts till some seven or eight years ago when he was converted to Christ. There is also a young black boy named Themba who seems to be about the same age as Skip."

"You have certainly been asking around, haven't you Mr. Nichol? I mean Raymond. May I ask why you are so intensely interested, and why you are here at all?"

Raymond waited till the waiter had taken their orders, then he said. "In my former involvement with witchcraft I became aware of certain plans and conspiracies that may be helpful to Skip. I came so he and whoever is with them will not go into this thing totally blind."

Reginald spoke up, "You said your inquiries have led you to believe Skip and the others have gone back into the jungle. "Do you have any idea why they would have done such the thing, especially after having finally arrived at their destination?"

"I believe," Angela said firmly, "it was because they were invited to some distant village to preach Christ."

....

Skip allowed his eyes to take in the entire gathering of black bodies in the open space surrounded by grass and mud dwellings.

It seemed that none had dared to defy the chief's command to assemble here at first light.

Indeed, nearly all the faces close enough for him to see were eager with anticipation. The combination of seeing angelic beings protecting this small company, and the promise of hearing about a Deliverer, had excited their curiosity. They appeared to be in a state between fear and hope, as if the forces of darkness and light were engaged in a tug-of-war with their emotions. Fear had dominated their lives for so long they could hardly believe deliverance was even possible. On the other hand word had spread from the warriors to the other villagers of the supernatural forces active in defence of these strangers. It was at least worth listening to what they had to say.

Such was Skip's assessment as he studied the expressions on the faces of those nearest him. There were, however, a number of faces exhibiting displeasure, even antagonism. He reflected that there were always those who would never submit to the truth. Images of his former friend Roger Wilson flashed on his mind's eye. James, standing beside him had turned from witchcraft when evidence of its evil had come to him. Roger's reaction had been exactly the opposite. The lure of power had blinded his eyes to the glory of a life lived in submission to Christ.

Skip and his friends stood behind Ntambo and Mazimbi, with Themba positioned himself so he could translate and explain the significance of what was taking place. There would be tribal customs that would need explanation.

A holy hush fell on the company gathered as they waited for proceedings to begin. The head-man then did something completely foreign to the culture of his people, except when defeated by the superior forces of an enemy. He advanced to where the newcomers were gathered and bowed his head. By so doing he was acknowledging the superiority of the powers protecting the visitors. He was giving them unspoken control of the village.

After the head-man withdrew Ntambo stepped forward. Opening his vernacular Bible he read from the Song of Solomon, while Themba translated.

Skip was familiar with the passage:

Put me like a seal on your heart,
like a seal on your arm.
Love is as strong as death;
jealousy is as strong as the grave.
Love bursts into flames
and burns like a hot fire.
Even much water cannot put out the flame of love;
floods cannot drown love.
If a man offered everything in his house for love,
people would totally reject it.[xl]

Ntambo proceeded to explain the passage, telling the people in tender tones that love is stronger than hate. He went on to tell them that hate rose up from the human heart because we have all sinned and our hearts are corrupt.

"Because God loves us," Ntambo continued, He has promised to give us new hearts: *Then I will sprinkle clean water on you, and you will be clean. I will cleanse you from all your uncleanness and your idols.Also, I will teach you to respect me completely, and I will put a new way of thinking inside you. I will take out the stubborn hearts of stone from your bodies, and I will give you obedient hearts of flesh.I will put my Spirit inside you and help you live by my rules and carefully obey my laws.*[xli]

"But God could not give us new hearts until the sinfulness of our hearts had been punished. That is why He sent us His only Son, Jesus, to become a Man. Jesus never sinned, so he was able to be punished for the sin of others. Jesus was punished for your sin and mine, and for the sins of the whole world, so that whoever believes in Him can have everlasting life, and a new heart that loves God." He quoted:

God loved the world so much that he gave his one and only Son so that whoever believes in him may not be lost, but have eternal life.[xlii]

"If you believe that Jesus died for you and paid for your sin, God will give you a new heart; He will take the hate out of you and cause His love to live in your heart."

What happened next was a shock to all of them, except perhaps to Mazimbi and Ntambo. A great wailing rose up from the gathered villagers. It began as a low moan and increased in intensity till no other sound could be heard. In it was a world of grief, like someone mourning over the tragic death of someone dearly loved. A verse of Scripture popped into Skip's head: *They are blessed who grieve, for God will comfort them.*[xliii]

That was precisely what these people were doing; they were grieving, but not for the death of someone they loved. The message of the Gospel had penetrated their hearts and their first response was to mourn for the sins of a lifetime. Tears were running down the faces of the head-man and the elders of the tribe, and down the cheeks of most of those within the Skip's field of vision.

He felt Nancy's hand grope for his and hold it tightly. The eeriness of the sound assaulting their ears was excuse enough for her action. He did not blame her for reaching for his hand, in spite of the conflicting emotions it stirred in him. He could not deal with them now while this amazing event was taking place before his eyes, so he did not react to it at all. He just focussed on what was going on ahead of him. He would deal with the sweet enjoyment he was getting from holding Nancy's hand later.

Indeed, the mournful sound was changing. Here and there a shout of victory could be heard, soon multiplying in number and intensity. And then, like dew settling on mown grass, an awed silence came upon the whole company.

Ntambo took a step backwards and allowed Mazimbi to take centre stage. The tall, former witchdoctor, now a faithful servant of Christ, seemed to grow even taller as he stretched his arms wide as if to embrace the people. His voice was strong, and its resonance commanding as he began to speak.

Themba translated, "Mazimbi is calling on them to put their trust in Christ alone, and to get rid of their charms and amulets, and all evidence of their ancestral worship. He is urging them to repent, and believe the Gospel."

The rest of the morning passed in a sober round of activity. A place was assigned in the open space where the people had gathered; into it men brought branches, grass, dry thorn bushes and all manner of kindling. Once this fuel was judged sufficient to create a blaze worthy of a village this size, a line of men, women and children started to troop past, throwing amulets, charms and carved images onto the pile of kindling. The head-man had told them once all the objects of idol worship, including witchcraft paraphernalia, had been placed on the pile, a formal ceremony would be held. The fire would be lighted to burn everything that connected the village with its past. The ceremony would also include a formal renunciation of witchcraft, and a dedication of the village to serve the living God, and to put its trust in Christ alone.

"Did you notice," James said to Themba, "that there hasn't been a witchdoctor present all the time we have been here?"

"I noticed," Themba said, "I saw him leave when we first arrived, and he did not leave alone. About fifty men left with him."

Skip said, "If I'm not mistaken, that group over there do not exactly approve of what is happening here."

"Did not my uncle tell you," Themba replied, "not all would believe. Still, those who have believed are greater in number than my uncle and Mazimbi have ever seen before."

"That must be because they saw the angels protecting us," Nancy said.

"I'm sure that must have helped," Ashley commented, "but I think it was mostly because of the power of the Gospel message. When Ntambo was preaching, and when Mazimbi was calling them all to repentance I could feel God's presence in a special way." Turning to Skip, she said, "Do you remember where that verse is in Jeremiah about God's Word being like a fire and like a hammer?"

"Skip pulled out his pocket Bible and turned pages till he found the verse he had underlined. "It says: *Isn't my message like a fire?" says the Lord. "Isn't it like a hammer that smashes a rock?"*[xliv]

"When the people started wailing," Nancy commented, "it was as if their hearts were being broken. God's Word was like a hammer that first broke in pieces, and then, when they turned to the Lord, it was like a fire that burned with love for the One who died for them."

By the time the sun was directly overhead they all returned to their assigned lodgings where Mazimbi announced his intention to remain in the village to instruct and encourage the new converts.

"But I thought you were going to show us the entrance to the Lion's Den," Skip wondered.

"I will give Ntambo directions. I dare not leave these new believers without instruction lest the enemy come in and corrupt the message they have heard. The drums will send a message to my village to send others to assist me."

"Then we should leave as soon as the ceremony and the burning is over." Ntambo said.

"Won't that mean," James asked, "that it will be dark before we can leave? Wouldn't it be better to leave in the morning?"

"A shadow passed over Ntambo's countenance, "Yes, James, you are right. We will be leaving and travelling after dark, but we cannot delay much longer. Not all in this village were pleased that the Gospel has reached these people. A number of them are already on their way to warn their masters of what has happened here. The ceremony and the burning will take place at sundown. After that the head-man will send some of his warriors to protect us and speed us on our way. By the time our enemies return we will be almost back to The Smoke That Thunders." You should try to sleep for the rest of the afternoon. We will be travelling all night."

Nancy put in, "Why do we need the village warriors to protect us? After all, we had angels protecting us before."

"Nancy, God's protection is there when we need it, but He also expects us to take every precaution ourselves, or we will be tempting God by putting ourselves in the way of danger."

"I just wasn't sure," Nancy said defensively.

"Well, I guess we had better try to get some sleep," Skip said, lying down on his mat and resting his head on his back pack. The girls retreated behind the partition, and soon the sounds of normal village life lulled them to sleep.

As it happened it was two hours after sundown before they were able to commence their journey back to the waterfall. The double ceremony of renouncing the old way of life and committing to the reign of Christ over the village had taken longer than expected. The entire event had been peppered with individual testimonies to the change Christ had wrought in their hearts. At last Ntambo had decided not to wait for the conclusion of the proceedings; the head man and the elders bowed low in gratitude for the message that had come to them with such power.

Mazimbi said his farewells a few hundred yards along the trail, having given Ntambo detailed instructions on how to find the entrance to "The Lion's Den."

Not much was said between the two black men before parting. Each had a deep understanding of the other's motivation, the one for staying, and the other for proceeding with the original mission. Mazimbi took the time, however, to say his farewell to each of the young people individually, laying hands on them in blessing.

"You, Nancy, will be bold as a lion as you enter into conflict with the forces of darkness. This boldness is a gift you must employ when your friends are overwhelmed or uncertain what course of action to follow."

Turning to Ashley, Mazimbi said, "Your sweet and quiet spirit will act like oil on troubled waters. Your presence among your friends will steady them and give them courage.

Laying his hands on James's head, Mazimbi proclaimed, "You are like a brand plucked from the burning, almost consumed by the powers of darkness, but snatched away to serve the living God. Never forget the kindness God has shown you, and bestow that kindness on others."

Mazimbi turned next to Themba, "You, nephew of Ntambo, are a warrior in the service of the King. You are called, not to attack, but to protect. There will be times when you must stand between the enemy and these, your friends from across the sea."

Skip could not help feeling a little nervous when Mazimbi approached him. The blessings the tall black man had pronounced over his friends sounded prophetic. It reminded him of the blessings Isaac in the Bible gave Jacob and Esau, and later, how Jacob in his old age prophesied over his sons, and the sons of Joseph. Was God using Mazimbi in the same way? Was God's servant merely speaking his own thoughts over them, or was it more than that? If it was God speaking through Mazimbi, then what he said had to be taken seriously.

When Mazimbi placed his hands on his head Skip felt a jolt that passed through his entire body. His scalp tingled and pleasant warmth radiated from his inmost being. A conviction settled on his mind: this was going to be more than a godly man expressing kindly sentiments over him. The man was being guided by a power beyond himself. God was using this man to express His will and purpose.

"You with hair the colour of fire," Mazimbi said, "are a chosen instrument in the hand of your God. You will prevail, not by any strength that lies within you, but by the very weakness you feel while engaged in conflict with the powers of darkness. To you God has given the gift of weakness." He then quoted a passage from the Bible Skip had long since memorized, one that had sustained him in his previous battles with the prince of darkness:

But God chose the foolish things of the world to shame the wise, and he chose the weak things of the world to shame the strong.He chose what the world thinks is unimportant and what the world looks down on and thinks is nothing in order to destroy what the world thinks is important.[xlv]

When Mazimbi removed his hands the feeling of hands resting on him remained. Skip dared to believe he had just received a divine touch. For reasons beyond his understanding God had chosen to lay His hand of blessing on his life, and Mazimbi had been His instrument in conveying the divine touch.

Far from making him feel proud the whole idea of being chosen gave him a profound sense of unworthiness. And the gift he had been given? Who could understand such a thing? What on earth was 'the gift of weakness,' and how would it reveal itself as he pressed on to embrace the mission that lay before him? He said to himself: "I guess I'm going to find out – sooner or later."

Chapter 18

Two Days of Rest

Fifty of the best warriors had been assigned to accompany them back to The-Smoke-That-Thunders, as they kept referring to it.

Half the warriors went ahead of the small company, and half brought up the rear, till they passed through the narrow jungle trails. When they came to the grassy plains they spread out, forming a ring of protection around them. The small lamps that each man carried flickered like stars in the darkness, till an almost full moon shed its silvery light over them and only a few leading men kept their lamps lighted.

When they were no longer walking in single file, but more or less bunched up together as they made their way across the plain, Ashley asked, "Ntambo, what is the meaning of the burning ceremony we witnessed in the village earlier?"

Ntambo cast a sideways glance at her, "You do not know, fair one?"

"Well, I guess I do in a way. The people who believed the Gospel were getting rid of everything associated with their former life and making a public display of embracing the truth."

"That is correct. So then, what do you really want to know?"

Ashley frowned, "It was all rather dramatic, and very public. My Dad is a youth pastor, and I've never seen anything like that happen in our church. In fact, I haven't ever heard of anything like it happening anywhere in Canada, or in the States for that matter."

"Neither have I," Nancy added.

"I guess what I want to know is it really necessary? Couldn't a new Christian do the same thing quietly and in private?"

Ntambo edged closer to Ashley before replying, "There are some things in your walk with God, sweet one, that need to be done in private, like your times of prayer where no one can see you, but God only. That is because there is the temptation to fall into pride. We can end up trying to impress other people with how spiritual we are. God is not pleased with such things. He knows the secrets of our hearts and we do not need to show off to others."

"But, what happened in the village was very public."

"It was public," Ntambo responded, "And it needed to be public. When the apostle Paul was preaching in Ephesus, something similar happened." He quoted directly from memory:

Many of the believers began to confess openly and tell all the evil things they had done. Some of them who had used magic brought their magic books and burned them before everyone. Those books were worth about fifty thousand silver coins.

So in a powerful way the word of the Lord kept spreading and growing.[xlvi]

"It was because of this public confession that the Word of God kept spreading and growing. Other people got to know about the change Jesus made in these people's lives, because they did not hide what was happening to them. When someone comes to Christ they need to do three things: they need to confess, repent and believe. There are two kinds of confessing. First we have to confess we are sinners and cannot save ourselves. Second, we must confess, or publicly admit that we are followers of Christ. Jesus said: *All those who stand before others and say they believe in me, I will say before my Father in heaven that they belong to me. But all who stand before others and say they do not believe in me, I will say before my Father in heaven that they do not belong to me.*[xlvii]

Ashley took a deep breath, "I guess those of us in the so-called civilized countries have a lot to learn from those living in more simple cultures."

Ntambo grunted assent, "I think there is a lot we can learn from each other, fair one. But yes, Christians living in more prosperous counties have forgotten some of the more basic things that matter most."

After that they entered jungle country once again and had to walk in single file. The upper foliage hid the light of the moon and the warriors re-lighted the lamps. Conversation ceased, and their progress was marked by tramping feet, the chatter of small creatures, and the occasional roar of a lion in the distance. It was going to be a long night. Skip's breathing became more laboured and he knew the same could be said for the others, Themba excluded. The black youth seemed to have inherited the hardiness of his race, or his way of life had tempered him to endure hardship. Skip could not help longing for some rest period along the way, and their speedy arrival at their destination.

....

Aunt May was awakened from a deep sleep by vigorous knocking on the cabin door.

She rolled over and tried to ignore the sound till its insistence finally penetrated. She glanced at her husband beside her and saw he was still soundly asleep. She envied his ability to shut out the world so completely. The clock on the bedside table said 6.00 am.

Aunt May shook Reginald awake, "Sweetie, I'm not dressed to open the door. Would you mind?"

Reggie yawned and resolutely got out of bed, "I can't imagine who could be knocking at this hour. After all, we are on holiday." Donning a dressing gown he went to the door, unlatched it and swung it wide. There in the doorway, looking still rather sleepy from early rising, were their two new friends, Raymond and Angela. Aunt May caught a glimpse of Angela raising her hand to her mouth to stifle a yawn.

Aunt May quickly threw the blankets aside and retrieved the gown she had thrown haphazardly over a chair the night before. Slipping her arms through the sleeves she buttoned it up hurriedly and moved to stand beside Reginald, "Why? What is the matter? "What has happened?"

Raymond seemed to have caught his breath, "Nothing bad. I promised to pay some of the locals if they could give me news of Skip and the others getting back from wherever they went. One of them just arrived to tell us they are here. He is waiting to take us to where they are camped. We thought you would want to come along."

"Just give us five minutes, OK?" Reggie said, "Where shall we meet you?"

"We'll wait for you on one of the park benches across the way," Raymond said, taking Angela's hand and moving along the path toward the park benches. Their figures created a silhouette against the spectacular display of a golden sunrise.

"They're quite the couple," Reggie whispered as he watched them walk away.

"I would say that would apply to us as well as to them," Aunt May said, planting a kiss on his cheek.

"Well then," Reggie said, leaning toward her to return the favour. "We had better get dressed and go and meet our adventurous young people, and their companions. They should be surprised to see us, seeing they think we're still far away exploring the wonders of the African continent."

"I guess we still are," Aunt May responded. "Exploring the wonders of Africa, I mean. There are very few places more wonderful than that amazing waterfall not two hundred yards away from us."

....

James removed the pack off his back and groaned, "If I fall asleep now I don't think I'll ever wake up. I've never been so tired in my entire life."

The others seemed too weary to respond. They had continued the gruelling march throughout the night with hardly a break and they were all bone weary. Only Ntambo and Themba seemed to have retained the appearance of freshness and vitality. Skip guessed they were as exhausted as the rest of them. However, a life-time of rigorous exercise, combined with a stoic refusal to acknowledge their vulnerability made them appear unaffected by the sleeplessness and tension of the night before.

Ntambo's refusal to halt their progress was not because of any urgency to arrive at their destination. How long it took them to return to the falls was less important than the need to avoid a surprise attack by the enemy. Stopping to sleep would expose them to danger for longer. The dense jungle growth made it much too easy for an enemy to come upon them unawares. It was better to shorten the time they were on the trail and find safety in a more populated area. The enemy was unlikely to attack near where the tourist trade was thriving.

Ntambo had halted the march in a clearing close to where they had observed the falls before. The fifty warriors had left them to return to their village. Their departure had been emotional amid expressions of gratitude for the message they had heard on the previous day.

Skip wondered aloud where they were going to sleep, since the sun was rising and would soon be blazing down on them.

"I guess we could find some shade under a tree somewhere," Ashley said doubtfully, "but what I wouldn't give for a nice comfortable bed, with clean sheets, an air conditioner, and curtains to shut out the sunlight."

"You can wish all you like," Nancy replied, wiping the perspiration from her brow and adjusting what she kept referring to as 'boy clothes' to achieve a measure of comfort. "However," she continued, "I don't think you are going to get your wish, any more than I'm going to get mine."

"And what may that be?" Skip put in, an amused smile curling his lips.

"Nancy gave him a challenging look, "A change of clothes, or should I say, several changes of clothes appropriate for a girl. I'd even settle for a dress with frills on it if it will enable me to get rid of this khaki shirt and shorts."

"Why Nancy," Skip teased, "I have always seen you as something of a tomboy. "What's this new you I'm seeing? My, what a transformation? I never thought I'd hear you longing for a dress with frills on it."

Nancy turned on him with mock anger, "Well, get used to it. I don't know whether you've noticed or not, I'm not a little girl any more wanting to be just one of the guys. I'm a woman now and I no longer have to pretend."

In spite of the teasing tone of Nancy's voice, her words silenced him. He had indeed noticed she was no longer a little girl, and he was well aware of the effect it was having upon him. It was all at once exciting, thrilling, and disturbing. He hardly knew how to deal with it.

A shout from James interrupted his thoughts.

"I can't believe it!" James exclaimed. "Are my eyes deceiving me, or is that Aunt May and Reginald coming toward us?"

"And who is that couple coming up behind them, Ashley said with just as much surprise in her voice. "The man looks familiar. No, it can't be!"

"If you think that is our former teacher, Mr. Nichol, I'd say you were right," Nancy said.

Skip was equally surprised by the sudden appearance of aunt May and Reginald. But shock was the best word to describe his reaction to the appearance of Raymond Nichol. The last he had heard his former teacher and practitioner of witchcraft had been committed to a lunatic asylum. What was the meaning of his presence now in the heart of Africa? He had arrived at the precise moment they were about to confront the powers of darkness in an attempt to rescue Roger Wilson. Was he here to oppose them? Was the battle to begin now, rather than later?

Skip's questions had to take second place behind the excitement generated by the reunion with Aunt May and Reginald. Raymond Nichol and the golden haired beauty at his side stood slightly apart as the girls' hugged Aunt May and shyly greeted Reginald. There was gladness at once again being reunited, and expressions of surprise that the newly-weds had returned early from their honeymoon.

Once the initial excitement had calmed down Aunt May noticed the exhaustion apparent on the expressions and body language of the young people. Turning to Ntambo, she enquired, "When do you intend to proceed on your journey? Will there be time for Skip and the others to rest? They look as if they haven't slept for a week."

Ntambo regarded Aunt May curiously. Her resemblance to Skip's mother was striking. It appeared to bring back memories of the missionary couple that had been instrumental in his conversion to Christ. They had nurtured his faith till he had become a giant of faith in his own right. Skip guessed Aunt May's resemblance to her dead sister triggered emotions even Ntambo found hard to repress.

"We will rest for two days," Ntambo replied, "We must regain our strength before proceeding."

Aunt May said, "I intend to rent some cabins for the young people, including your nephew, if that is acceptable. Would you like to join us?"

Ntambo shook his head, "I must spend time alone. There is a great battle ahead; it is one I do not expect to survive. I need to spend time in prayer."

So the matter was settled and they all made their way back to the tourist centre in town. On the way Aunt May and Reginald explained Raymond Nichol's presence, and introduced Angela to them as his bride.

Skip was not yet ready to accept Mr. Nichol in light of his previous involvement in witchcraft. He was sure the others felt the same way. It would take a much more detailed explanation before they would be convinced he was not still their enemy. It was entirely possible his friendliness was merely a cover for some evil intent. Enquiry into that would have to wait. They were all far too exhausted to delve into that now.

Ashley said to Nancy, "What was that you said about me not getting a shower, and you not getting your wish either? I would say a shower and a soft bed are entirely possible at this point. And I wouldn't put it past Aunt May to attend to your longing for a change of clothing either."

"What can I say?" Nancy replied smugly. "I am entirely willing to be wrong if it leads to a shower, a soft bed, and comfort beyond my wildest dreams."

True to her word, Aunt May and Reginald rented two cabins, one for Ashley and Nancy, and one for Skip, James and Themba. It was clear Themba felt strange in what were to him luxurious surroundings. Village life and tribal existence was rugged and offered not many creature comforts. Having known nothing else it had never occurred to him he was suffering any hardship. He nevertheless expressed pleasure in the friendship growing between him and these young people from across the sea. "We have much to learn from each other," he said seriously. "Your world and my world may be entirely different, but there is much to be gained by mixing them."

Exhaustion prevented any further discussion and they fell into a deep sleep minutes after laying their heads on their pillows.

The sun had already set when they awoke to a pounding on the door. At least, it sounded like pounding to Skip as he struggled to surface from a deep sleep. Still drowsy, he got out of bed and went to open the door. Reginald stood there with an amused expression on his face as he took in Skip's appearance.

"You had better smarten up and put a comb through that hair of yours. Meet us in fifteen minutes for dinner at the hotel restaurant."

It was then Skip noticed his uncle was holding a package wrapped in brown paper. He placed it in Skip's hands, "Your aunt bought these for Themba to wear. They should fit him. She's a good judge of sizes."

Skip thanked him and shook the other two awake, with groans of protest, mainly from James. Themba was fully awake in seconds.

When the package was unwrapped and Themba saw the khaki shirt and shorts he was expected to wear to dinner, he scrunched up his face in disgust, "How do you wear such things. They must be very uncomfortable."

"Only because you are not used to them," James said. "If I were to go around bare-chested like you, and with only a loin-cloth wrapped around my middle, I would feel uncomfortable. That would not be because there is anything wrong with the way you dress; it just does not fit into the culture I was raised in. I guess, if I were to live the rest of my life in your village I would end up dressing just like you do."

"Enough talking for now, guys," Skip said, lacing up his shoes. "The others are waiting for us."

When they entered the hotel dining room Skip was not prepared for the transformation he saw in Nancy and Ashley. It was obvious Aunt May had woken the girls early and headed for the clothing stores before closing. As accustomed as he was now to see them in 'boy' clothing, their feminine dress was both startling and disturbing. At almost fifteen, their new dresses and hair-dos made them look at least five years older than that. The colour and style of their dresses showed off their figures and made them look no less beautiful than Angela, Raymond Nichol's bride.

Aunt May saw the startled look on Skip's face and commented, "Don't worry, boys, "they won't be parading around like this when they're back on the trail with you. I bought jeans, blouses and footwear appropriate for everyday wear, and for walking in rough terrain."

Skip remained speechless.

Aunt May continued, "It is just that from time to time a women needs to look and feel special. I thought Nancy and Ashley needed to be spoiled a little, even if it was just for one night."

Nancy gave Skip a look that defied description, but one that made his head spin. James seemed to get a similar look from Ashley. Themba just looked awkward in his unfamiliar garb.

When Skip was able to breathe again he followed the others as the head waiter led them to a table in the corner of the room. Two tables had been moved together to accommodate the nine of them.

Skip made sure he was seated beside Themba whom he knew would be mystified by the array of cutlery to choose from when the time came to eat. In his own setting Themba would merely dip his fingers into a pot of stiff porridge, called Sadza, roll some into a ball, and dip it into a bowl of meat and gravy. Skip and the other young people had themselves become accustomed to eating in this manner while on the trail, and while visiting native villages. It was a fairly simple operation. For Themba, on the other hand, there was nothing simple about trying to choose the right knife, or fork, or spoon for a particular item on the menu. Skip guided Themba through the process by first catching his eye, then deliberately selecting the proper implement when it was needed. The African boy soon caught on and thus was spared any embarrassment.

Before they ordered, and while they waited for their meal to arrive, Skip determined to satisfy himself as to the reason for his former teacher's presence here, in the heart of Africa. With a suspicious edge to his voice he looked Raymond Nichol in the eye and asked, "You will forgive me Mr. Nichol if I wonder what someone so heavily involved in witchcraft would be doing here at the precise moment we have come to rescue our friend, Roger Wilson, from the very thing you declared so confidently? Indeed, it was you who mentored him and encouraged him to embrace witchcraft." He took a breath and continued, "You were certainly not our friend when we encountered you in the valley near Lake Torment."

Nancy intruded with a comment of her own, not seeming to care that she was being offensive, "We heard that you had gone mad, and had been committed to a lunatic asylum." She ignored the frown from Aunt May and the dig in her ribs from Ashley.

Raymond Nichol held first Skip's, and then Nancy's gaze, "I don't blame you for being suspicious, or for your need to ask such questions. I would do the same if our roles were reversed. But I think Angela here should be the one to explain." He turned to the golden haired beauty at his side, "My love, would you try to explain what happened to me and why we have come here?"

Angela Nichol's eyes seemed to fill with tenderness and understanding. She was immediately the focus of attention when she said, "Insanity is the clinical term for Raymond's condition when I met him, though 'meeting' him is not the best way to describe it. He was possessed with demons and was not able to meet with anyone in the true sense of the word.

"I was employed by the Bartlett Home for the Insane, and Raymond was just one of my patients. I don't know what made me recognize Raymond's case as different from all the others. In my early morning devotions it was his name and his face that kept coming to mind. As time passed I began to believe God had marked him for deliverance."

"How long did it take for this realization to come upon you?" Reginald asked.

"Several months, but it was more progressive and gradual than a sudden revelation. It came as a settled conviction that I was to pray for Ray's deliverance. One morning in my devotions I read of the conversion of Saul of Tarsus and what God told Ananias what He had planned for the man who was later known as Paul the apostle: *But the Lord said to him, "Go, for he is a chosen instrument of Mine, to bear My name before the Gentiles and kings and the sons of Israel; for I will show him how much he must suffer for My name's sake.*[xlviii]

"Two things became clear to me. First, Raymond was God's chosen vessel, an instrument God intended to use, and second, that the way ahead for him was to be full of suffering for the name of Christ."

"But you still married him, despite your knowledge of what lay ahead."

Angela cast a meaningful glance toward Raymond before answering, "I cannot choose my own path, any more than you can. Besides, I love him. Whatever lies ahead I will embrace as God's will for both of us."

Aunt May asked, "Could you tell us, in detail, what happened to bring about his deliverance from madness?"

Angela took a deep breath, "I can only tell you what I saw, and what I felt, but I believe there was a great battle in the heavenly places. There were times I felt torn apart by invisible forces battling for Ray's soul."

"So, tell us!" Skip blurted out, conflicting emotions warring inside him. "Tell us how someone who foisted witchcraft on unsuspecting young people, has now become a true disciple of Jesus Christ."

So Angela did. She started at the moment she first encountered Raymond Nichol, and continued till every detail of his remarkable transformation had been told. When she was done, a sense of the awesome Presence of God had settled on the company.

Chapter 19

Angels of Light

For several minutes after Angela Nichol had finished the account of her new husband's deliverance from madness and demonic possession, no one said anything.

The only sound was the muted conversation from other tables, the clatter of dishware, and soft music playing in the background. All had been moved by the dramatic tale and now all eyes were fixed on Raymond Nichol as if the ball was now in his court; whatever more there was to tell was up to him.

Mr. Nichol turned first to Skip, his former student and adversary, "You asked earlier why I was here and implied I have no business being here considering my past involvement in leading my students astray. I don't blame you for that. There is no excuse for what I did, but God has been merciful to me, and I am here in the hopes I can make up for some of the damage I have done."

"How do you expect to do that?" Nancy asked, still somewhat unsettled by the appearance of her former teacher.

"To provide you with some intelligence, Nancy, and to prepare you for the battle that lies ahead."

Reginald's soothing voice intervened, "I think we should give Raymond a chance to explain. After that, if we have any concerns, we can address them then."

Nancy nodded agreement.

Skip leaned back in his chair. Whatever Mr. Nichol had to say was going to receive all his attention.

"You will remember the story of Troy, how the Greek army was able to enter that impregnable city by practicing deception?"

Skip glanced at Themba, who obviously had never heard of such a thing.

Noticing the direction of Skip's gaze, Raymond Nichol said, "Well, since at least one of us may not know the story, and the rest may need a refresher course, let me tell the story from the beginning.

"A war had raged outside the ancient city of Troy for ten years. Paris of Troy had abducted Helen, a Greek queen, and the Greeks besieged the city for all of that time in an effort to get her back. The walls of Troy were so high and strong the Greek soldiers had been unable to achieve their goal – to recapture their queen and take her back home.

"At the end of the ten years they were faced with the options of giving up and sailing their ships away forever – or coming up with another plan to defeat the Trojans. Brute force had not worked, so deceit and trickery seemed the only way.

"A plan was concocted to build a gigantic wooden horse, fill it with soldiers, and sail away, leaving the impression that they had given up, and the war was over. One of them was left behind to tell the Trojans the Greeks had given up and gone home. In reality they had merely sailed to a place where their presence was hidden by an island.

"Fascinated by the horse and convinced it would be an ideal gift to their goddess, Athena; they brought the horse into the city and celebrated with revelry for most of the night. After ten years they thought the war was now over, and they were at last rid of the Greek army.

"When everyone was either asleep or drunk, a door in the wooden horse opened and the soldiers crept out. They opened the gates of the city, knowing that under cover of darkness the Greek army had sailed back to attack the city. Thus they achieved in one night by trickery what ten years of brute force had not been able to do."

After a few moments of silence, James asked, "You told us this story for what reason, Mr. Nichol?"

"I told it to explain the strategy the powers of darkness are using to attack the church of Jesus Christ. Their plan is to attack the church form the *inside*."

"Exactly how are they going to do that?" Ashley asked, "Though I think I've heard someone explain it before."

"I'm sure you have," Raymond Nichol responded. "However, I'll show you from the Bible what I mean. While Angela and I were waiting for you to arrive, we looked up some Scripture references that apply to what is going on in the church today."

Mr. Nichol removed a sheet of paper from his pocket, unfolded it, and read:

I went because God showed me I should go. I met with the believers there, and in private I told their leaders the Good News that I preach to the non-Jewish people. I did not want my past work and the work I am now doing to be wasted.Titus was with me, but he was not forced to be circumcised, even though he was a Greek.We talked about this problem because some false believers had come into our group secretly. They came in like spies to overturn the freedom we have in Christ Jesus. They wanted to make us slaves.[xlix]

"Here Paul is describing what happened when he went to Jerusalem and brought Titus with him. Titus was a Greek, and some Jews objected to them being brought into the fellowship of the church. These Jews pretended to be converted. The apostle Paul says of them:

...false believers had come into our group secretly. They came in like spies to overturn the freedom we have in Christ Jesus. They wanted to make us slaves.

"You mean Satan is sending false believers into the churches to corrupt the message of the church?" Reginald put in.

"I mean," Raymond said pointedly, "that is what is happening in the 'Lion's Den' you are planning to visit. You are planning to rescue Roger Wilson. The caves under the Victoria Falls are where he and others are being trained to pose as true believers, but their real mission will be to come into the church and pervert the message of the Gospel."

"That sounds incredible," Nancy said. "Do they really think we will be fooled?"

"Many churches are already being fooled, but this is not a new thing, as Jude found in the first century. He said: *Dear friends, I wanted very much to write you about the salvation we all share. But I felt the need to write you about something else: I want to encourage you to fight hard for the faith that was given the holy people of God once and for all time. Some people have secretly entered your group. Long ago the prophets wrote about these people who will be judged guilty. They are against God and have changed the grace of our God into a reason for sexual sin. They also refuse to accept Jesus Christ, our only Master and Lord.*[l]

"So you see, the danger is very real and the devil is using the same tactics as were used in the story of the wooden horse. If he can't defeat the church from the outside, he'll try to defeat her from the inside."

Skip said, "You are saying these people who are secretly entering the church really work for the devil, but they look like servants of God?"

"Yes, Skip. Paul the apostle explained it like this:

Such men are not true apostles but are workers who lie. They change themselves to look like apostles of Christ. This does not surprise us. Even Satan changes himself to look like an angel of light.[15] *So it does not surprise us if Satan's servants also make themselves look like servants who work for what is right. But in the end they will be punished for what they do.*[li]

"These false servants of God won't get away with it in the end, but in the meantime they will cause havoc, and turn many unstable souls from the way of truth."

"But," Ashley said plaintively, obviously shaken and overwhelmed by the implications of what Mr. Nichol had shared, "if the deception is going to be so strong, and will even come from the churches where we worship, what can we do about it?"

Angela Nichol spoke up, "Three things, Ashley. First we are to take warning, second, we are to remain alert, and third, we are to trust God to give us discernment." Reaching for her purse, Angela removed a well-worn copy of the New Testament, and leafed through it till she found what she was looking for, "Listen to the warning the apostle Paul gave right at the beginning of the Christian era:

I know that after I leave, some people will come like wild wolves and try to destroy the flock.Also, some from your own group will rise up and twist the truth and will lead away followers after them.So be careful! Always remember that for three years, day and night, I never stopped warning each of you, and I often cried over you.[lii]

"You see how serious the apostle was. God had revealed to Him how things would be. Satan would plant people *inside* the church to lead people away from the truth.

"You asked what you can do about it. Jesus told us how to tell the difference between the true and the false teachers." Angela flipped to another page and read:

You will know these people by what they do. Grapes don't come from thorn bushes, and figs don't come from thorny weeds.In the same way, every good tree produces good fruit, but a bad tree produces bad fruit.A good tree cannot produce bad fruit, and a bad tree cannot produce good fruit.Every tree that does not produce good fruit is cut down and thrown into the fire. In the same way, you will know these false prophets by what they do.[liii]

"If you watch carefully, and prayerfully, sooner or later the false teachers will give themselves away.

"And there is something even more important. God told his people:

You will search for me. And when you search for me with all your heart, you will find me![liv]

"Knowing *what* to believe is very important, but it is even more important to maintain a vital and living relationship with God Himself."

The restaurant was emptying and the waiters were clearing up and resetting the tables by the time discussion finally wound down. Skip's head was spinning from the sheer abundance of ideas passing through his mind. Glancing at Themba, he was surprised to see an expression of total comprehension on his face. What the Nichols had shared had not fazed him in the least. If he looked at all uncomfortable it was due to the unfamiliar clothing he was wearing, and not to the volume of truth coming at him.

Skip reminded himself that Themba had grown up in a church environment where there was constant conflict with witchdoctors. The church leaders and congregation had to be on the alert for all kinds of deception and the influence of demonic spirits. What Themba had heard here tonight was nothing new to him.

As they all rose to leave, Raymond Nichol caught Skip's eye. His eyebrow was raised in enquiry, as if asking if Skip believed he was a changed man. Skip gave him a half smile in acknowledgement. It wouldn't be easy to forget the conflicts of the past, or the teacher's former betrayal of the students entrusted to him. There was no doubt something radical had transpired in the man's life, and his new wife's testimony was impressive. However, it would take time and a lot of positive action for him to be completely convinced. He hoped fervently that the change was real and permanent, but he guessed he would just have to wait and see.

Chapter 20

The "Bridge"

Ntambo was waiting for them, standing regally on a large rock near the edge of the gorge and staring at the mighty flow of water before him.

It appeared as if the time he had spent alone in this place had etched some new lines of resolve on his face. His jaw was set and his lips pressed together in a determined line. Skip thought he saw an expression in his eyes that he had seen the future, knew it would end in in his own death, and had resigned himself to his fate.

Yet Skip knew Ntambo did not believe in fate. He would never call it that. He would call it "the will of God." Whatever lay ahead for Ntambo, he would embrace it, even if it ended in the tragic way Skip's dream had indicated it would. Skip felt suddenly ashamed he had been occupied with personal issues over the past few hours, and not even considered what Ntambo must be going through.

If Ntambo noticed the evidence of a change in the way the young people related to each other, he gave no indication of it. Instead he turned to Raymond Nichol, his tone direct and challenging, "You know what awaits you if you insist on accompanying us?"

Raymond Nichol stared back at the big black man with equal directness, "Yes I do."

"You know you may never return to your woman? You will be seen as one who has betrayed the cause, having once served the powers of darkness. A terrible fate will have been reserved for you."

"That much I know," Raymond said, "but I also know my new Master, Jesus, will protect me. But if not; if He deems it best to allow me to suffer death for His name, I cannot turn from what I believe is His will for me."

This speech seemed to satisfy Ntambo, and he spoke to the whole group, "We will camp here tonight and set out at sunrise."

Later, after Ntambo and Mr. Nichol had retired for the night, the young people sat together to talk. Skip wanted to hear what the others thought about Mr. Nichol and the almost unbelievable change they saw in him. Skip reflected that it was not so much that it was unbelievable, but that he was himself unwilling to believe it. If he believed the teacher had truly turned from darkness to light, then he would have to let go of the secret resentment he had been feeling toward him.

Watching the dying light of the campfire reflected on his friends' faces, Skip asked, "What do you think of this so-called transformation of our former class teacher?"

The question seemed to produce shocked expressions in the others, as if they had never thought to question what had happened to Raymond Nichol.

"I don't think there is anything 'so-called' about it," Nancy said.

"I agree," Ashley responded. "No one could doubt Angela's account of what happened at the mental institution, though you obviously have."

James leaned closer to the dying embers, "If God could deliver me from witchcraft, I don't doubt he can deliver anyone."

Themba smiled his enigmatic smile as he listened, but offered no comment.

Skip was miffed that his doubts had been dismissed so lightly, "Don't you think the enemy could be planting him among us to undermine our efforts to rescue Roger? That is if Roger even *wants* to be rescued."

"Skip, pull out that Bible of yours and turn to the book of Daniel. I think there is something in it that may convince you."

Nancy scuttled over with a flashlight, to aim it on the page as Skip flipped through the pages to where Ashley indicated. She couldn't restrain herself from passing a gentle caress on his arm, as if for support as she directed the beam over his shoulder.

Skip was familiar with the passage:

Nebuchadnezzar became very angry and called for Shadrach, Meshach, and Abednego. When they were brought to the king, Nebuchadnezzar said, "Shadrach, Meshach, and Abednego, is it true that you do not serve my gods nor worship the gold statue I have set up? In a moment you will again hear the sound of the horns, flutes, lyres, zithers, harps, pipes, and all the other musical instruments. If you bow down and worship the statue I made, that will be good. But if you do not worship it, you will immediately be thrown into the blazing furnace. What god will be able to save you from my power then?"

Shadrach, Meshach, and Abednego answered the king, saying, "Nebuchadnezzar, we do not need to defend ourselves to you.If you throw us into the blazing furnace, the God we serve is able to save us from the furnace. He will save us from your power, O king.But even if God does not save us, we want you, O king, to know this: We will not serve your gods or worship the gold statue you have set up."[lv]

Skip looked up from his reading, “How is that going to convince me Mr. Nichol is genuine?”

“Just think, and remember what you heard when Ntambo asked him if he knew what he was getting into. Doesn’t it sound familiar?”

“In what way is it familiar?”

Ashley sighed, “It was similar to the way the three Hebrews answered the king of Babylon when he threatened them with the fiery furnace. If I remember correctly he said, ‘I also know my new Master, Jesus, will protect me. But if not; if He deems it best to allow me to suffer death for His name, I cannot turn from what I believe is His will for me.”

“What a memory!” James said in an attempt to inject some humour into the conversation. “Remind me to get your help when we get back to school.”

Nancy brought her lips close to Skip’s ear, “Don’t tell us he was faking that, Skip. He’s leaving Angela behind, and going, as it were, into the jaws of death. He knows he’ll be seen as a traitor.”

“Then why risk it? What does he think coming with us will accomplish? This could all be planned, and they know he is coming to betray us. If that was true it wouldn’t be a risk at all.”

“You seem determined to believe him a fake,” Ashley said. “For myself, I think he is coming with us because we are going into this thing blind. He believes his inside knowledge with the powers involved can make a difference.”

A familiar voice spoke from the edge of the clearing, “Go to the top of the class, Ashley. That is exactly why I am going with you.”

Every head turned in the direction of the voice. Standing at the edge of the clearing, his features hardly visible, was Raymond Nichol.

"How... how long have you been there, sir?" Skip said, unconsciously slipping into student-teacher mode.

"I've been here long enough to hear how much you doubt my conversion, Skip. Is it so hard for you to believe the God you believe in would have mercy on someone like me?"

Recovering somewhat from the surprise of the teacher's appearance, Skip said, "That's not exactly it, sir. I believe God *can* do it. It is just that you were so ... so..."

"You still can't forgive me for leading your friends into witchcraft? Is that your problem? You think I was an instrument of the devil, and I was. From all I know about my involvement in witchcraft, and from Angela's account of my deliverance, I was most certainly demon-possessed. But I've been forgiven. I've been washed. The blood of Christ has cleansed me and made me a different person. All I want to do is to serve Him, and make up for my rebellion of the past."

As Raymond Nichol came to sit with them, Nancy directed the beam of her flashlight once more onto the Bible still clutched in Skip's hand, "Skip, you're not the first one to doubt the conversion of one of the enemies of the church. Turn to the ninth chapter of the book of Acts." She moved from behind him and eased back into her former position, keeping the beam of the flashlight in place. She waited for Skip to find the place and pointed with her finger to the verses she wanted him to read.

Feeling suddenly ashamed of his stubborn unbelief, Skip did as Nancy directed:

"*When Saul went to Jerusalem, he tried to join the group of followers, but they were all afraid of him. They did not believe he was really a follower. But Barnabas accepted Saul and took him to the apostles. Barnabas explained to them that Saul had seen the Lord on the road and the Lord had spoken to Saul. Then he told them how boldly Saul had preached in the name of Jesus in Damascus.*"[lvi]

When he had done reading Nancy switched the flashlight off, slipping her hand into his, "So if God could turn the apostle from being his enemy, why not Mr. Nichol?"

Skip said, somewhat impatiently, "I get it, but the Bible also says we will know people by the fruit of their doings. Forgive me if I just wait for a while to see just how much of a change there has been."

Skip was not proud of his little speech, but he felt intimidated by what he perceived as his friends' ganging up on him – Nancy in particular. He let go of her hand and suggested they all go to bed.

....

Joshua, tucked away in his reclusive cabin in Canada, had often felt the gracious influence of the Holy Spirit in a call to urgent prayer for needs he only half understood. He had learned not to question when these strong impressions came upon him. Invariably he had found out later that these seasons of intense prayer had contributed to the deliverance of groups or individuals he had been impressed to pray for.

However, this time the urge had come upon him so suddenly, and with such intensity, as he had never experienced before.

Joshua had been tending his small vegetable garden, taking advantage of few hours of sun reaching down into the gorge where his cabin was situated. He had half-filled his basket with potatoes, turnips and beans, when he was assaulted by a compulsion to prayer so strong he left the basket where it lay and staggered to the cabin. As tall as he was, he barely escaped banging his head on the cabin's cross-beams. He fell to his knees before his bunk and heaved out such prayer as he had never known. Even as his body was wracked with sobs a verse of Scripture passed through his mind:

Also, the Spirit helps us with our weakness. We do not know how to pray as we should. But the Spirit himself speaks to God for us, even begs God for us with deep feelings that words cannot explain.[lvii]

This time the overwhelming spirit of prayer was accompanied by visions so real they imprinted themselves indelibly on his mind.

Joshua saw in his vision the group of adventurers getting ready to enter the domain of the devil, what the Spirit revealed to Him was known as "The Lion`s Den." They were eager and excited at the prospect of rescuing their friend from the clutches of the enemy, but he saw on their faces a lack of comprehension as to the dangers that lay ahead. In spite of having encountered the forces of darkness before, he saw that Skip was struggling with personal issues, robbing him of the single-mindedness necessary for the fight ahead.

This was not true of the large black man Joshua knew to be Ntambo. He stood proud and sombre, contemplating the path he had chosen. It was clear from his expression that what he saw ahead was death – his own death.

The black youth at his side seemed to reflect the mood of his elder. He, too, stood solid and silent, sensing, if not realizing, the tragic events that lay not too far in the future.

The former teacher, Raymond Nichol, was there, too. On his face was the light of a holy zeal, like a Joan of Arc fulfilling her divine calling, or like the apostle Paul consumed with the inner compulsion to preach the Gospel.

Skip, Nancy, Ashley, and James seemed unprepared, simply because they had no idea of the malevolence of the forces arrayed against them.

The vision shifted, and Joshua found himself inside the vast network of chambers beyond the entrance, and he saw things not lawful to reveal. A sense of horror came over him, and his large body was shaken like a leaf in the wind. Prayer, such as he had never known before shook his body; sobs rose up in him from a well too deep to fathom.

For an hour Joshua remained in the grip of this powerful movement of the Spirit. When it subsided he lay prostrate and drained from the ordeal of body and mind he had been subjected to. Inwardly, however, he knew that a victory had been won. He knew not what the victory was, or what consequences had been avoided, but he knew he had been granted a singular honour in being allowed to fight in a battle taking place half-a-world away.

....

At first light they all gathered at a look-out point over the falls and prepared for the last leg of their journey. If Skip thought it would be easier to go over the modern bridge to Zambia on the other side, he did not mention it. Detailed instructions from Mazimbi probably meant there was only one safe entrance to the fabled caves most people said never existed.

After a quick check to determine they had all they needed, they put on their back-packs and waited for Ntambo's final instructions.

He warned them to stay close together and to only speak if absolutely essential.

"The steep paths and narrow ledges are not the only dangers. By far the greatest perils we face are the ones we cannot see. *For our struggle is not against [a]flesh and blood, but against the rulers, against the powers, against the world forces of this darkness, against the spiritual forces of wickedness in the heavenly places.*[lviii] "Keep praying every step of the way."

In spite of Ntambo's warning Nancy whispered to Skip, "Are you upset with me for not agreeing with you last night?"

"No," he said, not elaborating.

The truth was Skip was not upset with Nancy. He was just a little hurt she did not share what he considered reasonable caution regarding their former teacher's presence. After all, they were about to face their most critical challenge so far, and they could not afford a traitor in their midst.

Mr. Nichol brought up the rear and Skip could not restrain himself from the occasional glance behind. There was nothing in the man's expression or demeanour to indicate anything suspicious, yet his doubts persisted. Was he being foolish to question the sincerity of the man while the others accepted him without question? Skip found himself concentrating his prayers, not on the dangers ahead, but on his need for assurance that Mr. Nichol posed no threat. All he got for his intense praying was a fragment of a Bible verse that kept passing through his mind: *Then Jesus said to them, "You are foolish and slow to believe...*[lix]

Was he being slow of heart to believe God could change someone, even one deeply embroiled in witchcraft as Raymond Nichol had been? Another Scripture popped into his mind, *"God has made these things clean, so don't call them 'unholy'!"*[lx] Skip realised God is able to make anything, or any *one*, clean and holy, no matter how bad they were before. It seemed God was telling him to let go of his doubts and to trust Him to work out all things in his time.

With an effort, he wrenched his mind away from his doubts and concentrated on praying against the spiritual forces arrayed against them. This was not easy, for the path they were following was steep and dangerous, requiring extreme caution. They were headed down into the bottom of the gorge; rocks and shale strewed their path, which was only wide enough to proceed single file. Skip called to Nancy ahead of him not to look down to the right; he had found out that staring into the depths of the gorge caused his head to swim.

It took three hours to reach the bottom; their heads reeled from the intense concentration and frequent bouts of fear when someone's foot slipped. More than once Skip had had to grab hold of Nancy's arm to prevent her from falling. Several times he had narrowly escaped falling himself. Without shoes, Themba was much more sure-footed; he calmly extended a hand of support when he thought Skip was in danger of losing his footing.

Once they reached the bottom of the gorge, out of breath and trembling from the nervous energy expended on the descent, their troubles were not over. The raging torrent of water rushing downstream left them no way of crossing to the other side.

Thinking to lighten the mood, James said, "I guess we'll just have to swim across."

No one smiled at his remark, but Mr. Nichol offered, "Just take a look at Ntambo. He doesn't seem at all perplexed. It is my guess he has this all figured out."

"You don't know him as well as we do," Ashley said. "He never looks ruffled or perturbed, no matter what's going on. It's rather upsetting to tell you the truth. You can't tell what he is thinking and it makes me feel inadequate, and a little envious."

"Part of that has to do with his race," Nancy commented. "You notice Themba is developing some of the qualities of his uncle. He hardly ever seems ruffled either."

"Except when you put him in clothing he is not accustomed to," James said, and they all laughed.

Themba just smiled his enigmatic smile, and kept silent.

"I think it is more than that with Ntambo," Skip said. "I think he has learned to walk in the calm of God's presence. He told me once he puts his faith in a verse in Isaiah. He suggested I commit it to memory."

"Can you quote it now?"

"I think so. It says: *You, Lord, give true peace*
to those who depend on you,
because they trust you."[lxi]

"There is another one, too: *Those who love your teachings will find true peace,*
and nothing will defeat them.[lxii]

"I wish we could all learn to live like that," James said.

"I guess we can," Ashley said. "It just takes a little time and growth in maturity to reach that level."

Their discussion was interrupted when Ntambo returned from his gazing at the turbulent waters. "We will rest here for a while before proceeding," he said, totally ignoring the seeming reality that no way of proceeding was possible. Sensing their unspoken query, he continued, "There *is* a way across, though it is fraught with danger." He paused, "But we knew that before we set out. I suggest we use some of the time we have for prayer. God always has a way when there seems to be no way."

In spite of Ntambo's last words sounding like a cliché, Skip knew them to be true. None of the things he and his friends had been involved in for the past two years had been easy, but God had brought them through.

As he contemplated this his eyes strayed toward Nancy who was standing apart, staring blankly at the opposite wall of the canyon. He felt suddenly ashamed. He had not treated her very well, and why? He had been upset because she had not agreed with his expressed doubts regarding Mr. Nichol. Is that what he expected of her just because he knew she had special feelings for him? Was he expecting her to agree with everything he said, not giving her freedom to hold her own opinions and convictions? That wasn't exactly fair, was it?

Skip walked over to where she was standing and gently took her hand, "Will you forgive me?"

Nancy turned to gaze directly at him, her hurt expression melting slowly into a smile, "Should I?"

"I would be grateful if you would. I had no right to shut you out just because you have a different view to my own."

"Are you convinced now that Mr. Nichol's conversion is genuine?"

Skip hesitated, "I'm not sure I'd go that far, but I'm willing to reserve judgment till his sincerity is proved either way."

Nancy squeezed his hand, "That's good enough for me. And in answer to your question, I do forgive you. Just don't shut me out again. I couldn't stand it." With that they joined the others who were speculating on how they were going to reach their destination with white water and rapids barring their way.

"I wouldn't worry if I were you," Raymond Nichol commented. Turning his gaze toward where Ntambo stood apart, he said, "I think our guide over there has it all figured out."

Themba's only response was to smile. In spite of having been born in Africa, Skip had been too long removed from the tribal culture for him to understand it. Themba and his uncle reacted to situations in a manner far removed from his own, or what he had been able to observe in his short life. Somehow this difference was comforting, rather than disturbing.

James said, "There must be a bridge of some kind around that bend, or Ntambo wouldn't have brought us here in the first place."

James' comment later had some foundation in fact, particularly the phrase "of some kind." After resuming their journey they rounded a bend and were faced with a curious sight.

"I sincerely hope," Nancy said, "Ntambo doesn't expect us to cross to the other side on *that*."

The "that" Nancy referred to was indeed something to cause incredulity. It *was* a bridge, but only in the loosest sense of the term. The best way to describe it was as a "broken archway." Two columns of rock rose from either side of the gorge, arching toward each other, but ending over the raging torrent twenty feet short. On the extreme end of the nearest arch was a tree. It was gnarled and ancient; its many roots wrapped around the solid rock liked an octopus fearing for its life. Its trunk was bent toward the opposite arch, with gnarled branches reaching out as if to grab hold of something solid.

They all stood staring at this freak of nature. Only Ntambo and his nephew seemed un-intimidated by the prospect of clambering over it to the other side. If the bridge itself was not scary enough, the white water that rushed by beneath it was directed by a protruding rock only a few inches from the branches of the tree.

Seemingly unaware of the awed expressions on the faces of his charges, Ntambo raised his voice above the sound of the torrent, "Let us cross over. We must reach our next stop before dark."

Chapter 21

Into the Lion's Den

There was a tremor in Ashley's voice when she shouted to James, even while she clung to the knotted roots of the ancient tree, "I... I'm so scared I could die without even falling."

"Just go slow and hold on tight," James responded. It was sound advice, except that the spray from the white water made the tree and its roots slippery. "Dangerous" seemed a very mild word to describe what they were doing.

Ntambo had gone across first; after him Mr. Nichol, then Nancy and Skip. James followed Ashley, ready to grab should she be in any danger of falling. Themba, as was his custom, followed behind. In their favour was the width of the granite arch. It was much wider than they had thought while observing it from a distance. The uneven surface afforded them some stability as they crawled forward. The wet surface of the tree was much more intimidating, as were its branches that swayed under their weight. Ashley and James made it across, but having almost slipped into the raging torrent on three occasions, made Ashley speechless with imagining what might have been.

It took half an hour for all of them to cross and stand shaken but relieved on the other side of the gorge.

"It felt closer to a week for me," Nancy said, still breathing deeply, more from stress than from physical effort.

"But we made it," Skip said, giving Nancy's hand a comforting squeeze. "Don't relax too much though. There may be just as many challenges ahead of us as what we've been thorough already. Now that we're near our destination I expect things may get worse."

"Well, thank you," James said with a note of sarcasm. "Thank you for those encouraging words."

"I was only trying to be realistic," Skip said. "This is not a game we are playing, neither is it just an exciting adventure. If what we have faced before should teach us anything, it would be that the enemy is out to destroy us."

Mr. Nichol spoke up in Skip's defence, "Skip is right. Remember, I've been on the other side. I know how dark and devilish the forces of darkness can be. Our only hope is to trust Christ for His strength, and to remain alert."

Further discussion ended when Ntambo beckoned to them to follow him on the next leg of the journey. Since the path was steep and rugged no one had breath to spare for talking; their approach to the roar of the main falls further restricted conversation. Two hours later the fading light forced them to seek a slightly broader section of the trail and to settle down for the night.

"We must stay here," Ntambo said as they huddled together. "It is too dangerous to go the rest of the way in the dark."

Spray from the waterfall had already wet their clothing. The waterproof coverings they drew from their backpacks, while preventing any further spray from reaching them, merely aided the dampness of their clothing in penetrating their skin.

Nancy shivered, "I can see we are not going to get much sleep tonight."

But she was wrong. Huddled together as they were, the concentrated heat from their bodies created damp but comfortable warmth, allowing them to drift off for some time. They only half emerged from sleep when someone moved or changed position, so they were surprisingly alert when the first light of dawn found the ledge where they lay.

"I dreamed a horrible dream," Nancy confessed when they huddled together, eating a breakfast of bread and sour porridge. "I think Skip is right. The trouble ahead of us is going to be much worse than what we've been through already. I would like to say I am not afraid, but there were things in my dream that scared me silly."

Skip reached for her hand, "Tell us what you saw, Nance."

Taking a breath before speaking, Nancy's voice trembled, "Most of it was all confusion, but there were a few flashes of clarity I can't forget. I saw a throne constructed out of human bones and skulls. There was no one on it, but I seemed to know instinctively that it was intended for Satan himself, or some manifestation of his presence."

"That is no more than we know already," James said. "We know it is the devil's lair we are going to, or 'The Lion's Den,' as Mazimbi called it. We know from the Bible that the devil goes about like a roaring lion seeking whom he may devour."

"There is more," Nancy said. "You won't believe what I saw. I just hope my dream is not a warning of what is going to happen."

"Go on," Ashley encouraged,

Nancy hesitated. It was clear she doubted the wisdom of sharing all she had seen in her dream. The others urged her on.

"Well," Nancy continued reluctantly, "There were three crosses in a chamber. It was just like the pictures depicting the crucifixion of Jesus and the two thieves on either side of Him, except that the crosses were empty."

"That is surprising," Mr. Nichol put in, "In the circles I moved in, the cross was a hated symbol."

"I don't think the crosses were meant to symbolize Jesus or his sacrifice to bring sinners back to God. I think they were erected for an evil purpose." She would not say any more, but Skip thought she was holding something back. Whatever it was caused a troubled look to pass over her countenance, and she was mostly silent for the rest of the day.

Soon, they donned their back-packs and set out on the steepest part of the climb. A lot more rocks and loose shale lay in their path. Every step had to be negotiated with extreme care; a misstep could end in tragedy.

"I think there must have been several rock-falls here since Mazimbi was here last," Skip muttered between long periods of holding his breath. "We must be mad taking this path. There must be a safer route."

Nancy, who was the only one who could hear him above the roar of the falls, moved her lips close to his ear, "I don't think there is another route, at least not one any safer than this one."

No other conversation was possible after that. The noise of the falls blotted out all other sounds. Their progress was so slow, and the fear that gripped them so intense, it took more than three hours to reach the ledge immediately below The Devil's Cataract. " By this time they were so exhausted even if there had been no noise to prevent speech, they would have been too weary to utter a word.

The spray from the falls was so intense it was more like rain and they all looked more like drowned rats than a party of human hikers.

Skip could not say anything, but he thought they had come to a dead end. There seemed no way to proceed. Under the overhanging ledge there was only a blank wall. Memories flooded back of the blank wall that had blocked their entrance into the tunnel leading to the witchcraft retreat before. He, Nancy and Ashley had only been able to overcome the magic barrier by prayer, fasting, and an act of faith. In this case he knew Mazimbi and the other former witch-doctor's had marshalled enough prayer support to bring down the gates of hell. The thought comforted him, and he fully expected the barrier before them to simply melt and give them entrance.

Instead, Ntambo merely moved to one side and disappeared. As the others followed, they, too, disappeared. As Skip and Nancy approached the point of disappearance they saw a narrow crack in the solid rock. It had been masked from their view by a jutting projection of granite. Only close proximity could reveal its presence. As they peered into the crack they saw their companions had lighted their lamps, or turned on their flashlights. They did the same. Squeezing past jutting projections they at last came to a cave where the noise of the mighty falls became only a steady droning in the background. Speech was once more possible.

The cave they had entered was not large, but its irregular walls and ceiling created shadows that shifted in the flickering light of the lamps. It gave Skip an eerie feeling. Nancy's hand in his felt clammy. A glance in her direction convinced him she was feeling the same way he was. It was nothing tangible that could be explained, just a presence that insidiously seeped into the senses – malevolent and threatening.

James was up front where Ntambo was staring down at something below him, "We'll never get down there in one piece," he said.

"What are you talking about?" Ashley responded, moving up to stand beside him. The rest of them did the same. They stared in wonder at the sight that met their eyes.

Just below where they stood was a black hole, only the upper edges of it being lit by the lamplight. Below the edges of light it was so black they got the feeling it wanted to suck them into it. It took an effort of mind to fight the urge to just let it draw them in.

Stepping around the hole, Skip directed his flashlight ahead. Another wonder met his eyes as he became aware of the others gathering around him. Stretching ahead and downward was a narrow tunnel, its floor so smooth and steep Skip knew it would be suicide to attempt to go down it. There was no knowing where it led, or if it ended suddenly at some point to plunge one into an abyss. It was madness even to consider it.

Nancy turned to Ntambo who just stood silently with a mysterious smile on his face, "I hope you don't expect any of us to go down that thing."

Ntambo just smiled without comment, as if to say, "Wait and see."

Mr. Nichol commented, "There has to be a way to proceed safely. If this is the way, and there seems to be no other, there must be a way to follow that tunnel safely."

"I can't imagine how," James said, "I don't suppose we can float down on a cushion of air? That's the only way I can imagine going down it without breaking our necks, and a number of other bones as well."

Ashley, with her usual perception, said, "I don't think we have to worry. If you look carefully at Ntambo, he doesn't seem at all perturbed. I think he is waiting for something." Glancing toward her former teacher, she continued, "I even think Mr. Nichol suspects what the answer to our dilemma is."

Ntambo looked approvingly at Ashley, but still said nothing.

"I don't think Ntambo looking unperturbed means much, Ash. He never looks worried, or anxious. I think it's just a characteristic of his race. Whatever he may be feeling on the inside, he doesn't show it. If you've noticed, Themba acts in much the same way."

"That's true, Nance, but usually when that happens he doesn't have that half-smile on his face, as if he has a secret to share, and just does not care to share it."

"That's very perceptive of you, Ash, and I'm inclined to agree with you." Turning toward Ntambo, Skip challenged, "Out with it, Ntambo. What secret are you keeping from us?"

"With a grin of amusement he said at last, "You'll just have to wait. In the mean time we should all move back. The "secret," as you call it, is not long in coming, and you had better get out of the way."

They all made an involuntary movement away from the intimidating slope before them, being careful to step around the black hole that still gaped menacingly at their feet. Safely away from both dangers, they waited, uncertain what to expect, but strangely comforted by Ntambo's enigmatic smile. Surely he would not be smiling if they were in any immediate danger.

They waited in silence, giving Skip time to notice a subtle change in Nancy's demeanour. She seemed pensive and somewhat troubled. It was a contrast to her usual confident assertiveness.

Drawing her further back toward the entrance, out of earshot of the others, he whispered into her ear, "What's going on, Nancy?"

"What do you mean?"

"Come on, Nance, I can tell you are disturbed about something."

She sighed, "I may just be imagining things."

"Imagining what?"

"Nothing definite, but I can't get those three crosses I saw in my dream out of my head. I know there is something sinister about them."

Skip said, "You think your dream was a warning, and there are actually three crosses down in the chambers below?"

Nancy nodded.

"You think they are going to be used for a sinister purpose?"

She nodded again.

"Nancy, you *do* know what they are going to be used for, don't you?"

But she shook her head and would say nothing more. Her reaction gave Skip an odd sense of doom, but before he could speculate any more, the "something" they were all waiting for intruded.

It began with a distant sound that seemed to be coming from the black hole. It increased in intensity till they all identified it as a gurgling and splashing of water. Skip did not realize he had been holding his breath till a mighty shaft of water shot out of the black hole and soaked them all to the skin again, then he gasped and spluttered as he choked on the water he had involuntarily drawn into his throat. The others had similar reactions, except for Ntambo and Themba, who apparently had known what to expect. The reason for

Ntambo's warning to keep back from the hole was apparent. The gush of water shooting out of the hole would have jammed them against the ceiling of the cave and spat their broken bodies down the chute. For that was the direction the water took. The walls of the well-like hole must have been angled, so the water flowed naturally in that direction.

After the initial gush, the water more or less swelled out of the hole and ran down the chute like a fast flowing stream.

"We only have a few minutes," Ntambo said urgently, "the water will stop flowing and we will have to wait for several hours before we can try again."

Ashley's face was white as she asked, "You don't expect us to get down *that* way, do you?" But she knew by the look he gave her that that was exactly what he expected,

"It shouldn't be too bad," Nancy said, trying to control the tremor in her voice. "Grams and I went on a trip to New Brunswick once, to the city of Moncton. They had a park there with a water chute. We watched people slide down it, but grams couldn't get me to try it."

James said, "I bet it wasn't as long and twisted as this one appears to be."

Mr. Nichol urged, "I think we had better reserve the chatter for later. As Ntambo says, the flow of water will only last a few minutes."

Ntambo started giving instructions, "Take your back-packs off and hold them in front of you, close to your chest. Skip, you and James go first, and wait to help the girls as they come off the chute at the bottom."

The thought occurred to Skip that no one was likely to be at the bottom to help *him* when he got to the bottom, wherever *that* was. Slipping the straps of his back-pack over his shoulders, he walked past the gushing well and stood near the edge where the water began its journey to the bottom. With a piece of string he tied his flashlight to his back-pack, hugged its bulk to his chest, and hesitated.

"Go!" said Ntambo.

The command sounded loud in the confined space. It acted almost like a physical blow and he found himself hurtling feet first down a winding cataract. It varied in steepness, at times plunging down at a forty five degrees angle; at other times it levelled off to an only slightly downward spiral. For spiral it was; it plunged downward in a circular motion that made Skip dizzy.

This was not the worst of his troubles. The chute was not as smooth as he had at first imagined. Sometimes it dipped so sharply he was actually airborne for some seconds before landing once more and continued his downward journey he knew not where to. Also, due to the irregular nature of the chute, he was either sliding in shallow water or being nearly drowned by the volume of water going over him. At last he landed, sputtering and disoriented, in a roiling pool that in turn spat its contents over its edge to continue on to an unknown destination.

Skip scrambled to get out of the way as James shot out of the shoot, narrowly avoiding a kick to the head by mere inches.

James had just managed to stand upright when they heard the girlish yells of delight or terror as either Nancy or Ashley followed them. Positioning themselves on either side of the chute the two prepared to make their companion's landing slightly less chaotic than their own had been.

It turned out to be Ashley, whose wide eyed expression and open mouth testified to the emotional stress she had experienced on her way down. The boys gripped her by her arms and hoisted her away from the path of the gushing stream. They were just in time to receive Nancy as she hurtled over the edge of the chute and was dumped unceremoniously into the roiling white water. She bore a defiant, rather than a distressed expression, as if she had determined feminine squeals were beneath her. She seemed about to express this attitude to the others, but Skip and James pulled her out of the way of whoever was to follow her. In any case, she would have had to shout to be heard above the noise of the rushing stream.

As they had guessed, Raymond Nichol was the next to come down the chute, then Themba, and finally Ntambo.

Ntambo had barely managed to stand upright when the gushing stream lessened, then ceased altogether, and the relative silence hung in the air like a physical presence.

Skip broke the silence when he said, "We just made it. The water flowed just long enough to get us here."

Ntambo explained, "The next flow of water will not come for another two hous."

"Well, I suggest, before the next gush of water comes down the chute," Nancy said, trying to wring the wetness from her hair, "that we all get out of the pool and try to get dry again." There was not a lot of space in this chamber not occupied by the pool, but it was sufficient for them all to get out, stamp their feet and get their backpacks out of the water.

Mr. Nichol, as though once more faced with a class of students, said, "There is no way we would have survived trying to come down that chute without the water. It shot us over the rough places, and prevented injury."

"We'll never be able to go back out the same way," Nancy said, "Even if we managed to climb those impossible drops, the water flow would sweep us back down again before we could get to the top."

"We'll have to find another way out," Ashley said. "However, the people who use this place must know of other entrances and exits."

Skip interrupted the flow of speculation, "Have you noticed something strange?" he asked.

'What?"

"We've turned off our flashlights, Ntambo and Themba have not lighted their lamps, and yet this place is still full of light."

"He's right," James said, "we're so deep underground the light could not possibly come from outside. There must be something else causing the light."

"That's not too hard to guess," Raymond Nichol said.

They saw Mr. Nichol was examining the walls of the chamber, "The rock here is full of crystalline content. The light is reflective. There must be a light somewhere."

Themba pointed, saying nothing.

Following the direction of Themba's finger Mr. Nichol examined the wall in that area. Behind a jutting rock formation, he found a small lamp. The crystals in the walls multiplied the effect of the lamp's tiny flame and filled the chamber with light.

Ntambo merely smiled, as if he had known this all the time and was amused at his companions' process of discovery.

"You know, of course," Ashley asked, "what this means? It means that we have been expected. Whoever they are who inhabit these caves knew we were coming. They're making sure we find our way. I find that rather ominous."

"I don't think I ever believed we would take them by surprise," Skip said. "And I agree with you, Ash. It *is* an ominous sign. Have you noticed there hasn't been any obvious attack of the enemy since we left the village? I think their intent was to lure us here. I think they have something rather nasty waiting for us."

James said sarcastically, "Well, thanks Skip. That was really encouraging. Now we can go and meet our fate with confidence."

"Sarcasm doesn't suit you, James," Nancy said. "Skip is just preparing us for what we will have to face."

The shadow Skip had noticed before crossed her eyes again. He had the distinct impression she was withholding something from him – from them all. He was certain it had something to do with the dream she had dreamed last night. It must have been something to do with the three crosses her dream had revealed to be in one of the chambers.

Just the presence of those crosses in this habitation of evil, if Nancy's dream proved accurate, was disturbing enough. That Jesus had died on the cross for his own sins was a precious thought to him; to have that cross enthroned in a den of evil was a mockery. However, he sensed Nancy's secretiveness was over something far more ominous than mere mockery. He tried not to be hurt that she was withholding something from him. Knowing her as he did, she no doubt had a good reason for holding something back. At least, that was what he tried to convince himself of. He determined to put it out of his mind for the present and concentrate on what lay ahead.

The thought had barely crossed his mind when a once familiar voice echoed from some place hidden from their eyes, "You should not have come here. You have no idea how much danger you are in. You will never get out of here alive."

The voice belonged to none other than their old friend, Roger Wilson.

Chapter 22

Imprisoned

The realization it was his old friend's voice speaking to them at first delayed Skip's reaction. He and the others had come this far for this specific reason, to rescue Roger from the powers of darkness. Still, to find him so soon after entering this domain surprised him, and it caused a thrill of alarm. When things went smoothly in spiritual warfare, Joshua had warned him, it usually meant the enemy was preparing a trap.

"Come out and let us see you, Roger. There is no need to hide."

The shimmering crystals in the walls made Roger's appearance seem magical. The reflected light masked the jutting outcrop that had hidden him from view.

"I am not hiding, Skip. I actually came to find you. Not that it will do any good. We're all doomed now."

"What do you mean?" Nancy snapped. "You're one to speak of doom after all the trouble you've caused."

Skip squeezed her hand as if to prevent her from saying anything else: "Let him speak, Nance. Can't you see how different he is from the last time we saw him?"

Roger Wilson was indeed different. More accurately, he was more like the Roger they had known before the evil of witchcraft had captured his mind.

For one thing he was dressed differently. Gone were the black robes of a wizard; in their place he wore khaki shorts and safari jacket, conventional socks and rubber-soled sandals. For another, behind the spectacles his eyes reflected the intelligence of the Roger they had once known. In spite of this, the gloom and despair in his eyes drew a shadow over his entire countenance. He looked sad and defeated. Regardless, the glimmer of his friend more as he had known him before was heartening. It stirred a hope in him that their efforts to rescue him may not be hopeless after all. At least they did not have to fight Roger's hostility any more.

Roger stared at Mr. Nichol, and some of the hostility resurfaced, "What are you doing here? I thought you were in some kind of lunatic asylum."

"I was," the former teacher and deceiver said, "For many months I was demon-possessed, just as you are."

The brutal statement surprised Skip, but it drew no denial from Roger, only a question, "And you're not?"

"No! And neither do you have to be. There is deliverance through Christ."

"So I've heard." There was no vestige of hope in the statement.

Ashley asked, "If you are demon-possessed, why do you seem so normal now?"

"They don't always plague me. They become active when I have to do their bidding."

"And what is that?" Skip asked.

"You'll see," Roger said, and turned with a gesture to follow him.

Donning their back-packs they made no protest, and set out in obedience. This time Ntambo brought up the rear. Their way was now lighted by a lamp in Roger's hand. It seemed likely to Skip he had been sent to bring them to the domains below.

The tunnel led downward for some time, then levelled off. At times they had to bend and almost crawl; at other times they could walk upright, and see holes at regular intervals. From these holes a waft of air stirred the girls' hair as they passed.

Presently the tunnel widened into a cave, not large, but filled with small stalactites and stalagmites – their columns shimmered with reflected light. At the extreme end of the cave they came to a ledge that overlooked a vast chamber such as Skip had never imagined before.

Below them was an amphitheatre with a natural shelf of rock acting like a stage where speakers could command the attention of any crowd gathered below. The scene was awe-inspiring. Whoever inhabited this place had taken full advantage of the natural phenomena created by the crystalline content of the rock. The stalactites and stalagmites, and the extensive walls of the chamber scintillated with rainbow colours. Skip guessed lamps had been placed beneath glass globes of varying colours to create this spectacular effect.

Roger turned and regarded them all with an ominous expression. When he spoke there was a tremor in his voice, "I have to take you down now. The leaders want to welcome you."

Despite his words, he sounded more like he was announcing their imminent execution. Skip had never known Roger to act in this way before. It was as if the shadow of death loomed over him. Following this pronouncement he turned and led them down a steep spiral staircase.

No one spoke, for two reasons. First, the steepness of the descent required complete concentration. Even though the steps were well constructed they were extremely narrow, and there was no railing to hang onto. Second, the ominous tone of Roger's words made them all feel like they were marching toward their doom.

So when they reached the amphitheatre at the bottom of the staircase, what they found there was so much more of a surprise. There were perhaps five hundred people gathered there all looking toward them as they approached. That was not remarkable. What was remarkable was the complete normalcy of every individual they were able to make eye contact with. The crowd parted to allow them passage toward the base of the naturally raised platform. There stood what appeared to be a mild-mannered fuddy-duddy professor type. To one side exactly as Nancy had described it from her dream, was a throne constructed out of human bones and skulls. There was no one on it, but as she had intimated before it seemed to have been designed for Satan himself.

They had all expected, with the possible exception of Raymond Nichol, to find the typical gathering of witches and wizards in their flowing robes and conical hats. What they found was quite different. They were dressed as they would have been in their own living rooms and in the normal pursuit of their everyday lives. They also seemed to represent every nation on the face of the earth.

Noticing the expression of wonder on Skip's face, Roger moved closer and whispered conspiratorially into his ear, "Don't be fooled. This is all part of the deception."

Roger's words caused Skip conflicting emotions. On the one hand he felt joy that his old friend was once more acting like the friend he once knew. On the other hand there was something hopeless in Roger's demeanour, as if he had discovered the truth too late and had given up all hope of deliverance.

There was no more time for reflection for he found himself standing before the mild-mannered professor type. He was gazing at Skip with the curiosity and interest of a scientist observing the behaviour of a lab-rat.

"So this is the red-headed boy wonder we have all been hearing about." There was a note of disappointment in his voice, as if he had been expecting someone more charismatic, and not this gangly adolescent whose only remarkable feature was his curly red hair.

"You are aware that you have caused us all a great deal of trouble?" he said. "You have caused more trouble than one would have expected from someone of your kind."

Skip found himself irritated by the man's tone of contempt. Something rose up within him that caused him to speak out boldly, "I hope so," he said. "I hope I have caused you more trouble than you know, and will cause you more trouble than you can ever imagine."

Skip was astounded at his own words. He had had no intention of responding in such a manner. He had to believe the Holy Spirit was involved, and had given him the words to speak. He had no time to reflect if his words were either kind or consistent with the Christian faith, but a fleeting thought passed through his brain. Perhaps the words were not directed at the fuddy-duddy professor at all, but at the demonic entity that controlled him.

The professor, as Skip now thought of him, seemed stunned by the response from someone he considered to be no more than a boy. He chose a distraction rather than a direct answer to Skip's word. In a tone of rebuke he said to Roger, "You didn't tell me your friend was so objectionable, especially considering he is encroaching on territory not his own. And you haven't even thought to introduce him, or to inform him who I am."

Roger cowered at the rebuke, "I... I was waiting for an opportunity," He said. "I think you know this is Skip Jordan. The girls are Ashley and Nancy, and Mr. Nichol..."

The professor cut him off, "I am well aware of who Raymond Nichol is, a traitor to the cause."

"I don't know who the others are," Roger said apologetically.

"They are Ntambo," Skip cut in, "and Themba his nephew. They too are soldiers of the army of light. This is the army that will finally defeat you."

Skip was vaguely aware that Nancy, Ashley and James were looking at him in astonishment, as if he was displaying a side of his nature they never knew existed. Of a truth, he was as astonished as they were. Perhaps Joshua back in Canada, Aunt May and the others across the gorge, and the host of praying people in the scattered villages were having an effect upon him. He was sure of one thing: this uncharacteristic boldness was not coming from him.

It appeared as if Skip's words triggered a fear in Roger of some impending doom, for he said quickly, "This is professor Lucifer Andronicus. He is the Chief Sorcerer, heading up all activities here."

Suddenly the professor's mild manner evaporated. A malevolent glow emanated from his eyes. A phrase current among his schoolmates occurred to Skip as he observed the transformation: "No longer Mr. Nice Guy."

Indeed, the man seemed to grow taller and his gaze enveloping the small band of Christians distilled into pure hatred, "You do not know whom you are dealing with. You are doomed. You have come here thinking to rescue this pitiable creature," he pointed in Roger's direction, "but you are powerless to rescue even yourselves. You will die here, but first you will experience the torments of knowing what we are doing to your Christian beliefs."

It was a shocking monologue but did not go unchallenged. Ntambo, spoke up, bold and courageous, looking directly into the professor's glowing eyes. Scripture rolled off his tongue as he pronounced his own judgment, "And you," he declared, *are like springs without water and clouds blown by a storm. A place in the blackest darkness has been kept* for you. You *are like wild waves of the sea, tossing up their own shameful actions like foam.* You *are like stars that wander in the sky. A place in the blackest darkness has been kept for* you. You will *suffer the punishment of eternal fire, as an example for all to see.* (2 Peter 2:17; Jude 13; Jude 7 – NCV)

The glow in the professor's eyes died at Ntambo's words. He seemed to shrink back into his former mild-mannered demeanour.

He nevertheless put an end to what he evidently considered was a useless exercise. A hand waved toward the gathered crowd drew a dozen pre-selected men who, it turned out, were assigned to escort the intruders to an as yet unknown destination. It was no surprise to Skip that the place they were escorted to was a prison, one without gates and bars, but with equally effective means of holding them captive. They were ushered into a cave and one of their escorts, a handsome man with pleasant features, and a mane of golden hair, drew a wand from inside his shirt. A wave of the wand seemed to produce no effect. Nothing visible appeared to prevent them from leaving. After the escort had departed, however, Nancy tried to move into the passageway and slammed into an obstruction. The wave of the wand had created an invisible barrier. They were, after all in the domain of demonic activity. Magical activity was only to be expected.

From previous experience Skip knew that the barrier was a lie, and the truth would always find a way of counteracting its power. For now, he decided, there was no point breaking out. They had nowhere to go, and they needed time to reflect and discuss their situation.

Nancy said, "I should have known they'd use magic. I could have saved my nose from serious injury if I'd been thinking."

Nancy's attempt at humour produced a few chuckles, but Ashley was more concerned about something else. Turning to Roger, she asked, "What are you doing here with us? I thought you were part of all this... this magical stuff."

"Not any more, I'm not. I've been stripped of all my powers, and I'm afraid there's no hope for me, or for you either."

"What do you mean?"

"I mean," Roger said, "there is only one end for those who have second thoughts about their involvement in this devilish business."

"And what would that be?"

"It can only be death! And believe me it won't be simply that we will die. They will concoct some evil scheme to make it memorable."

"And how have you offended them?" Ashley asked.

"I've told you. I've had second thoughts about all this. No, more than that, my eyes have been opened to what's really going on here, as well as the whole witchcraft thing that Mr. Nichol got me into." He glared at his former teacher.

Raymond Nichol spoke up defensively, "I was as deceived as you were, but I'll admit I went into it willingly. It seemed the only good way to punish those who had betrayed me in that church I attended long ago. But, like you, my eyes have been opened."

"Does that mean you now believe in Jesus?" Skip asked Roger.

"Well, not exactly."

"What do you mean, not exactly?"

"Well, I believe everything you say about Him is true. None of the things they teach in this place would be necessary if the Gospel you preach were not true. They have hundreds of ways to twist the truth.

"And then there is professor Lucifer Andronicus."

"What about him?"

"That's not his real name, or at least, it's not the name his mother gave him."

"The moment I heard it," Nancy said, "I knew it was phoney."

"It's not exactly phoney," Roger said. "It describes him perfectly."

When the others raised their brows quizzically, he continued, "Andronicus is a word meaning "wind." So the professor's name basically means: wind of Lucifer, implying that he has the *spirit* of Lucifer – the devil. And, believe me he may look mild and harmless, but there are times you could swear you can see the devil in him."

Skip said, "I think I saw that briefly when I told him he would finally be defeated by the army of light."

"Yes, you did tell him didn't you?" Ashley said with a touch of wonder. "I don't think any of us have seen you act like that before. Whatever came over you? "

"I'm not sure," Skip said. "it was like Someone else was using my tongue. I felt something well up in me and the words just came out."

Ntambo, who had stood silently in a corner of the cave till now, stepped forward, "It was the Spirit of God speaking through you. You would not have been able to overcome the power that is working in that man by yourself. There is something evil working in him, even the devil himself. You saw how he reacted to your words."

"I also saw how he reacted to *your* words, Ntambo," James said. "You almost shut him down when you quoted all that Scripture."

"It was the Spirit of God who shut him down," Ntambo said, and retreated back into silence.

Nancy reached for Skip's hand, "So, what's going to happen to us now? Is Roger right? Are they really going to kill us?" The tremor in her voice communicated her fear to the others, and in a manner, passed it on to them all."

Raymond Nichol answered Nancy's query, "I don't think so. At least I don't think they are going to kill us yet. From what this Andronicus fellow said, I think we are first going to be shown all they are doing to pervert the Gospel. As Roger said, their efforts to twist the Gospel message are evidence of the truth and power of it. If it were not true, they would not go to so much trouble to undermine it."

"But they do intend to kill us eventually?" James asked.

"Yes, I think that is their intention," Mr. Nichol said.

....

Aunt May and Angela Nichol stood together holding onto the railing overlooking Victoria Falls.

"I think I understand," Angela said, "why the natives call these falls 'The Smoke That Thunders.' They have a much more graphic way of naming places, don't you think?"

"I do," Aunt may replied, "I've heard them call a moped 'Isi-tu-tu-tu,' referring to the noise it makes. But I don't think your mind is much occupied with the Victoria Falls, or how the natives refer to it. I think your mind is occupied with something far more personal. Am I right?"

"You are very perceptive, though I don't suppose it would be too hard to guess. I confess I am worried about Raymond, and the others, too, of course. I think they are in mortal danger."

Aunt May glanced at this beautiful young woman's silhouette, "And on top of everything else, it is all happening on your honeymoon."

"It is happening on your honeymoon, too." Angela returned.

"Yes, but my husband is safe and sound in the cabin, and yours is somewhere out there facing who knows what onslaughts from the enemy."

"But you also have your nephew, an adopted daughter, and a close friend of both of them. You can't tell me you are not carrying a heavy burden of prayer and concern for all of them."

"You'll get no argument from me about that," Aunt May said. "So I guess you and I are sisters in more than one way. The Lord has no doubt put us together so we can bear each other's burdens, and so lighten each of our loads."

Angela quoted: *Bear one another's burdens, and thereby fulfill the law of Christ.* (Galatians 6:2 – NASB)

After that there was a comfortable break in their conversation, until Angela asked, "So why are we standing here then? I don't imagine it is to watch the falls. There's a wonderful view from just about anywhere along here, even from our cabins. You and Reginald seem to be taking turns gazing at some point above the falls. And you spend hours here. Also, you keep using those binoculars." She indicated the powerful lenses hanging around Aunt May's neck. Is there any reason you are doing this, beyond your love of the outdoors? If there is, I'd be happy to take a turn."

Aunt May did not reply immediately. She turned her gaze on this lovely young woman who had married a former wizard for two reasons. She loved him, and she had heard God's voice urging her to do so. She deserved to be taken into their confidence.

Pointing above the falls, she directed Angela gaze toward a small hill with piles of rocks at its summit, "Ntambo has made an arrangement with us in case of an emergency. He doesn't know how he will get there, but he will make the attempt to place a red linen cloth, secured by a rock, at the top of that hill. Perhaps you've seen it wrapped around his middle. Reginald and I are taking turns to watch that hill in case the others get into some real trouble."

"OK, I get it. So what are you going to do if the red linen cloth suddenly appears at the top of the hill?"

"We've informed the local police that our friends are exploring, and may need to be rescued if they get into trouble. They have access to a helicopter if it is needed.

"But what if the trouble they are in is in some hidden place?"

Aunt May dug into the pocket of her jeans, retrieving a crumpled piece of paper, "Ntambo gave us Mazimbi's detailed instructions of how to get where they most likely will be. "We'll do what we can to rescue them, if the need arises."

Angela sighed, "It's very dangerous what they're attempting, isn't it?"

"It is *very* dangerous," Aunt May said.

Chapter 23

School of Seduction

It seemed odd to be imprisoned in a cave with no visible means of confinement.

They could see into the corridor and occasionally see people passing, but any attempt to exit the cave was met by an impassable barrier. It was undetectable, but solid.

Further exploration revealed a passage to a smaller cave that provided some privacy for the girls. They had no idea how long they would be confined, but it seemed reasonable to make use of what comforts were available. They dragged their back-packs into it and hung a rug over the entrance.

Breathing did not seem to be a problem. However deep these caves were under the surface there was an adequate flow of air to sustain however many people lived here. Skip doubted the five hundred or more people they had seen in the main chamber were the full complement of residents. If they survived much longer, he suspected hundreds, or thousands more would emerge. They were likely outnumbered a thousand to one. Escape would be well-nigh impossible.

"How long do you think they will keep us here?" James asked.

Raymond Nichol said. "Until they are ready to show us what they're up to in this place. Whatever it is it can't mean anything good for the Christian Church."

"But why would they...?" Nancy cut off her question as the answer came to her, "Of course, they can tell us anything they like since they don't intend for us to leave."

"Exactly," Roger said. "I told you, you shouldn't have come here. We are all doomed now. And it's my fault. What a fool I was to believe all those cheap tricks Mr. Nichol showed us were the way to power." He glared once more at his former teacher.

Skip spoke with in a conciliatory tone, "You were deceived, Roger, as was Mr. Nichol. You were both victims. It is no good playing the blame game. As for why we came, isn't friendship a good enough reason?"

"But you had no way of knowing I was having second thoughts. You could have come here only for me to betray you and blast you with all the demonic power at my disposal."

"Which you no longer have," Ashley observed.

"Yes, it is a power I no longer have. Believe me I am glad to be rid of it. I came to see it was not I who had the power, but the power that had me. Still, it was a risk for you to come here. However did you manage it? This place is half-way across the world from Canada."

"We'll explain that later, but let me answer your question. We came here because of a secret power we all have."

"And what is that?"

"I think I can explain it best by quoting something from the Bible: *If we are out of our minds, it is for God. If we have our right minds, it is for you.The love of Christ controls us, because we know that One died for all, so all have died.Christ died for all so that those who live would not continue to live for themselves. He died for them and was raised from the dead so that they would live for him.*[lxiii]

"Our secret power is the love of Christ. It is a power that compels us to act in ways that would normally be beyond our ability and seem like madness to anyone outside the Grace of God.

Roger sounded disgusted, "Why on earth didn't I believe you when you first told me these things?"

"You were drunk with power," Mr. Nichol said. "I know all about it since it happened to me. Of course, it was all a delusion. As you said, the power we were promised was a trap, so it could take control of us."

"So let me understand this, Roger," Skip said. "You now believe the Gospel? You believe Jesus died on the cross for your sins, and that he rose again to come and live inside you? So why are your eyes so empty of hope? Your whole attitude is one of doom."

"Because it is too late," Roger said. "Christ will never receive me now. Isn't there something in the Bible about the unforgivable sin? You have no idea how deep I went into the things of darkness."

"That is a very specific sin, Roger. It applies only to those who speak against the Holy Spirit and finally reject Christ. The Holy Spirit revealed to you how false witchcraft is, and all the other deep things of Satan, so you obviously have not committed the unforgivable sin. The Holy Spirit is still at work in your life."

Further conversation ended when their escort arrived to conduct them to some undisclosed destination. They all bore a smile that seemed to imply some secret knowledge that did not bode well for their charges.

They were taken first to a place where they could attend to their personal needs. It was built over what appeared to be a bottomless pit, with separate facilities for men and women. It was a great relief to them all. These caves had obviously been inhabited for a long time, perhaps hundreds of years. Every human need seemed to have been provided for. It was still unclear how food was brought here, especially for so many people. If Skip's guess had been correct the amount of food needed would be considerable.

It became evident as they trudged along they were being taken to the chamber where they had first been introduced to Lucifer Andronicus. Along the way Roger edged closer to him and spoke in a conspiratorial tone, "Skip, I need to warn you of something. There is a girl you will meet soon. Her name is Angelica. Do not be put off by the way she talks to us. She has to be somewhat abusive so she won't be discovered."

Skip said, keeping his voice low, "I'm not sure I know what you're talking about, Roger. Why would this girl put on something like that?"

"Come now Skip, don't act like a dimwit. You must know what's going on here. When I started to have second thoughts and considered getting out of here, I wasn't careful enough. They soon figured me out. From that time on I've been doomed. I'm not sure what exactly they have planned for me, but I know it's not good. Angelica is in the same position I am, except that she has been much wiser than I have. She has to pretend she is still committed to the cause."

Skip had been watching Roger's face as he spoke, "And what is your interest in this girl, Roger?"

Roger blushed, but tried to hide it, "Oh, nothing..."

Skip chose not to press the matter. However, Angelica's presence as a secret dissenter intrigued him. To find two people in this den of deception, Roger, and now Angelica, suggested there may be more. Professor Andronicus may be under the impression he had the total devotion of those under his control, but the very nature of a lie lays it open to exposure. The truth has a way of revealing itself. Unless one has an entirely seared conscience, the hunger of the human heart will inevitably seek it out. Perhaps this was indeed a place where haters of God were concentrated. Even so, there would be exceptions. Fear of reprisal may prevent them from exposing themselves, but his gut feeling was that there would be more.

And then again, professor Andronicus would know this. It is the nature of evil to be continually on the lookout for betrayal. Barring a miracle, anyone entertaining doubts concerning their decision to participate in what was going on in this place, would sooner or later be exposed. And exposure would mean...?

Skip was jolted from his reverie when they entered the main chamber and his ears were assaulted by a shout that sounded like it was coming from a thousand voices. Indeed, there may well have been more than a thousand. The few hundred people they had seen on arrival had swelled to a multitude, filling up the open space beneath the natural podium. However, it was the figure that stood atop that elevated tower that commanded his attention. She was tall and beautiful, though perhaps a trifle thin. She wore a long white robe that reached her ankles. Her features seemed cut from alabaster marble, and her demeanour was one of command. Her dark hair reached to within a foot of the ground.

The fact that Skip could see her so clearly was itself remarkable. He thought it might have something to do with the reflected crystal light of the chamber, but he guessed it was more than that. After all, they were in the company of witches and wizards who may be using their arts, as illusory as they were, to create a close-up view of the speaker even at a distance. A movement from Roger at his side convinced him that this was Angelica, and he immediately understood his friend's fascination with her.

Lucifer Andronicus stood behind her, but it was Angelica that commanded the attention of the crowd. She could have been no more than fifteen years old, yet she spoke with a voice that rang with authority, "Intruders have come into our midst," she said, sweeping an arm in the direction of the newcomers. "They have come, not only to spy on our activities, but to subvert those among us with uncertain commitment to our cause." She took a breath and threw her question at the crowd, "Shall we endure such an invasion of our privacy?"

A deafening roar erupted in answer, "No!"

"Shall we allow them to subvert our cause?"

"No!" came the response once again.

"What, then, shall we do with them?" This last was obviously a rhetorical question, for the crowd waited in anticipation for the answer.

"I'll tell you what we will do," Angelica continued, "We will entertain them."

Silence followed this declaration.

"You know these are followers of the Christ we have sworn by any and every means to oppose. They are members of the Church Christ sent to do His work on earth. So this is how we will entertain them: we will introduce them to all we are doing to pervert the Gospel they are so eager to preach. We will show them how we have sent our agents into the churches to twist and confuse its message. We will reveal to them the "Trojan Horse" we have introduced into the Church, the new Age ideas we have propagated under different names. We will show them the Pagan ideas we have injected into the teaching of the Church. We will reveal the sorcery that is being practiced in the Church under the guise of discovering the unlimited potential each person possesses.

"We will do more," Angelica said with a dramatic sweep of her arm, "We will show them what all of you have come here to learn – how to invade the Church with the occult, subtly introduced with charismatic gifts acquired from our lord, Lucifer. You are the 'angels of light' that will invade the domain of our enemy and turn His followers into puppets under our own control. We will let them roam freely here to explore the different aspects of this great school of deception."

A roar of approval followed Angelica's speech, yet there was an element of wonder in it, too. Were all their secrets to be revealed? Were the hidden mysteries of evil they had sworn never to make known to the uninitiated to be thus revealed to those in the camp of the Enemy?

Angelica was not yet done. She raised her voice a decimal higher, "and then what will we do with them?"

Again, the only response was anticipation.

"Once we have twisted this knife of knowledge into their souls; when they are grieving for the fate of the Church they love, we will deal with them according to our code."

A thrill of comprehension ran through the multitude.

"And what will that be?" Angelica demanded.

If possible, the shout that issued from the crowd was even louder than before, "Death! The sentence upon them is death!"

Through the shiver of fear that passed unbidden through Skip, he thought what a masterful performance this was. If Angelica was, as Roger claimed, a secret dissenter, she could not have been more convincing to the contrary if she had tried.

"They will be given freedom to roam freely," Angelica said above the murmurs of approval, "precisely because there is no escape from this place. No one has ever left here without our approval, and neither will these enemies of our cause. And when they have full understanding of the scope and intensity of the deceptions we are foisting on the Church, they will die."

The strange visual phenomena that operated in this place gave Skip a clear view of the expression on professor Andronicus' face. Standing to one side and slightly behind Angelica, he beamed with delight at Angelica's address. She was obviously being primed for leadership in this habitation of demons, and the mild-mannered professor was closely following her development.

Patting Angelica approvingly on her shoulder, he stepped forward, "So there you have it," he said. "Angelica has ably presented the manner in which we are to deal with these intruders, particularly with the one known as Skip Jordan."

The shocked expression on Skip's face, and of the faces of his friends, was not lost on the professor, "Oh, you did not know your fame had spread abroad, did you, my red-headed wonder boy?" His tone was at once mocking and contemptuous. "Don't be deceived, however. You are not known in the world at large. No one there knows anything about you. You are of no account there.

"But among those in the Craft; among those sworn enemies of the Church, you are quite famous. We know about your miraculous deliverance by the big black man who hid you on the night of your parent's death, and who is with you now. We know of your mother's prayer as she was dying that her God would use you to defeat the powers of darkness. A rather useless prayer in my opinion, though admittedly you have had one spectacular victory against the Wicca division of our forces, and have won a few skirmishes along the way. There are too many of us and we have the prince of darkness on our side, so you will not prevail"

Andronicus seemed no longer to be addressing the crowd, but Skip only, "Your teacher, who is a traitor by the way, was not up to the task of defeating you, but be assured, he will be dealt with appropriately. That snivelling friend of yours will meet his fate as well. I know you thought you were coming here to rescue him, but I assure you, it is a vain hope.

"In fact, we have a singular fate planned for all three of you."

Skip felt Nancy flinch at his side. Whatever dark thoughts had affected her mood since her dream the night before intensified now. She looked terrified and would not meet his gaze.

Lucifer Andronicus now turned to the gathering at large, "You can now all go to your places of instruction." He turned to leave, and then, as if a new thought had occurred to him, he came back and addressed the little group of intruders, "Oh, in case your friend has not informed you, this is indeed a school of seduction."

As if they had not had enough surprises, another was waiting for them. As the crowd dispersed, Angelica swept into view from somewhere at the base of the podium. She came directly up to them and said, "I have been appointed as your guide. I will take you to all the areas of instruction and answer all your questions."

She still maintained her officious stance, but Skip saw her cast a secret glance in Roger's direction. There was no doubt that these two were in silent communication.

....

It was not often Joshua was reduced to the condition he was in at that moment – sobbing and crying out in agonizing supplication to God.

Ensconced as he was in this remote cabin in the woods, living the life of a hermit, he had learned to conduct his spiritual life generally on an even keel. He did not believe many of God's people should live as he lived. Though Christians were not to be part of the world system, they needed to be very much in it, exerting a holy influence on those around them.

In his own case, however, Joshua had been virtually driven by the Spirit into solitude, as Christ had been driven by the Spirit into the wilderness, and John the Baptist into the desert.

In this secluded place he had sometimes been the recipient of visions and dreams, though these were rare. They enabled him to intercede for particular world events, or individual men and women with a unique call upon their lives. Such had been his part in the lives of Skip Jordan and his companions. Young as they were it seemed his Lord delighted to use them. Indeed that was the very reason He chose them. He recalled that Bible passage outlining the manner of God's choosing: *Brothers and sisters, look at what you were when God called you. Not many of you were wise in the way the world judges wisdom. Not many of you had great influence. Not many of you came from important families.But God chose the foolish things of the world to shame the wise, and he chose the weak things of the world to shame the strong.He chose what the world thinks is unimportant and what the world looks down on and thinks is nothing in order to destroy what the world thinks is important.God did this so that no one can brag in his presence.*[lxiv]

The visions and dreams he had been having in the last few days, however, had driven him to his knees for longer and caused him to weep more than he could remember having happened before. Something momentous was about to take place.

The children (for so he still thought of them) were in such great danger as they could never imagine. The forces of evil were gathered in such numbers, and in such a concentration that Joshua could hardly see through them as his vision showed him the great chamber in the hidden caves. It was not just the numbers of demons gathered that caused him distress; What wrung tears from his eyes and caused sobs to wrack his body, was the malicious glee and the triumphant cries that issued from them. This demonic host expected a victory against the forces of Light. Skip and his companions were right in the middle of it.

As if this was not enough, the final vision that passed before his eyes was ten times more horrific than all that had come before. As he knelt on the rough boards of his cabin, his vision focussed on three crosses. They were so real he felt he could touch them. The Central cross could well have been the same on which his Lord had bled and died. The other crosses, too, seemed crafted to bring about agony and death. And then Joshua knew the purpose for which these crosses had been made, and the knowledge caused an agony he could not endure. In a voice that sounded more like a scream, he cried out, "No!. Dear Lord, no! Anything... anything, but not that!"

Chapter 24

The Scarlet Woman

Angelica proved to be a most efficient tour-guide, though the term did not exactly fit what she was doing. This place did not feel like a tourist's paradise; they were increasingly aware that what she showed them was more like a chamber of horrors.

"Not that what we are seeing is anything that *looks* like it," James observed. "Everyone looks so mild and ordinary. It is what they're being trained to do that's creepy."

Nancy reacted, "It's much more than creepy. It is downright evil!" Skip thought her passionate outburst was fuelled by something more than she was willing to reveal. He had caught her staring at him when she thought he was pre-occupied with something else. He thought he had detected a combination of fear and grief in her expression.

"You may think these people are mild-mannered creepy folk," Nancy continued, "But they are dedicated to the destruction of our Faith. Sooner or later, when the training is over, they are going to be let loose on the Church. They will distort its teachings and lead many to stray from the Faith. And as for that witch who is supposed to be our guide, there is nothing mild about her. She is full of venom, and I would sooner trust a snake."

Nancy had chosen to make her remarks in Angelica's absence. She had not been near enough to hear Roger's remarks concerning the girl's deliberate show of hatred for the newcomers. She had also not noticed the secret glances of communication between Angelica and Roger. So she was quite taken aback when the subject of her remarks appeared suddenly from around the corner.

"I am quite flattered by your description of me, Nancy. I must be doing a better job that I thought I was doing."

Nancy swung round to face the girl, her face flushed, "I... I..."

"Don't apologise. That was precisely the impression I was trying to make, but we have to be careful. You have heard the expression, 'the walls have ears?' That may be truer than you realize."

"You mean...?

"Yes, but keep your voice down. Roger and I have been planning our escape for some time, though he seems to have given up hope. The consequences of turning against these people are quite severe."

"You can say that again," Roger said. "And this place is completely escape-proof."

"I must admit, Roger, I have doubts of my own, but we must not despair. Perhaps your friends will come up with something that will get us out of this place."

Skip was impressed with her changed demeanour. He said, "If Roger had not warned me you had misgivings about this place, I would never have guessed it. You gave a sterling performance back there."

"And she'll have to continue to give one if she is not to be discovered," Raymond Nichol said.

Angelica turned to him, "You yourself have been involved in the deep things of Satan, haven't you?"

"Not as deep as seems to be going on here, but deep enough to be powerless to free myself."

"But you have been freed, haven't you?"

"Yes, but not by my own doing, and only by the faith and dedication of someone who would not give up on me."

Angelica sighed, "I'm afraid I have gone too deep to be delivered now. The best I can hope for, and that hope is almost gone, is to get away from here and try to forget the evil I have seen."

It was then Ntambo broke his silence, and asked, "You understand the Gospel, fair one?"

"Yes I do." She stared up into the black man's face, "We all do. It is the one thing we are all taught most carefully, but only in order that we may twist and distort it. I am afraid, though, that though I understand it, and even admire it, I have sunk too low now for it to do me any good."

Ntambo fixed his eyes on her perfect features, "Then you do not understand it as you might. The Gospel has more power than you can imagine."

A light of hope seemed to flare up in her eyes, then died, "I could wish that were true, but you have no idea how far a soul can sink into darkness. However, I cannot discuss this now. I have come to conduct you to another 'Chamber of Learning.' " At that she moved out into the corridor, beckoning for them to follow her.

As gentle and sweet as Angelica's demeanour had been the past few minutes, it changed to the hard and bitter manner that was her only protection against discovery. The mask of hatred had been dropped for a while, but now it was firmly back in place. She could not allow anyone else to see that under the malicious exterior there beat a heart that longed for truth and light.

Nancy sidled up to Skip, and said, "Can you believe this girl? She gives a speech that could wither an oak, and then comes on with this 'understanding the truth,' stuff, but having gone too deep for it to work for her."

Ashley, who was near enough to hear, touched her friend on the shoulder, "Have you noticed the looks Angelica and Roger have been giving each other?"

"Not really. Why?"

"Roger trusts her. Don't you think he would know if she were not genuine?"

Nancy shrugged, "She acts rotten, says rotten things. It's reasonable to expect she's rotten to the core."

Ashley gave some thought to this before speaking, "Are you sure your dislike of her is not just because she is so incredibly beautiful?"

'What do you mean?"

"Do you remember once before, in the valley of the witches, both of us were jealous of Julia? We thought she was charming Skip, and we didn't like it."

Skip had moved ahead by this time to walk beside James, so Nancy was able to speak her mind, "That is not what this is about."

"Are you sure?"

Before Nancy could respond Roger moved up from behind and drew the girls' attention, "I heard what you've been talking about – some of it anyway. You seem suspicious of Angie, Nance?"

"Angie? Is that what you call her?"

"We have, you would say, a connection. But answer my question. You have a problem with her?"

Ashley answered for her friend, "I don't think Angelica is really Nancy's problem."

Nancy jerked her head around, "What on earth do you mean Ash?"

"You haven't been yourself ever since you had that dream." Turning to Roger, she explained, "Nancy had a dream about this place yesterday, and she's been unsettled ever since. I think her reaction to Angelica may be connected to what she saw in her dream."

"What did you see, Nance?"

Nancy was still trying to adjust to Roger's return to his former self. Her memory still flashed images of the vitriolic Roger, the one who cast spells with his wand and lusted after the power witchcraft had offered him. She also remembered the super intelligence she had recognized in him before he had been seduced by the forces of darkness. It was still there, though it was now dulled by the shadow of regret. Would he ever get beyond the remorse of having been deceived? But of course, he didn't expect to get beyond it. She saw in his gaze the despair. Angelica may still have a vestige of hope; in Roger, hope had died. Her voice was gentle when she said, "It doesn't matter Roger. Nothing will be gained by revealing it now."

"Has it got something to do with us getting out of here alive?" Ashley asked.

"I said it doesn't matter. I don't want to talk about it."

"Well, at least tell Skip. He is worried about you."

"I have to keep it a secret – especially from Skip. I want you to promise you'll say nothing to him about this. Don't even *hint* there is anything significant about my dream." She accepted the reluctant nod of their heads as agreement and quickened her pace to catch up with the others.

The chamber they entered was relatively small. Crystalline content in the walls provided adequate light from only two oil lamps set on pedestals on either side of the chamber. There were perhaps thirty students of various ages, seated lotus fashion on the floor. Their instructor was a man who seemed too thin, his sunken cheeks and protruding bones giving his head the appearance of a skull, rather than that of a living person. He was nevertheless passionate about what he was sharing with the group, swinging his arms and stamping his feet for emphasis. But it was not his reed-like voice or his energetic movements that captured Skip's attention.. What stopped him in his tracks and caused an intake of breath was the vivid picture set up behind the instructor.

Skip sensed rather than saw the reaction of his companions. Nancy gasped; Ashley's face set in a mask of astonishment; James mumbled under his breath, "Oh, dear God!" Skip guessed, due to their cultural background, that Ntambo and Themba registered no outward reaction at all, or perhaps they were not aware of the significance of the picture at all. The reason for the shocked reaction of the others was clear to him. They had all recently participated in a Bible study regarding the very image that stared back at them now.

In vivid colours and with a reality only a master artist could create, was the life-size painting of a woman riding a horrific beast. The beast had seven heads, and between them were ten horns protruding from their foreheads. As spectacular as the image of the beast was, the depiction of the woman was even more so. Raised high in one hand was a golden chalice with wine spilling from it. It was a perfect depiction of that described in the seventeenth chapter of the book of Revelation.

Skip dug into his pocket and retrieved his New Testament. He could quote the two verses almost word for word, for the study had made a deep impression upon him. Yet he felt the need to verify that his senses were not deceiving him. Turning the pages till he found the place, he read:

Then the angel carried me away by the Spirit to the desert. There I saw a woman sitting on a red beast. It was covered with names against God written on it, and it had seven heads and ten horns.The woman was dressed in purple and red and was shining with the gold, precious jewels, and pearls she was wearing. She had a golden cup in her hand, a cup filled with evil things and the uncleanness of her sexual sin.[lxv]

There was no doubt the picture was meant to illustrate the verses he had just read. What was a representation of a biblical passage doing in a place dedicated to deception and lies? Skip knew the answer to the question would not turn out to be anything good.

Skip was suddenly assailed with a sense of incredible evil settling over his spirit. Having experienced something similar in the past he immediately cried out in a voice that startled the others. Though he uttered no words, he knew God would interpret his cry as a call for help. The answer came swiftly. As quickly as it had settled on him the evil presence lifted and he felt he could breathe again.

In response to the expressions of alarm on his companions' faces, he said, "I'll explain later."

None of this had escaped Angelica, "You know about this?" she asked

Skip gave her the same answer as he had the others, "We'll discuss this later. Please continue your tour."

....

May was awakened by loud pounding on their cabin door. She and Reginald had elected to have an afternoon nap while Angela kept watch from the railing at the edge of the gorge. They wanted to be ready if Ntambo's signal appeared on the hill opposite, though they had only a vague idea what they would do should one appear.

The pounding continued, and May stumbled to the door, only half awake. Reginald groaned on his side of the bed and merely waited while May opened the door.

Angela stood trembling on the doorstep, "M...May... something is h...happening over there."

"Why, Angela, you are trembling. What has happened?"

"Well..."

"Just come in and tell us what is upsetting you so."

When they were all seated around the small table set in the centre of the room, Angela took a deep breath, "I was watching that rise you pointed out across the gorge when it happened."

"What happened?"

"Something like a cloud and it wasn't smoke. Though it poured out of the ground like smoke from a chimney, it didn't rise like smoke does. It is dark and ominous like a host of demons gathering before some onslaught on humanity."

"Angela, you're not usually as emotional as this. Remember how the Lord used you to bring deliverance to Raymond. Whatever you saw is not beyond the Lord's power."

"I know... it's just that when I asked one of the locals what it was that caused that black cloud he said..."

"What did he say?"

"He said that it only happened when... It only happened when strangers intruded on the domain of the devil. He said his people had always known that beneath the rumbling of the Smoke-That-Thunders, the devil had his lair."

"What else did he say?"

"He said it didn't happen very often, but whenever it did the dark cloud meant the intruders had come and were going to be punished. Oh May! Reggie! Wherever Ray and the others have gone, they are in mortal danger."

Reginald said, "The cloud is still there?"

"It was just before I came to your door."

"So why don't we go and have a look at this cloud." So saying Reginald pushed back his chair and moved toward the door. May put her arm around Angela's shoulders and they followed.

It was now late afternoon and the beginnings of an African sunset began to paint the sky with spectacular hues of gold and orange. Strangely, it tinted the clouds above, but left the brooding dark mass Angela had described, untouched.

May understood why Angela had been so unsettled by the sight. She felt it herself. The interpretation the local man had given would not normally be taken seriously. There were all kinds of stories and superstitions, part of the tribal culture that had no foundation in fact. Considering all Skip and his friends had encountered in the past, and that she herself had encountered, something told her this was an exception. The old adage, 'there is no smoke without fire' may apply in this case. She felt a chill in her bones and she began to reproach herself for letting the young people, for letting any of them, embark on so dangerous an undertaking. After all, they were little more than children. What had possessed her to lend her support to such an undertaking?

At the same time May knew there was nothing she could have done to prevent it. She believed in the Providence of God – she believed He ordered human events, and led his children in a path that would ultimately glorify His name. She must not lose faith. She had to believe that, however dark things may get, God would ultimately get them through this.

That argument held until a cry from Angela brought her attention back to where the dark cloud had been swallowed up by the shades of night. A green glow, luminous and eerie, sent out a tendril that rose up in the night air. It was like an evil finger getting ready to point out an enemy, and it was coming straight toward them.

....

They had visited three 'centres of learning,' as Angelica called them. Though they had seen and heard things that angered them, and filled them with loathing at the way their Christian Faith was being twisted, nothing had made a deeper impression than the life-size pictures displayed at each location. The woman in the pictures was described in the Bible as 'The Mother of Prostitutes' Skip had verified this by reading more of the chapter where she was described. He remembered Reginald explaining this when they were all gathered around the kitchen table back in Canada.

He had read the passage Skip had read that morning:

On her forehead a title was written that was secret. This is what was written: the great babylon mother of prostitutes and of the evil things of the earth

Then I saw that the woman was drunk with the blood of God's holy people and with the blood of those who were killed because of their faith in Jesus.

When I saw the woman, I was very amazed. Then the angel said to me, "Why are you amazed? I will tell you the secret of this woman and the beast she rides—the one with seven heads and ten horns.[lxvi]

Reggie had explained that the woman represented the false church that would rise to prepare the way for the anti-Christ. And the Beast represented the anti-Christ himself who would rule the world for seven years. Here in this habitation of demons, the woman, and the beast she rode were revered. They were being displayed almost as objects of worship.

When they returned to their lodgings Angelica followed them in and again dropped her pretence. The softness returned to her features and her smile rested on them. Skip thought it was going to be hard to trust someone who could change so radically at will.

"You seem to be familiar with the Prostitute riding the Beast," she said as she settled herself on a convenient shelf of rock in their cave.

"She is well known among Bible believers as the false church that will arise at the end of the age," Ntambo said in his deep, measured tones. "She will assist in bringing the Man of Sin to power, and finally be destroyed by him."

Angelica regarded the big man with interest, "You are referring to what Christians refer to as the anti-Christ?"

"Yes, that is his other name." Raising his eyes to the roof of the cave, but apparently seeing right through it, he began to quote Scripture: *Do not let anyone fool you in any way. That day of the Lord will not come until the turning away from God happens and the Man of Evil, who is on his way to hell, appears. He will be against and put himself above any so-called god or anything that people worship. And that Man of Evil will even go into God's Temple and sit there and say that he is God.*

I told you when I was with you that all this would happen. Do you not remember? And now you know what is stopping that Man of Evil so he will appear at the right time.The secret power of evil is already working in the world, but there is one who is stopping that power. And he will continue to stop it until he is taken out of the way. Then that Man of Evil will appear, and the Lord Jesus will kill him with the breath that comes from his mouth and will destroy him with the glory of his coming.The Man of Evil will come by the power of Satan. He will have great power, and he will do many different false miracles, signs, and wonders.He will use every kind of evil to trick those who are lost. They will die, because they refused to love the truth. (If they loved the truth, they would be saved.)For this reason God sends them something powerful that leads them away from the truth so they will believe a lie.So all those will be judged guilty who did not believe the truth, but enjoyed doing evil' "[lxvii]

When Ntambo stopped speaking Angelica's face reflected mingled shame and remorse, "I no longer believe the lie," she said.

Ntambo's gaze was full of compassion as he asked, "But do you believe the Truth, child?"

"I *know* the truth. Strange as it may seem we are taught the truth in this place. We have to know what the truth is in order to distort it. Do I believe it? I suppose I do, but I cannot see how it applies to me. I have been introduced to the deep things of Satan. There can be no redemption for me."

"Then you do not know the truth as it should be known," Ntambo said, his large hand touching her shoulder reassuringly, "But, do not fear, child, you *will* understand, for the God of Heaven has had mercy on you."

A thrill passed through Skip as he felt God's Presence enter the cave like a gentle breeze. He glanced at the others and knew they had sensed the same thing. Even Roger seemed to feel it. For the first time since coming here a faint light of hope shone from his eyes. He was gazing at Angelica with something akin to wonder. Her face seemed to glow in a manner that defied description.

A holy hush settled in their midst and Skip knew he was witnessing a miracle. Angelica was in the throes of being reborn. However, he also knew that, by virtue of the new life entering her soul, the sentence of death had also settled upon her. Barring a miracle, Angelica would never get out of this place alive.

Chapter 25

Chambers of Deception

In the days following Angelica's transformation she introduced the group to many "centres of learning." These left them all shaken for she explained how each one was meant to train people in the art of deception. Each group would target some specific teaching from the Bible. They would study how to twist the teaching so it no longer represented clear Bible truth. The plan was to present it in such a way that it still *sounded* like the Truth.

The trainees would then be sent out to infiltrate churches, pretend to be genuine converts to the faith. They would then sow their subtle lies from within. Skip remembered the story Mr. Nichol had told of how the enemy had used a wooden horse to get their soldiers inside the city of Troy. This was precisely the tactic being used against the Church.

That Angelica was allowed to explain all this to them was proof they would never be allowed to leave here alive. As she had said in her first dramatic speech in the main chamber, explaining the deception was a form of mental torture. Once their captors had caused them enough anguish of mind and grief of heart, there was no longer any reason to keep them alive. Skip guessed their deaths had already been planned. Anyone who entertained thoughts of turning would have ample warning of the consequences of doing so.

Angelica in particular would be made an example of, for there was no longer any hope for her to pretend allegiance to the powers of darkness operating here. The light of love was now upon her; she had lost the ability to pretend. The students gathered at each venue began to look at her strangely, their expressions changing from that of fearful respect to suspicion. Angelica, however, seemed oblivious to this change of attitude and conducted the tour with skill, displaying a store of knowledge that seemed remarkable given her tender years.

At one venue the instructor was smartly dressed in a business suit, as were those under his tutelage. The whole thing was set up like a business seminar.

Angelica answered their unasked question, "Every effort is made to make the training as realistic as possible. They are wearing business suits because their job is to introduce sorcery into the church through business seminars."

"How in the world are they going to do that?" Ashley asked.

Angelica motioned to the instructor who was presently using a pointer to indicate a diagram displayed on a white board. He nodded his head in acknowledgment, finished the explanation in progress, and came over.

He was a handsome man, such as you might find in the executive boardroom of a thriving company in the business district of a large city. He exuded confidence, flashing a smile that acknowledged them all but singled out the girls in particular.

"This is Allan Maitland," Angelica said. "He is in charge of the Seduction through Business module of our school. He will answer your question Ashley." Turning again to the man she said, "Our friend wants to know how conducting business seminars can be used to seduce Christians, and pervert the teachings of the church."

Allan Maitland's smile broadened, "Elementary, my dear." He was obviously turning on the charm. "It is simply a matter of getting to church members who have to attend business seminars sponsored by the companies they work for. In that way we can get to them outside the walls of the church. When they go back to church they will go with adjusted attitudes and different ideas. These attitudes will ultimately undermine the traditional values and Biblical principles they have been taught from their youth."

James asked, clearly horrified by what this man was saying, "You mean you will teach doctrines against their Christian convictions? How are you going to convince them to accept ideas that are clearly against their faith in Christ and what they know the Bible teaches."

Allan gave James a condescending look, "Oh, they won't *know* the ideas they are taking back are un-Christian."

"You mean you will convince them that your teaching is better than Bible teaching?"

"No, that is not what I mean."

Raymond Nichol interrupted, "What he is saying James, is that the business seminars will present New Age ideas in such a way they will *appear* to be the same as what the Bible teaches. They will teach sorcery, and call it faith. They will teach unlimited human potential and Positive thinking, passing it off as a way to live fuller, more effective Christian lives. Those attending the seminars will hardly realise they are shifting their focus from faith in God, to faith in themselves."

"Very well put," Allan said, giving Mr. Nichol a look that clearly accused him of being a traitor to the cause. "You see," he turned his gaze back to the young people, "there are many Christians who earn their living in the world of business. They naturally want to be successful. The companies they work for require them to attend business seminars to increase their effectiveness and make more money for the company. So we get to teach them ideas from the occult – doctrines of demons, if you like – only we call them by different names."

"So you tell them that these teachings are better than Christian teaching?"

"No, we convince them that these ideas are the *same* as what the church teaches, only in a more interesting an effective way."

Nancy gave a snort of disgust, "That... that is... evil!"

Allan Maitland grinned, "It is, isn't it? You have no idea how much delight I take in twisting the teachings of the Church. You can call it pay-back for what those hypocrites did to me when I was a boy."

Skip realized this man's story was not very different from what had happened to his former teacher Raymond Nichol. Bitterness over what so-called Christians had done to him had driven him into a thirst for revenge, and ultimately into witchcraft. Some regrettable incident in Allan Maitland's past had caused him to follow the same path.

Mr. Nichol's response was striking in that it was gentle, and filled with compassion, "I fully understand how you feel. I myself went down that road. If it had not been for a singular act of God's mercy I would have perished in my bitterness. I went over the edge into madness. It was not God who betrayed you, Allan, only those professing to serve Him. You know the Truth, or you would not know how to pervert it. It is not too late. Turn to Him now."

Skip could hardly believe the suddenness of the change that came over the instructor's features, or how extreme they were. The smiles and the charm disappeared completely. In their place a mask of hatred took hold. There was also malicious delight in what he said next, "Oh yes, Mr. High-and-Mighty-Nichol, traitor. You turn to the Enemy and expect to escape your fate?"

"What fate are you talking about, and who are you calling the Enemy?"

"You must know you are fated to die. You could not possibly have come here and expected to get out alive. But it is not an ordinary death you are going to die. Oh no, it is going to be singular in the extreme." His eyes strayed to Skip, and then to Roger, "You will not suffer it alone, either."

No one but Ntambo noticed the gasp that issued from Nancy at the instructor's declaration.

Mr. Nichol said, "You are talking in riddles Allan. Why don't you just come out and tell us what you are referring to?"

"That is not my place. You will find out soon enough. However, I will answer your other question. Who do you think the enemy is? It is Jesus Christ. He is the One who ruined my life. If he had not come there would not have been a Christian Church, and there would not have been a bunch of hypocrites who turned a blind eye to someone who abused little boys."

Skip could no longer hold his tongue. The drama being played out here was a tragedy, and he no longer saw Allan Maitland as a perpetrator, but as a victim. He said, "Sir, the Lord Jesus is not your enemy. He is your Friend. He wants to offer you forgiveness and new life. Those who abused you were not His true followers."

Now the eyes of the embittered instructor fixed themselves on Skip, "Oh, now the golden boy Skip Jordan speaks. Oh yes, don't be surprised. I know about how the Enemy saved you from death when you were only a small boy. Why would he save you, and let me be abused in a place bearing His name. Why didn't He save *me*?"

"He still wants to save you," Skip said. He wants to save you from your bitterness. He wants to set you free from the hatred that is twisting your soul."

Allan Maitland spat contemptuously on the ground, "Even if that were true, it is far too late. I must get back to my class." He turned and strode confidently back to his class, once more the confident, charming executive.

There was a stunned silence amongst the group as the tragedy of one man's life sank in. Angelica, as deeply affected as the others, said, "There are many here just like him, but we must proceed. There is much more to see and hear." So saying she led them along paths and through tunnels to several other 'centres of learning,' On the way she explained further, "Actually, this whole place is modelled after the apostle Paul's declaration in one of his letters. He says: *Such men are not true apostles but are workers who lie. They change themselves to look like apostles of Christ.This does not surprise us. Even Satan changes himself to look like an angel of light. So it does not surprise us if Satan's servants also make themselves look like servants who work for what is right. But in the end they will be punished for what they do.*[lxviii] From here the trainees are sent out to infiltrate the church, presenting themselves as sincere followers of Christ."

"And that is what this Allan character is training his students to do?" Ashley asked.

"They are all doing that here, Ashley. Allan's task is to sell the church on the idea that success is to be sought at any cost, even if that means buying into methods that are not taught in the Bible. Business practices based on ancient sorcery, and rooted in the occult, are re-stated and made to sound scientific. They are passed off as part of human psychology, and therefore the most natural means on the way to success."

"So," Skip commented, "success is the name of the game."

"Yes, those sent to infiltrate the church will emphasise being successful. They will recommend any means to bring numbers of people into the church – except place emphasis on sin, repentance and salvation.

"I heard of one earnest preacher who attended a ministerial meeting. A very successful minister was there who had one of the largest churches in the district. He was going on about how God wanted every Christian to be successful, and that success was to be measured by the number of people in your church. If your church was small and struggling, you were clearly a failure.

"The preacher admitted he would love to win great numbers to Christ, but that numbers did not necessarily indicate success. He wanted everyone who came to be soundly converted to Christ, and be passionate about sharing the Gospel. He then asked the minister of the large church what he thought of Jeremiah. 'Did you know,' he asked, "that Jeremiah never had anyone *ever* respond positively to *anything* he ever preached, even though he was a true messenger of God, and spoke only what God told him to speak?"

The minister ignored the question, so the preacher continued, "In spite of his apparent failure to influence his audience Jeremiah was a success. His success was not measured by the number of people who responded positively to his message, but how faithfully he discharged what God had called him to do.

"I am sure you know what God said to Jeremiah when he was in prison. He said: *Then the word of the LORD came to Jeremiah the second time, while he was still confined in the court of the guard, saying, "Thus says the LORD who made the earth, the LORD who formed it to establish it, the LORD is His name, 'Call to Me and I will answer you, and I will tell you great and mighty things, which you do not know.'"*[lxix]

Skip was amazed at Angelica's knowledge of Scripture, and he told her so.

"It shouldn't surprise you, Skip. We do not only study methods of deception here. We have to be thoroughly acquainted with sound Biblical teaching. If we were not, we would not be able to make subtle changes to the message without the average church-goer being aware of it."

"I would think," Mr. Nichol said, "it is risky for the leaders here to do that. After all, they are actually giving them the truth before they teach them to preach a lie. There is the danger that the students would respond to the truth, and refuse to pervert the truth."

"I think they know that," Angelica said, "and they are willing to take the risk – for two reasons. First, they only enrol people who are already disenchanted with the church. They choose people who are bitter, and filled with hatred for the Church. They are people who have already rejected the truth. Their only thought is revenge."

"And what is the second reason?"

"The second reason is that once anyone arrives here they will never ever leave. The penalty for accepting the truth of the Gospel is death."

"And, knowing that, you still accepted it? You went ahead and received Christ into your life?"

"Yes, I did," Angelica said, with a determined set to her lips. After that she fell silent. Coming to another fork branching off in two directions she took the tunnel leading to the right.

....

Professor Lucifer Andronicus gazed across the room at the members of the high council gathered around the stone table. He had called this meeting to discuss matters relating to those who had intruded into their midst. They had also gathered to pass judgment on those who had turned traitor to their cause.

One of the members of the council, a too thin man with angular features, rubbed his hands together with glee, "I think, Mr. President, that the fate you have determined for these despicable followers of the Enemy is truly appropriate. Indeed, I think it is a delightful demonstration that will be a slap in the face to the forces arrayed against us."

The professor's eyes glowed with the unearthly light his council was accustomed to seeing whenever he was filled with passion, or zeal, or rage, "It was not my idea Aristarchus. It came directly from the Ruler of the Power." That was always how they referred to their invisible ruler, who was the real director of operations in this place. He thought it was a good name, in spite of its having come directly from that accursed book Christians always referred to.

Andronicus was well acquainted with those passages in the Bible referring to his lord and master. He thought of the term the apostle Paul had used: *In the past you were spiritually dead because of your sins and the things you did against God.Yes, in the past you lived the way the world lives, following the ruler of the evil powers that are above the earth. That same spirit is now working in those who refuse to obey God.*[lxx]

Then there was the term Jesus Himself had used: *Now is the time for the world to be judged; now the ruler of this world will be thrown down.*[lxxi]

The professor did not believe his master would be thrown down. He believed in the triumph of evil against good. He *had* to believe that, or he would have to accept the inevitability of his own damnation. No, he would rule together with his master, Lucifer, and he would have his revenge against the Christ who had stolen the affections of his wife and overturned his presidency at the university. No, the 'Prince of the Power of the Air' would not be cast out. He would finally overcome the forces of Light and he, Lucifer Andronicus, would rule with him.

The voice of Aristarchus brought him out of his reverie, "What was that?"

"I was just saying," Aristarchus replied, "that we will need to send out a missive summoning our devotees to witness the humiliation of our Enemy."

"The missive has already been sent," said a small, bearded gnome of a man, sitting on the professor's right. By the time the Celebration begins there should be five thousand devotees to witness the event."

Aristarchus nodded his head, a satisfied smirk on his face, "That, of course, does not include the 'others' who will be there."

The professor knew the man was referring to the demonic host that always hovered over this place, and inhabited every space, as well as every individual who had surrendered to his master's influence, but they must get on with the business at hand.

"That is enough!" Andronicus took charge of the meeting. "We now have to deal with the particulars. There is the matter of what to do with the traitors to our cause. There are far too many of these. It pains me to inform you that Angelica, one in whom we placed such confidence, and gave so much responsibility, has deflected to the Enemy."

A gasp issued from all present.

"Yes, it is indeed a shock. She was particularly skilled in hiding her changed loyalties. She was at one time as committed as you and I. I do not know how the Enemy gained an entrance into her soul. I suspect it was through that turn-coat Roger Wilson, who was himself influenced by that abominable youth, Skip Jordan." He paused while assuring himself he had the full attention of the council.

He continued, “We must cut out this cancerous growth quickly and finally, before anyone else of our number is infected.” Everyone nodded in agreement.

“There are eleven others who, like Angelica, have switched loyalties, not including Roger Wilson. These will be sacrificed in the usual way after the main event.”

“Who will take the central place in the demonstration?” someone asked.

“Obviously the Jordan boy must occupy that place. He has been a thorn in our side long enough. It is appropriate that he should die in the most significant manner.”

“And which ones are those who are to die on either side of him?”

“On his right will be his former teacher, Raymond Nichol.”

“And who will be on his left?”

“Oh, that will be that contemptible creature, Roger Wilson. The others in the group will be positioned around the central display to complete the scene. Afterwards, they, too, will die.

Chapter 26

The Sorcerer's Apprentices

Angelica next led them to a chamber occupied by a large group who were quite obviously presenting themselves as preachers of the Gospel.

Some were in casual dress, others with suits and ties; still others wore clerical collars. There were those who wore the traditional robes and paraphernalia of the high church with their ostentatious hats and gold embroidered borders. It looked like the gathering of an Ecumenical council called to discuss ways and means of uniting the church.

As in the other chambers they had visited, the picture of the Prostitute riding the Beast was prominently displayed. The vivid colours and masterful art struck the eye immediately on entrance. This picture was larger than the others, Skip reflected, because this was the chamber where the plot to establish the false church was being hatched.

"Our goal is not only to unite all the many denominations that represent Christianity", the leader was propounding from a podium set up near the painting, "but also to draw in other faiths. We no longer care what each group is teaching, just so long as we are not divided.

"Especially the Evangelical Church has been guilty of dividing the world's religions by insisting on what they call 'sound doctrine,' and holding to a strict adherence to 'Bible teaching.' By so doing they have alienated homosexuals and the Gay Rights Movement. They have insisted upon absolute moral values and alienated those who believe human sexuality is a God-given gift. As such they are free to express it in any way they choose.

"They have labelled many Christian groups as 'cults,' because they were creative, and adjusted the restrictive pronouncements of the Bible to something more in harmony with human nature.. They have condemned other religions and so have caused hatred and resentment against the Christian faith. I do not hesitate to say they are the cause of many of the terrorist acts that have devastated our world.

"Thankfully, many evangelicals are beginning see our point of view. And you," he swept a hand to indicate those seated before him," have been chosen to infiltrate the ranks of Bible believing churches, and undermine their bigoted views."

The passion of the leader, who was dressed in clerical garb, struck Skip as being very like that shown by evangelists he had heard preaching the true Gospel. This man was proclaiming false teaching with as much zeal as any he had seen calling for sinners to repent and turn to Christ.

When there was a break, Angelica called the leader over. He had white hair and a white beard reminiscent of Moses, or of many of the Old Testament prophets.

Angelica introduced him as the very reverend Oscar Windercott.

From the outset the man displayed open hostility to their group, and to Angelica herself in particular. Word had no doubt filtered down that she had put her trust in Christ and was to be tolerated only till she could be dealt with later.

"I cannot say it is a pleasure to meet you," the man said abruptly. "You, and all you stand for, are the epitome of all I despise and all I have sworn to destroy."

Skip was not so much surprised by this man's vitriolic attack, as he was by the response it drew from Ntambo. The large black man was in the habit of keeping his own council, until, that is, the occasion demanded a more aggressive response. This was obviously one of those occasions.

Raising himself up to an even greater height, Ntambo stepped forward and confronted the reverend Oscar Windercott with a voice that seemed to role like distant thunder. Quoting Scripture, he said, "*You have no part or portion in this matter, for your heart is not right before God. Therefore repent of this wickedness of yours, and pray the Lord that, if possible, the intention of your heart may be forgiven you. For I see that you are in the gall of bitterness and in the bondage of iniquity.*[lxxii]

"The speech you made when we entered this chamber is an indication of how far you have strayed from the truth, and of how swift your judgment will be if you do not repent. I call to you in the same way the apostle Peter appealed to Simon the Sorcerer: *repent of this wickedness of yours, and pray the Lord that, if possible, the intention of your heart may be forgiven you.*"

Oscar Windercott's reaction was to scowl in contempt. His face turned red, and the veins in his neck stood out with the intensity of the anger he directed toward Ntambo, "You arrogant, stupid man. You have no idea what you are dealing with. The forces on our side are stronger than you can imagine. You will be squashed like an insect and cast out like rubbish while we will create a church that is not bigoted and narrow."

"I know exactly with what, and with whom I am dealing," Ntambo returned. "It is you who are ignorant of the dire consequences of the path you have chosen. You may prevail for a season," Ntambo replied," but in the end you will be destroyed by the very forces you trust in now. As for being bigoted and narrow, we are following the Truth, for Scripture tells us: *The temple of God cannot have any agreement with idols, and we are the temple of the living God. As God said:*

'I will live with them and walk with them. And I will be their God, and they will be my people.'

'Leave those people,
and be separate, says the Lord.
Touch nothing that is unclean,
and I will accept you.'[lxxiii]

"We are called to be separate from all that is unclean, and from all false teaching. The Gospel is not something that can be played with and adjusted to and conformed to our own desires and weaknesses. It is a fixed thing. You cannot twist it without serious consequences."

Reverend Windercott almost spat at this outpouring of Biblical truth, but Ntambo was on a roll and could not be stopped. He quoted another passage: "*I am amazed that you are so quickly deserting Him who called you by the grace of Christ, for a different gospel; which is really not another; only there are some who are disturbing you and want to distort the gospel of Christ. But even if we, or an angel from heaven, should preach to you a gospel contrary to what we have preached to you, he is to beaccursed! As we have said before, so I say again now, if any man is preaching to you a gospel contrary to what you received, he is to be accursed!*"[lxxiv]

The effect of this on the reverend was dramatic. He placed his fingers in his ears and turned to flee back to his podium. Ntambo raised his voice still higher so the others in the chamber could hear. "Hear what the apostle Jude had to say*: Beloved, while I was making every effort to write you about our common salvation, I felt the necessity to write to you appealing that you contend earnestly for the faith which was once for all handed down to the saints. For certain persons have crept in unnoticed, those who were long beforehand marked out for this condemnation, ungodly persons who turn the grace of our God into licentiousness and deny our only Master and Lord, Jesus Christ.*[lxxv] I call you to repent and do not listen to this man who means only to lead you to damnation. I call you to turn to Jesus Christ, who is the true Master of the Universe."

The only sound after Ntambo's monologue was over was of water dripping from the chamber's stalactites and of the exhaling of breath from all who had heard him. Everyone had been holding their breath. Those under Windercott's tutelage were no doubt relieved the biting words of Scripture had ceased and they could once again devote themselves to their studies.. Skip wondered, however if the truth of God's Word may not have penetrated some hearts. Spoken under the power of God's Spirit, as Ntambo's words had been, they could not have been lightly dismissed. He had himself felt the words cutting like a sharp knife, awakening his conscience, and making him feel exposed. The cutting, he knew, was like a surgeon's scalpel, ultimately intended to bring healing. Only if the truth was rejected could it bring harm to the hearers.

Angelica motioned for them to an alcove at the extreme end of the chamber. There she sought to explain further. She looked somewhat shaken herself by Ntambo's outburst. New as she was to the Holy Spirit's work in her life, she could not fail to be startled by it. She nevertheless seemed determined to continue with the tour, and explain the intent and purpose of each segment of this school of deception.

"As I've explained before," Angelica said, a slight tremor to her voice, "the goal is to infiltrate the church and replace sound teaching from the Bible with something different, but which can be passed off as the same thing."

"So what are these students been taught?' Ashley asked. They are all dressed as ministers of different denominations."

"Basically," Angelica replied, "they are being taught sorcery."

"You mean witchcraft," James put in.

"In a way it is. All witches and wizards use some sorcery among, other things, but sorcery is a very handy tool in the hands of a deceiver. If presented in the right way, it can be made to look very much like the faith taught in the Bible, but is actually a doctrine of demons."

"I'm not sure I understand what you are saying," Nancy said.

"Sorcery is all about becoming masters of our fate. Through sorcery you can control your destiny and make things happen the way you want them to. At least, that is what sorcery teaches. You are the one who controls your life, not God." Reaching into a pocket she drew out a piece of paper, "This is a computer print-out of something on a sorcery website." She turned it so the light from the chamber shone on it and read:

"Now you can master the art and science of commanding omnipotent supernatural beings, including: fallen-angles, demons, the rulers of unearthly mystic dimensions, and even the embodiments of the elements (sylphs, salamanders, gnomes, and so on.)

You'll discover how normal people have learned to enlist the service of spirits -- entities -- and elementals to get what they want out of life. Whether it be the destruction of a terrible menace, the whereabouts of a powerful occult artifact or perhaps an increase of money and popularity."[lxxvi]

"How can they pass that off as the faith taught in the Bible?" James asked.

Raymond Nichol cut in, "Quite easily. My wife Angela and I were studying this while we were waiting for you all to arrive." Angelica waved a hand for him to continue, so he said, "Many prominent Christian leaders are teaching faith is a force that can make things happen simply by the act of believing. To them faith is a force. It doesn't much matter how you direct it; it is a power enabling the user to manipulate people and events for their own benefit without reference to the will of God.

"They quote verses like: *"All things are possible to him who believes."* (Mark 9:23 – NASB) What they don't tell you is that the faith taught in the Bible is not a force, as sorcery teaches. It is faith *in* God based on promises He has already made. Faith is putting your trust in God to perform all He has promised. It is meant to enable you to do God's will, not a tool to act as if you are yourself God.

"Many Christians find it hard to know the difference. They are seduced into looking for ways to control their own destiny, rather than putting their destiny in the hands of God who loves them and has promised to work everything together for their good."

It was quite a speech, and Skip was impressed; it helped to diminish the suspicion he had harboured regarding his former teacher. It seemed this former wizard's conversion had been genuine, and that he had indeed put his trust in Christ.

Angelica returned to her task, building on what Ntambo and Mr. Nichol had said before, "Those in this class are what you might call Sorcerers' Apprentices. They are learning the principles of sorcery, and how to present it in ways that will make it seem indistinguishable from biblical faith. The goal of sorcery is to make God a kind of 'Cosmic Force' to do our bidding. It is making use of our words and thoughts to make us masters of our fate.

"You must understand two things about this school of deception, and its need for absolute secrecy. Everyone being trained here is to be sent out to infiltrate the church as 'angels of light.' Their natural gifts will be developed, but more than that, they will be inhabited by evil spirits. They will be able to pass themselves off as genuine servants of God. Some will even be able to perform lying signs and wonders."

Turning to Skip, Angelica asked for his pocket New Testament. Once it was in her hands she found the place she wanted, and began to read: "*The secret power of evil is already working in the world, but there is one who is stopping that power. And he will continue to stop it until he is taken out of the way.Then that Man of Evil will appear, and the Lord Jesus will kill him with the breath that comes from his mouth and will destroy him with the glory of his coming.The Man of Evil will come by the power of Satan. He will have great power, and he will do many different false miracles, signs, and wonders.He will use every kind of evil to trick those who are lost. They will die, because they refused to love the truth. (If they loved the truth, they would be saved.)For this reason God sends them something powerful that leads them away from the truth so they will believe a lie.So all those will be judged guilty who did not believe the truth, but enjoyed doing evil."*[lxxvii]

"It seems incredible to me," Skip said, "that the leaders know this. They know they are not going to win; they know the antichrist will be destroyed and they are going to share in his destruction, and yet they persist in following these lies."

"Some know it Skip," Ntambo put in, "but most do not. You have not yet understood the power of a lie. The apostle John spoke of the *spirit* of error, and the *spirit* of truth. A powerful delusion has fallen on all in this place, and they are all under the power of a *spirit* of delusion. The only hope is for God to reach out in mercy, as he did to your former teacher, and to this sweet child," his eyes settling on Angelica.

"What is the second thing you said we need to understand about this place?" Mr. Nichol asked her.

"The second thing," Angelica replied, "is the ultimate purpose behind everything that goes on here. No one here believes that the whole church will be deceived. God, who knows all hearts, knows those who are His, and He will protect them even against strong delusion. No the purpose behind all this is to bring about the world church, which is described in the book of Revelation as the great harlot – the prostitute." She swept a hand in the direction of the painting. "The false church, which will be a mixture of all religions and all faiths, will enable the lawless one, the anti-Christ, to rise to power."

Ashley said, "What we have seen here is just the tip of the ice-berg, isn't it? It is not just bringing error into the church through business techniques and sorcery. There must be hundreds of ways the evil one uses to twist the truth and delude Christians into believing they are still following the true faith."

"You have no idea," Angelica said. Everything, from psychology to possibility thinking, positive thinking, and a host of other ideas rooted in the occult, are being streamlined to adjust the Christian mindset. In subtle ways Christians are being steered away from absolute reliance upon Biblical teaching. They are being seduced to adopt

Pagan ideas redressed to appear Christian. The apostle Paul called these 'doctrines of demons.' But we must proceed. I have much more to reveal to you."

....

May, Reginald, and Angela stood transfixed as they watched the green menace coming toward them.

There was no doubt in Angela's mind that her new husband was in peril, together with all those who had ventured into the enemy's domain. The green finger was pointing directly at them, and it came to her like a revelation just why they were being targeted. They, and perhaps many others, were the only back-up the group had. Her thoughts were confirmed when the finger of mist suddenly divided and went off in several directions.

Angela grabbed hold of May's arm and urged her to move toward their cabins. The action served to snap both May and Reginald out of the trance the appearance of the menace had brought them under, "Quick, we have to get back to the cabin," Angela cried. That thing does not mean us any good."

"Come to our cabin," Reginald said, "we can resist this evil better if we stay together." So saying he spread his arms protectively and urged them to hurry. They stumbled into May and Reginald's cabin and closed the door moments ahead of the menace. Not that it did them any good. The green mist seeped in under the door and through the edges of the windows, revealing the less than perfect skill of whoever had built these cabins.

As the green cloud enveloped them they fell to their knees on the circular rug in the middle of the room and began to pray. Reginald had snapped up his Bible before landing on the rug, but the mist prevented any reading. Instead, they quoted Scripture from memory, not in a quiet, ordered manner, but with the desperation that comes with the knowledge of immanent peril.

So give yourselves completely to God. Stand against the devil, and the devil will run from you.

The devil, your enemy, goes around like a roaring lion looking for someone to eat.Refuse to give in to him, by standing strong in your faith.

...everyone who is a child of God conquers the world. And this is the victory that conquers the world—our faith. So the one who conquers the world is the person who believes that Jesus is the Son of God.[lxxviii]

And our brothers and sisters defeated him
by the blood of the Lamb's death
and by the message they preached.[lxxix]

It took an hour, and at the end of it they were exhausted, but the green mist had retreated and the peace of God ruled once more in their hearts. When they went outside the evil mist was nowhere to be seen.

"What was that all about?" Angela said. "I don't mean the mist. I know we were targeted by the evil one, but..."

"But you wonder whether the victory we won back there in the cabin made a difference to whether or not we will see the others again?" May said, her voice sounding hoarse from an hour of pleading with God to intervene.

"That's putting it rather brutally, but yes, that is what I mean. You think there is a possibility we *won't* see them again?"

"There's always that possibility, Angela, but we can't even think that way. We've done our part. We have to leave the rest to God and trust that He will bring them out safely."

"That's true," Reginald said solemnly, "but we can't afford to let our guard down. The devil really is like a roaring lion, and I don't think he's done roaring yet."

Chapter 27

The Voice of the Beast

Over the next two days they visited at least a dozen groups like those first two. Through them all was a recurring theme; they all referred to the coming of a powerful leader who would counteract the teachings of Jesus Christ. He would be one who was in their view one who deserved to be worshiped more than the Christ revealed in the Scriptures. He was, in effect, the anti-Christ.

More than this, those leading the teaching sessions made no bones about identifying this coming one. He was the beast being ridden by the prostitute, so prominently displayed in each of the chambers where the training was conducted. They did not even hide the fact that the picture was taken directly out of the description given in the seventeenth chapter of Revelation.

Ntambo was familiar with the New Testament prophecy regarding this leader immediately before the coming of Jesus Christ to judge the world: *Do not let anyone fool you in any way. That day of the Lord will not come until the turning awayfrom God happens and the Man of Evil, who is on his way to hell, appears. He will be against and put himself above any so-called god or anything that people worship. And that Man of Evil will even go into God's Temple and sit there and say that he is God.*[lxxx]

Through all these sessions Ntambo was aware of something else that disturbed him – the way Nancy was reacting to it all. They were all upset by what they were seeing and hearing, but it seemed to him it was affecting Nancy far more than the others. She kept glancing at Skip and looking away, as if each glance brought her pain. Knowing in some measure Nancy's feelings for Skip, such pain made no sense – unless she knew something the rest of them were not privy to – something that put Skip in greater peril than the rest of them.

Ntambo remembered the dream Nancy had had, and the way she had clammed up when they had pressed her for details. It had something to do with three crosses she had seen in her dream. All she would say at the time was that her dream had revealed them to be in one of the chambers in this underground domain of darkness. He would have to get her alone and persuade her to reveal the details of her dream to him.

The opportunity presented itself when Angelica suggested a more leisurely tour of some of the places they had not yet seen. She assured them they would not have to witness any more of the deceptions to be foisted on the church, just see some of the natural wonders of this place. Nancy, clearly growing more depressed, elected to stay behind. Ntambo did the same.

Nancy had retreated to the smaller cave she shared with Ashley. Ntambo stood at the entrance and saw this beautiful child, as he viewed her, kneeling on the rough stone surface, her head bowed and her long hair almost touching the ground. She was praying, but the only sound the big man heard was that of restrained sobbing, as if she were trying to hide her distress from him. She no doubt thought he was in the larger cave. He could see her body tremble under the powerful emotions that gripped her.

"You need to tell me, now," Ntambo said.

Nancy jerked up in alarm, almost losing her balance as she turned to face him. Her cheeks were wet with tears and there was redness around her eyes, "Wh... what..." she stammered.

"You have been carrying this burden too long, child. It is time you told me all about it."

His words seemed to release the flood-gates of emotion. There was no restraining the sobs that wracked her body and periodically a wail escaped her lips. This was more than sorrow; it was unmitigated grief.

Ntambo went to her, raised her up and cradled her head against his shoulder, "What terrible things have you seen, child that would bring you such pain?"

It was a while before her sobs diminished enough for her to give any kind of answer. At last she stammered, "I... can't.... tell you."

"Of course you can. Ntambo is your friend, and he has seen worse things than you can imagine. You cannot bear this burden alone anymore."

"It wouldn't matter. We... we are all going to die anyway."

"All the more reason for you to tell me what is breaking your heart. You don't really believe our Lord will abandon us in our time of need, do you?"

"But... but..."

"But you doubt God's love for you?"

"No, but isn't it true that God does not always deliver his people from death?" Many have died when persecution has come upon them, and God has not delivered them."

"In that case child, you will need to have courage. You need to follow the example of Shadrach, Meshach and Abednego."

"You mean the three friends of Daniel when they were commanded to worship Nebuchadnezzar's golden image or they would be cast into a fiery furnace?"

Ntambo held her by the shoulders at arm's length and looked into her eyes, "Yes, and do you remember what reply they gave to the king?"

"Not in their exact words."

"The Scripture tells us: *'Shadrach, Meshach, and Abednego answered the king, saying, "Nebuchadnezzar, we do not need to defend ourselves to you. If you throw us into the blazing furnace, the God we serve is able to save us from the furnace. He will save us from your power, O king.But even if God does not save us, we want you, O king, to know this: We will not serve your gods or worship the gold statue you have set up.'* "[lxxxi]

"So you are telling me not to be such a baby?" She dried her eyes with the back of her hand.

"Not exactly. I am just reminding you that we all need to have faith and continue to serve our Lord whether we are to live or die." He released her and led her to a ledge that served as the only seating available. "Now you have to tell me everything you saw in your dream."

So Nancy told him in detail, her jaw set determinedly lest her courage failed her. And with every word Ntambo's countenance grew more troubled, and a shadow passed over his eyes. It was worse, much worse than he had imagined.

....

Lucifer Andronicus rubbed his hands together, a satisfied smile on his face. Everything was coming together and soon he would have his revenge on the Christ who had stolen the heart of his beloved.

However, his revenge was not centred entirely on one event alone, one that was to take place within the next twenty four hours. It had been an ongoing revenge. He had begun exacting it, not at his wife`s death, but five years earlier when she had come home from some church meeting to tell him she had given her heart unreservedly to Jesus Christ.

The shock of her declaration had impacted his emotions with the force of a hurricane, or an earthquake, or an erupting volcano. He could not see, as she had reminded him often that her commitment to Jesus Christ caused her to love him more, not less.

He began to resent her times of early-morning prayer and Bible reading, as well as her church attendance on Sundays and the mid-week Bible studies. In his mind this dedication to Jesus Christ was worse than if she had been unfaithful to him by sleeping with another man. All the time she took in private devotions and church attendance were like time she was taking to meet with her lover. He even found some Bible verses that supported his claim:

My lover has gone down to his garden,
to the beds of spices,
to feed in the gardens
and to gather lilies.
I belong to my lover,
and my lover belongs to me.
He feeds among the lilies.[lxxxii]

Searching through some Bible commentaries he found the Beloved in the book written by King Solomon referred to Christ's love for His Church, and of each person in it. That included his wife, and her corresponding love for Christ solidified the idea that He was her lover.

In the New Testament he found something even more telling:

"Don't think that I came to bring peace to the earth. I did not come to bring peace, but a sword. I have come so that
'a son will be against his father,
a daughter will be against her mother,
a daughter-in-law will be against her mother-in-law.
A person's enemies will be members of his own family.'

"Those who love their father or mother more than they love me are not worthy to be my followers. Those who love their son or daughter more than they love me are not worthy to be my followers.[lxxxiii]

That the passage did not specifically mention husbands was to him immaterial. Jesus Christ demanded total devotion from his wife and thus had stolen her affections. So he began to see her as an adulterous woman and treated her as such. He banished her to her own room and vowed he would not take her back till she had abandoned her devotion to Jesus Christ and gave it to him alone.

He saw the devastating affect this was having on her but refused to attribute it to his own actions. Unable to abandon her devotion to Christ, and cut off emotionally and physically from the man she loved, her health deteriorated. She told him his hatred of Jesus Christ would be the death of her, and finally it was. Five years after her conversion she succumbed to various ailments the doctor's attributed to emotional distress. Her friends called it another name – a broken heart.

To Lucifer Andronicus' way of thinking she would still have been alive if Christ had not stolen her affections.

Shaking himself from his reverie, Andronicus brought his mind back to all that had been accomplished in the years he had given his devotion to Lucifer.

This centre of deception in the heart of Africa was not the only one of its kind. There were others in Europe, in Asia, and in various centres around the world. All of them were protected with codes of secrecy that if violated resulted in penalties that included death, and others that were, in his view, worse than death.

But this one beneath the Victoria Falls had been singularly successful in infiltrating pagan and occultist practices into the church. They had done this almost without the church being aware of it. There were pockets of resistance, of course, but nothing in the way of upsetting the overall plan – creating a world church that would ultimately include many religions with conflicting ideologies.

The professor thought how successful psychology had been in diverting Christian leaders from total dependence upon basic Biblical teaching. Psychology subtly counteracted the Biblical idea that people need to be convicted of sin, called to repentance, and be saved by an act of God's Grace. The teaching that mankind is unworthy of God's love was being ridiculed by the psychological community and replaced by the doctrine of mankind's innate goodness.

Clear teaching like the one in the letter of Paul the apostle to the Romans was no longer being taken seriously by many Christian leaders:

But God shows his great love for us in this way: Christ died for us while we were still sinners.[lxxxiv]

Psychology further counteracted the idea of self-denial so strongly taught by Jesus Himself: *Then Jesus said to His disciples, "If anyone wishes to come after Me, he must deny himself, and take up his cross and follow Me. For whoever wishes to save his life will lose it; but whoever loses his life for My sake will find it.*[lxxxv]

In its place psychology espoused the doctrine of self-esteem almost to the point of self-worship. Andronicus wondered what the average Christian's reaction would be if they knew that many of the ideas being foisted on them by psychology had their roots in Hinduism. No genuine Christian would allow a Hindu priest to teach his pantheistic religion from the pulpit of their church, yet those very ideas were being accepted, simply because they had been re-dressed as 'science.'

All of this, and a thousand other deceptions had only one purpose – to bring about a false church that would in turn help to bring about the rule of the coming world leader Christians identified as the anti-Christ.

Yet Lucifer Andronicus knew that even this was not the whole truth. To him it had been revealed who the prime mover was behind all the future chaos that would overwhelm the world. Indeed, it was time to have his audience with that supernatural being in only a few minutes. Turning to a curtained recess in the rock wall he unveiled the picture of the Prostitute riding the beast. Seating himself and bowing in an attitude of obeisance, he waited.

Even though he had done this many times before, the prelude to his encounter with the Prince of Darkness was always harrowing. The atmosphere in the cave became thick with a presence that caused his nerve endings to tingle. In a mirror placed at an angle beside the picture of the Beast he could see his own eyes begin to glow with a greenish light, and bile rose up in his throat, transferring a bitter taste to his tongue. It was a taste he knew well – it was the taste of fear. One never entered casually into the presence of this evil majesty.

The Beast in the picture began to move, its seven heads undulating in time to the movements of the Prostitute on its back. One of the heads, the one with three horns, turned and fixed its gaze on Lucifer Andronicus. As it did so shafts of green light shot out and connected to the same light in the professor's eyes. Once that connection had been made the voice of the Beast was communicated to his brain. Anyone entering the cave would have heard nothing, but the words of the Beast resounded like the sound of thunder inside an empty drum.

"You have allowed too many of your people to defect to the Enemy," the voice said, and Andronicus shivered.

"The... the arrival of the intruders had... it had a disturbing influence on some of the more unstable members of the group."

"You should have sifted those out before they were admitted."

Andronicus did not dare to say anything in his defence. You did not argue with the Prince of Darkness.

"They must all die, but have you made adequate preparations for the Celebration?"

"I have my lord?"

"Have the three candidates been prepared for their fate according to my instructions?"

"No. Lord. That will happen in the hour preceding the main event. We thought it better the victims did not know the details of their fate till the last moment. The shock of discovery will make their deaths that much more painful. The costumes have been made for all the players, and the instruments of death are ready for use. Nothing can prevent the final scene from playing out as you have directed."

"Make sure the red-headed one has suffered appropriately. He has been a constant thorn in my side."

"He will so suffer, my lord."

"You will be rewarded if your performance is according to your words. If not...."

There was no need for the voice to complete the sentence, and Andronicus trembled as the picture returned to its former immobility and the shaft of green light disappeared. His course had been set, and even if he wished to choose a different path, there was no going back. His final destiny was imminent – and unchangeable.

....

In the aftermath of Nancy's detailed description of her dream, Ntambo was overwhelmed with a sense of shock and alarm. He knew, in spite of appearances, the evil one was not in control of events. However, as he had shared with Nancy, God, for reasons of His own did not always deliver his people from trial, or from death. That he often did so did not guarantee he would deliver in this particular instance.

Also, there was always a path of duty that had to be followed. The extreme danger they were all in, and the uncertainty of whether or not they would come out of it alive did not absolve him from taking action. He would do all in his power and leave the rest to God. The question was what *could* he do?

He sat cross-legged on the stone floor and prayed for guidance. His arrangement with May and Reginald to leave a red flag flapping in the wind at the highest point above Victoria Falls depended on one thing – his ability to escape these caverns and get there. By all he had heard it was considered to be impossible to do so.

That did not mean there *was* no way, or that God could not *make* a way. It just meant he had to resort to desperate measures and to a level of prayerful intercession he had not been called upon to enter for years. Now he allowed himself to be carried by the Spirit to regions he had only visited once before. Up there on the mountain, with wind and rain swirling around him, and lightning flashing, he had been granted a vision. That had been when he had first been called to intercede for Skip and his companions. Now, in the quiet of this underground network of caves he was taken up once more into the realms of the Spirit.

Though no words issued from his lips, unspeakable groaning came from a deep place inside him and spread throughout his body in the same manner described by the apostle Paul: *Also, the Spirit helps us with our weakness. We do not know how to pray as we should. But the Spirit himself speaks to God for us, even begs God for us with deep feelings that words cannot explain.God can see what is in people's hearts. And he knows what is in the mind of the Spirit, because the Spirit speaks to God for his people in the way God wants.*[lxxxvi]

For half an hour he sat, gripped by the power of the Spirit. At last, in the visions of his head he saw it – a map intricately painted on the rock wall of one of the caverns. He had no idea where this cavern was situated, but as the agonizing intercession faded he felt an inner compulsion to get up and start walking. The details of the map seemed imprinted on his brain.

Just as the others returned from their tour he walked stony-faced past them, intent on following the inner urging of the Spirit. They stared at him as he brushed past them, a lighted lamp in his hand. His odd behaviour caused them to frown, but caused no further reaction. The black man did not express his emotions much in any case, so marching off like this was not all that remarkable. They never guessed he was never to return.

Leaving the others behind, Ntambo found he was able to follow the map by memory. He identified one possible exit point, though the name designated to it was not inspiring: "The Devil's Chimney." Still, it seemed the best option both in distance, and as the most direct route.

A sense of urgency gripped him. He felt it in his bones that all of them were in mortal danger and that the time and manner of their death had already been decided. There was no time to waste. He had to get out and tie his red cape on the higher ground above the falls. May and the others would then see it and know they were in danger. It was a faint hope at best, for even if the authorities launched a search for them as missing adventurers, the directions he had left for Reginald to pass on were too complicated.

It had taken Ntambo and the others a day and a night to reach the secret entrance. But with helicopters and a rescue team equipped with climbing gear there was still a chance they could reach the ledge immediately outside the secret entrance.. However, no matter how quickly the rescuers arrived it could still be too late. Nevertheless, he knew he would still have to try.

Chapter 28

Passion Play from Hell

Angela burst in to May and Reginald's cabin. "Something strange is happening across the gorge," she blurted. She had been at the look-out post where they were taking turns to watch for the signal Ntambo had arranged to give them. Now she was out of breath, having run to inform May and Reginald what she had seen.

"What is it Angela?"

"There was no red flag on the higher ground above the falls," she replied, still breathing hard.

"There must have been something to cause you to run so hard to tell us," Reginald said.

"There was no red flag where Ntambo arranged to place it, but I could see it flapping in the wind as he ran."

"You mean you saw Ntambo from so far away?"

"I'm sure it was him, but that is not what alarmed me. Come and see. I believe Ntambo is in mortal danger."

They were all a little out of breath when they arrived. The place they thought was best suited to keep watch for Ntambo's signal gave them a perfect view. Raising their binoculars to their eyes they watched the drama playing out across the gorge and it drove everything else out of their minds. It was a scene any epic moviemaker would delight in capturing on film. It had all the elements of drama to delight an audience. It drew the opposite reaction from the three watchers, causing them to gasp in alarm.

Ntambo was the focal point of the scene, running with a horde of pursuers behind him. The red cloth he normally wore around his waist was tied like a cape around his shoulders and flapped in the wind as he ran. He may not have been able to tie it up on higher ground but it was serving the same purpose as originally intended. It announced as clearly as anything could that Skip and the others were in trouble, and that knowledge caused a chill through the watchers' bones.

Above and beyond the action being played out dark clouds were gathering. Already lightning flashes could be seen lighting up the sky, thunder rolling as if to announce a great conflict. The conflict was in progress, it seemed, in the heavens as well as on the ground. Ntambo's pursuers were gaining on him, those on the edges moving faster in an attempt to cut off any attempt he made to move to either side. They were succeeding and it became clear what the intention of the pursuers was; they meant to drive him over the edge of the falls into the raging waters below.

In the meantime, as the drama on the ground played out, the clouds had advanced and darkened, shutting out the light of the sun. Thunder and lightning intensified and rain began to fall. It seemed to Reginald a fight was going on in the heavenly regions. He could not see angels and demons in conflict above the falls, but he could imagine them. Indeed, his mind conjured up images of a mighty battle between light and darkness. These images only endured for a moment, for events on the ground drew his attention.

He could see what was about to take place before it happened. When it did, he heard the cries of alarm from the women on either side of him. The press of bodies behind Ntambo forced him to the edge of the precipice.

Their binoculars pressed hard against their eyes to the point of pain, the watchers saw the giant black man tumble over the edge, the red cloth streaming behind him as he plunged to the waters below. A mighty man of God had fallen and Reginald could not help but think he had gone to his reward. Yet the manner of his going was stamped indelibly on their memories. Their hearts stood still as they played the scene over and over in their minds.

When they thought to look again the pursuers that had driven Ntambo to his death had disappeared. Their dark design accomplished they had retreated to whatever evil occupations they were engaged in. "God have mercy on you," Reginald muttered as they turned, heavy hearted, to their cabins.

....

"Where in the world has Ntambo got to?"` Ashley asked. "It has been hours now since he left."

Nancy emerged from the inner cave, her eyes still showing evidence of grief, "I think he has gone." She said.

"Gone where?" Skip asked in alarm."

"Just gone, and I don't think we will see him again."

"Whatever do you mean, Nance?" James retorted. "What's the matter with you? You look strange. Come to think of it, you've been acting strangely for some time now. What's going on?"

Angelica said, "I think Nancy has seen what is going to happen to us. She must have seen a vision or a dream, or something."

Skip said, "It was a dream. Nancy had a dream about three crosses, but so far she has refused to tell us the rest of it." He turned an appealing eye toward Nancy, "Come on Nance. It's been weighing you down for a while now. Why won't you tell us?"

"I told Ntambo, and he's gone, perhaps forever. Besides, there is no need to tell you now."

"Why is there no need to tell us, Nance?

"Because," Nancy said forlornly, "what I saw in my dream is already happening. You can experience it for yourself."

As if Nancy's words were some sort of queue for backstage hands in a theatre, people began to appear. They were all in costume as for a movie production, and their costumes were not amateurish or contrived. They looked real.

First were the soldiers, like Skip had seen in pictures and in movies. They represented the temple guards assigned to the Temple in Jerusalem. After them came men in long robes and white beards, and wearing expressions of rage. Skip identified these as Scribes and Pharisees. There was one with the robes, headgear and bearing of a High Priest.

Three soldiers came and grabbed hold of Skip, Roger and Mr. Nichol, their gloved hands digging into the flesh of their arms. Skip was certain there would be bruises to show for this, but he thought that bruises would be the least of their troubles. He suddenly understood where this was leading and it struck terror into his heart. He knew now what Nancy had been so depressed about lately. She must have seen a re-enactment of the Crucifixion of Jesus. The only thing was that he, Roger and Raymond Nichol were to be literally crucified, as Jesus and the two criminals on either side of him had been. This was all an elaborate Easter Passion Play to be performed here in this spectacular setting. He could not evade the thought that this was to be a passion play straight from Hell.

Strangely, Skip felt only an initial twinge of fear. After that calm settled over him that was unimaginable under the circumstances. His intelligence told him he was in mortal danger but his heart told him a different story. A Scripture verse sprang to mind:

Good people will always be remembered.
They won't be afraid of bad news;
their hearts are steady because they trust the Lord.[lxxxvii]

A glance at the girls, however, showed expressions of alarm, though he knew their distress was not for themselves. Nancy could not have been surprised by the turn of events; she had obviously been carrying the knowledge of it in her heart for some time, ever since her dream a few nights ago. The actual fulfilment of it was nevertheless a shock to her. She cried out when the guards started stripping their clothes from the three intended victims. He, Roger, and Raymond Nichol, were left bare-foot and clad only in boxer shorts; they were given cloths to wrap around their loins. This was indeed going to be a realistic re-enactment of the Crucifixion.

Ashley's expression was one of anguish, even while James stood by her side to support her. She gave James a glance that was anything but reassuring.

The guards prodded them forward to an as yet unknown destination without regard to the effect the roughened stone surface had upon their feet. The girls were pushed ahead of the guards with James doing his best to encourage them even while he was evidently in distress himself. Behind the guards the elaborately bedecked Scribes and Pharisees and High Priest strode in procession, their noses held high and their lips set in a contemptuous line.

Skip's feet, scraping on the rough surface as he walked, drew blood. The prodding would produce bruises if they survived long enough for the bruises to appear. He twisted around as he stumbled forward and saw both Nancy and Ashley with tears streaming down their faces. Ashley's expression still bore some hope; in Nancy's face there was none. No doubt she felt her dream had been an accurate depiction of what was going to happen. She looked as if she were staring death in the face. Angelica walked behind them, her head held high and her step sure. She had known this would be the consequence of her rebellion. Now she embraced it, if not gladly, at least with determination and courage.

A particularly vicious prod from a guard turned Skip's attention back to the way ahead, "Keep moving, fool!" he said cruelly.

Their destination turned out to be the same cavern they had first entered on arrival. This time it was packed with what Skip estimated must be around five thousand devotees. Before their entrance was noticed there was a steady buzz of conversation that seemed to bounce back and forth on the stalagmites and stalactites in the great chamber. The natural wonders were lit up in rainbow colours. He was sure his earlier guess had been right. The colours were accomplished by placing coloured glass before the open flame of each lamp. The colours flickered with the flickering light of the lamps, creating a spectacular effect similar to the Northern Lights .

Once they began their procession down the corridor dividing the crowd, the buzz became a roar, whether of censure or excitement was uncertain. In any case, what drew Skip's attention was what looked like a movie set built at the end of the corridor. As movie sets go it was a masterpiece. The scene painted on the vast backdrop was no mere impressionistic work; it seemed equal in quality to some if the best Dutch painters. To add to the reality of the set, actors dressed as Roman soldiers stood waiting, presided over by a Centurion with regal armour and headdress.

All that was missing from the scene were the crosses as depicted by artists through the centuries. The hill of Golgotha was there; the darkening clouds on the horizon were there; the actor's dressed as the observing crowds were there – every detail of that ancient scene had been attended to – except the three crosses.

Before he could think any more on the matter a shadow loomed to his right; it was the shadow of a cross. Two soldiers bore the cross and halted beside him. The guards pushed him to his knees and the cross was laid on his shoulder, its weight and sharp edges cutting into his flesh. The guards prodded him to rise. Try as he would he could not raise it more than a few inches, crying out in pain and aware of Nancy's cry of distress.

Skip's inability to raise the cross was anticipated. A large black man, he supposed meant to represent Simon of Cyrene who carried the cross of Jesus, appeared. Removing the cross from Skip's shoulders he carried it to the stage-set and laid it down. The guards prodded Skip forward.

By this time Skip had no doubt what the purpose of this gathering was; he was to be nailed to the cross in the same manner his Lord had been two thousand years before. It was not to be a celebration of the death of Christ, but a mockery that would end in death for him and for his companions. Two crosses were laid on either side the one he was to be nailed to, one for Roger for his betrayal of the cause, and Raymond Nichol for having been delivered from the powers of darkness so spectacularly. Skip felt a sense of shame for having doubted his former teacher's conversion. It must have been real, for here he was about to pay the ultimate price for his allegiance to Christ.

The procession arrived at last at the place of crucifixion, and everything stopped.

The crowd grew silent, and all eyes lifted toward the podium. They appeared to be waiting for someone to appear and officiate before the proceedings could continue.

That someone turned out to be Lucifer Andronicus, this time dressed in robes of officialdom, such as a governor under Roman rule. Though he may have looked like Pontius Pilate who had reluctantly given up Christ to crucifixion, his manner was anything but reluctant. Glaring down at the almost naked victims he said viciously, "At last we come to the final reckoning. You dared to invade our territory as representatives of the Christ. Now you are going to represent Him in very deed. You are going to die as He died, and believe me if I say you will not rise again as He did. You are in over your heads."

Skip heard a whimper of distress escape Nancy's lips, a sound that drew Lucifer's attention, "Oh, come now pretty maid. You will not have long to grieve for your red-headed friend. You, too, will be sacrificed together with those who have betrayed our cause."

It was then Skip's attention was drawn to a group of young people whom he had assumed were simply extras meant to add to the sense of reality of the Passion play. Now he realized, as Lucifer swept a hand in their direction, they were fellow victims in this hellish charade.

At this point guards took hold of Angelica, Ashley and Nancy and dragged them to join those who were to share the same fate they were to suffer.

"Oh yes!" Andronicus boomed over the crowd, "There is always a price to pay for those who betray their master. As all of you know we are worshipers of Satan, however much we cloak this reality to those we are called to deceive. We are sworn to prepare the way for the anti-Christ – the one who will overturn all the Christ came to accomplish on earth. These who stand before you, including Angelica, who once aspired to the position of high priestess, will suffer the death of all betrayers.

"Judas, who betrayed Jesus before His death, went out and hanged himself. These will not hang *themselves*, but they will be assisted to that end. This will be a warning to all those who would follow in their footsteps."

Andronicus then turned his attention to the three to be crucified, singling out Skip for his most venomous words, "You have been a thorn in my side you pitiful excuse for an adversary. How your Master dared to use such a weak vessel is beyond me. It was a fatal error in His Plan. Today I will be rid of you."

A green light now shone in the professor's eyes, and it dawned upon Skip that it was not the professor who had spoken. The devil himself was using him as a mouthpiece.

With this realization Skip felt the power of God rest upon him. A holy boldness rose up within him and words came to him he had never thought he would speak, "I am indeed a weak one, oh my enemy. But it is through weakness you will be brought down. For: *God chose the foolish things of the world to shame the wise, and he chose the weak things of the world to shame the strong.He chose what the world thinks is unimportant and what the world looks down on and thinks is nothing in order to destroy what the world thinks is important.*[lxxxviii]

"You will be defeated, as you well know, your victories will only be what God allows, and will be of short duration. God is able to deliver us from your hand, but be aware we will resist you to the end, even if He chooses not to deliver us."

Skip's words (he hardly recognized them as his own) seemed to spark rage in Andronicus. The green light in his eyes intensified and he appeared to grow in height. Looming over them he said, "Enough! I will listen to no more drivel from such contemptible creatures. Let the proceedings continue."

Those on the stage, dressed in the garb of Roman soldiers, came down and literally dragged the three condemned to where the crosses lay. Large mallets were handed to them. After Skip and the others were laid on the crosses, they reached for the spikes that lay ready for use.

Five thousand voices rose in a roar of approval that was deafening. Terrified out of his wits, Skip cried out, again with words that seemed not to be his own, "Have mercy on us, oh God, and deliver us, for we are like sheep brought to the slaughter. We cannot endure this unless you come to aid us."

As Skip's words faded there came a mighty clap of thunder and flashes of lightning struck the elaborate set designed to mock the death and resurrection of the Living Christ.

A fleeting thought flashed through Skip's brain: "So this is how we are all going to die."

Chapter 29

Fire and Brimstone

Death did not come as Skip had expected.

That in itself was an incomprehensible wonder. The natural podium, on which Lucifer Andronicus had stood, was suddenly gone. The stage, elaborately constructed to set the scene, was nothing more than smouldering timbers and ash.

All that was left were the three crosses on which he and his companions still lay.

In a daze, Skip rolled off his cross and rose to his feet. Raymond Nichol and Roger were doing the same, while Nancy Ashley and Angelica rushed to their side. The other eleven intended victims followed them.

Pandemonium reigned in the great chamber around them; there was a confused babble of voices with the occasional scream as someone was trampled beneath someone's feet. The only place free of panic was where Skip and the survivors of the lightning strike stood. Come to think of it, a lightning strike hundreds of feet below the surface was impossible. When he uttered the thought aloud, Ashley said, "Perhaps it was not lightning at all, at least not of the sort we are used to. King David prayed for lightning to scatter his enemies. I memorized the verses for a science project at school. It says, '*Lord, tear open the sky and come down. Touch the mountains so they will smoke. Send the lightning and scatter my enemies. Shoot your arrows and force them away.*'"[lxxxix]

"Of course!" Nancy exclaimed, "God made lightning. He can cause it to strike anywhere He likes."

"I think lightning is the least of what we have to worry about," Angelica said. "Have you noticed how hot it is getting? It looks like smoke, or steam is rising up from the ground."

"I know what it is," Angelica said ominously. "It was rumoured when I came here that there's a direct link somewhere in these caves to the molten core of the earth. Some said it was connected to hell itself."

"You mean you believed the rumour?" James asked.

"Believe it or not, there must be an explanation for what is happening now." She swept an arm in the direction of the now almost empty chamber. Cracks were beginning to develop in the rock surface; from these cracks steam rose, followed by liquid fire Skip recognized as volcanic lava. Fine volcanic ash rose into the air.

"So," Nancy said, her voice hoarse with dread, "if we are not going to perish as sacrifices to the devil, we'll perish in the fires of hell."

Skip reached for Nancy's hand, "Don't panic, Nance. The Lord has delivered us from crucifixion and human sacrifice. I'm sure he will deliver us from this, too."

"The only thing is," Raymond Nichol said, "is that three of us are almost naked, and our feet are bare at that. Have you felt how warm the ground is becoming?"

Angelica pointed to a pile of discarded clothing on the as yet unscathed portion of the movie set, "Those discarded soldier's costumes will have to do, don't you think?"

Strangely, only three costumes had been left behind; stranger still, each one was a perfect fit for each of them . Skip thought this just one more piece of evidence they were under divine protection, though he was as much at a loss as to what to do as the others seemed to be.

Roger turned to Angelica, "Do you know of any way out of this?"

Angelica shook her head, "I have absolutely no idea what to do. I guess we will just have to trust God to show us a way out."

One of the eleven who had been condemned to die with them, a girl Angelica later identified as Sophia, stepped forward. She bore the same expression of relieved terror and renewed uncertainty as her companions. She said, "We're doomed, aren't we?"

"I won't lie to you," Angelica replied, "Without a miracle we are. I know of no exit that will not be automatically shut down in the case of an emergency. I think this is an emergency."

"You don't think the panic and confusion may have prevented any such shut-down?" Roger asked.

"No. The few exits there are known only to Lucifer Andronicus and the ruling council. This knowledge was to be given me before I was exposed as a traitor to the cause."

While this discussion had been going on two things had taken place. First, the vast chamber where they stood had emptied. The backs of only a few were seen scurrying to whatever safety they thought may be available. Second, the cracks in the floor of the chamber had widened and molten lava spewed out.

The heat in the chamber had intensified and the place where they stood, though free of lava, was hot beneath their feet. The heavy soldier's boots Skip, Mr. Nichol and Roger wore, were not enough to prevent their feet from becoming uncomfortably hot. Skip knew his feet were sweating. He could only imagine how hot it would be for those with lighter footwear. They had to get to somewhere cooler before it was too late. Yet there seemed nowhere to go that promised more safety than they enjoyed at present.

It was while these thoughts were passing through Skip's mind that it happened. He was suddenly transported into a dream-like state, but the images he saw were sharper than any dream he had ever experienced before. He knew he was fully awake, but he saw images passing before his eyes. It was like watching a classic movie production on wide screen. Over the images verses from the Bible scrolled down:

At dawn the next morning, the angels begged Lot to hurry. They said, "Go! Take your wife and your two daughters with you so you will not be destroyed when the city is punished."

But Lot delayed. So the two men took the hands of Lot, his wife, and his two daughters and led them safely out of the city. So the Lord was merciful to Lot and his family.After they brought them out of the city, one of the men said, "Run for your lives! Don't look back or stop anywhere in the valley. Run to the mountains, or you will be destroyed."[xc]

Simultaneously a voice in his mind explained the significance of the vision he was seeing.

Once the vision faded Skip realized he and the others were in grave danger. The boiling lava had not yet encroached on the small area where they were standing, but it was slowly advancing.. The heat of the ground beneath them was increasing at an alarming rate and he knew they did not have much time before the heat and the lava converged. They would not survive for long. It was then he became aware the others were staring at him oddly. While the vision had lasted they must have noticed some oddity in his behaviour.

"Are you alright Skip?" Nancy asked, gripping his arm with evident concern. "You looked as though you were in some kind of trance."

There was no time to explain the details, so Skip just said, "Someone is coming to lead us out of here."

"How do you know that?"

"I just know. They will be here any moment now."

"What do you mean, 'they?' " James enquired.

"There will be two of them, like when the two angels led Lot and his family out of Sodom."

Before the words were out of his mouth, the beings he had spoken of appeared, startling them all. They looked just like the two men he had seen in his vision. They had the same long robes, but otherwise looked no different to anyone they may have passed on the street back home. Their sudden appearance had robbed their small company of the power of speech, at least temporarily. All except Skip himself, who had been expecting them to appear. Still there seemed nothing he could say that was appropriate for the occasion, so he kept silent.

One of the two men spoke directly to Skip, "You must follow closely behind us. He-Who Knows-All will do nothing till you have been led to safety."

Skip would never be able to explain what he did next. He felt overwhelmed with a sense of dread and, taking hold of the speaker's robe, began to plead, "My Lord, what is going to happen to all these people?" Sweat broke out on his brow, and his whole body felt clammy. He was in the grip of fear, but not for himself, or even for his companions. In his mind's eye he saw the thousands who had been gathered in this chamber to witness his death and that of his companions. His heart seemed to break with the thought that they were to die such a horrible death as the boiling lava and flashes of lightning seemed to indicate.

The man paused as Skip held on to his robe. His eyes seemed to burn as he looked down at this youth with the red hair and a tearful countenance, "That is not to concern you. We must leave immediately." However, he made no attempt to release himself from Skip's grip.

Skip found himself unable to let go, or stop his pleading, "But sir, the Word says God does not wish *any to perish but for all to come to repentance.*[xci] Is it not possible to delay God's judgment to give these people another chance to repent?"

In spite of the urgency of the moment the man did not show impatience or try to release himself from Skip's grip. He answered Skip's pleading in measured tones, while his companion stood silently by observing, "They have all had many chances to repent, and only these few (he indicated Angelica, Roger, and the eleven others, "have taken heed of the warnings."

Skip still would not let go, his mind desperately trying to remember Bible verses to back up his appeal, "Did not the prophet Jonah say that God is *a gracious and compassionate God, slow to anger and abundant in lovingkindness, and one who relents concerning calamity?*[xcii]

The man with the burning eyes looked down at Skip, and with an altered expression, said, "Oh Skip, son of two of your Lord's choice servants, your pleading has prevailed and your desire has been granted. However, this place, and the deeds that have been committed here, will be utterly destroyed, to the point where it will never be known to have existed. The volcanic lava will rise up and fill every space." So saying, he turned and beckoned them all to follow.

Skip's grip on the man's robe had involuntarily loosened and with Nancy and Roger's assistance he struggled to his feet. He felt drained, yet euphoric. Who would have thought the pleadings of a mere youth would prevail with the Almighty God? It was only one more proof of the greatness and glory of the living God his parents, and now he, served.

Nancy said, "Skip, look what's going on up ahead!"

"And behind us," Ashley put in.

Brought out of his reverie Skip let his gaze fix on the two men ahead of them. In spite of their average appearance, apart from the long robes they wore, Skip knew they were angels. So he was not entirely surprised to see the phenomena taking place ahead of them. They were walking across chamber floor that had become a mass of boiling lava with the attending smoke, steam and the pungent odour of sulphur. Yet as their feet touched the glowing lake of fire it solidified; a firm path for the rest of them to walk on was opening. What was more, as they proceeded, the path thus created was returning once more behind them to a bubbling mass of molten lava. So long as one of their company remained to tread upon it, the path remained solid. As soon as the last one had passed, it melted away.

"That's not all that's happening," Mr. Nichol said. "Have you noticed the path is cool and is no longer burning our feet."

Angelica's eyes and those of the eleven who had been spared were wide with wonder. She said, "The smoke and steam is also not intruding on the path as we pass. What exactly is going on here, guys? I am familiar with magic and deception, but this is real."

Roger, who had been mostly silent till now, said, "It's the real thing this time, Angie. This is not the lying signs and wonders we have been taught. I was a fool to follow the guidance of a teacher I should have been able to trust." He cast a resentful glance in the direction of his former teacher. Raymond Nichol appropriately cast his gaze downward, acknowledging the shame of what he had done to his former students.

Skip found himself speaking up in Mr. Nichol's defence, "Don't hold it against him, Roger. He was himself deceived even while he was deceiving. God has had mercy on him, just as He has had mercy on you, and the rest of us."

"I guess," Roger said, reluctantly acknowledging the truth of Skip's words, "but it's going to take me a while to forget that someone in a position of trust violated that privilege and led me astray."

"You have to take responsibility for that, too, Roger." Angelica's words were mildly reproving. "You followed Mr. Nichol's guidance willingly, just as I did those who deceived me. From what I hear, Skip, Nancy, and Ashley, tried to warn you, but you would not listen"

Roger appeared humbled by the reasoning of the one person in their company he wanted most to please, "You're right. I've been a fool right from the beginning. I was seduced by the promise of power."

The discussion ended when they reached the far end of the chamber and the robed figures beckoned for them to follow them into a tunnel hitherto made invisible by a jutting sliver of rock. Once inside they were introduced to another wonder. None of them had a lamp. And the walls of the tunnel had no crystalline content, yet they could see perfectly where they were going.

There seemed to be no explanation for this until Angelica pointed to an effulgence that seemed to surround their two guides.

"It looks like the halos you often see in paintings to show a person's saintliness," Ashley said."

"That's because they are angels, and not ordinary men," Nancy put in.

Angelica said in a voice filled with wonder, "So the light we can see by is coming from them? It is so soft, and yet radiant and … comforting."

Themba broke his silence of many hours and said, "I have seen this before."

They all turned their heads to look at him, surprised by this revelation. How could a teenage African boy, living in the wilds of Africa, have seen this miraculous light?

"How?" Someone said.

"Where?" came from someone else.

"When did this happen?" Skip asked.

"I was with my uncle," Themba replied, using his usual economy of words, "He was facing a witchdoctor who was opposing his preaching in a village. Suddenly this light shone around us. The witchdoctor was so frightened he never spoke against us again. Soon, my uncle thinks, he will find his way to worship the living God."

There did not seem to be much that could be said to this. No one doubted Themba's word. It was spoken in such matter-of-fact tones as one participating in the event might describe. In any case, the opportunity for discussion ceased when the tunnel they were traversing came to a sudden end. Their guides stood before a solid rock wall. There was nowhere else to go. They were trapped in a tunnel down which molten lave would soon come, leaving them no way out. A thrill of panic passed through them all.

Chapter 30

Deliverance

Lucifer Andronicus was trembling, gripped with such fear as he had never experienced in his more than sixty years.

He had been deathly afraid before, when he had offended the Prince of Darkness, though he had not been able to figure out how he had offended him, or why. When that evil entity was angry, no mere human dare ask why. The only option was to cringe, and bear his ire till it passed – if it passed.

But the fear he was in the grip of now was like nothing he had ever experienced before.

The lightning flashes in the bowels of the earth, the stench of sulphur and volcanic ash had hardly registered on his brain before he found himself transported to another realm. Whether he was in the body or out of the body he had no idea. In one portion of his brain he recognized what was happening to him as similar to the experience of St. Paul. That servant of Christ had described it in one of his letters:

I know a man in Christ who was taken up to the third heaven fourteen years ago. I do not know whether the man was in his body or out of his body, but God knows.And I know that this man was taken up to paradise. I don't know if he was in his body or away from his body, but God knows. He heard things he is not able to explain, things that no human is allowed to tell.[xciii]

Andronicus had studied that portion of Scripture and concluded the apostle was speaking of himself, but for reasons of modesty, was describing it as something that had happened to someone else.

One thing he was sure of, however, was that he himself had not been caught up into paradise. He was equally certain he was not in hell, at least, not yet. No, he had been caught up to some other plain of existence. The thought occurred to him that he was on his way to hell, and that the place he was in was a place of reckoning, a kind of judgment hall where he would be confronted with the sins and rebellion of a lifetime. Then he realized he was not standing on anything solid. He was suspended in a cone of light that, while not blinding, prevented him from seeing anything beyond.

What terrified Lucifer Andronicus, however, was not the isolation, or the bareness of his surroundings; what terrified him was his knowledge of what was to come. If what was to happen would follow the pattern of what St. Paul experienced, he was soon going to hear things that were not for human ears. For the apostle those things heard were no doubt wonderful, since he had been a servant of the Light. For Andronicus, the things he was about to hear would follow the pattern of his own choices, since he had been a servant of the powers of darkness. The very idea of such an audience with the Creator of the Universe was terrifying in the extreme.

And then he heard it – the Voice he could only describe as being comparable to the rushing of water plunging into a gorge below – like the noise of the Smoke-That-Thunders not far from the caverns where he had served the Prince of Darkness. He saw no form, unless it was an intensifying of the light in one area of the cone of light surrounding him.

"Percival Winthrop," the Voice intoned, echoing in the cone of light. "Why have you resisted Me for so long?"

Andronicus had not heard his given name for so long he hardly recognized the Voice was referring to him. He was speechless before this Voice he had expected to be full of wrath and condemnation. Instead he was overwhelmed with its tenderness such as he had never expected to hear from his Enemy, the One for Whom he had harboured resentment and hatred for half a lifetime.

The Voice continued, "I have loved you with an everlasting love, and yet you have spewed out the venom of your hatred toward Me, colluded with the forces of darkness, and drawn many onto the path of destruction."

All Lucifer could manage was, "My wife... You stole her love from me..."

"Oh poor deluded Percival. I did not steal her love from you. I invaded her with the love that enabled her to love you more, and you spurned it, shut it out, and caused her to die of a broken heart. It was you, Percival, who killed her. If you had not shut out her love, and Mine, you would have known joy beyond comprehension."

No one had called him Percival for many years. The last time had been at his wife's death-bed. "Percival," she had said, "I have not been taken from you. I have always been yours. And I am not being taken from you now. I am going willingly, for I cannot bear to see the pain in your eyes, nor can I endure the pain of your rejection. I ask only one thing of you dear one."

"What is that, my love?" he asked, his heart breaking. "I'll do whatever you ask."

"Promise me you will not be bitter. Promise me you will try to understand and do not shut the love of Christ out as you have shut out mine."

"Anything you say, my love," Percival had answered, willing to say anything if it would in some way change the look of mingled love and reproach in her gaze. Instead, he watched the light die in her eyes, and she was gone.

Percival, now Lucifer Andronicus, had not kept his promise to his wife. He had allowed the bitterness of his loss to fester. It had driven him to seek revenge in any way he could. He could not seek the revenge he desired if his wife's lover had been another man on earth. He could not load a gun and shoot his wife's lover to death, but he would seek some means to steal the devotion of millions who worshiped the Son of God. He would seduce them to the love of other things, and to worship other gods.

Percival had found the means to accomplish his goal through witchcraft, through sorcery, through New Age teachings, through devil worship. He sought to infiltrate the Church, plotting to send angels of light into the church to pervert its teachings. If he could introduce subtle changes to the Gospel, Christ's followers would continue to think they were continuing in the true Faith, but would actually be turned to a different Gospel. He had found the inspiration for his game plan in the New Testament: *I am amazed that you are so quickly deserting Him who called you by the grace of Christ, for a different gospel; which is really not another; only there are some who are disturbing you and want to distort the gospel of Christ. But even if we, or an angel from heaven, should preach to you a gospel contrary to what we have preached to you, he is to be accursed! As we have said before, so I say again now, if any man is preaching to you a gospel contrary to what you received, he is to be accursed!*[xciv]

This Lucifer Andronicus had done, and it had led him down the twisted path that had brought him to this moment. He knew he was accursed. He knew he was condemned. He knew he was damned, and there was no way of escaping the terror that he knew he would suffer for eternity.

The Voice spoke again, not as something his ears heard, but as something that reverberated in his spirit, "You have two things that speak for you, Percival. The first is that, however misguided it was, you truly loved your wife; the second is that your wife poured out prayers and intercessions for you while she was alive. Because of these things you have been granted one more chance to choose."

"You ... mean..." Percival stammered, I... I... am not ... condemned?"

"You have the chance to choose, once more, between *condemnation* and *transformation*."

Percival could hardly process the meaning of these words. He had always assumed that, by aligning himself with the Prince of Darkness, his destiny was fixed. It was a path from which there was no returning. A verse of Scripture flashed into his brain: *But God demonstrates His own love toward us, in that while we were yet sinners, Christ died for us.*[xcv]

As the meaning of the verse registered he had a sudden vision. He saw Jesus Christ dying on the cross, then an empty tomb. Words ran like a banner over the whole of it: *"I have loved you with an everlasting love;*

Therefore I have drawn you with lovingkindness.[xcvi]

Superimposed on these images, was the shadow of another realm, and he knew it was the realm of the damned. He knew he was being given the chance to choose once again between death and life. He chose...

....

The two guides stood before the solid wall of rock imprisoning them all in this vast network of caverns and tunnels.

There seemed no alternative to death by fire, but Skip did not despair. He, Nancy and Ashley had faced this kind of challenge before, and God had shown the way. This would be no different, except that the outcome was not in his hands. These messengers of God, angels as he believed them to be, had been sent to deliver them, and he was not going to give in to fear. He turned to give a reassuring smile to his companions. Nancy and Ashley did not seem to need it. He saw in their expressions that they remembered their previous encounter with solid walls, and were not intimidated.

Their confidence was not misplaced. One of their guides raised his arm and pointed directly at the rock before him. A stream of fire shot out from his index finger and the rock melted, revealing a passage beyond.

The path ahead was straight, and angled upward. Their guides turned, pointed to a tiny point of light gleaming like a star in the distance, and simply vanished.

It took a moment for them to process the sudden disappearance of their angelic visitors before speech was even possible. Raymond Nichol was the first to speak, "Our source of light is gone. All we've got is that pin-prick of light up ahead to guide us."

"That should be enough," Ashley said, "the tunnel is narrow, so we can touch the sides to steady us. Just be careful. The ground under our feet is uneven, and there are rocks and pieces of shale that could trip us up.

For the next twenty minutes they stumbled forward, the pin-prick of light all the while growing larger. Soon they had enough light to see the path ahead, and sounds began to penetrate – sounds of voices and engines and the bustle of activity.

When they at last came out into full daylight they realized they were the focus of a search and rescue operation. Two helicopters, one bearing the insignia of the Zambian Air Force, and the other that of the Zimbabwean Air Force, were in the process of landing. Once the latter helicopter had landed, three figures emerged from it and ran toward them. The figures turned out to be Aunt May, Reginald, and Angela Nichol.

Shouts of joy and relief were all that was possible when the two groups met. Nancy and Ashley almost hugged the breath out of Aunt May. Angela and Raymond Nichol were locked in an embrace that was almost desperate in its intensity, and it was some time before things settled down enough for introductions to be made.

Aunt May hugged Roger, letting him know how delighted she was that he was once more back to being the Roger she had known.

"I'll never be quite the same as I was, Aunt May," Roger told her. I've been the worst kind of fool. I... I've done some terrible things. I can only hope the Lord will forgive me."

"Of course He will, Roger. Of course he will!"

Angelica stood beside Roger. She waited for introductions, and then turned to regard Themba, who stood silently observing.

Aunt May grew suddenly silent. She told them later how her heart constricted at the task that lay before her. She would have to tell Themba that his uncle, Ntambo, had plunged over the falls into the raging waters below.

"But Themba seemed to know. He just stood there, his face so emotionless it could have been carved from stone. The time would come when he would express his grief, but that time had not yet come. Till then he would simply lift his heart to God, as his uncle hat taught him to do.

The reunion was interrupted by a disturbance around the exit point of the tunnel from which they had lately emerged. It seemed Skip and his companions were not the only ones to find the escape route opened up by their angelic visitors.

First, they saw a few straggling individuals came out of the tunnel; after that a steady stream of humanity poured out onto the island of ground dividing the mighty Zambezi River. The water rushed by them and plunged into the mighty chasm below. Skip threw up a prayer of thanksgiving as he realized his request of the angels had been granted. None of those who had inhabited the chambers would die. They were being given time to repent. He thought of what the apostle Peter had said: *The Lord is not slow about His promise, as some count slowness, but is patient toward you, not wishing for any to perish but for all to come to repentance.*[xcvii]

Among the streams of people issuing from the tunnel to escape the volcanic lava below may be some who would reconsider the path they had chosen and turn to the Lord. After all, besides Angelica and Roger, eleven young people had made that choice despite the threat of suffering a horrible death if they did so. Skip could only hope and pray that others would do the same.

The stream of humanity spewing from the tunnel slowed into a trickle. At last a few stragglers stumbled onto the island skirted by the Zambezi River and no one else followed.

"Do you think they all escaped? Ashley asked.

Skip shrugged, "I'm sure they have. Even though only a few hundred followed us through the tunnel, the angels must have opened other avenues of escape. I received a promise from the angels that no-one would be lost."

"Are you sure that's a good thing." James put in. They're free now to spread out into the churches now to become angels of light and deceive many others. We've seen and heard all that is planned by these evil people. All they're going to do is spread their poisonous teachings far and wide."

"That may be true," Angela Nichol said, but look what God did for Ray. God had mercy on him and there may be others in this group," she swept an arm in the direction of the several hundred gathered, "who will find the same mercy Ray found. Besides, nothing can frustrate God's final plan for the ages. Even if they all spread their lies, the truth of God will prevail in the end."

Aunt May interrupted, "We have to go now. The helicopter is waiting to take us back to the other side."

Chapter 31

Three Months Later

The group was once again gathered in Aunt May's kitchen.

It wasn't quite the same as before, since cardboard boxes were stacked around the walls, including a few where the table and chairs had been. The moving van had moved everything else to Reginald's new house, and they were waiting for it to return for the boxes.

There were some new faces among those gathered.

Angelica was perched on a box beside Roger who looked inordinately pleased with being exactly where he was. Themba was also with them, still looking awkward in city garb. Reginald had suggested Themba come to Canada to stay with them and offered to pay for his education.

Angelica herself looked content as she answered a question someone had posed, "As I told you before, my parents were killed in a traffic accident when I was ten. Having no other relatives, I passed through several foster homes till, at the last one, I couldn't take it anymore, and I ran away."

"Why did you do that?" Nancy asked.

"Angelica blushed, "I... I... was abused."

"Don't press her for any details," Aunt May interrupted, "that's all we need to know."

Angelica glanced gratefully at Aunt May before continuing, "By that time I was full of bitterness toward God for taking my parents from me, and at society for putting me in such unacceptable circumstances. Those who abused me claimed to be Christians, so I was mad at the church as well."

"So you were in the perfect frame of mind to be influenced and drawn into witchcraft," Reginald commented.

"I guess I was. I wanted revenge and once I had been initiated into a coven, I realized witchcraft, with its promise of power through spells and incantations, was one way to get it."

"What convinced you to at last to turn from it?"

"Actually, it was Roger who convinced me." She cast a look of gratitude his way, "He basically repeated the arguments Skip and the others had given him when he was first buying into witchcraft. Together with the doubts I was already having, it was enough for me to see where the path I had chosen was leading."

"And how do you feel," Aunt May asked, "about our offer to bring you to Canada and adopt you into our family?"

Angelica beamed, "I think it is the most wonderful thing in the world, but there is something else I need to tell you."

"What is that?"

"You remember the eleven young people who were scheduled to die with us?"

"We sure do."

"Well, one of them, a girl named Rose, wrote to me. She said she heard that Lucifer Andronicus has renounced witchcraft and has become a follower of Christ."

They all gasped their amazement.

"His real name is Professor Percival Winthrop. Apparently he had some kind of epiphany, some kind of dream or vision in which Christ spoke to him. Apparently he is planning to write a book exposing all that went on in the caves, and the plans certain groups have to infiltrate the church. He'll be exposing his own part in it too."

"That's amazing, and wonderful, too." Ashley said. "The only thing is I'm not sure anyone will believe him."

Angelica continued, "Rose also said the volcanic lava had completely filled the caves and scientists are trying to figure out why there was lava there in the first place, and why it did not result in an eruption."

While they were all processing this information Skip reflected on how his family was growing. He and Aunt May had lived alone at one time. Then Aunt May had adopted Nancy. After that, Aunt May had married Reginald. Now Reginald and Aunt May were adopting Angelica. And that was not the end of it either. Themba was to live with them until he had completed his college education. Considering he had been plucked from his natural environment he was adjusting remarkably well. Besides himself, he now had three siblings.

Turning his gaze to where Themba was leaning against a stack of boxes Skip noticed the African youth was fidgeting with an envelope in one hand, while tapping his fingers on a box with the other.

Skip addressed them all, "I think Themba has something to share with us."

All eyes turn on the tall youth from across the sea.

Self-consciously Temba said, "I have a letter. It came in the mail this morning. It is from my home and the writing is that of my uncle, Ntambo."

In response to this declaration there was a collective drawing in of breath.

Gripping Raymond Nichol's hand tightly, Angela expressed the consternation of them all, "But Ntambo is dead. May, Reginald and I saw him go over the falls. No one could have survived that."

"What does the letter say?" Raymond asked.

"I have not yet opened it," Themba replied.

"Then open it quickly!" James blurted. "There must be an explanation. Perhaps he fell onto a ledge and survived."

"Even if that had happened," Aunt May said, "he could not have survived without a miracle. He had fallen out of sight before he could have struck a ledge. The ledge would have killed him after falling that distance."

"Please just open the letter, Themba. We're all dying of curiosity."

"It's a private letter to Themba, not to us. We shouldn't pry." Ashley objected.

Themba extended the letter to Skip, "You read it for me, my friend. My uncle writes in English. I am not yet so good at reading English."

Skip reached into his pocket for his jack-knife, slit the envelope, and extracted three sheets of paper. As far as he could judge, the writing was the same as the writing Ntambo had included in a letter he had sent with the box belonging to his parents. That had been over two years ago, before their first encounter with witchcraft and the forces of darkness. He turned to the last page and read the last line, "It is signed, 'Your uncle, Ntambo.'

"This letter is definitely from your uncle," he told Themba."

"Just read it," Nancy urged.

Drawing in his breath, Skip began.

My dear nephew, and the good friends who have taken you to the land of plenty,

I know you did not expect to hear from me again. I myself expected to die, for Skip Jordan had seen a vision of the manner of my death. When I went to escape through the devil's chimney I knew my last act was to warn the others in the manner we had agreed upon. I did not expect to live after that. I did not even get the chance to tie the red flag on the top of the hill as arranged. All I could hope for was that the wind would cause it to fly as I fell to my death, and so warn May and the others you were in danger.

Skip paused in his reading, his eyes stinging with unshed tears.

"Keep going," Roger said. "You can't stop now."

"I'm just catching my breath, and you must admit this is something of a shock. Reading this is like getting a letter from a ghost."

"Just read it!" James said.

Nancy turned to him, "Stop badgering him, James. Skip is just trying to process an event that is totally unexpected."

"It's OK, Nance. Everyone is just keyed up to hear what else Ntambo has written." He turned his gaze back to the letter in his hand.

What I am going to tell you now will be hard to believe, but I am telling the truth about what happened. As I was falling I was waiting for death, but death did not come. The raging torrent below seemed to rise up to meet me, and drag me into its deadly embrace. It may seem strange that, falling at such speed my brain was able to process things, but at the edge of death time does not move at the same pace. I had time to stare death in the face, and to consider with joy my soon entrance into the Presence of my God.

Just when I should have struck the rocks over which the rapids roared, I was borne up by invisible arms and carried to a place of safety. For a split second I seemed to see the vague outline of angels wings, and of gigantic arms. They set me down on a shelf of rock and then vanished. It was more like awareness than an actual vision. This awareness was so swift that I doubted at first whether I had really seen what I had seen, but on reflection I knew I could not have imagined it, or the reality of my miraculous deliverance.

As I was considering these things, the passage of Scripture the devil quoted to Jesus during his temptation in the wilderness flashed into my mind:

...it is written,

'HE WILL COMMAND HIS ANGELS CONCERNING YOU';

and

'ON their HANDS THEY WILL BEAR YOU UP, SO THAT YOU WILL NOT STRIKE YOUR FOOT AGAINST A STONE.'"[xcviii]

I knew this referred to the Son of God, but it came to me as an explanation of what had happened to me, and how I had been delivered from certain death.

This is a true account of what happened, my nephew, and I am sure you will share it with your new friends, but there is more. Soon after landing on the shelf of rock, when I had barely processed the miracle of my deliverance, Mazimbi and a dozen warriors from the village where he had been instructing the new converts, arrived. An impression he could not deny urged him to come and look for me, though he had no knowledge of all that had transpired in the caves. They took me to the village and tended to the injuries I had sustained in my escape.

I had not been aware how severe my injuries were, and it took me several weeks before I was fully recovered. During that time the Lord has revealed to me how near we are to the fulfillment of all God said will take place before the end. The false church, as depicted in the picture we saw displayed in the caverns, is already arising. The prostitute riding the Beast, which is the anti-Christ, will not be long in coming. I felt I must warn you, and those with you, to be on the alert.

Finally, my nephew, I have a deep conviction that God has a mission for me to fulfill, or He would not have prolonged my life so miraculously. I do not know in what manner, or in what time-frame, but I believe you, Skip Jordan, and your other companions, will also be involved in the end-time battles that are to come. I call on you to be alert and prepare yourselves while there is still time.

I, Mazimbi, and the other faithful servants of Christ, send you greetings

I am your Uncle,

Ntambo.

The impact of Ntambo's letter caused silence for a full minute. It was as if the implication of his words had robbed them of the power of speech. Even beyond the fact that Ntambo was still alive was the looming menace they all felt from his warning of things to come.

At last, Ashley spoke her mind: "We have to *do* something," she said.

Skip gave her a curious look, "What do you think we should do?"

"I... don't know.... just something. Ntambo said we must be prepared. We ought to organize some kind of a watch – to keep an eye on things."

"You mean some way of tracking events taking place in the church, so we can identify the activities of the angels of light?"

Angelica said, "I can help with that, and so can Roger. We both know of people who have been sent out to infiltrate churches, though I've been at it longer. I could give you a list right now."

Aunt May held up a hand, "Now hold it. Let me understand what you are saying. You want to form some kind of group, or society, dedicated to exposing the forces spreading deception and lies into the church. For one thing that is a monumental task; for another it could be very dangerous."

"We don't have to do it alone, "Roger said, excitement in his voice. We can start websites on the internet and enlist the aid of other like-minded Christians."

Reginald said with incredulity, "And you are going to do all this while you are involved in your studies? You are at the age when school, and later, College, is going to demand more and more of your time. You're not going to neglect your studies to form a kind of underground resistance movement, are you?"

"We could spread the load," Nancy put in, catching the general enthusiasm spreading through the group. "As Roger says, we can enlist the aid of others. As you say, we could be part of an underground resistance to counteract the work of the angels of light. We could set up prayer groups, and study groups all over the country."

Raymond Nichol glanced at his young wife, and said, "I was wondering what I could do now that my teaching career has ended."

Angela looked up at him, "I'm with you, my love."

"Now hold it," Aunt May said. "Things are moving far too fast for my liking. None of you are thinking clearly. You have to consider what a mammoth undertaking this would be."

"I'm sure you're right," Reginald said, but how is this that different from what Jesus told us to do in the end times? He said: *"Be on guard, so that your hearts will not be weighted down with dissipation and drunkenness and the worries of life, and that day will not come on you suddenly like a trap; for it will come upon all those who dwell on the face of all the earth. But keep on the alert at all times, praying that you may have strength to escape all these things that are about to take place, and to stand before the Son of Man."*[xcix]

"It makes sense to band together to help ourselves, and others in the church to be on our guard. With the right kind of prayer and planning we could become instruments in the hand of God to counteract the deception already infiltrating the church. We need to pray that the Finger of God will move to defeat the forces arrayed against us. According to prophecy we can't prevent the false church from rising, but we may be able to encourage and strengthen the true followers of Christ."

Aunt May drew in a breath, "Oh no! Don't tell me you are also being swept away by this madness?"

"Oh yes, my love," Reginald said softly, "me, too."

Skip stood to stretch his legs and flex his muscles, "Uncle Reggie," he said, "You just said something that would be a good name for our website."

"And what might that be?"

"The Finger of God; since we will be working to awaken the church to the great delusion that is coming over the earth, we could call our website 'The Finger of God.com.' "

Index

[i] Judges 16:28-30 – NCV)
[ii] (1 Corinthians 1:27 – NCV)
[iii] (Jeremiah 1:4-8 – NCV)
[iv] (Jeremiah 1:5 – NCV)
[v] (Acts 2:16-17 – NCV)
[vi] (1 John 5:14-15 – NKJV)
[vii] (Genesis 41:28-32 – NCV)
[viii] (Genesis 41:33-36 – NCV)
[ix] (Acts 9:3-6 – NCV)
[x] (Acts 1:8 – NCV)
[xi] (John 20:21-22 – NCV)
[xii] (Acts 1:8 – NASB)
[xiii] (Luke 11:9-13 – NCV)
[xiv] (John 14:12-14 – NCV)
[xv] (Daniel 4:10-18 – NCV)
[xvi] (Daniel 4:28-37 – NVC)
[xvii] (John 1:11-13 – NCV)
[xviii] (John 3:36 – NCV)
[xix] (James 4:7 – NCV)
[xx] (Psalm 46:10 – NCV),
[xxi] (1 Corinthians 1:26-29 – NCV)
[xxii] (Psalm 46:10 – NCV)
[xxiii] (John 10:4-5 – NCV)
[xxxiv] (John 10:27-28 – NKJV)
[xxv] (Deuteronomy 33:27 – NCV)
[xxvi] (Numbers 16:20-35 – NVC)
[xxvii] (Jude 9-10 – NCV)
[xxviii] (Matthew 17:14-20 – NCV)
[xxix] (1 Peter 5:8 – NCV)
[xxx] (Exodus 17:8-13 – NCV)
[xxxi] (Colossians 3:2-3 – NKJV)
[xxxii] (Ephesians 4:11-13 – NCV)
[xxxiii] (Romans 10:17 – NCV)
[xxxiv] (1 Corinthians 1:21 – NCV)
[xxxv] (Psalm 16:6 – NASB)

[xxxvi] (Ecclesiastes 3:1-8 – NCV)
[xxxvii] (2 Kings 6:15-17 – NCV)
[xxxviii] (Ecclesiastes 4:9-12 – NCV)
[xxxix] (1 Samuel 7:12 – NCV)
[xl] (Song of Solomon 8:6-7 – NCV)
[xli] (Ezekiel 36:25-27 – NCV)
[xlii] (John 3:16 – NCV)
[xliii] (Matthew 5:4 – NCV
[xliv] (Jeremiah 23:29 – NCV)
[xlv] (1 Corinthians 1:26-27)
[xlvi] (Acts 19:18-20 – NCV)
[xlvii] (Matthew 10:32-33 – NCV)
[xlviii] (Acts 9:15-16 – NCV)
[xlix] (Galatians 2:2-4 – NCV)
[l] (Jude 3-4 – NCV)
[li] (2 Corinthians 11:13-15 – NCV)
[lii] (Acts 20:29-31 – NCV)
[liii] (Matthew 7: 16-20 NCV)
[liv] (Jeremiah 29:13 – NCV)
[lv] (Daniel 3:13-18 – NCV)
[lvi] (Acts 9:26-27 – NCV)
[lvii] (Romans 8:26 – NCV)
[lviii] (Ephesians 6:12 – NVC)
[lix] (Luke 24:25 – NCV)
[lx] (Acts 10:15 – NCV)
[lxi] (Isaiah 26:3 – NCV)
[lxii] (Psalm 119:165 – NCV)
[lxiii] (2 Corinthians 5:13-15 – NCV)
[lxiv] (1 Corinthians 1:26-29 – NCV)
[lxv] (Revelation 17:3-4 – NVC)
[lxvi] (Revelation 17:5-7 – NCV)
[lxvii] (2 Thessalonians 2:3-12 – NCV)
[lxviii] (2 Corinthians 11:13-15 – NVC)
[lxix] (Jeremiah 33:1-3 – NASB)
[lxx] (Ephesians 2:1-2 – NCV)
[lxxi] (John 12:31 – NCV)
[lxxii] (Acts 8:21-23 – NASB)
[lxxiii] (2 Corinthians 6:16-18; Isaiah 52:11; Ezekiel 20:34, 41 – NCV).

[lxxiv] (Galatians 1:6-9 – NASB)
[lxxv] (Jude 3-4 – NASB)
[lxxvi] (http://www.academyofsorcery.com)
[lxxvii] (2 Thessalonians 2:7-12 – NCV)
[lxxviii] (James 4:7 – NCV)(1 Peter 5:8-9 – NCV)(1 John 5:4-5 – NCV)
[lxxix] (Revelation 12:11 – NKJV)
[lxxx] (2 Thessalonians 2:3-4 – NCV)
[lxxxi] (Daniel 3:16-18 – NCV)
[lxxxii] (Song of Solomon 6:2-3)
[lxxxiii] (Matthew 10:34-37 - NCV)
[lxxxiv] (Romans 5:8 – NCV)
[lxxxv] (Matthew 16:24-24 – NASB)
[lxxxvi] (Romans 8:26-27 – NCV)
[lxxxvii] (Psalm 112:6-7 – NCV)
[lxxxviii] (1 Corinthians 1:27-28 – NCV)
[lxxxix] (Psalm 144:5-6 – NCV)
[xc] (Genesis 19:15-17 – NCV)
[xci] (2 Peter 3: 9 – NASB
[xcii] (Jonah 4:2 – NASB)
[xciii] (2 Corinthians 12:2-4 – NCV)
[xciv] (Galatians 1:6-9 – NASB)
[xcv] (Romans 5:8 – NASB)
[xcvi] (Jeremiah 31:3 – NASB)
[xcvii] (2 Peter 3:9 – NASB)
[xcviii] (Matthew 4:6 – NASB)
[xcix] (Luke 21:34-36 – NKJV)

CPSIA information can be obtained at www.ICGtesting.com
Printed in the USA
LVOW050230100712

289379LV00001B/8/P

9 781619 963870